QUEEN OF STONE

A Novel of Boudica

MELANIE KARSAK

Clockpunk Press

For those who follow the old paths...

MELANIE KARSAK

QUEEN
· OF ·
STONE

· A NOVEL OF BOUDICA ·

MAP OF THE CELTIC TRIBES A.D. 42

GLOSSARY

THE NORTHERN ICENI

Oak Throne, seat of the Northern Iceni
Aesunos, deceased king of the Northern Iceni
Albie, kitchen boy
Balfor, housecarl of Oak Throne
Belenus, deceased druid adviser of the King of the
Northern Iceni
Bran, second son of Aesunos
Brenna, first daughter of Aesunos
Cai, leader of Bran's warriors
Can, brother of Saenuvax
Children from Oak Throne: Eiwyn, Phelan, and Birgit
Cidna and Nini, cook in Oak Throne and her dog
Conneach, jewel crafter in Oak Throne
Davin, one of Bran's men
Damara, deceased wife of Aesunos

Ector, guard in Oak Throne
Ectorus, one of Bran's men
Egan, father of Aesunos and Saenunos
Foster, Bran's horse
Kennocha, widow in Oak Throne
Mara, illegitimate daughter of Kennocha and Caturix
Moritasgus, stablemaster in Oak Throne
Riona, maid in Oak Throne
Riv, Brenna's horse
Saenuvax, grandfather of Aesunos and Saenunos
Tadhg, stableboy in Oak Throne
Ula, wisewoman of Oak Throne
Varris, warrior of Oak Throne
Ystradwel and Arddun, helpers to Cidna

FROG'S HOLLOW
Cien, sister of Lynet
Children from Frog's Hollow: Tristan, Henna, Aiden, Kenrick, Aife, Connel, Glyn, and Glenndyn
Gaheris, deceased son of Rolan and Lynet
Gwyn, deceased daughter of Rolan and Lynet
Lynet, chieftain of Frog's Hollow
Rolan, deceased husband of Lynet
Villagers from Frog's Hollow: Egan, Becan, Turi, Oran, Guennola, Kentigern

THE GROVE OF ANDRASTE
Dôn, High Priestess of the Grove of Andraste
Priestesses of the Grove: Bec, Grainne, Tatha

HOLK FORT

Arixus, arch druid of Seahenge

Bowen, housecarl at Holk Fort

Condatis, patron god of Seahenge

Saenunos, deceased brother of Aesunos, chieftain at
Holk Fort

Seahenge, holy site of the druids near Holk Fort

Vian, Fan, and Finola, servants at Holk Fort

STONEA

Brigthwyna, cook in Stonea

Caturix, king of the Northern Iceni

Einion, druid of Stonea

Innis, a stableboy in Stonea

Melusine, queen of the Northern Iceni

Oran, messenger for King Caturix

Pellinor, messenger for King Caturix

THE GREATER ICENI

VENTA, SEAT OF THE GREATER ICENI

Ansgar, chief druid of the Greater Iceni

Antedios, deceased ancient king of the Greater Iceni, father
of Prasutagus

Ardra, novice druid of the Greater Iceni

Ariadne, midwife of Venta

Artur, son of Esu

Betha, Ronat, and Newt, kitchen staff in Venta

Boudica, Queen of the Greater Iceni

Brita, Boudica's maid

Elidir, messenger of the Greater Iceni

Enid, deceased mother of Prasutagus

Esu, deceased first wife of Prasutagus (From Coritani tribe)

Ewen, leader of Prasutagus's warriors

Galvyn, Prasutagus's housecarl

Ginerva, mother of Esu

Isoldee, stable hand in Venta

Madogh, Broc, spies of King Prasutagus

Nella, servant in the house of Prasutagus

Prasutagus, King of the Greater Iceni

Raven, Prasutagus's horse

ARMINGHALL HENGE, HOLY NEMETON OF THE GREATER ICENI

KING'S WOOD
Henwyn, chief priestess at King's Wood

RAVEN'S DELL
Brangaine, daughter of Chieftain Divin
Divin, chieftain of Raven's Dell

YARMOUTH, VILLAGE AND HARBOR IN GREATER ICENI TERRITORY

THE ATREBATES

CALLEVA ATREBATUM, SEAT OF THE ATREBATES

Cadell, messenger for Verica

Druce, messenger for Verica

Tiberius Claudius Cogidubnus, son of Verica

Verica, king of the Atrebates

THE BRIGANTES

Cartimandua, queen of the Brigantes

THE CANTIACI

DUROUERNON, THE SEAT OF THE CANTIACI
Anarevitos, king of the Cantiaci

THE CATUVELLAUNI

VERULAM, SEAT OF THE CATUVELLAUNI
Cait, priestess of the Catuvellauni

Caratacus, king of the Catuvellauni, brother of Togodumnus

Cunobelinus, deceased king of Catuvellauni, and father of Caratacus, Togodumnus, and Imogen

Dindraine, high priestess of the Catuvellauni

Epaticcus, deceased brother of Cunobelinus

Imogen, daughter of Cunobelinus, sister of Caratacus and Togodumnus

Phelan, messenger for Togodumnus and Caratacus

Rue, priestess of the Catuvellauni

Togodumnus, king of the Catuvellauni, brother of
Caratacus

THE CORITANI

Ruled by three kings: Volisios, Dumnocoveros, and
Dumnovellaunus
Fimbul, a chieftain in the lands under Dumnovellaunus
Gwri, druid adviser to King Volisios
Varden, chief man to King Dumnovellaunus=

THE DOBUNNI

CORINIUM DOBUNNORUM, SEAT OF THE DOBUNNI
Stokeleigh, fort near the Avon Gorge in Dobunni territory
Abandinus, king of the Dobunni

THE PARISII

BROUGH, SEAT OF THE PARISII
Cailleacha, queen of the Parisii
Ruith, king of the Parisii

THE REGNENSES

NOVIOMAGUS, SEAT OF THE REGNENSES
Urien, king of the Regnenses

THE TRINOVANTES

CAMULODUNUM, SEAT OF THE TRINOVANTES
Aedd Mawr, exiled king of the Trinovantes
Camulos, patron god of the Trinovantes
Diras, grandson of Aedd Mawr
Julia Vitellius, Roman mother of Diras

MAIDEN STONES, HOLY SHRINE TO THE TRIPLE GODDESS
Arian, Brigantia, Dynis, and Mirim, priestesses of Maiden
Stones

THE DRUIDS OF MONA

Caoilfhionn, current Arch Druid of Mona
Rian, deceased Arch Druid of Mona, grandmother of
Caturix, Brenna, Bran, and Boudica
Selwyn, High Priestess of Mona

AVALLACH (AVALON)

Venetia, High Priestess of Avallach

THE ROMANS

Atticus Julius Scato, officer of Rome

Aulus Plautius, Roman general, leader of the Claudian forces in Britannia

Britannia, the Roman name for ancient Britain

Darius Volusus, Roman soldier

Drusus Titus Flamininus, officer of Rome

Felix Arixis Isatis, legate of Rome

Gaius Marcellus, praefectus of Londinium

Mithras, Roman god of war and obligation

Narcissus, secretary of Aulus Plautius

Ocean, the Roman name for the English Channel

Sai, mahout serving the Romans

Silvis Hispanus, Roman soldier

Titus Carassius, messenger for Aulus Plautius

Victory, Aulus Plautius's dog

CHAPTER 1

"Rome."

The word hung in the air.

All around us, the torchlights flickered as if the fire itself had taken a breath. The visions had proven true. Rome had come.

"Where?" Prasutagus asked.

The fire from the torches made patches of orange light and black shadows dance across the messenger's face. "A rider came from King Anarevitos of the Cantiaci. They've landed at the mouth of the Thames. The Cantiaci are resisting. King Anarevitos reports thousands of soldiers, horses, and war elephants. A force the likes of which have never been seen before."

"*I've* seen a force like that before," Pix said in a low sing-song.

I turned to her. "Please, go find Caturix. Send my apologies for the interruption."

Pix nodded to me and then disappeared into the darkness.

"King Prasutagus," the messenger continued. "The Cantiaci king asks for your help. King Anarevitos's fort in Durouernon is besieged by the Romans. King Anarevitos and Kings Caratacus and Togodumnus are raising the alarm all across the land, asking every tribe to fight with them."

"And King Verica. Any sign?"

"King Verica pleaded with King Anarevitos to stand aside, let them make their way inland, but the Cantiaci king rejected his request."

"Of course he did. Anarevitos is always ready for a fight," Prasutagus said in frustration.

I stilled. My father was dead. Murdered. His body lay on a cart like a forgotten carcass. He had not yet been sent to the Otherworld. And my uncle had masterminded the whole affair—but had he done so alone? I still wasn't sure. My tribe was in upheaval. Everything in the Northern Iceni territory was undone. Romans or not, I couldn't just leave them like this.

My gaze went from the messenger to Bran.

Bran's brow was knitted in worry. "But someone must go to Holk Fort to deal with Saenunos's treachery. We must get the Northern Iceni in hand. And Father, Belenus..."

"Let's go inside," I said, looking back to the rider. "You look faint from hard riding. You find us in upheaval with bodies on the floor, but we still have ale and meat."

The man nodded.

"This way," Bran said, gesturing to the rider to follow him. "Cidna," he called to the maid, motioning for her to join him.

I turned to Prasutagus, meeting his gaze.

He joined me, taking my hand. "The battle has already begun."

I exhaled deeply, trying to calm my mind.

"Your father said that your grandfather Saenuvax made promises to Rome that were not kept. My grandfather made similar arrangements. We sent our yearly tribute in wealth but not in slaves as promised. If the Romans get a foothold, there will be a reckoning for both our people," Prasutagus said.

"And yet, Verica is not wrong to seek to reclaim what is his."

"Caratacus and Togodumnus have brought this upon themselves, but what they have brought on us in tandem is not yet clear."

"And Anarevitos?" I asked.

Prasutagus frowned. "Anarevitos... Quick to get angry, slow to listen. And now, he and those Catuvellauni brothers would have us all rally to war."

I frowned, then looked back at the carts holding my father and Belenus's bodies.

"You should return to Venta at once. There can be no delay," I said, feeling pulled in multiple directions.

"Yes," Prasutagus said, but the expression on his face told me he understood my quandary. He paused and gave me a soft smile, touching my cheek. "And you must stay here and help your family. Days-old marriage, and already, we must part ways for a time."

"Boudica," a voice called.

I turned to see Caturix hurrying my way, Pix following alongside him.

"Is what this mad woman told me true?" Caturix asked.

"Mad?" Pix shot back at him, but Caturix ignored her.

"Yes. The Romans have landed," I replied.

"Where?"

"In Cantiaci territory, Verica along with them. The Cantiaci and Catuvellauni are calling for allies to stand against Rome," Prasutagus explained.

Caturix frowned so hard I thought his face might close in on itself. "Convenient for them. What of Aedd Mawr?" my brother asked, referring to the ousted king of the Trinovantes.

Prasutagus shook his head. "The last I heard, he is in Gaul. Aedd Mawr is very old. The trip across the sea would surely kill him."

"Where is Bran?" Caturix asked.

"He's gone with Prasutagus's rider inside. Let's join him."

Caturix, Pix, Prasutagus, and I made our way into the roundhouse. As we went, I noticed that Ula was sitting on the side of Belenus's cart, the druid's hands in hers. I could just make out her voice in the wind. Across the square, I spotted Lynet.

"Lynet," I called to her, gesturing for her to join us.

4

Excusing herself from the others of Frog's Hollow, she followed our party.

Within the roundhouse, I found that the bodies of Saenunos and his men had already been cleared. The servants were busy scrubbing the blood from the floors. Prasutagus's rider sat drinking and talking to Bran.

The color had drained from Bran's face.

When we entered, Bran looked up. "Caturix."

"You must ride to Holk Fort," Caturix told Bran. "Assemble as many men as you can. We do not know how deep Saenunos's deception runs. We must clear the fort of traitors, question his people, and subdue any pending rebellion."

Bran nodded.

"When it is done, you will return to Oak Throne, where you will take charge."

"Me?" Bran asked, looking surprised.

"I will return to Stonea," Caturix said matter-of-factly.

"But the king of the Northern Iceni—"

"I will rule from Stonea," Caturix replied sharply, then moderated his tone.

While Bran was confused, I understood Caturix's reasons. He would not have Melusine here in Oak Throne, where Kennocha and Mara lived.

I turned to Caturix. "And a crowning?"

"There are more important things to worry about. When I get to Stonea, my druid will perform the rite and be done with it. Tonight, we must see our father and our people to the pyre, and then turn our faces to what is happening in the south."

"Dôn is still at Arminghall. I can send to the grove for another of the priestesses to come for the funeral rites," Bran suggested.

"There is no time," Caturix replied. He turned to me. "Will you ask Ula?"

"She will complain, but she will consent."

"Good. Boudica, it is too much to ask, but I want you to ride with Bran."

My brother held my gaze. In it, he spoke a thousand words. Bran was a good fighter, but my brother was not always the quickest to see the problems under the surface. If trouble lurked in Holk Fort, it must be rooted out and quickly.

I looked from Caturix to Prasutagus. "I..."

"Your family needs you," Prasutagus said gently. "Venta will be there when the matter is settled."

I gave him a grateful nod and then turned back to Caturix. "All right."

"What of Oak Throne? We cannot leave it empty, especially not with the Romans on the move. Not even for a day," Bran said.

Caturix turned to Lynet. "The Romans have landed in the south. We must act quickly on all fronts. Can I ask for your help in this, Lynet? Will you and the people of Frog's Hollow see Oak Throne secured until Bran can return?"

"Of course, my king," Lynet said, inclining her head to my brother.

"Good. Now, I will see my father to the fires."

I looked up at my husband. "Will you go at once?"

He shook his head. "I will stay to see King Aesunos safely to the Otherworld."

Which only left convincing Ula...

"I'll be back," I told them, then made my way outside, Pix dogging my shadow.

"I tried to warn ye," Pix told me as we went.

"You did."

"My fox nose can smell 'em from here. Whatever these Romans tell ye in the days to come, don't believe a word of it."

"Of course not."

"And make ye ready."

"For what?"

"To fight."

CHAPTER 2

To my great surprise, it didn't take much to convince Ula to help with the funeral rites. Everyone in Oak Throne banded together to build the pyres. A hush had washed over the crowd as word spread about the Romans.

Rome.

Rome.

The word was on everyone's lips.

And from the look in their eyes, it had stricken terror into their hearts.

When Caesar had come, the Romans had taken us by surprise. The united clans, the druids, and our gods had sent them back. But this time, the Romans had landed in a divided country, a country at war. And they had done so at the side of at least one tribal king.

Once Aedd Mawr and Verica reclaimed their thrones, then what?

We had all seen what had happened in Gaul. Barely a

hundred years had passed since the Romans had defeated Gaulish King Vercingetorix. With Vercingetorix defeated, Gaul became Rome. And the people had suffered. Enormously.

And now, they were here. Invited. The kind of guest who had no interest in leaving.

Where would this lead us?

Once the pyres were prepared and the bodies of the people of Oak Throne placed thereon, we all gathered to say our goodbyes.

My mind felt like it was splitting.

My heart ached for my father.

And for the first time, the reality of what had happened began to sink in.

My father was dead.

Belenus, who had loved us like we were family—since we were—was dead.

And with them, many of the good people had died.

All over one man's foolish ambition.

At Ula's urging not to offend the gods, Saenunos's body and those of his men had also been prepared for the pyre.

"Will ye not entomb the druid and the king?" Pix asked.

I shook my head. "No. In Oak Throne, we send the bodies to the Otherworld in flames."

Gaheris, Rolan, and the men of Frog's Hollow had been entombed, as was the tradition in their village. In Oak Throne, we did things differently. It had always been that way. I remembered watching my mother's fire burning. As a little girl, I was shocked and horrified as I watched the flames catching her gown on fire, burning it away, and the smell of burnt hair and flesh. The memory and the pain lived just below the surface. I had loved my mother, and I had watched her burn.

With my father, things were different. In recent years, my father had become difficult. He was not the sweet man I remembered from my childhood. I knew now that he was trying to protect us, but he had done so with no regard to the cost—to him or to us.

I scanned across the crowd, spotting Kennocha. She held little Mara. The child now had a full head of black ringlets, her hair the same color as my brother's. Kennocha stared at Caturix, who stood not far from me.

I looked back to the fire.

My father's willfulness had cost us all.

But in the end, I loved him. I mourned the man I loved.

"People of Oak Throne," Ula's gravelly voice called out. "We come to see our dead to the fires. It is not a chore any of us relish, but death comes for us all. We mourn when lives are taken from us too soon, as has happened this night. But we cannot control our fates. Our destinies lead us to the ends always meant for us, whether they come early or late in our lives.

"So, we have come here with our dead. This is the night of the dark lady. Ancient Andraste, kingmaker, weaver of darkness, has drawn close. She has come to see Aesunos, Belenus, and all of the men and women of the Northern Iceni to the Otherworld. There, they will feast with our ancestors until they are reborn into this world once more. Do not weep for the dead. They are beyond pain now.

"As their spirits drift to the Otherworld, their deaths come to us as a warning. A dark cloud has spread—not just on the lands of the Northern Iceni, but on us all. Rome has come once more. The eagle is shrieking. And these deaths," she said, turning to my father and Belenus, "are but the first of many to come. Guard your families. Prepare for the winters ahead. As Aesunos and Belenus go to darkness, so do all our people. Make no mistake, Oak Throne, the gods whisper, and the greenwood speaks in warnings. These events are the beginning of a dark time for us all."

No one said a word.

No one moved.

Ula was not one for idle chatter or mindless conversation. And she did not mince words. Ula told the truth, even when it hurt.

"Let us send these loved ones on to the Otherworld where they may begin their journey. King Caturix," she said, gesturing for my brother to come forward.

Ula lifted a torch from the fire and handed it to my brother.

"Send your dead to the dark lady, and in so doing, claim your throne," she told him.

My brother took the torch from her and then made his way to my father's pyre.

The flames flickered in the breeze.

Caturix paused.

I could see his lips moving but could not hear his words. Then, he set the pyre aflame. Leaving Father, he went to Belenus, whispering a farewell to the druid, then on to the others. Soon, bonfires were roaring as the people of Oak Throne burned.

Caturix turned to the crowd. "May the gods watch over all the Northern Iceni in the days ahead."

"Hail, King Caturix," Ula called.

"Hail, King Caturix," the crowd answered.

My brother turned back toward the pyre.

Then, we all stood in silence, watching the past burn before our eyes.

THEREAFTER, CIDNA AND LYNET, HAVING THE FORESIGHT that I had forgotten in all of the mess, called for the mourners to return to the king's roundhouse for ale and food.

Prasutagus turned to me. "I cannot delay any longer. I'm sorry. I must collect my men and ride south."

I nodded. "I understand. I will join you as soon as I can."

"Be careful at Holk Fort, my May Queen," he said, setting his hand on my cheek. "Everywhere I look, I see trouble."

"What will you do?" I asked Prasutagus.

"I am not keen to make enemies out of Togodumnus and Caratacus, but this war is not mine. Verica has a right to his throne, and he has a son who is of age. Aedd Mawr was also pushed from his lands. Verica and Aedd Mawr must think of their tribes' futures. The Greater Iceni did not interfere in Togodumnus's and Caratacus's wars. But now... The presence of the Romans changes everything. I must see what I can discover. I, too, have a wife and my own children's future to consider."

"Children, King Prasutagus?" I said, raising an eyebrow at him.

He chuckled. "Once you are done running the countryside, I presume we can continue our practice in that matter."

I chuckled.

Prasutagus kissed my forehead and pulled me close. "Be safe," he whispered.

"And you."

He let me go, then turned and rejoined his men.

As I watched him go, Ula joined me.

"So, you are the queen of the Greater Iceni now."

"I suspect that doesn't come as a surprise to you."

She shrugged. "A king needs his queen."

I turned and looked at her. "Thank you for your words," I said, my gaze drifting back to the pyre.

"There are dark times ahead, Boudica. Do not let the moments when the sun breaks through the clouds deceive you." She turned and walked away.

"Ula," I called to her. "When all of this is done, Bran will be alone here in Oak Throne. You will watch over him?"

"Bah," she huffed, turning to me. "What does he need me for? He'll have the help-maid he needs here soon enough," she said, then made her way back to her cottage.

My gaze went back to the fire. Amongst the flames, I could see the narrow silhouette of my father's body—at least, what the fire had not yet taken.

"Farewell, Father," I said, then returned to the roundhouse.

THE MOOD IN THE ROUNDHOUSE WAS SOMBER. AFTER THE mourners had gone and Lynet and the warriors from Frog's Hollow settled in for the night, Bran and I sat glossy-eyed at the table, each of us with a mug of ale in our hands.

"Where has Caturix gone?" Bran asked.

I shrugged, then shook my head, not meeting Bran's gaze. I knew where Caturix was, but I dared not say. Nor did I dare look at Bran. I didn't want him to read the expression on my face.

After a long time, Bran whispered, "Brenna."

"Once Holk Fort is settled, we can send a messenger."

Bran nodded, and then rose. "We will ride out at first light. I'm going to bed. You should get some rest too."

I gave him an absent nod.

"Good night, Sister."

"And you."

"Queen of the Greater Iceni," he added with a tired smile, then went to bed.

Setting my ale aside, I went back outside to Oak Throne's palisades. When this business was done, I would return to Venta as queen. And yet... I turned my attention once more to the fields surrounding the fort. A mist had risen off the river, covering the land in a blanket of fog.

"Great Andraste," I whispered. "As the fog shelters this fort, so let it shelter all of the Iceni from Rome's gaze."

"Rome looks on with an eagle's eye.

"There is nothing in our lands it cannot see."

CHAPTER 3

I woke the following day before dawn. I hurriedly dressed, grabbed my gear, and headed to the main room, where I found Caturix finishing off his morning meal.

"Boudica," he said, nodding to me. He took the last swig of his ale and then began pulling on his gloves. "I will stay to see Lynet settled and ensure all is calm at Oak Throne before I depart this morning."

"For Stonea…"

"I need to ride to Venta first. Melusine is still there. I don't want her riding back to Stonea on her own, not even with an escort. I'll fetch her myself."

"That is… I'm glad to hear it."

Caturix met my gaze. "It is early days still, so she did not want to tell anyone, but she is with child."

"Oh," I said, surprise in my voice. "I see."

Caturix paused, and then lowered his voice. "Kennocha told me how you looked after her and Mara. Thank you, Boudica."

"I think I'm going to have a lucky day."

"Why?"

"My brother thanked me for something."

Caturix smiled lightly, but then sadness swept over his features once more. "You advised me rightly before. I should have fought against Father. If I had, now I could wed Kennoc—well, it's no matter now."

I was stunned by Caturix's openness. I knew well enough to handle it delicately. "I'm sure Kennocha was comforted to see you. And I am glad you had a chance to see Mara. She is the sweetest thing."

"I hate to leave them here alone with things so unsettled, but I cannot bring Melusine here."

"Bran will get things in hand. They will be safe."

Caturix frowned. "Bran isn't ready. He is not tempered enough."

"No, but Bec is."

Caturix held my gaze a moment as he came to understand my words. He nodded. "Yes, so she seems. By the gods, why now? Saenunos. Ambitious bastard. Not only do we have our own troubles, but Rome is at our door. When I ride to Venta, I will speak further with Prasutagus. I don't trust those brothers. They pressed their finger on the scale in Saenunos's favor, even if they did not lift a knife."

"Yes."

"I must see to some things. Get Bran out of bed and get

going. Be careful on the road. And it goes without saying, at Holk Fort as well.

"Thank you, Caturix."

My brother nodded and then departed.

After stuffing a few bites of food in my mouth and washing it back with ale, I went to my brother's bedchamber.

"Bran," I said, knocking on the door and then entering.

My brother groaned in his sleep and rolled over.

Bran was usually up early. The loss of our father and Belenus was hanging on him, even if he didn't speak of it. It was unlike Bran to linger.

"Bran," I said, shaking his shoulder. "I'll go to the stables and begin preparing the horses to ride."

"Boudica… wha-what's happening?"

"We're riding to Holk Fort."

"Yes. I forgot. I mean, I'm getting up now."

I nodded then left.

When I arrived at the stables, I found Pix and some of Bran's men already there. They had started readying the horses. I fetched Druda, who paused on his way out of the stables to bump noses with Mountain, then we made ready.

"Mornin', Strawberry Queen," Pix said with a grin.

It didn't escape my notice that she was fully outfitted for battle. I eyed her over. "Are you wearing *more* weapons?"

She nodded. "That silver ye gave me went far."

"What silver did I give you?"

Pix merely grinned at me.

Davin, who overheard the conversation, chuckled.

"First Cai's horse, now Boudica's silver."

"Watch yerself, or I'll find something belonging to ye I like. Come to think of it…" she said, eyeing him up and down.

Davin's cheeks reddened. "I've got a woman."

"Why not have two?"

Davin merely laughed, then turned to me. "What do you think we will find in Holk Fort, Boudica?"

"Honestly, I don't know. But either way, we must be ready to meet with resistance."

"Why do ye think I have all these?" Pix asked, gesturing to her weapons with a grin.

"Considering you've dubbed yourself my protector, I won't complain," I replied.

Davin nodded. "Bran told us to be ready, full at arms."

"That's right."

"My cousin went to the pyre last night," Davin said, the mirth leaving his voice. "If we find resistance in Holk Fort…"

"I feel the same, my friend," I said, setting my hand on his arm.

It was not long after that Bran and the rest of the warriors joined us.

Lynet came to see us off.

"I'll keep the gate closed and put my men on the walls. I've sent a rider back to Frog's Hollow this morning, telling them to keep things quiet and be watchful. Caturix has done the same for the other small villages and farms."

"Will you send someone to the grove as well? Dôn will

return soon, but they need to be cautious in the mean-time. I'm not worried about Saenunos's people, but I don't like them being on their own with the Romans afoot. They can come to Oak Throne if they don't feel safe."

"I'll see to it," Lynet said as she took Druda's reins so I could mount. "May Epona go with you and keep you safe, Boudica."

"And may the gods watch over you."

"Let's ride," Bran called.

Lynet stepped back.

I waved goodbye to her and then clicked to Druda. We rode out. I didn't know what we would find when we arrived at Holk Fort. But if there was one sure thing, my patience for intrigue had reached far beyond its limits.

I was coming with a reckoning.

THE RIDE TO HOLK FORT WOULD TAKE A LITTLE MORE THAN half the day. The fort sat near the sea, with salt flats and marshes surrounding it. Not far from Holk Fort was another holy place of our people. The druids who worshipped Condatis, a god of waters, war, and change-able places, had a temple to the sea god along Wash. Their holy site, Seahenge, sat somewhere deep in the marsh between Holk Fort and the Wash. I had never been there before, but Belenus once described the holy site as a great circle of ash trees with an altar at the center made of the roots of a sacred tree.

With our party of two dozen, we rode quickly across the landscape. We were nearly there when I caught the scent of salt in the air, which made Druda quicken his step. I felt sorry for the horse. This was not the galivanting on the beach he was expecting. But the farther we went, the stranger Druda's behavior became. He flicked his ears, his nostrils flaring, and his steps quickened.

Something was wrong.

I was about to call out to Bran, who was riding in front of me, when the first arrow went whizzing by.

"Ambush!" I screamed.

But my voice was drowned out as a warrior in the tall grasses around us shouted, "Attack!"

A moment later, men wearing my uncle's colors emerged from the grass, swords swinging.

Pulling my spear from my back, I swung Druda around. When the first warrior rushed toward me, I gripped my spear hard and jabbed, piercing the warrior's throat before he could get within arm's length to swing. Another man ran toward me, attempting the same move, but met with the same grizzly end. My gaze swept quickly across the men. Pix had already leaped from her horse and was fighting, her twin blades whirling, as she launched herself headlong into the fray. Bran, still ahorse, was battling one man while another rushed toward him.

I clicked my heels against Druda's sides, and then raced in Bran's direction. Hoisting my spear, I took aim and then threw. The spear knocked the man advancing on

Bran from his feet and to the ground. Riding quickly, I collected my spear and then regrouped with Bran once more.

Our warriors battled hard. We outnumbered the men who'd ambushed us. But the surprise attack had worked to some effect. Two of Bran's warriors had taken damage. One of them, Boden, lay dead on the ground. Another, Aterie, was severely wounded.

Two burly warriors rushed Bran and me. This time, however, my rage had the better of me. Hoisting my spear, I sent it flying. The man moved to dodge, but he was too late. Seeing his comrade fall, the other warrior turned and raced down the road toward the fort.

I clicked to Druda and rushed after him.

The man ran, but Druda was faster.

My heart pounding in my chest, we rode him down. I snatched up my spear and threw it once more. It stabbed the man in the back, knocking him off his feet. The rage within me made my hands shake. My father was dead. Belenus was dead. Everything was a mess, and the Romans were coming. I wanted to murder every last man standing. My fury startled me.

Willing my heart to be silent, I yanked my spear from the man's body, then turned Druda and raced back to rejoin the others. Many of Saenunos's men had been defeated. A handful of them retreated and were running off through the high grass.

"We should go after them," Bran said.

"No," I said, reining in the fierce emotions. I, too, wanted to chop down every man. "They know the marshes here. We don't. We'll be swallowed by the mud. Let's press on quickly to Holk Fort."

"All right, but I must see to my men first," Bran said, then dismounted.

I followed my brother.

Bran went first to Boden, but it was clear the man was dead. Working together, Davin and Bran lifted Boden's body and placed it on the back of Davin's horse.

As they worked, Pix joined me.

"Ye have a man injured," she said.

I nodded, and then the two of us went to Aterie.

The warrior lay on the ground. He was one of the younger men in Bran's warband. His long, blond hair was pulled back at the nape, his face painted with blue woad designs. He looked the part of a warrior but was still green. He held his side.

Pix pulled a cloth from her vest and pressed it against the wound. "Ye will survive. Keep pressure on it," she told him.

"Can you ride?" I asked.

Aterie looked uncertain. "I…I don't know."

"If we leave you here, you'll bleed to death. Holk Fort is a hard ride across the marsh. We may find trouble there, or we may walk into the fort with no resistance and be able to get you some help." I looked at his wound. "You'll die before we get you back to Oak Throne."

"I don't like those options, Boudica," he told me with a wince.

"Nor do I, but that is what they are."

"Get me up."

"You'll ride with me," Ectorus, one of the older men in Bran's crew, told him. "I have him, Queen Boudica. We will be ready to ride." Ectorus reached out for the young man, helping him to his feet. Then the pair went to Ectorus's horse, Ectorus helping Aterie up.

Leaving them, I went to Druda and mounted once more.

Bran and Pix joined me after that.

I nodded to my brother.

Bran whistled to his men, and then we rode off once more.

CHAPTER 4

After some consideration, Bran and I decided to hoist the banner of Oak Throne and approach the hillfort with the confidence of a king's children. After all, the worst was that they could try to kill us, and they'd already tried once today. Both mine and Bran's patience had run thin.

We followed the road toward the ancient fort. Like Oak Throne, Holk Fort had massive ditches that protected it on three sides. A bridge passed over the wide earthen embankment. The fort was walled, and even from a distance, we could see men on the palisades.

"Are you sure we shouldn't have come in by nightfall?" Bran asked me for the hundredth time.

I chewed on the inside of my cheek as I considered, then said, "No. Saenunos brought most of his fighting men with him to Oak Throne. We just defeated the rest on the road. The men on those walls will have been waiting to see which banner would return. Let's show them."

Bran looked toward Pix.

Pix, who was taking a swig from her water pouch, wiped her mouth with the back of her hand and then shrugged. "Let them see ye, Prince. Show them ye are not afraid."

Bran nodded.

We rode boldly toward the fort.

The gate was closed.

Clicking to his horse, Bran moved to the front of our party.

"Hold!" a man on the watchtower called. "Who approaches?"

"Prince Bran of Oak Throne. Open your gates," my brother called.

The man on the watchtower paused then said, "No, Prince Bran. We are under orders from the chieftain not to open these gates to anyone but himself."

"You will do as I command. Open this fort."

The man on the watchtower did not move.

Frowning, I coaxed Druda forward. "I am Boudica, Princess of the Northern Iceni and Queen of the Greater Iceni," I called in a firm voice. "Chieftain Saenunos went to the pyre last night with his brother's blood on his hands. Your chieftain is dead. Only his spirit will ever approach this fort again."

At that, the man paused. He looked over his shoulder at the others standing nearby.

I continued, "The good people of Holk Fort do not deserve to be punished for my uncle's treachery. We have much larger and far more urgent issues at hand. Rome has landed in the south. In the name of my brother, King Caturix of the Northern Iceni, you *will* open these gates."

The man stood stone still in contemplative silence for a moment, then retreated.

"Do you suppose that scared him sufficiently?" Bran asked.

The gates began to swing open.

"There is your answer," I replied. "Now, let's see what we find within."

At that, Bran and I led the others into the fort.

HOLK FORT WAS SMALLER THAN OAK THRONE BUT STILL home to a sizeable population. Within the fort were a marketplace and many small houses. A wall surrounded three sides of the fort, but the west of the fort was protected by a jagged, rocky cliff that looked out into the salt marsh below. Within the fort were three massive retaining ponds. Natural aquifers deep in the ground fed water into the ponds.

The chieftain's roundhouse sat at the end of the lane to the north.

As we rode into the fort, we found the place silent.

The market was closed.

No one was outside.

No children were running amuck, nor workers carrying on about their business.

Everything was quiet.

Druda's feet stuck in the mud, making a sucking sound with each step as we made our way down the muddy lane to the roundhouse. Somewhere in the village, a dog barked, only to be shushed by someone inside.

Bran and I exchanged a glance.

"Cheerful place," Pix mused.

When we arrived at the chieftain's roundhouse, we were met at the door by an aged man I recognized as Saenunos's housecarl, Bowen. He had held that position at Holk Fort for as long as I could remember. In every memory I had of him, he was old. He had served Saenunos well, but from where had that loyalty come? From his dedication to the Northern Iceni or to Saenunos?

"Prince Bran, Princess Boudica, you are welcome to Holk Fort. Please accept my apologies for your unhospitable welcome," he said with a bow, and then motioned for an attendant—a young man barely out of his teen years —to open the door to the roundhouse.

Bran moved to dismount, but I gestured for him to hold. I turned back to Pix and motioned to the house.

"Right," Pix told me, then turned to Davin. "Come on, pretty. Let's see if they've got men inside waiting to kill us."

"I say," Bowen exclaimed in protest. "Princess Boudica, we would never..." he said, but his voice fell flat as Pix and David pushed past him, blades drawn.

Scowling, Bowen turned back to me. "What is the meaning of this?"

"Will you truly claim ignorance?" I asked him.

"Ignorance?" he replied.

I sighed, already annoyed by his game. Turning, I gestured to our party. "We have an injured man here."

Bowen turned to the boy and said, "Go get the healer."

No questions on how he'd been injured.

A few moments later, Davin reappeared. "The house is clear. Only the kitchen staff—three women—are inside."

"Where is Pix?" I asked.

"In the kitchens. Eating."

I shook my head and then turned to Bran.

"All right. Let's get Aterie inside," Bran said.

Two of Bran's men helped the injured warrior down and led him into the house.

"I heard the news from the gate. Is it true what was said, that the chieftain and King Aesunos are dead?" Bowen asked Bran and me.

I studied the man. Bowen was a slim, short man with a bald head and beady, dark eyes. He looked at me over his long, pointed nose. His eyes revealed he was not entirely surprised.

"It is," Bran said firmly.

"Hmm," Bowen mused, rubbing his hands together. "I am very sorry to hear such dire news. And the Romans?"

"They are with King Verica in the south," I replied.

"That will get Caratacus's and Togodumnus's attention," Bowen said absently. "This is dire news all at once. Come have some ale."

Bran met my gaze. He was uncertain what to do.

"No," I replied. "You will summon the people of Holk Fort. Now."

Bowen stared at me. "I will *what*?"

"You heard me."

Bowen looked confused.

"Now," I repeated.

Bowen glared. "Very well, Princess Boudica."

"Queen," Bran corrected. "Boudica is Queen of the Greater Iceni now. She is *Queen* Boudica."

"Is that so?" the man asked with raised eyebrows. "Interesting," he said, then made his way to the central square where a bell hung on a pole. The sound of the sharp bong of the bell rolled across the fort as he pulled on the rope.

"Well?" Bran whispered to me.

"We shall see," I replied.

Slowly, the people of Holk Fort gathered. I was aghast to see their condition. Never in Northern Iceni lands had I seen so many thin frames, hollow cheeks, sallow skin, and raggedly dressed people. Those who gathered were worn raw from work and hunger. And for the most part, it was women, children, and aged men who answered the bell's call.

Bran stepped forward. "I am Prince Bran, and this is my sister, Queen Boudica. We are the children of King Aesunos. Our father is dead, killed by his own brother— your chieftain," he said, and then let the words settle.

A murmur ran through the crowd.

Bran said, "Oak Throne was taken by Saenunos and a warband from this fort. But they do not hold the fort now, and those who rode with our uncle are dead, alongside their chieftain."

That brought a wail from several people in the group, and many of the women burst into tears.

"Our brother, Caturix, is now king of the Northern Iceni. Those who conspired against my father will pay the price for their trespasses," Bran added.

I scanned the crowd. Besides the gate watchman and the other men who had been on the wall, there were no abled-bodied men in the group.

"Where are your menfolk?" I asked.

There was silence from the group. No one would meet my gaze. I met the watchman's eye, but he looked away. Frowning, I studied the group once more. Dressed in drab gray, the hems of their gowns covered in inches of mud, the women were a sorry lot. One woman was heavily pregnant. I went to her, standing before her.

She would not look at me.

"Good woman," I said, tipping her chin gently so she would meet my eye. "Where are the menfolk?"

The others around her look nervous.

The woman stammered as if unsure what to say.

"Bran and I are here to ensure the safety of all the Northern Iceni. There must be no more lies. We need one another now. Where is your babe's father?"

"Gone, Queen Boudica. He went to Oak Throne with the others at Saenunos's command on pain of death or banishment of our whole family from Holk Fort if he did not comply," she said in a sorrowful moan.

"On pain of death?" Bran asked, his voice sounding alarmed.

Another woman, emboldened by the first speaker,

stepped forward. "The chieftain forced our menfolk to ride with him to Oak Throne. He threatened to send the families out, kill us, kill them... there was nothing the chieftain did not threaten," she said, setting her hand on her child's shoulder, pulling a small boy protectively toward her.

"Is this true?" I asked Bowen waspishly.

The old man merely shrugged and then laughed nervously.

Glaring, I turned back to the watchman. "Is this true?" I demanded.

"It is," he said tersely.

The emboldened crowd spoke up in a chorus.

"Aye, Queen Boudica. It is true."

"It's true."

"He threatened to kill my boys."

"Saenunos threatened to send us out of the fort with nothing but the clothes on our backs."

"The chieftain beheaded my husband for refusing to go," another tearful woman said.

"And mine," another added.

I turned and looked at Bowen, my gaze demanding an answer.

"You know your uncle, Queen Boudica. He listened to no one when he had something in his mind. I could do nothing to dissuade him."

"Nor did you do anything to warn King Aesunos," I replied sharply.

The man lowered his gaze.

I surveyed the surviving villagers. Perhaps some

amongst them were complicit in Saenunos's plan, but the threadbare women and children were not to blame.

I turned back to Bran. With a tilt of the head, I motioned for him to speak to them.

"Friends," Bran began gently. "More than ever now, we must stand together. You may have heard the news. Rome has come once more. The Northern Iceni must be strong. Now is not the time for infighting. Saenunos is gone, and so is our father. We must unite behind my brother, King Caturix."

"Yes, Prince Bran," the watchman called. "We are with you."

"Thank you, Prince," a tearful woman called.

"Hail King Caturix," one old woman shouted.

"Hail King Caturix," came a chorus of voices in reply.

Bran nodded. "Go in peace, friends. Go in peace. The terror is over. You are safe now."

The people dispersed, whispering to one another about the news.

I turned to Bowen. "The people of this fort are skin and bones," I said sharply.

"Was a hard winter, Queen Boudica."

"As you should have expected. As we always plan for in Oak Throne. But our people do not go hungry. Plans are made. Crops are planted. Game hunted. Meat preserved. This place is a muddy mess. What has my uncle done here? Did he give any thought to his people?"

"Well," the man said, running his hand over his bald head, "the chieftain had other things on his mind."

Furious, I turned to Bran. "We must make an

accounting of Saenunos's provisions," I said, turning back to Bowen. "We will see the grain stores, the livestock, and everything else. Now."

The housecarl appeared to take in the tone of my voice and did not protest.

"Very well, Prin—Queen Boudica. Follow me."

Bran gestured for two men to accompany us, the rest going into the roundhouse.

Bowen led us around the fort. My boots stuck in the mud as we went. Around the roundhouse, the land had been reinforced with dirt, gravel, and grass, preventing the mud. But the rest of the fort was like a pig's wallow. Bowen toured us about, showing us the well-stocked ponds, the bursting grain stores, the supply sheds loaded with salted fish and cured meat, and the animals' pens.

"The fort is very well supplied. Why are the people starving?" Bran asked.

"These are the chieftain's supplies," Bowen explained.

"The *chieftain's* supplies? Saenunos kept all of this for the chieftain's house? None of this is for the people?" I asked pointedly.

"That's correct."

"Saenunos was letting his people starve," I told Bran.

"How many people are in Holk Fort?" Bran asked.

Bowen shrugged. "Don't rightly know."

"How about a guess?" my brother retorted. It was unusual for Bran to get angry, but I could hear from the tension in his voice that he'd seen and heard enough.

"Maybe twenty or so families. Can't say for sure."

"It is your job to say," I told him. "You are the chieftain's housecarl, master of his roundhouse, and go-between from the chieftain to the people. It is literally your job to know."

"Chieftain had me busy with other matters, Queen Boudica."

"As chieftain, his people were his *only* concern," I replied, then turned to Bran. "We need to send some men to go around and get an accounting of the number of families here. I'll go to the roundhouse and look over Saenunos's notes."

Bran nodded. "All right. I'll get the men on it."

"Let's get the place secured for the night. Gates closed. Guards on the roundhouse," I said.

"Agreed."

I tuned to Bowen. "You will take me to the chieftain's meeting room."

"As you say, Queen Boudica," the man said, and then waved for me to follow him.

Saenunos, lost to his own greed, had forgotten his purpose. He'd wanted to be king. Dear Uncle would have been surprised to find the same responsibilities waiting for him on the other side of my father's crown, only on a larger scale.

With Bran working to secure the fort and get a census of Saenunos's people, I took over my uncle's meeting chamber. The small space was well appointed, with a large desk and comfortable chair. Bearskins lined the stone floor, and a brazier burned at the center of the room. There was a table at the opposite end of the room. On it was a display of antlers, the tips covered in silver. On the walls hung wolf pelts and other adornments.

Saenunos let his people live like swine while he lived in opulence.

Bowen stood at the door, shifting nervously as I shifted through correspondence between Saenunos and Melusine's father, King Volisios of the Coritani. I also found letters between Saenunos and Caratacus and Togodumnus about possible alliances between ourselves and the brothers, mainly concerning the marriages of Brenna, Bran, and myself. But amongst the letters, I found one obscure line written in Caratacus's hand: *All things will come to pass much more easily in the days to come.*

I stared at the note, suddenly sorry I had complained endlessly when Belenus had taken the time to teach us all Latin. Without it, I would not be sitting here with the Catuvellauni king's words in my hand.

"When were Togodumnus and Caratacus last in Holk Fort?" I asked Bowen.

"The Catuvellauni kings?" he asked, feigning stupidity.

I held the man's gaze.

"Been some years."

"Stop lying. Your master is dead, and your words make you complicit in his crimes. Speak the truth now or be condemned with your master."

"Hmm," the man considered. "I'm old, Queen. You must forgive me. I did forget. They were here last autumn, those brothers."

"What did they talk to Saenunos about?"

"Oh, can't rightly say. I was not in the room."

"I repeat my warning to you."

"It's true, Queen Boudica. I don't know much about it except your uncle hoped to see a good match between our people, you or your sister married to those brothers. That's all I know."

"Swear it by the gods."

"Swear what?"

"That you have told me all you know."

The man balked a moment, and then said, "I swear it."

"Then may Andraste punish you if your words prove a lie. Go. I will call you if I need you."

Bowen opened the door, revealing one of the kitchen maids on the other side. She was holding a tray full of food.

"I... I'm sorry to interrupt," the girl stammered. "That funny lady with the fox tail in her hair said I should bring food for the queen."

"Always underfoot. Nuisance," Bowen grumbled at her. "Go on with you, then," he said, pushing past her as he departed.

The girl stepped into the room. She was a tall, slim girl with straight black hair that hung to her hips. "My apologies, Queen Boudica," she said, her eyes cast downward.

"Please, do not apologize. You have my thanks."

The girl set the tray down on the edge of the table. On it, she had left me a round of freshly baked bread, cheese, and thin cuts of beef. Along with those sat a bowl of butter and another of something orange-colored.

As the girl poured me a mug of ale, I lifted one of the bowls and sniffed. "Is this orange marmalade?"

"It is," the girl said brightly. "A trader came from the south with a crate of oranges. They cost the chieftain a sack of silver, but he bought them all."

"Smells of sunshine," I said, setting the bowl back down. "What is your name?"

"Vian."

"How many people work in the kitchens here, Vian?"

"It's me, my mother, and my sister."

"I am so sorry to find the people of Holk Fort in such dire conditions. It appears my uncle did not look after the people of the fort as he should have."

The girl looked over her shoulder to see if Bowen was still there. Even though the housecarl had gone, the girl looked nervously at the floor. She opened her mouth to speak, then closed it again. Twiddling her fingers anxiously, she lingered as if she was working up the courage to say something.

I went and closed the door.

"What is it? You can tell me," I encouraged her in a low voice. "Bran and I are here to help."

"Chieftain Saenunos called the villagers swine. The chieftain always said he would not waste his supplies on hungry-mouthed hogs. That's what he called us. Trouble was, everything was his. Our grain. Our game. Even the fisheries, which the people had always used and tended, he kept for himself. So much has changed these last few years."

"We will set things to right here. We truly are here to help."

Vian looked uncertain.

"What is it?"

"The people are afraid. The men were forced to join the attack on Oak Throne. King Caturix... Will he take revenge upon us?"

"Saenunos's duty was to look after his people, not abuse them. As far as I can see, he let the people of Holk Fort suffer and misused their loyalty. They have nothing to fear. Caturix will not punish people who were used against their will. And I will not leave this fort until the people here are looked after."

"Thank you, Queen Boudica," the girl said, a deep tone of gratitude in her voice. "I will make sure the others know."

"Thank you, Vian."

With that, the girl turned to go. When she got to the door, however, she paused. "Queen Boudica," she said, then came and stood close to me. "I'm sorry. When I came with the tray, I lingered at the door, trying to open it with my hands full. I heard what you and the housecarl were saying. I wasn't trying to spy. I just... the tray. Queen Boudica, you should know that Bowen lied to you. Those brother kings have been here many times, including just before the chieftain rode to Stonea for Beltane. The three of them spoke of your father. I heard them when I served their dinner. That Togodumnus had hands like an eel. It was all my sister and I could do prevent him from—well, you know. Anyway, they whispered about what might happen if your father died. The chieftain suggested that your father's death could occur sooner than expected. Those brother kings encouraged the idea. And they

MELANIE KARSAK

promised the chieftain their full support if King Aesunos died. I'd heard King Aesunos was ill, so I didn't think anything more of it. Now... I'm sorry. I never suspected what they were plotting. I didn't hear any more of the conversation, but Bowen *did*. He was there the entire time. He lied to you."

My heart thundered loudly in my chest. I cleared my throat then said, "Thank you. Thank you for your honesty, Vian."

She curtsied to me, and then exited once more. Returning to the desk, I sank slowly into my chair.

They had plotted together.

They had plotted my father's murder.

While they may not have known what Saenunos was going to do, they had fanned the flames.

The Catuvellauni's treachery had sealed their fate.

Rome could burn them to the ground.

King Verica could take their heads.

I would never support Caratacus and Togodumnus.

The Catuvellauni were on their own.

CHAPTER 5

I'd worked myself bleary-eyed going through all of Saenunos's notes, looking for further proof of their involvement in my father's death. When I could not keep my eyes open any longer, I rose to find Bran.

"Queen Boudica," one of the serving boys said, crossing paths with me. "Can I help you?"

"I was looking for my brother."

"He's gone to bed."

"There is a woman in our party…she has a fox tail in her hair."

The boy grinned. "She dozed off in the kitchen drinking ale."

At that, I laughed. "Don't let her stay there all night, okay?"

He nodded. "The ladies in the kitchen made up a room for you," the boy told me, then waved for me to follow him. He led me down a hall to one of the chambers.

The boy opened the door to a small chamber that was

decadently adorned. A brazier had been lit. The bed was nicely made up with furs and rich coverlets. Elaborate tapestries hung on the walls alongside antlers and carved wooden pieces. While Saenunos kept his people impoverished, he spared no expense on his own desires. His roundhouse was fully stocked with food and expensive imports. Every room was elaborately adorned. While the fort looked like a pig's wallow, the roundhouse looked fit for a king—as Saenunos saw himself.

"There's no maid here, but Vian said you could call her if you need anything."

I ruffled the child's hair. "Thank her for me, but there is no need. I'm so tired I can barely keep my eyes open. The bed is enough. My brother's men are on guard here at the fort?"

"Yes, Queen Boudica. At the door to the roundhouse, the gate, and the walls."

I nodded. "All right. Then, I am settled. Thank you."

The boy grinned and then ran off.

Closing the door, I leaned my spear against the corner and then sat down on the bed. My whole body ached, the tensions of the last days seeping into my bones. I should be in Venta with Prasutagus. I was a new bride. What was I doing so far from my husband?

"Aye, Saenunos, what a mess you have created for us all."

I pulled off my boots and then lay back. Removing the dagger from my belt, I slipped it under my pillow.

No sooner had I closed my eyes than sleep took me.

I quickly drifted off into dreams.

I walked barefoot down the path in Frog's Hollow leading to the catacombs. As I approached the opening to the shrine, I heard voices within. My eyes lingered on the empty eye sockets of the skulls looking back at me. But then, from within, I heard a familiar voice.

"Boudica…"

"Father?" I whispered.

Ducking low, I entered the crypt. Under my feet, I felt the crunch of bones as I made my way to the center chamber. The air was cold within the catacomb and smelled of earth and minerals. I approached the main room. There, I found the pale, translucent figure of my father.

He turned and looked at me. "Boudica."

"Father?"

"Boudica, you must protect the Iceni. You must watch over them *all*. Protect the people. Protect the greenwood. Protect the stones." He stared at me, his ethereal hand reaching toward me. "Queen of ash and iron." His gaze shifted behind me. "Boudica! Wake!"

My eyes popped open in time to find a face close to mine. I felt hot breath on my cheeks and a blade on my neck.

"I will finish what my master started. Death to Aesunos and all his progeny," Bowen hissed.

Gasping, I reached for my knife under my pillow.

But then the housecarl jerked.

He grew perfectly still, his eyes going wide, and a moment later, blood leaked from the corner of his mouth.

I clawed away from him.

Bowen's body then fell to the ground, his knife clattering along with him.

Wide-eyed, I looked behind him to find a man I didn't recognize. He was a tall, thin man with stringy black hair. He had dark kohl around his eyes and Ogham symbols tattooed all over his face.

"Queen Boudica," the man said. "I am Arixus, Arch Druid of Seahenge."

"Banshees be cursed," I whispered. "You just saved my life."

"As the gods demanded."

CHAPTER 6

"**Y**ou'll want to come with me," the druid said, lending me his hand.

Not resisting, I went with him.

Pausing a moment to pull his long, crooked blade from the base of Bowen's skull, the druid wiped the blood off on the end of his cloak, slipped his knife back into his belt, then led me from the room.

Stepping over the body of Bowen, I exited the chamber. The druid led me from the roundhouse. Just outside waited at least two-dozen druids holding torches. I had expected to find men in robes, but they were dressed like warriors, with knives and swords on their belts. Like Arixus, their faces were marked with dark kohl. They wore dark, hooded cloaks. Many had their hoods up, the light from the torches played in patches of darkness and orange firelight on their shadowed faces. Along with the druids were half a dozen men who had been bound by their hands and were on their knees. All of them were muddy.

Many were bleeding. I scanned them over, recognizing them from the attack on the road that morning. These were the men who had run.

"What's happening?" I heard Bran ask.

Turning, I looked back to see my brother being accompanied by Pix. The warrior woman had her sword drawn and looked like a muddy, bloody mess.

"Pix," I said, alarmed. "Are you all right?"

"Ding here and there, but ye cannot catch this fox."

I turned from Pix to Arixus.

"Queen Boudica," Arixus said, gesturing to the cloaked men. "My brothers, the druids of Seahenge. We druids have long divorced ourselves from Chieftain Saenunos and are loyal to the line of Aesunos."

"So you have proven," I said, touching my neck where I still felt the shadow of steel.

"We aided your warrior maiden in subduing these men," Arixus continued. "What would you have us do with them?" the druid asked, gesturing to the captives.

I turned to Bran. While it was clear that many of the men of Holk Fort had been pressed into service by Saenunos, these men were not of the same ilk. They wore fine armor and my uncle's colors. These were his trusted soldiers. These men had tried to kill us on the road. And from the looks of Pix and the druids, had they not been stopped, they would have killed us tonight.

Still, Bran looked uncertain.

"Do you have anything to say in favor of these men?" I asked the druid.

"No more than I had for the chieftain's housecarl."

Bran said nothing.

Behind us, a crowd of servants had gathered. Amongst them, I spotted Vian. I gestured for her to come to me.

"Queen Boudica?"

"I will not make the same mistakes my uncle made," I told her in a whisper. "Anyone innocent will be spared. Were *these* men forced into service, or are they loyal to Saenunos?"

Vian's eyes glimmered in the torchlight as she surveyed the men gathered there. "They are Saenunos's men, part of his warband. He left them behind to keep us in line. They are cruel, beastly creatures."

I knew what must be done.

"Thank you, Vian."

I turned and looked over the men.

Protect the people. Protect the greenwood. Protect the stones.

I turned to the druids. "Execute them."

Bran said nothing, simply stared.

Not waiting another moment, the druids pulled their blades and dispatched the men.

I turned to Arixus. "Join me inside. I suspect we have much to discuss."

"So we do, Queen Boudica. So we do."

WHEN WE ALL RETURNED TO THE ROUNDHOUSE, PIX CLEARED the confusion about what had transpired.

"Aside from a wee nod off in the kitchen, it wasn't a good night for sleeping," Pix explained, "so I walked the fort. On the cliffside, I found the party creeping back into the fort. One of 'em spotted me. They tried to kill me, but ye cannot kill Pix. The gods brought the druids to help."

"Why did you come tonight?" Bran asked Arixus.

"Condatis sent me here to protect Queen Boudica," he said, referring to their patron god.

Confused, Bran looked at me.

"I woke to Bowen's blade on my neck. If Arixus had not come, I would be dead."

"Bowen tried to murder you?" Bran asked, his eyes going wide.

"Tried. He's dead now."

"Banshees be cursed," Bran whispered under his breath, causing me to laugh lightly.

"We are here to help," Arixus told Bran and me. "Condatis has shown us many visions. Is it true? Has the eagle returned?"

"The Romans landed in the south," I said. "King Verica was seen amongst them. That is all we know besides that they arrived with a considerable force."

"As the gods have shown us," he said to his brothers, who nodded.

I studied the druid. "You and your brethren did not come south for the Beltane rites. Why were you not at Arminghall with the others?"

"We walk a different path, Queen Boudica."

I eyed the druid's attire once more. Warrior druids. I *had* heard Belenus speak of these men before. They prescribed to a path not often followed by our druids. While druids generally served as priests, advisers, or bards, the druids of Seahenge followed an older path. "Sons of Condatis," Belenus had called them with a shake of the head. "A god of water and war."

I met the druid's gaze. "As Condatis wills?"

"As Condatis wills, Queen Boudica."

Vian and her sister appeared with tankards of ale. I gestured to the men to take their seats while Bran and I settled in with Arixus.

"This is not how I expected the day to start," Bran said, rubbing his temples.

"It is done now. At least we've cleared the rats from the house," I replied.

"Well said," Arixus told me. "In our visions, we saw both the chieftain and King Aesunos dead. Is it true?"

"It is. Our uncle masterminded our father's death."

"We shall mourn the king's loss. Your elder brother, Caturix, is king now?"

I nodded. "Yes."

"What shall be done with Holk Fort?" the druid asked.

"There is much to be done here," I told Arixus. "Saenunos has left the fort in disorder."

"It has been crumbling for years, Queen Boudica. As your uncle aged, his ambition grew, and his duties to his people declined. Many families left the fort and built homes in the countryside. Where the chieftain once offered aid to the people during difficult times, the task fell onto our brotherhood. We have mended houses and aided in constructing more animal pens than I can count these last few years. Aside from Condatis's decree, that is why we have come. They are *our* people. We are here to help and protect them."

"Good," I said with a grin. "Then today, you and your men can assist us."

"With?"

"Redistribution of grain, livestock, mending more houses, and building more animal pens. We will see Holk Fort set back to right. If Condatis is in agreement with me."

The druid grinned. "His waters are flowing, racing to keep up with you, Queen Boudica. And we are ever his servants—and yours."

The druids were true to their word. At sunup, Arixus and I went to the granaries, along with some of the druids. I sent Vian into the village to spread the word that the people should come to collect their rations. Bran led another group of the holy brothers, along with Bran's warriors, to do something about the muddy mess the roads had become. Pix led the third group to examine the fisheries.

Not long after we began our work at the granaries, Holk Fort's people appeared with baskets and carts.

Vian, looking bright-eyed and sweaty, joined me.

"I asked all my friends to help spread the word," she said, then turned and gestured to the people. "Everyone has come. Queue up, Holk Fort. There is plenty for everyone," she called, motioning for them to form a line. "Queen Boudica. In one of the out sheds at the chieftain's house, we have a stock of wool. I sent two learned women from the village to determine how much is there. I hope that was all right?"

"It is very well done," I said, eyeing the long line of villagers with baskets and bags.

The girl beamed with pride. "My mother always said I could make fleas line up in a row," she said with a light laugh. "It was no easy feat to help keep the pantries organized, especially when the chieftain would buy crates of Roman imports but forget to purchase salt for the beef and fish. How we ever managed, I don't know. My mother left it for me. I never cooked all that well anyway."

"It is no easy feat to manage such things. Thank you, Vian."

She smiled at me.

I stayed for a time, watching the work underway. The people of Holk Fort seemed reassured by the presence of Arixus and the other druids. Once I was sure the granary was well in hand, I signaled to Arixus that I was departing, and then went to Vian.

"Come with me," I told her, then the pair of us made our way back across the fort to where Bran was working.

"Stones and reeds must be laid on the main thoroughfares," one of the druids explained to Bran. "With some luck and a little sun, it will dry out."

Bran turned, seeing Vian and me approaching. "Boudica," he said, "is all well?"

"Arixus has the grain well in hand," I said, then turned to the druid. "You have advised my brother rightly that the roads must be reinforced, but I had a thought. In Frog's Hollow, there were problems with flooding in one section of the village. A ditch was dug to drain the water into the stream." I turned to Vian. "Where does the water lie after a hard rain? Are there any places here in the fort that flood?"

"Yes," she said, then began pointing. "There and there. Water collects near the animal pens and then floods down the road toward the gate. Perhaps a ditch can be dug from the road to the northwest fishery. And in the southwest corner, another dug toward the cliff," she said, gesturing as she surveyed the land. "Is that right? Is that what you were thinking?"

"I was only thinking of the ditch, not how it worked. That's why I asked you."

Vian grinned.

"I will get my men to work digging the ditches if you can see to the roads," Bran told the druid, who inclined his head to him.

My brother, his hands, clothes, and face grubby with mud, turned and looked at me. And for the first time, I saw a flash of happiness in his eyes. I knew Bran. No doubt, he liked the hard physical work. But in that glimmer, I saw something more.

"I was thinking," Bran said. "The druids... Maybe it would be good if the holy people took charge here. With the druids' guidance, they could fare well."

I turned to Vian. "Do you think the people would agree to such an arrangement?"

"Yes. Arixus is much respected here. And with the men gone, the women will need the extra help."

Bran nodded. "Good. Let's get this work finished so we can return to Oak Throne in the morning."

"What has you so motivated all of a sudden?"

Bran grinned. "The realization that my future wife is likely on the road home by now."

"Does Bec know she's riding home to become your future wife?"

"I'll be sure to tell her when she gets there."

I set my hand on Bran's shoulder. "I am glad to see this glimmer of light in the darkness."

"Me too," Bran agreed. "Now, I need shovels."

"I can help with that," Vian offered.

And with that, the pair of them departed.

I stood for a moment, surveying the scene. We hadn't known what would await us in Holk Fort, but we hadn't expected this. How had my father missed the conditions here? Had he known and done nothing? I frowned. While Saenunos's lack of care was reflected here, so was the weakness in my father's leadership. My father had trusted his brother. But just because someone is part of your family, it doesn't mean they are loyal or trustworthy. My father's brotherly love had cost him his life. It was a hard lesson but one I would not forget.

My gaze drifted down the road.

My brother was eager to get to Bec, but my thoughts lay farther south.

Prasutagus.

I sighed heavily, then turned, pulling my foot from the sucking mud, and went after Bran. If I had any hope of getting back to my husband soon, I'd better grab a shovel.

CHAPTER 7

The sun beating down on us, we worked until nightfall. My arms aching, my back tense, I returned to the roundhouse with the others. Vian's mother and sister had prepared a hearty meal, and I was glad. As we settled in to eat, I listened as Bran talked with Arixus. Apparently, at some point that day, Bran had taken the initiative to speak to the druid about providing leadership to the people of Holk Fort in the absence of a chieftain. The druid, it seemed, had agreed.

I smiled at my brother. Perhaps Caturix and I had both underestimated him. Bran was friendly and got along well with everyone he met. Where he was lacking in shrewdness, he was not lacking in willingness to ask for help and befriend just about anyone. That was a quality that would take him far, even if he would need Bec's discernment from time to time.

At my insistence, the servants settled in along with us to eat.

Vian's mother and sister, Fan and Finola, sat across from me, Vian settling in beside me.

"It is a fine meal," I told them. "You have my thanks for your hard work today."

"We used up everything that would go bad and tried to give out the rest," Fan told me.

"I hope you will stay at the roundhouse to look after the place. With Bowen gone, it would be good to have someone competent looking after the chieftain's house. In Stonea, the housecarl was found keeping pigs in the roundhouse. That caused some discomfort to all involved."

"Except the pigs," Pix said with a snicker.

Fan laughed. "I would be honored to see to the place, Queen Boudica. There will not be much work here for my daughters and me, but we will manage."

"I had a thought on that matter, actually," I said, my gaze drifting to Vian. "If she is interested, I would like to ask Vian to come with me to Venta. I could use someone with a mind like hers to serve as my secretary."

Fan and Finola looked at Vian in surprise.

Vian stared at me. "Me?"

I chuckled. "Yes. You."

"But I... Of course, I would love to come if my mother permits it, but I don't see how I could be of help to you."

"Venta will be new for me, and I would be glad to have someone with me I can trust."

"'Tis good living," Pix told Vian. "Best bed I ever slept in. And King Prasutagus has many fine-looking warriors."

At that, Vian's cheeks rose into a blush.

"So, like a maid? She would be your maid?" Finola asked, looking confused.

"Not exactly. More like an assistant," I replied. I looked at Fan. "What do you say?"

"It is for Vian to decide. I am happy to let her go with you, Queen Boudica. The gods know; the girl has more mind than just for making dough and pickling vegetables."

"Vian?"

"I will come," she told me with an eager smile.

"Good," I replied with a grin. "Make ready to leave by morning."

"To Venta," Fan said, lifting her tankard, "and the future that awaits."

"To Venta," I agreed, clicking my cup against the others.

Oh, how I long to get back to Venta.

THE REST OF THE NIGHT, I SPENT MY TIME ORGANIZING THE last of Saenunos's papers. When I had the chieftain's meeting room settled, I went back to the main hall. I found the druid Arixus sitting alone. He sat holding the fire poker, gently moving the embers in the firepit.

"Queen Boudica," he said, inclining his head to me. "So, you will return to Oak Throne tomorrow, then to Venta."

I nodded. "There is much to be done, but I'm sorry I won't have time to visit your holy site at Seahenge. Belenus told me it is an awe-inspiring place."

The druid smiled weakly. "Perhaps, one day, you will find yourself there," he said, his eyes on the fire. The expression on his face was soft, as if he was seeing something beyond himself.

"Will I?"

The druid stared into the flames. "The future grows increasingly dark and unclear. But you have a friend in us if there is ever need."

"Thank you, Arixus."

"You should rest, Queen Boudica," he told me, gesturing with his chin to the back of the roundhouse. "The coming days will be difficult."

I grinned at him. "For you as well. You will be chieftain here in all but name."

He chuckled lightly. "Until the people are settled. We have begun the work together. I will finish what we started here."

"May Condatis bless your endeavors."

"And yours. You will need him."

I paused. He was right. With the Romans upon us, it might not be long before we called upon Condatis to give us strength. "Do you see them there?" I asked, looking toward the fire. "The Romans..."

"They are coming," he said, his voice sounding hollow, "in great waves. Blood on the land. Blood on the land. Beware of Roman lies," he said, and then blinked hard.

"Thank you for your council."

He nodded to me.

My heart feeling heavy, I turned and made my way back to my chamber.

Blood on the land.

War had come.

For Caratacus and Togodumnus or for us all?

CHAPTER 8

The following morning, we made ready to ride out. After making a quick stop in the kitchens, I checked on Bran's wounded warrior, Aterie, before we departed.

The chamber smelled of heady herbs, but Aterie's color had improved already.

"Boudica," he said, moving to sit up.

I lifted my hand. "Rest. I wanted to check on you before we depart."

"I'm healing. The druid Arixus tells me I should be well enough to take a wagon back to Oak Throne within a week. Don't worry about me. Ectorus will stay, and I am in good hands with the druids here," he said, then smiled. "Not to mention, Finola has been attending me."

"Is that so?" I asked, raising an eyebrow.

He grinned at me. "I can't say I am sorry to stay another week."

"Well, if you are sure. Otherwise, I can send Ula to check on you," I told him.

He laughed. "Please, no."

I chuckled. "Very well. Then I wish you a speedy recovery."

"And you, a safe return to Venta. Guard yourself well, Boudica. We seem to have enemies where we least expect them."

"Rest. Recover," I told him, setting my hand on his shoulder. "When I next come to Oak Throne, I will see you there."

He smiled at me and then nodded.

Leaving him, I exited the roundhouse, joining Pix, Vian, Bran, and the others.

Druda nickered at me when he spotted me.

"Send word to Oak Throne if you need anything," Bran told Arixus.

The druid bowed to him then said, "Ride safely, Prince Bran, Queen Boudica. May the gods keep you."

"And you," I replied.

Bran turned and looked over the party. Apparently, I was the last to arrive. Seeing us all in place, he motioned for us to head out.

Vian, who was riding a fine horse—undoubtedly one of Saenunos's own steeds—trotted alongside Pix. Vian turned and waved to her mother and sister. Fan blotted her cheeks with the corner of her apron, wiping away her tears. Finola waved to her sister.

As we rode away from Holk Fort, the people stopped to watch. While their eyes were still haunted by their losses, I also saw a glimmer of hope. Their loved ones had been pressed to war—and lost in the process. Sadly, I knew that had come from our hands. But what choice did any of us have in this? Saenunos had constructed the entire problem with ample encouragement from the Catuvellauni. But Saenunos was gone. We all had to look toward the future.

My gaze shifted to Bran.

He would do just fine in Oak Throne because he cared.

Sometimes, that was all that was needed.

WE RODE ACROSS THE COUNTRYSIDE, ARRIVING ONCE MORE IN Oak Throne. The sun had just set. Everything was quiet save the sound of croaking frogs. The mist had settled on the river and in the fields around the fort. The fog bank was so dense that it made my skin, clothes, and hair wet. While it was common for the river to evoke such fog at this time of year, something about the mist felt unnaturally dense. Had Ula conjured the weather? Was she keeping Oak Throne hidden?

We crossed the land bridge and approached the gate.

"Hold," the guard on the gate called.

"It is Prince Bran and Queen Boudica," Bran called in reply.

The gate swung open.

We entered the fort to find Oak Throne secure and

quiet. Everyone was in bed. The lamps in the little houses had been extinguished. The children were asleep. We made our way down the lane to the roundhouse. There, Lynet met us.

"Boudica. Welcome. I am glad to see you unharmed," she said, holding Druda's reins as I dismounted.

"Not for lack of trying," I said as I dismounted. "But Holk Fort is settled."

"I am glad to hear it. Dôn returned from the south. She's inside."

"Dôn is here?"

Lynet nodded. "And the priestess, Bec. The rest went on to the grove."

I turned back toward the roundhouse in time to see Bec appear. Her hair hung in a loose tangle. She hurried to Bran, who pulled her into an embrace.

I smiled at the pair, and then turned back to Lynet. "Thank you for seeing to the people. It is too much to ask of you, but Bran and I both appreciate it."

"It is nothing to ask of me, Boudica. Even if I've become so by marriage, we are all Northern Iceni," she said with a light laugh, setting her hand on my arm. "You are chilled in this fog. Come inside."

Leaving Druda with the servants, I gestured to Vian to come with me.

"Vian, this is Lynet. She is the chieftain of Frog's Hollow. Vian will journey with me to Venta."

Lynet smiled at the girl. "Very good. Come, Vian, Boudica. Ula has us all drenched in mist. Let's get inside."

Within, I found a sleepy-looking Cidna setting out food

on the table. She had placed baskets of bread and cheese. From the back, I smelled fish cooking.

"Cidna," I said. "Please don't trouble yourself. Bran and I can see to it well enough."

"Oh, no. I won't have Bran rambling around my kitchens, getting into who knows what. Your brother will have half the kitchen eaten if I don't put some limits on him. Set yourself down. I'll go get the winter mead. That will knock the weariness from the long ride off of you."

Vian and I sat. Soon, the others joined us. The warriors crowded around the table, grabbing a bite to eat and drinking a bit of ale before saying their goodbyes. Beside me, Vian eyed Cidna's bread suspiciously but ate the underdone and partially burnt offering anyway. It was some time later when Bran and Bec joined us.

"Oh, Boudica," Bec said, setting her hand on my shoulder. "Such terrible news met us here. I am sorry for it."

"As am I. But I am glad to see you well."

"These are dark times."

"Yes."

Bec's gaze went toward the back of the house. "Dôn was tired from the long journey. It took more out of her than she would admit. I'm sure she will be glad to see you come morning."

I nodded.

Pix pushed in beside me.

"Where have you been?" I asked her.

"Ye don't need to know all of me business," she replied, refilling her plate with meat, cheese, and bread.

Exhausted from the long ride, the warriors ate and

drank their fill, then headed back to their homes. Pix, seemingly uninterested in conversation, finished two full plates, and then rose. "That's enough for one day. I'll be taking yer sister's bed. Try not to make too much noise when ye come in," she told me, then wandered off.

I chuckled. "I guess I should just be glad she hasn't taken my bed."

"Riona settled Dôn in your father's chamber," Lynet told me, then looked to Vian. "If you are finished here, I can have the servants show you to a bedchamber."

Vian, who had been studying the underside of her very burnt fish, nodded. "Yes, I think that's quite enough for one night."

Giggling, I said nothing. Poor Cidna was a mediocre cook on the best of days. I had grown used to her burnt, undercooked, and over-salted food. Waking her in the middle of the night did nothing to improve her culinary skills.

"Do you need anything, Lynet? What can I do to help?"

"Finish that cup of mead and put yourself to bed," she told me. "Nothing is happening here that cannot be settled in the morning."

Vian and Lynet then disappeared toward the back, leaving me alone with Bec and Bran, who had been talking in low tones. I suddenly realized it was in everyone's best interest if I left. Slugging back what was left of the drink, I rose to go.

"We shall see you in the morning," Bec told me.

"Good night, Priestess."

"Good night, Prin—*Queen*."

At that, I laughed. When I arrived in my chamber, I found Pix sprawled on Brenna's bed, a low snore coming from her. Morfran squawked loudly when I entered.

"Morfran," I said, pausing to stroke the bird on the head. "I'm glad to see you too. Brenna has taken Bear and left us, I'm afraid. Though I don't think you'll miss that dog."

The bird fluttered his wings then settled in to roost once more.

Exhausted, I slipped onto my bed and pulled off my boots. I should change, but I didn't care. For the moment, I was home—at least, what had always been my home—and all I wanted to do was sleep.

CHAPTER 9

I t must have been late when I woke the next day. Pix and Morfran had already gone, and Riona had left a clean gown for me. I hadn't even heard the woman in the room. As I looked around, I saw that she had been busy. All of my things had been reordered and packed. She was preparing for me to go to Venta.

I rose, feeling groggy, then redressed. Pulling my tangle of red hair back into a braid, I slipped on the mossy-green dress Riona had laid out for me, then made my way to the main room of the hall only to find it empty.

Curious.

Snatching a round of bread, I went outside.

The fort was humming along quietly. There was no sign of Bran, Bec, Dôn, Pix, or anyone else. My feet, impassioned by habit, turned in the direction of Ula's little cottage.

When I arrived, I could hear her rummaging around inside.

"Ula?" I called.

The clattering stopped, and the door opened.

Ula studied me a moment.

I pushed the bread in her direction.

She took the loaf and then motioned for me to come inside.

When I got inside, I discovered that Ula had torn the place apart.

"What's happening here?" I asked.

"Looking," she said, going through her things as she took a bite from the bread. "Gah, did she dump the whole bowl of salt in the dough?"

"Probably. Can I help you find anything?"

"No. What happened at Holk Fort?"

"The place was a disaster. Saenunos forced the people to fight with him. We managed to get things in order with the help of Arixus."

Ula paused and looked back at me. "The druids of Seahenge came?"

I nodded.

"Must be a change in the world to bring them out of the mist," she said, then pulled down a basket. "Ah," she said, lifting an oddly shaped root. "Here."

"What's that?"

"A root, you stupid girl."

"Queen. I'm a queen."

"A root, you stupid queen."

At that, I laughed.

Ula sat down by her fire and pulled out a knife. She cut slivers from the root, mixing them into an odd-smelling brew she had bubbling. She stirred them around with her fingers, touching the hot liquid gingerly. After a long moment, she slowly poured the mixture into a cup and handed it to me.

"Drink."

"That's for me?"

"Sit down and drink."

"How did you know I was coming?"

"You are here. Of course, you will come to harry me. Now, drink."

"What does it do?"

"Let's see what will come."

I sat down and then took the drink from her. Tilting the cup back, I swallowed the hot liquid. It burned my throat and tasted horrid, but I had learned that it was best to get it over with.

I handed the cup back to Ula.

She stared at me. "You drank it all? All at once?" she asked, aghast.

"Why, wasn't I—" I began when the room started to spin. "Ula..."

"Better lie down," she said as black dots appeared before my eyes.

The last thing I saw was Ula reaching out to grab me before I fell forward into the fire.

Then, everything went black.

I woke up sometime later, my stomach feeling sick, to the sound of tapping.

Confused, I sat up.

"Ula?" I called, but there was no one there.

Puzzled, I rose.

For a moment, I swayed. Once I got my bearings, I made my way outside. Oak Throne was silent and covered in mist. I walked down the lane from Ula's house to the main route through Oak Throne.

There was no one there.

Everyone—*everyone*—was gone.

Then, I realized.

I was not really in Oak Throne.

I was somewhere beyond, in the realm in between.

In the distance, I heard the hammering once more. I followed the sound, walking away from Oak Throne, across the land bridge, and into the fields surrounding the city.

Thunk-thunk.

Thunk-thunk.

The first sound had a low tone, the second higher pitched. I followed the sound into the mist.

Walking across the field, I went deeper into the fog. Everything around me fell into shadow, but the sound grew louder.

Thunk-thunk.

Thunk-thunk.

Then, through the mist, I began to make out the shape of...a building. No. Not a building. A tent.

Thunk-thunk.

Thunk-thunk.

I walked toward the tent. As I drew closer, I saw movement. Someone was there. I could just make out the shape of the person—a man. He stood before a workbench. On it, I could make out the outline of armor. He lifted and lowered the hammer, tapping twice.

Thunk-thunk.

Thunk-thunk.

He must have sensed me. Looking up, he stared into the mist, pausing his hammering.

The two of us stood in the mist, staring at one another for a long moment.

Then, the man moved forward, hammer in hand.

He passed through the mists, coming close to me.

I was barely able to make him out.

When he drew close, however, I saw that he was tall, with shaggy black hair and pale blue eyes. He wore the armor of a Roman.

I opened my mouth to speak, but only a shriek came out.

Something lifted me from the ground, and my body— my clothes, hair, and limbs—

burst into flames.

I could see the image reflected in the man's eyes.

He stared at me in wonder.

"Britannia," he whispered.

I gasped, and then opened my eyes.

I found myself lying on the dirt floor of Ula's house.

I had never left.

"Slow," Ula cautioned. "Go slow," she said, helping me sit.

I put my hand to my head. "Banshees be cursed. What was that?"

"What did you see?" Ula asked, ignoring me. She went to her table and poured me a glass of spring water. "What did you see?"

"I... I'm not sure. First, Oak Throne. But I heard a noise. I followed it," I said, taking the water she handed me. I sipped it, clearing away the terrible taste in my mouth. "It led me deeper into the mist."

"And?"

"There was a man there, a Roman."

"Did you know him?"

I paused. He *had* looked familiar to me. But how could I know a Roman? "I... I don't know."

"Did he speak?"

"Yes. He called me Britannia, and then I burst into flames."

"Into flames?"

"Yes," I said with half a laugh, then drank again.

Ula sat down beside me once more.

"What does it mean?" I asked her.

"I don't know," she said, sounding annoyed. "The Dark Lady Andraste is playing. I feel her smug grin in the darkness. She is keeping the future from us."

"What should I do?"

"Be wary. That is all you can do. Be wary."

"Caratacus and Togodumnus encouraged—if not more —Saenunos to kill my father. I discovered the truth in Holk Fort. Let the Romans have at the Catuvellauni. I won't stand in their way."

71

"Don't be guided by your anger. Listen to the green-wood. *It* will guide you. Don't be stubborn."

"So says the most stubborn person I know."

Ula pinched me.

"Ouch!"

"Don't be stubborn."

"Yes, Ula."

"Good. Now leave me. I have my own things to attend to."

"Do you want me to help you clean—"

"I said go on."

"Very well," I replied, then rose to go. My head was still feeling woozy.

"Go slow. The tonic will remain with you for a time."

"Always drugging me with something. I don't know why I come here."

At that, Ula huffed but said nothing more.

I stepped out of her small roundhouse, glad for the fresh air.

There was no mist now. The sun was shining. I inhaled deeply, soaking in the spring breeze and feeling the sun on my face.

Whoever the man was, he was a stranger to me.

Or was he?

Rome.

Who had set me on fire.

I RETURNED TO THE ROUNDHOUSE TO FIND BEC, DÔN, AND Bran standing outside.

"Boudica," Bran called, a broad smile on his face.

Behind him, I saw Albie hurrying off toward the market. Vian had just returned from somewhere with baskets full of flowers.

"What's happening?" I asked, eyeing all the commotion.

"A wedding," Bran replied, giving me a sheepish grin.

"Wedding," I repeated. I turned to Bec. "A wedding?"

Bec nodded.

"Since the gods agree, we will see to it before I return to the grove," Dôn told me. "Ah, Boudica, what dark news greeted us here in Oak Throne. I am sorry for your losses...your father, Belenus."

"Thank you."

"Lady Bec," Riona called from the door. "I'll be needing you inside."

"I..." Bec began, confused as she studied Riona, who was holding a gown in one hand and gesturing to Bec wildly with the other.

"Best get on with it," I told her. "Riona will chide you if you don't listen to every bit of her dressing advice, even if you are the new Lady of Oak Throne."

"But I…" Bec began then turned to Dôn, who motioned for her to go on.

Bec gave Bran a wary smile, then disappeared back into the roundhouse.

Grinning, Bran turned to me. "I'll have everything set up in the square. I'm going to get the men to help," he told me, then hurried off.

Everything was happening so quickly that I felt dizzy. Or was that the lingering effect of Ula's tonic? I set my fingers on my temple, willing the world to be still.

"Bran tells me the druids of Seahenge are bringing order and leadership to Holk Fort," Dôn said.

"Ah, yes…"

"Boudica, are you all right?"

"I was with Ula," I said by way of explanation, then laughed lightly. "Holk Fort. Yes. I woke the first night at the fort with a blade on my neck. Arixus was kind enough to dispatch the wielder."

Dôn nodded slowly. "Arixus is close with the gods. No doubt, it is their will he was there."

"Have we done right, leaving the fort with the druids?"

"I am certain they will be good shepherds for the people of the fort. It's only…" she began, then paused for a long moment.

"Only?"

"Like us at the grove, they are a quiet sect. They have always kept to themselves. This news from the south has everyone stirring, from kings to druids to gods to Seelie. I don't like what it portends."

Her meaning was not lost on me. The gods were

moving all of us where they wanted. To what ends, I couldn't say. But as the Romans began their movements, so had we.

Dôn sighed heavily, and then chuckled. "Let's not dwell on such things, Boudica. Tonight, Bran and Bec will wed. It is a happy time. Come," she said, taking my arm. "Let's find a way to make ourselves useful. No doubt, Cidna can use a hand in the kitchen."

"Are the gods moving us to the kitchens—a queen and a high priestess?"

"For today? Yes," she told me, then grinned. "Even the gods know that Cidna needs help."

CHAPTER 10

We spent the rest of the day weaving garlands, baking, and preparing the square for the festivities. It had been comical to listen as Dôn subtly made suggestions to Cidna on how to tweak her baking. Cidna, feeling very in control of her element, corrected the priestess and carried on as usual. Dôn eventually gave up. It was a somber time to wed, but I think the spot of light—and the semblance of normalcy—was a welcome reprieve from all the recent tragedies for the people of Oak Throne.

I floated between baking and preparing the square around the ancient oak for the wedding.

But the square wasn't the only thing festively adorned with flowers.

I sat patiently as Eiwyn and Birgit fixed my hair, weaving flowers into my long locks. The girls worked their magic on anyone willing to comply. Vian received violets for her long, ebony hair. Dôn wore a crown of flowers.

Even Pix had consented to let the girls adorn her short blonde hair.

"Why is your hair cut so short?" Eiwyn asked her.

"All the warrior women of my people kept their hair short. It keeps it out of the way during battle."

"Who are your people?" Eiwyn asked.

At that, I'd perked up. Who *were* her people?

Pix looked mildly confused, and then said, "I come from the west."

"West where?" Birgit had asked innocently.

"So far west, ye fall into the mist and disappear into the Summer Country. Now, get on with yer work. And not those snowdrops. Ne'er use snowdrops."

"Why not?" Eiwyn asked, lifting the delicate white flowers.

"The wee people are scared of them," she said, then grinned. "That said, best make Boudica a crown of them."

I laughed. "Please do. At Caturix's wedding, I couldn't keep the piskies away from me."

Eiwyn giggled. "Boudica. You always have such stories."

"What stories? One threw an acorn at me and knocked me unconscious."

At that, the children laughed and laughed.

I grinned at them, but Dôn caught my gaze and raised a questioning eyebrow at me.

"It was my own fault. Ula gave me a charm to ward them away, but I took it off," I explained.

"A charm that repels piskies?" Eiwyn asked.

"Yes. Of course."

At that, the girls giggled. "There is no such thing."

"I have not seen Ula today," Dôn said, her gaze drifting toward the old woman's house.

"She is… preoccupied," I replied.

"With?"

"Romans."

Dôn frowned but said nothing.

As it grew toward dusk, Riona appeared from the roundhouse. "Bec is ready," Riona told Dôn. "Balfor will bring her from the roundhouse when you call for her."

"Very well," Dôn said, then turned to the girls. "You have done very well, sweet children. We are all looking like Blodeuwedd herself. We thank you for your efforts. May the Maiden bless your hands."

"Thank you, Mother Dôn," Eiwyn said.

"Thank you, Dôn," Birgit echoed.

Eiwyn signaled to the other children who lingered nearby. "Come on. Let's get a place in the front before the others."

And with that, the children disappeared.

"It is time to attend to the matter," Dôn said. "I will sound the horn momentarily."

I turned to Pix. "Where is Bran?"

"In the stables," Pix said.

"Stables? Does he want to go to his bride smelling of horses? I'll go get him."

I made my way to the stables. When I pulled the door back, I was surprised to find Bran alone. I had expected him to be surrounded by his warriors, all of them toasting to my brother's good fortune. Instead, Bran stood stroking Foster's neck.

Bran was nicely dressed in a green tunic, leather jerkin, and tan trousers. His hair was neatly combed, and his jerkin's silver buckles were polished to a shine.

"Boudica," he said, pulling his attention away from his horse. He wore a strange expression on his face.

"It's almost time," I said, studying him. "Dôn will call for your bride in a moment."

Bran nodded.

"What is it?" I asked. "Is there something wrong? Bec..."

"No. Not Bec. There could never be anything wrong with Bec. It's just..."

"Just?"

"I am suddenly feeling the weight on my shoulders. With Caturix at Stonea, I'm left to manage Oak Throne, watch over Holk Fort, offer guidance and help to Frog's Hollow and all the farmsteads in between. All that, and I need to take good care of my wife. My wife! Boudica, I'm not up for all these tasks."

I crossed the stable, set my hands on Bran's shoulders, and looked him in the eyes. "You are Northern Iceni. You are the son of this house. And more, you are a good person. You have people who want you to succeed, people who will help you... Lynet, Dôn, Arixus. But more, you have that within you to rise to the task. I know you, Brother. Riding, hunting, training...that has been your life. But you can do this. You did well in Holk Fort. You earned the respect of the people there."

"That was your doing."

"No. It wasn't. I simply helped. You underestimate your gifts. You will find your way. You have to, for your children's sake."

"Children?" Bran asked.

I grinned at him. "I hear it's a natural side effect of marriage."

From the square, we heard the long, low sound of the carnyx.

"Your bride is coming," I said, straightening his jerkin and smoothing back a stray curl. I offered my brother my arm. "Shall we go greet her?"

Bran's tense demeanor softened. He smiled and then took my arm. Leaving the stables, we made our way across the fort, back to the tree. There, all the people of Oak Throne had gathered. I spotted Kennocha, little Mara in her arms, amongst the crowd. She smiled and nodded to me.

Dôn stood under the limbs of the ancient oak.

Torchlight flickered, casting an orange glow on the scene. The garlands of flowers, including the flower balls hanging from the trees' limbs, gave the place a magical glow. It was hard to believe that such darkness had occurred here only days before. The ashes from the pyre had been raked away, but the memory remained.

And yet, here was a sign of hope. Of something new.

I walked with Bran, meeting Dôn, and then left my brother before the priestess.

It was not long after that when I heard the tinkle of a

small silver bell. The sweet, melodious sound announced Bec's arrival.

For the first time in my memory, Bec had changed from her priestess gown to a pale pink dress embroidered with flowers. As I studied the gown, I realized it was familiar. It had belonged to our mother. Riona must have found it for Bec. At the sight, tears pricked at the corners of my eyes. I felt my mother's presence. But of course. Her son was marrying a daughter of the holy grove.

Balfor led Bec to Bran, and then stepped aside.

"People of Oak Throne," Dôn called in a clear, crisp voice. "The days behind us have been dark ones, and uncertainty lies in our future. But on this night, the Lord and Lady, the Great Mother and the Stag Lord of the forest come to us once more in the form of Prince Bran and the priestess, Bec. Let this night be proof that even in dark times, light can prevail..." Dôn began. She continued eloquently, calling on the gods to bless their marriage, binding their hands with ivy.

The torchlight shone on the couple, making Bran's hair shimmer red in the firelight. The leaves of the great oak tree glimmered golden. And above them, the moon shone silver against a background of deep blue and silver stars.

I could feel the presence of the Lord and Lady there.

I could feel the gods weaving, plotting.

And yet, from far to our south, I felt a weight of darkness.

A soft wind blew through the limbs of the ancient oak, making my hair and gown flutter.

"*Boudica...*

"Protector of the oaks…

"Protector of the stones…"

"May we all cheer Bran and Bec. May their bonds stretch beyond time, from life to life. So mote it be," Dôn called, her voice bringing me back to the moment.

"So mote it be," we called in reply.

"Prince Bran, kiss your wife. *Lady* Bec, kiss your husband," Dôn said.

Smiling, Bran and Bec leaned toward one another and exchanged a loving kiss.

The crowd cheered, me along with them.

I smiled softly.

With Bran settling into his life here, I was ready to return to my own husband.

I would ride for Venta in the morning.

CHAPTER 11

W e spent the night in cheer. Music rang out from all around in Oak Throne, the sound of fiddles, drums, horns, harps, pipes, and every other imaginable instrument filling the air. After the darkness of the assault on the fort and the news of the war to the south, people seemed to lose themselves in this single moment of happiness.

Everyone ate and drank, especially Pix, who had rediscovered Cai in the crowd. The two, it seemed, had developed a fondness for one another.

I would have joined the merriment if it weren't for the distinct lack of a cantankerous old woman whose absence nagged at me like a splinter.

Leaving the others to their revels, I went to Ula's cottage in time to see her exiting her little roundhouse, a wiggling sack in her hands.

"What's that?" I asked.

"Sacrifice," she said nonchalantly. "Why aren't you with the others?"

"Sadly, I found myself preoccupied with thoughts of you."

"Bah," Ula grumbled, and then paused. "No. May be better for it anyway. Come on," she told me, then hurried off toward the gate.

"And where are we going?"

"Mossy wood."

I stopped. "Why?"

But Ula didn't answer me. Instead, she carried on, her wiggling bag along with her.

I hurried my steps after her, but asked nothing more. We approached the gates. When we arrived, Ula looked expectantly at me.

"Open the gates, please," I called.

"Queen Boudica?"

"Ula and I... Open the gates, please."

The watchmen paused and then did as I asked.

Ula and I slipped out, the sounds of laughter and merriment fading behind us. We passed over the land bridge and made our way downriver until we turned into the dark forest.

"Your vision told me nothing," Ula muttered. "Andraste is riddling. We have no time for riddles. Omens are everywhere: the attack on Frog's Hollow, the death of your father, your marriage, the movement in the south. Darkness is coming. We must learn how to stop it."

"The Romans?"

"Of course, the Romans, you stupid girl. Do you think

they are so loyal to Verica? Do you think they'll just leave once Verica has his throne?"

I said nothing more. Ula was right to worry.

Moving quickly and quietly, we entered the forest. Ula led us over fallen logs, around trees, and into the deep hollow of the mossy wood. Winding through the forest, Ula led us to the cave entrance that led back to the well at her cottage.

"Ula…"

"Kneel," Ula told me.

Both of us knelt on the ground. The moonlight illuminated the forest in shades of deep green and black. As I looked deeper into the woods, I saw balls of blue light bouncing through the woods. Somewhere in the distance, an owl called.

"Brothers of the hollow hills, we honor you," Ula called toward the cave. "Ancient spirits of the stones, we honor you. Masters of the dark lands, the place between the worlds, we honor you. Show us. Show us what must be done. Lend me your magic so we may see what is to come."

A breeze came from within the cave.

I smelled the deep scents of fern, moss, and loam.

"Give me your hand," Ula said, snatching it. Pulling her dagger, she quickly drew it across my palm.

I winced but said nothing.

She then turned and grabbed her sack. From within, she pulled out a hare.

"The hare is a messenger between the worlds," Ula told me. "They can show you signs. The little people of the hollow hills are watching. Do you feel their eyes?" she asked me as she held the hare by its neck.

I nodded.

Ula took my bleeding hand and placed it on the hare, wiping my blood thereon.

"Brothers of the hollow hills, show us what must be done to protect this land," Ula said, then let the hare go.

The animal quickly scrambled away, but it ran into the cave rather than rushing off into the woods.

My heart pounded in my chest when I heard the sound of movement inside. Then, I heard an odd, loud, screeching sound. My skin rose in gooseflesh. I had heard that sound only once, when Cidna had prepared rabbit stew for my father. It was the sound the rabbits had made before they died.

My body trembled with fear.

"Watch," Ula whispered.

I sensed movement in the cave.

The ferns just outside the cave entrance twitched. Then, I saw a hand. Long fingers with elongated black nails pushed the greenery aside. In the darkness, I saw the mirror reflection of their eyes. And then, the creature tossed something.

A hare landed at Ula's feet.

But it was not the hare we had sent into the cave. This creature was pitch-black...and dead.

Ula took the hare to a stone nearby and slit its belly. The entrails poured out. Ula leaned over them, gently touching them with her fingers as she studied the signs there.

I stared at the cave, watching the hand pull back. The glimmering eyes stared out from the darkness at me for a long time.

I bowed to the creature.

Then, it disappeared.

Turning, I went to Ula.

Her fingers pink with the sticky blood and bodily juices, she pored over the signs then sat back, working her lips together as she considered.

"Ula," I whispered.

"Ride south to Venta. Tell Prasutagus to arm the people. You must rise alongside Caratacus and Togodumnus."

"Never. I will *never* stand beside them."

"You must."

"I will not. Caratacus and Togodumnus are conspiring killers. My father is dead because of their coaxing. Let Verica have his throne. Let the Romans crush them."

Ula slapped me hard.

When I opened my mouth to protest, she slapped me again. "Foolish girl. Foolish, stubborn girl. You will doom us all if you do not do as I say. Stand against the eagle now. Now. Or we will all perish."

"What do you mean?"

"It is there, in the message from the hollow hills. You have but one chance, Boudica, to stop this tide. One. That time is now."

"That can't be right." I shook my head. "No. I will not conspire with my father's killers."

"Then you conspire with the Romans."

"Ula," I protested.

But Ula said nothing more. Instead, she turned to make her way out of the mossy wood.

"Ula," I protested once more. "Wait. There must be another way."

"There is no other way," she replied gruffly. "If you do not stand now, Boudica, you will live to regret it."

"But Ula—"

"Do not *but* anything me. Listen to the voice of the ancient ones. Andraste riddles, but the creatures of the hollow hills speak nothing but the truth. They are never wrong. If we are to survive this, you must stand against the Romans now."

"I cannot."

"Then you doom us all."

"Ula."

She didn't turn back.

"Ula!"

Again, she did not respond.

In silence, I followed along behind her back to the fort.

Recognizing us, the watchmen opened the gate so we could enter.

Without speaking another word, Ula set off on her path toward her cottage.

"Ula?" I called to her, but she did not stop.

I knew well enough when Ula was truly angry. She spent so much time being difficult and cantankerous, it might have been difficult for others to tell, but I could see... My words had infuriated her.

I let her go. There had to be a better way, because I

would not fight alongside the Catuvellauni. I would stop in the morning before I left, talk to her then, and make her understand.

Letting Ula go, I turned and made my way back toward the roundhouse. The wedding festivities had ended—how much time had passed?—and everything was quiet once more.

The Romans would be dealt with. I would see to it when I returned to Venta, but I would have to find another way. Because I swore on my father's memory, I would never support Caratacus and Togodumnus, no matter what the little people of the hollow hills had to say.

CHAPTER 12

I rose early the following day, my head aching from ale and Ula's strange root brew.

Pix lay in Brenna's bed snoring.

I shook her shoulder. "Wake up."

"Aye, Strawberry Queen, what hour is it?"

"We must get on the road early to make Venta before nightfall."

Pix yawned groggily, and then sat up. "Easy for ye to say. Ye didn't spend the whole night dancing."

"Neither did you. The square was empty by the time I returned to the fort."

"It wasn't that kind of dancing."

I chuckled. "Regardless, we must make ready. I will go to the stables. Go and wake Vian, then get something to eat."

Pix yawned tiredly, motioning for me to go on.

I got dressed, pulled on my riding clothes, and then walked outside. It was just before dawn. The sky was a purplish-gray color, but I saw the glimmer of golden sunlight on the distant horizon. When I entered the stables, several horses huffed in protest at the disruption. When I got to Druda's stall, however, I found him waiting expectantly, his head hanging over the gate.

"Good morning to you too," I told him, stroking his face.

I fetched the grain pail. Filling it with the golden-colored grain, I slipped into Druda's stall. The horse nosed me hungrily.

"Stop pushing," I told him. "I'm hurrying." I poured the grain into his bin, then grabbed a brush and brushed the horse down. When I was done, I pressed my cheek against his side and closed my eyes.

Ula's words came to mind once more.

If I didn't act now…

I had to act now.

But how could I?

I honored the ancient voice of the land, but I could not stand at the side of those men. I would talk to Prasutagus when I reached Venta. We would have to make the decision together. As it was, we had no idea the extent of the invasion or its true purpose.

"Queen Boudica," Tadhg, the stableboy, called, leaning over the stable door to look at me. "You didn't have to do that. I was coming."

"I know," I told him. "Thank you, Tadhg. I just didn't want Druda to feel neglected."

Tadhg laughed. "Yes. He's a particular one."

I patted Druda's side. "All right, my spoiled boy.

You're in good hands now," I said, exiting the stall. "I need to talk to Bran about an escort south, but prepare those two as well," I said, pointing to Saenunos's horse we had liberated and a buckskin with black boots Pix had ridden from Venta.

"Very well," the boy replied, and then got to work.

I made my way back out of the stable, pausing to visit Mountain, who'd stuck his head over his gate.

"Good morning, old friend," I said, pausing to hug his neck. When I did, the scent of the horse struck me hard. It reminded me so palpably of Gaheris that I ached physically.

"Ah, Gaheris," I whispered. "How simple it would have been had you not gone on before me." I clutched the frog pendant still hanging on my chest.

Mountain sniffed my hair, and then shifted.

I pulled back. "You miss him too." I stroked the horse's neck. "Be well, dear one," I said, giving the horse a kiss before I departed.

Back down the hall, Druda whinnied at me.

"He saw that," Tadhg called. "Didn't take his eyes off you."

"Jealous boy," I yelled over my shoulder with a laugh and then left the stables.

When I got outside, I discovered that the sun had risen. Golden light shimmered through the soft, gray clouds, sending rays of sunshine toward the land.

Unhappy with how I had left things with Ula, I made my way to her cottage. A light trail of smoke spiraled from the roof.

"Ula?" I called, knocking on the door. "I know it's early, but I am riding for Venta. Can I come in?"

There was no answer.

"Ula?" I called, knocking again. Was she asleep?

I waited a few moments more. Still, she didn't come.

Moving quietly and carefully, I opened the door. If I woke her, she would scold me, but it would be better than leaving without making amends between us. Ula had only been truly mad at me a handful of times in all my recollection. But somehow, this felt different.

"Ula?" I called into the dark house.

A fire burned in the central hearth, but the logs had burned down to almost nothing. Ula's bed was made. There was no sign of her in the house.

"Ula?"

Nothing.

Leaving the cottage, I went around to the garden in the back, but she wasn't there.

I frowned.

Hopefully, I would be able to find her before we departed.

I returned to the roundhouse once more. I found everyone awake when I got there, including the newly married couple.

"There you are," Bran said, greeting me with a hug. "You smell of horses."

"I was in the stables."

"Of course you were. Where did you run off to last night? We had ale and food aplenty, but you were nowhere to be found."

I shrugged.

Bran chuckled. "No matter. Come. Eat something. I sent Albie to wake Cai, Davin, and the others to ride as an escort with you south. They will be ready within the hour."

"Thank you, Brother," I told him, my gaze turning to Bec. "*Lady* Bec," I said, bowing to her.

She chuckled. "*Queen* Boudica."

I settled in with the others to eat. I hated to leave the matter with Ula unsettled. And worse, I had no idea what news I was returning to in Venta.

Dôn, who had been seated across from me, met my gaze.

"You are distracted."

I gave her a forced smile. "Yes. I'm sorry."

Dôn raised her hand, dismissing my apology. "You are right to be distracted. There is much on the horizon."

"It's just..." I said, then paused. I cast a glance at the others who were busy in conversation. "Ula... she has read the signs. She told me we should stand. Now. Or pay the price. But how can we stand alongside such cutthroats? Caratacus and Togodumnus inflamed Saenunos to action. How can we ally with them?"

"Hmm," Dôn mused. "The Dark Lady riddles, Boudica. And Ula... Ula often walks the edge with creatures whose intentions are not always clear."

I frowned. I knew well that the golden troupe and the good neighbors were not to be trusted. But the ancient ones of the hollow hills? Ula called them honest. Was she right?

"What of the creatures of the hollow hills?" I whispered to Dôn.

Down the table, Bec shifted her gaze toward me for a moment, then back to Lynet, to whom she was speaking.

Dôn's brow furrowed. "It is unwise to traffic with such creatures as those who hate humans. Their motives cannot be trusted. After all, mankind is the reason they live in darkness."

I sighed heavily, and then sat back. I didn't know what to believe. Neither Ula nor Dôn had ever been dishonest with me.

"Trust your heart, Boudica. It will guide you," Dôn told me.

I nodded to her. "Thank you."

After a few moments, Pix rose. "Ye best get going, Strawberry Queen."

With that, we all rose and made ready to depart.

Cidna met me as we made our way outside. "I sent supplies out with the others, but here's a bag just for you. Be safe, Boudica."

"Thank you, Cidna," I told her, kissing her cheek.

She chuckled lightly. "Ah, Boudica. I will miss having you underfoot."

"Perhaps Bec will prove equally problematic."

"Her? No. She reminds me of your mother, that one. Be well, my dear."

"Thank you," I told her, squeezing her hand once more before leaving her.

Riona was waiting for me outside beside Druda. The horse had been packed with my bags. Morfran sat on the horn of my saddle. "Packed the things you like," she told me. "Left the rest. Make that new husband of yours buy you some dresses."

I chuckled. "Thank you, Riona."

"And I brought your noisy bird. I assume you want him with you. Packed his food as well."

I grinned, and then reached out for Morfran. "Coming to Venta, Morfran?" I asked.

The bird squawked at me, and then hopped up my arm to my shoulder.

Riona shook her head. "I also saw to your new girl. Slip of a thing, but Brenna had some nice dresses for her. Wanted her to look the part in Venta."

"Thank you... And thank you for giving Bec mother's gown. She looked beautiful."

"Bran thought it would be all right. I'm glad you were not bothered."

"Not at all," I said, and then added, "Bec will not be accustomed to someone looking after her. You'll have to teach her how."

Riona laughed. "If that is my worst problem, I will take it."

At that, Riona gave me a half-hug, avoiding Morfran, and then let me go.

I said goodbye to the others in turn, Dôn, Lynet, and Bec, all offering me their blessings. Bran held Druda while I mounted. Morfran took off, flying out beyond the fort.

"Be safe in Venta. Send a rider when you know anything."

"Thank you, Brother. I will."

"And if the Romans give you trouble…"

"I know which end of my spear is sharp."

At that, Bran laughed. "I'll see you again soon. May the gods watch over you, Boudica."

"And you."

With that, I adjusted myself in the saddle and then turned to look over the party. We were ready to go. A small crowd had come to wave goodbye, but I didn't see Ula amongst them. I scanned the square, but she wasn't there.

"Let's ride out," I called, then gestured to Pix to take the lead.

Giving Bran one last wave, I tapped my heels on Druda's side.

The children ran alongside me, calling to me.

"Goodbye, Boudica!" Birgit called.

"Farewell, Princess—no, Queen!" Eiwyn added.

"May the Mother watch over you!" Phelan said with a wave.

I grinned and waved at them. "And all of you."

As we passed the last of the crowd, I spotted Kennocha there holding Mara. She lifted the little girl's hand, waving to me. I smiled at her, returned the gesture, and then set my gaze south.

There was much to be done. With the Northern Iceni settled, it was time to set my face toward the future.

CHAPTER 13

W e arrived in Venta just as the sun began to sink toward the horizon. Once again, I was taken by the city's massive size—now, my city. Riding with the banners of the Northern Iceni before us, we crossed into Venta. Even though the marketplace was quieter now that the revelers from the Beltane festival had gone, the place was still teeming with activity and people. Citizens hurried to and fro with children, ducks, goats, donkeys, horses, dogs, and carts behind them. Many stopped to watch our party, but others simply carried on about their business.

Several people called as we made our way down the road toward the king's compound.

"Queen Boudica!"

"Queen!"

"Our queen has returned!"

"Like the Morrigu herself!" someone called, spotting Morfran sitting on my shoulder.

I stopped Druda for a moment and waited for Vian.

She was staring wide-eyed at everything.

"Well?" I asked. "Regretting your decision?"

"Not in the least. In fact, I am thanking all the gods at once for bringing me here. My mind is bursting."

I chuckled. "Good. I was afraid you would see this crowd and want to race home."

"Never, Queen Boudica. You have honored my family and me by asking me to come. I will stand beside you until the day I die."

"Let's not rush that day any time soon."

She grinned then gaped once more, her eyes lingering on some of the vendors in the marketplace who had clearly come from the continent. Everything from their dress to their physical appearance looked new and different.

I scanned the crowd. In Oak Throne, I knew nearly everyone's name. The same was true of Frog's Hollow. I loved the people of both places like they were my family— because they were, at least in my mind. How would I ever be able to manage in Venta, which was ten times the size of Oak Throne?

I would start first with my own house, where Esu's young son and mother waited.

As we approached the king's compound, I heard one of the guards shout to a runner below.

"The queen has come! The queen is here."

The gates swung open. We rode into the king's compound in time to meet Prasutagus, who was coming from one of the outbuildings, a pack of dogs trailing behind him. This time, he had a young boy with him. He held the dark-haired child's hand.

He paused, then spoke softly to the boy, who nodded.

This was, no doubt, young Artur.

Servants rushed out to meet us, including Galvyn, Prasutagus's housecarl.

"Welcome returns, Queen Boudica," he told me. Galvyn was an older man with a stout frame. He was balding, a circle of silver and gray hair around the lower portion of his head. His beard had been trimmed short. He wore a red tunic and a multi-colored cape pinned at the shoulder.

"I am pleased to be back," I replied, sending Morfran flying so I could dismount.

"The king is waiting for you," he said. "I shall see to your party and your things."

"The two women in our party will be staying here. The rest will return to Oak Throne."

"I understand."

"Thank you, Galvyn. Melusine. Is the queen still here or…"

"King Caturix and Queen Melusine left Venta two days ago."

I nodded. "Very well. Thank you," I said, clapping the man on the shoulder.

Adjusting my spear and my satchel, I turned and caught Pix's attention, gesturing that I would meet with Prasutagus and that she should go on.

"Come along," Pix told Vian. "Ye shall see. Prasutagus is as rich as a faerie king. Ye will not believe yer eyes."

Leaving the others, I made my way to Prasutagus and the boy.

"Boudica," Prasutagus called. "Welcome home. I am glad to see you safely back in Venta. Holk Fort?" he asked.

"In hand."

Prasutagus nodded. He held my gaze for a long moment. There was more that we both wanted to say, but now was not the time. Prasutagus flicked his eyes toward the boy.

"Boudica, I would like you to meet my son, Artur. Artur, this is Boudica of the Northern Iceni."

The boy did not look up at me.

I squatted to meet his gaze. He had thick, dark hair and bushy eyebrows that he had scrunched together in a scowl.

"Hello, Artur," I said. "I'm glad to meet you. Prasutagus has told me much about you…and your mother."

He lifted his gaze just a bit to look at me.

Prasutagus's dogs, excited to see me so low to the ground, also came to make my acquaintance. The biggest of them, a brown-and-black creature with white spots, wiggled around me, nearly knocking me over.

I laughed, and then ruffled his ears.

"Is this your dog?" I asked Artur.

"No. He is Prasutagus's."

"Hmmm. Are any of these beasts yours?"

The boy simply shrugged.

"It is far more complicated than that, I'm afraid. Artur is the pack leader," Prasutagus said. "They follow him as if he were their alpha."

I laughed. "Then they are loyal creatures. I bought a

marshland terrier when I was in Stonea, but my sister Brenna stole him from me. But I have Morfran," I said, pointing overhead where the raven was flying.

"That bird?" the boy asked.

So, he had been watching, at least a little.

"Morfran is my raven. He's quite smart. If you train him, he can deliver messages and even speak a few words. I'll show you one day, when we have time."

Artur shifted, a glimmer of excitement lighting up his eyes. It seemed as though he wanted to say something, but instead, he scowled once more.

"May I go now, Father?" he asked Prasutagus.

"Yes, but I will see you inside for the evening meal."

At that, the boy sprinted away, the dogs following behind him.

"That...went better than I expected," Prasutagus said. "I've been warming him up for days."

"It's all right," I said with a soft smile. "It will take him time to see I am not here to erase Esu's memory."

Prasutagus smiled gently at me. "Boudica."

Wrapping my arms around him, I exhaled heavily, feeling the weight of everything that had happened lift from me as I melted into Prasutagus's arms. We stayed like that for a long time, just feeling one another. Finally, Prasutagus kissed the top of my head and set his cheek thereon.

"Come inside. You must tell me everything," he said.

I nodded. I cast a glance toward the skyline, but Morfran had gone. No doubt, he would return soon.

Prasutagus took my hand and led me to the roundhouse.

Within, I was greeted by the familiar faces of Prasutagus's household staff. Pix and Vian were in the main dining hall, Pix making Betha and Ronat, Prasutagus's cooks, laugh. When we entered, Pix turned to my husband.

"Well met, Strawberry King," she told him with a naughty wink, making Prasutagus chuckle.

"Vian," I said, gesturing to the girl. "This is King Prasutagus."

"King Prasutagus," Vian said, rising quickly. She fidgeted nervously, and then tried a curtsey, a challenging task while standing near a bench.

"Vian will serve as my secretary," I told Prasutagus. "She is exceptionally bright. I look forward to seeing what she makes of Venta."

"You are welcome to Venta," Prasutagus told her. "Galvyn will ensure you are settled in comfortably."

"I... Thank you, King Prasutagus," she said, trying to curtsey once more.

"Please, be at ease," Prasutagus told her. "This is your home now. We don't stand on formality here."

"Thank you," Vian said, a smile lighting up her face as she sat once more.

"I told you, I want to see who has come!" an angry voice shouted from the hallway. A moment later, Ginerva appeared, Nella trailing behind her.

"Prasutagus, what's all this?" Ginerva asked, waving at us.

"Ginerva, the king is busy," Nella told the old woman. "Let's go to the garden."

Prasutagus motioned to Nella to wait.

"Ginerva, this group has come from the Northern Iceni," Prasutagus told the old woman.

Ginerva looked us all over. "Yes. Yes. I see it now. Here is Queen Damara," she said, looking at me. "Queen," she said, curtseying to me.

I smiled gently and then went to the old woman. "I am glad to see you again, Ginerva," I said, setting my hand on her arm.

"You remember me?" she asked with a surprised expression.

"I do."

"Well, won't Antedios be surprised at that." She laughed as she clapped her hands.

"I brought you something," I told her, dipping into my satchel. From within, I pulled out one of the crocks of orange marmalade I had taken from Holk Fort. I handed it to the old woman.

"What's this?"

"A gift."

She opened the lid, and then lifted it to her nose. "Orange marmalade," she exclaimed. "My favorite! How did you know?"

"A lucky guess."

The old woman smiled at me. "Guess? No. You were a priestess at the Grove of Andraste. The gods told you to bring this for me." Grinning, she looked around the room. "Esu? Esu? Where is my daughter? She loves this even more than I. We'll share it when she returns. Thank you, Queen Damara."

I inclined my head to her.

"Come, Ginerva," Nella said. "We will see if there are any scones left from the morning meal."

"Excellent idea," Ginerva said before shuffling away.

Nella's gaze drifted to me. For the first time, her features softened. She gave me a grateful smile then the pair disappeared to the back.

"It was kind of you to remember Ginerva," Prasutagus told me.

"There is more," I said, gesturing to my satchel. "Courtesy of Saenunos. At her age, it is the small comforts that matter most."

Prasutagus smiled at me, and then turned to Davin and the others. "My Northern Iceni friends, we shall see you lodged for the night. Please, take your rest. Eat. Drink. You can take to the road again in the morning. I won't have you traveling in the dark."

"Many thanks, King Prasutagus," Davin told the king.

At that, my husband took my hand and led me to a seat a little way away from the others.

"Now," he said. "Tell me everything."

CHAPTER 14

Prasutagus listened patiently as I explained the events that had unfolded at Holk Fort, including the attempt on my life, the assistance of the druids, and the news Vian had shared about the Catuvellauni's treachery.

"I've had messengers from Togodumnus and Caratacus. They are eager to mobilize forces."

I frowned. "What of the other tribes? What are you hearing?"

"When your brother left, he told me he would send word to the Coritani, inquiring about their stance. I have men elsewhere, watching and waiting," Prasutagus said, then shook his head. "I have spread the word here amongst our people. The smaller villages will close their gates and stay on alert. The Romans may not want anything from us. If this is truly about Verica and Aedd Mawr, then this is a war that has nothing to do with the Greater Iceni."

"After learning they were, to some extent, behind my father's death, I can never support Caratacus and Togodumnus. But I am not ignorant of what happened in Gaul."

"Nor am I. So, we will wait."

"For now."

Prasutagus nodded. "For now."

WHEN THE EVENING MEAL WAS SERVED, TALK OF WAR dissipated when Nella, Ginerva, and Artur reappeared again. Along with them arrived Ansgar, Prasutagus's druid, and Ardra, the novice druidess I had met briefly when I first visited Venta.

"Queen Boudica," Ansgar said, giving me a short bow. "We are pleased to see you back in Venta."

"Thank you, Ansgar." The druid reminded me much of Belenus in his gentle manner. Ansgar wore his silver hair long. He had an equally long, silver beard that lay on his chest. Within his beard, he had woven small bells and silver pieces.

"You will remember my novice, the druidess Ardra?"

"Welcome, Queen Boudica," the girl said. This time, I was able to assess the girl more closely. She was, perhaps, sixteen years of age. She had wide, blue-green eyes and curly, pale blonde hair, which she had pulled back into a tight braid. Unruly curls framed her pretty face. She had a pinched nose and heavy eyebrows. While she gave me a light smile, something in her eyes bid me to be cautious.

Ronat, Betha, and the kitchen boy, Newt, set a feast before us.

Artur took a seat beside his grandmother, who kissed the boy.

"Where is Esu?" Ginerva asked Prasutagus.

"She's not here," he replied simply, a pinch of pain in his voice.

"But she will miss the evening meal," Ginerva said.

"She feasts with the ancestors, Grandmother," Artur told the old woman.

Ginerva looked confused, and then turned to me, a distinct lack of recognition on her face. "Who are you?"

"I'm Boudica," I told her.

"Boudica?"

"She's father's new wife," Artur told the old woman. I didn't miss the bitter tone in his voice.

Ginvera laughed. "*Esu* is his wife. No, no. Boudica is Esu's new maid," she said confidently then turned to Pix. "What is in your hair?"

"Hair," Pix replied with a grin.

Ginerva laughed, shook her head, but asked nothing more. "Prasutagus brings strange people about," she told Artur.

The boy merely shrugged.

"Was your ride south quiet, Queen Boudica?" Ardra asked politely.

"Oddly quiet. As if the whole world has taken a breath," I replied.

"I find the greenwood greatly unsettled," Ardra said as she poured herself a mug of ale. "From the songs of the birds to the shape of the clouds, everything feels off to me."

"It is nearly Yule," Ginerva told Ardra. "That is why."

"Yes," Ardra replied simply, then turned to me. "I was sorry to hear of your father's death and that of ancient Belenus. The druid was much respected in our order."

"It is a great loss on both counts," Ansgar agreed. "We were very sad to hear of it."

"Thank you," I told them.

Feeling eyes upon me, I looked up to find Artur staring at me as he considered the news. After a long moment, he turned back to his food and ate his meal as quickly as possible. Watching him, I was reminded of Bran. I thought no one could eat faster than my brother, but I was wrong.

Artur shoved the last bite of food into his mouth, then rose. "May I be excused, Father?"

Prasutagus looked surprised but motioned for him to go on.

Artur moved to go but then paused and looked at me. "And...Queen Boudica. May I?"

I smiled gently at him. "I would not delay a boy who has things to do."

Making no reply, he turned and rushed off.

"You have come from Holk Fort, is that right?" Ardra asked Vian.

"I have."

"As Boudica's maid?"

"Vian will be my secretary," I told the novice.

"Oh," Ardra said, her eyebrows lifting. She turned to Vian once more. "So, you read and write? Ogham, Latin, and…" Ardra said, gesturing.

"I do read *some* Latin," Vian said, shifting nervously. She looked to me for help.

"Not that kind of secretary," I told Ardra, annoyed at her for laying a trap for Vian. "I have other tasks with which I want Vian's help."

"Such as?" Ardra asked.

"I am certain that's the queen's business," Ansgar told the girl, halting her questions.

"Yes. Of course," Ardra said, and then turned back to her dish, a light smile dancing on her lips.

Pix, however, had not missed the slight. "What do ye do here?" Pix asked Ardra.

"I am a novice to Ansgar, and I serve as a tutor for Artur. And you…your role?" she asked, needling Pix.

"Hmm," Pix mused. "Ye see, when I look at this table," Pix said, gesturing to the spread, "I can see about thirty different ways to kill a person who would cross me or mine. And that's not counting me weapons, of course."

Ardra gave Pix a sly smile. "I guess we all have our talents."

"That we do, novice."

Beside Pix, Vian lifted her drink and sipped, hiding her smile.

"The priestess Henwyn has asked Ardra and me to join them at King's Wood tomorrow," Ansgar told Prasutagus. "Will that be all right for you, my king?"

Prasutagus nodded. "Of course," he said, and then

turned to me. "The druids of Arminghall have a small village not far from the nemeton. Ansgar is arch druid of the Greater Iceni, but since he serves as adviser to the king, King's Wood is led by the priestess Henwyn."

"I hope to pay a visit one day," I said.

Prasutagus nodded. "We will see to it."

Our party lingered at the table awhile longer, the druids leaving shortly after that. Ginerva grew tired, so Nella took her to bed. The rest of us filled ourselves with the delicious food. When I noticed Vian's eyelids growing heavy, I nudged Prasutagus.

He nodded.

"You have had many days on the road, Vian," I said. "Perhaps you should take your rest."

"Yes. Yes, I think you're right."

Galvyn stepped forward. "We have Lady Vian's chamber prepared. If you are ready, Lady."

Vian rose.

I joined them.

"This way," Galvyn said, motioning for Vian and I to follow him.

A moment later, Pix appeared behind me.

"Nella has lodged Lady Vian and Pix in the servants' quarters," he said, gesturing to the hallway. "It's just outside."

"Wait. In one of the outbuildings?" I asked.

Galvyn paused. "Yes, well, that is where the servants stay."

"I see," I said tersely, then paused. "And Nella? Is she housed there as well?"

"Well, no. Nella, myself, and a few close attendants are here in the roundhouse with the family."

I bit the inside of my cheek and willed the flicker of flame in my heart to be silent.

"As will Pix and Vian," I said. "I will not have my people so far from me, especially when we are all so new to this place. Is there room for them in the king's house?"

"Yes, Queen Boudica," he replied, gesturing to a waiting servant. "Fetch the Northern Iceni's things and bring them into the house," he told the man, then turned to Vian and Pix. "Will you mind sharing a room?"

"Not me," Vian said.

Pix shook her head.

"You may change your mind once you hear how loudly Pix snores," I told Vian with a grin.

Galvyn laughed. "I am sorry for the confusion, Queen Boudica. Nella has always managed the queen's things. I had assumed she had asked you."

"No. She hadn't."

"In the morning, I will give you a full tour of the roundhouse. We have many guest chambers, storage rooms, and more that you should see. Queen Esu had a day room where she kept busy. She was quite adept at spinning and sewing. Perhaps you would enjoy the space?"

Pix laughed. "Ye will never find Boudica at the loom. More likely up to her knees in mud in the stables."

I chuckled. "She's right. Had Prasutagus actually married Brenna, perhaps there would be a need. But for me? No."

Galvyn smiled. "I see. Well, Ginerva spends a good deal of time there. I will show you where the room is, in case you change your mind or wish to pay her a visit."

We arrived at a chamber not far from that belonging to myself and Prasutagus. Galvyn opened the door to reveal a small but comfortable room with two beds. It was well appointed with furs, wall hangings, trunks, tables, benches, and more.

Vian gasped. "Is this your room?" she asked me.

Galvyn laughed lightly. "No, Lady. It is your room now."

"Told you," Pix said, elbowing Vian. "Rich as a faerie king."

"I will go check on your things," Galvyn told the women.

"Thank you," Vian said politely.

Pix nodded to him.

"Galvyn," I said, causing the man to pause. "When it comes to anything about my people, my horse, or anything else concerning me, if I am not available, you or Vian should make those decisions, not Nella. Nella would not choose for Prasutagus, nor will she choose for me. I honor the late Queen Esu, but I am not her and don't need her maid's input. Do we understand one another?"

Galvyn grinned. "We do indeed, Queen Boudica. And may I suggest, Your Majesty, that you employ a maid of your own choosing to see to your personal effects. Maybe... maybe Nella has enough to do with Ginerva? Maybe you don't want to overburden her..."

"You're right. I don't want to overtax her."

"And, maybe, you would not mind me employing such a person on your behalf. My brother has a teenage daughter. Quiet girl, but skilled. Perhaps…"

"I eagerly look forward to meeting her."

"Very good," Galvyn said, then turned and went on his way.

"There's a rat in yer barn," Pix told me.

"Just one? I think Galvyn just helped me find a way to handle one of them."

"Best watch yerself, Strawberry Queen. Rats always find a way to sneak back where they aren't wanted," Pix told me with a wink, then turned to Vian. "Well, don't stand there with yer mouth hanging open. Let's test the beds. Nice room, but ideal for my male guests."

"You will not bring male guests in here with Vian," I told her.

"What about female guests?"

I rolled my eyes at her.

"I will be just down the hall," I told them. "Don't hesitate to wake me if there are any issues."

"Good night, Queen Boudica," Vian told me.

"Good night."

I gave Pix a knowing grin, which she returned, then shut their door behind me.

When I turned, I found Artur standing at the end of the hallway.

"Artur," I said. "Are you… Do you want to meet Morfran? I was about to call him to come in for the night."

The boy hesitated. I could see his curiosity was urging

him to say yes, but his wariness won out. Shaking his head, he hurried off in another direction.

I frowned.

I loved children—all children—I *would* find a way to win him over yet.

Esu, be with me. I will look after your boy as if he were my own. Help me gentle his heart.

THAT NIGHT, PRASUTAGUS AND I WITHDREW TO OUR chamber. My stomach fluttered with nervous butterflies as I slipped into bed with him. How strange it all was—we were wed, yet we were still strangers to one another in many ways.

"In the days to come, I want you to make this place your home. Change things. Reorder things. Make things as you wish."

"Including forcing you to keep a raven in your bedchamber?" I asked, looking over where Morfran had roosted on his makeshift perch, a broom stuck into a barrel.

Prasutagus chuckled. "Even that."

"Galvyn helped me situate Vian and Pix down the hall. They had originally been placed in the outbuilding."

"In the outbuilding?"

"Nella had them in with the stable hands."

In the darkness, I felt Prasutagus frown. "Nella was

never an easy woman, but she and Esu were close. Nella took Esu's death hard."

"Galvyn suggested I bring on my own maid to see to my things. I agreed."

Prasutagus laughed lightly. "I understand. Nella will not, but I understand."

"I have no wish to make enemies here. Quite the contrary."

"You are very different from Esu. They will learn in time."

I rolled over, placing my chin on Prasutagus's chest. My fingers danced across the markings thereon. "And you? Are you adjusting, King Prasutagus?"

He grinned at me. "I've had little time to practice. I won my wife only to have war snatch her away."

"Hmm," I mused. "Then I guess we should make up for lost time before something finds its way between us again."

Prasutagus stroked my hair. "Nothing will come between us, Boudica. We are twin souls. Not time, distance, or death can separate us. You are mine. And I will always be yours."

With that, I crawled on top of him and set a kiss on his lips. And then another. And then another. And then another...until we were lost in each other.

CHAPTER 15

I t was very early the next morning when Galvyn knocked on the door. "King Prasutagus, Queen Boudica, riders at the gate."

I awoke groggily.

Prasutagus rose, pulled on a robe, and went to the door.

I nestled down into the blankets and listened.

"I'm sorry, King Prasutagus, but this could not wait."

"Who is here?"

"A messenger from King Verica. It is a small party of Atrebates…and three Romans."

"Romans?" I asked.

"Yes, my queen," Galvyn replied.

"We will meet them in the courtyard. Have the formal meeting chamber prepared."

"Yes, my king," Galvyn said, then departed.

Prasutagus closed the door, pausing a moment, his

hand resting on the handle. Then, he turned to me. "Will you meet them with me?"

"Of course."

Prasutagus nodded. "Good," he said, nodding to himself, then went to dress.

A moment later, there was another knock on the door. "My...queen. It's Nella. May I be of any assistance to you this morning?"

She had done little to hide the fact that she'd come begrudgingly.

Prasutagus looked at me.

I shook my head.

Prasutagus, who had nearly finished dressing, went to the door once more. "Good morning, Nella. No. We are well. Can you find Artur for me? We have guests. I don't want him wandering this morning. Tell him he'll get a better look if he stays in the roundhouse anyway. But inside, he shall stay."

"I understand," Nella replied, and then paused. "Is it true? Romans?"

"Yes."

"May the gods watch over us. And the queen?"

"She will accompany me to the meeting chamber."

"Oh," Nella said in surprise. "Very well."

At that, Prasutagus closed the door.

I crossed the room to help him lace up his tunic. It had not escaped my notice that he had chosen very fine clothes. Taking his signal, I selected my favorite deep purple gown. I was sorry Riona was not there to see me affix my hair with a pin and put on matching earrings. She would have been impressed.

"Here," Prasutagus said. "I had something made for you," he added, handing me a wrapped bundle.

"What is it?"

He laughed. "A wedding gift. Late, but a gift for my queen all the same."

Chuckling, I took the parcel. "Heavy," I said then and unwrapped it. Within, I discovered a massive golden torc. The ends were trimmed with horse heads, the eyes flickering to life with green gemstones. "Prasutagus," I whispered.

"You are the queen of the Greater Iceni, Boudica. Here, let me help," he said, taking the torc from my hands.

I pushed my hair aside and let him place the item on my neck.

"Weighty," I said, my fingers lightly touching it.

"Yes. As I feel the weight of mine, I tell myself it is a small reminder of the weight of my duty to my people."

When he was done, I shifted my hair once more, then Prasutagus pulled on his cloak, fastening it with a golden brooch.

He nodded to me, and then took my hand.

When we exited the room, I found Pix waiting. She was fully dressed, including all her weapons. Vian, dressed in a pale blue gown, waited with her.

"Heard we have guests," Pix said with a grin.

"Shall we say hello?" I replied.

Pix nodded.

"Boudica..." Vian said.

"Come with us. Look and listen."

She nodded.

With that, we made our way toward the front door of the roundhouse. Galvyn and several guards waited for us. On Prasutagus's signal, his men opened the door. With four guards in front of us and four behind us, Pix and Vian following, we made our way outside.

There, Rome waited.

"KING PRASUTAGUS AND QUEEN BOUDICA," GALVYN SAID, introducing us.

The strangers bowed deeply.

I scanned the party. Two men, whose capes and brooches indicated that they were Atrebates, King Verica's people, bowed to us. Behind the group, waiting with Prasutagus's soldiers, were more Atrebates warriors. Their banner, which depicted a grapevine leaf and Verica's name, written in the Roman fashion, fluttered in the breeze.

Along with the two Atrebates men were three Romans. They were dressed in an unfamiliar fashion. The men wore knee-length tunics that showed their legs. Over the tunics, they wore armored pieces that protected their chests and backs. Additionally, they wore high boots and heavy belts. Pinned at the shoulders were long, red capes. The three men, whose hair was cut short and had no sign of beard or mustache, held their helmets under their arms.

The sight of such men gripped me with equal parts terror and fascination.

The elder of the two Atrebates, a man with shoulder-length white hair, turned to Prasutagus. "King Prasutagus, I am Cadell, attendant to King Verica. It is an honor to meet you," the man said. "I was sorry to learn of your father's death. I was fortunate enough to meet King Antedios in my youth and was impressed by him. It is a great loss."

"Thank you," Prasutagus said stiffly.

"This is Druce, another adviser to King Verica," he said, gesturing to the other Atrebates man, a smaller gentleman with red hair cut in the Roman style. Then, he turned to the Romans. "As well, may I introduce Silvius Hispanus, Darius Volusus, Titus Carassius. These men are here under the direction of General Aulus Plautius."

My eyes danced across the men. Of them, the man introduced as Silvius Hispanus stood out to me due to his appearance: dark eyes, olive skin, and curling brown hair. Darius Volusus had short, brown hair and a severe expression. Titus Carassius, however, was a jovial-looking man with curly silver hair, plump cheeks, and a round physique. Despite his armor, I sensed he was not a soldier.

"Gentlemen," Prasutagus greeted them. "Please, come inside. You will be parched from your ride."

Prasutagus turned, and we led the strangers into the roundhouse. We went to a room I had not yet explored. Therein, I found two thrones seated at the back of a well-appointed chamber. Everything from shields, swords, horse hides, bearskins, and décor made of wood and silver decorated the walls. The braziers had been lit in anticipation of our arrival. At a table in the very back of the room, the servants worked busily preparing a table with food and drink.

Prasutagus led me to one of the thrones and held my hand when I sat. He then took a seat beside me. Once we were seated, he gestured for the men to speak.

It was the Roman, Titus Carassius, who stepped forward. "We are honored to be welcome into your hall, King Prasutagus and Queen Boudica. I bring warm greetings to you from our general, Aulus Plautius, who hopes he will soon be able to make your acquaintance."

"We thank you for his greetings and return them in kind," Prasutagus replied.

The man bowed to Prasutagus.

Druce, Verica's second man, then said, "I am delighted to be received by you here, Queen Boudica," he told me, then turned to Prasutagus. "We just learned of your wedding to the daughter of King Aesunos. You have our congratulations. We were rather surprised by the news, having heard a rumor that the daughters of Aesunos would wed to the Catuvellauni brothers. Instead, we find a joining of the Northern and Greater Iceni. That is something I never thought I would live to see," he said, then turned to the Romans. "The Iceni people, in all their great history, have never joined as one. And now, we find them bound by blood."

Cadell clapped his hands together. "Yes, indeed. It is

excellent news. That shall make a firm allegiance for King Verica here in the east. In fact, Queen Boudica, we intend to ride north to your father after our visit here."

The conversation revealed two things. First, Verica had spies amongst the tribes. Otherwise, rumors about Brenna and me wedding to the Catuvellauni would have no way of reaching him. It also revealed that they had expected the Northern Iceni to be allied with the Catuvellauni. Verica—and the Romans—were not the only ones trying to determine whose loyalty lay where. It also revealed that they had not yet heard of my father's death, despite their spying. I shifted, uncertain for a moment. It would be better if they knew nothing of my people. But if they already planned to ride north, they would discover the truth, and Bran would be unready to face the challenge of what to say.

"I am sorry to share the news that my father is in the Otherworld," I said. "My brother, Caturix, is now king of the Northern Iceni."

"Alas, I am sorry for your loss. I arrive in a great period of change for the Iceni, loyal friends of the Atrebates," Cadell replied.

"And King Verica, he is well?" Prasutagus asked.

"He is, and he sends his regards. These are exciting times for our people. With the help of our Roman allies, soon, our king will retake his rightful throne. And the lands of your neighbors, the Trinovantes, will soon be restored to Aedd Mawr and his heirs."

"Is Aedd Mawr here as well?" Prasutagus asked, fishing for news.

Cadell paused, as if realizing he'd said too much.

Titus Carassius stepped in to say, "Rome has come on his behalf. Age has prevented the king from crossing Ocean to return to his homeland once more. But our emperor and Aulus Plautius intend to see his people liberated, his lands and home secured."

"The Trinovantes and Atrebates are lucky to have such loyal allies," Prasutagus said.

"And we hope for more," Silvis replied, a rich accent in his voice.

Darius smiled. "Emperor Claudius cares deeply about his client kings here in Britannia. Since the time of Julius Caesar, you have been left alone too long. The rebel Catuvellauni have impeded on the rights of Rome's allies and have unwantedly set their sights on other tribes. We are glad to be able to offer Rome's friendship and protection."

"In exchange for?" I asked.

Darius simply smiled at me, ignored my question, and redirected his gaze to Prasutagus. "We are foremost here to aid King Verica and to restore the rights of the Trinovantes people. Envoys such as ours travel across the land, meeting with other great kings."

"Indeed," Cadell added. "Already, offers have been made to the Cantiaci and Regnenses."

"Offers of what?" I asked.

"Protection, Queen Boudica," Cadell replied. "From the Catuvellauni who have threatened their borders."

"The Cantiaci," Prasutagus said, and then smiled. "And how has King Anarevitos received your offers?"

Cadell shifted uncomfortably, then said, "I don't think

it will come as a surprise to you that King Anarevitos was less inclined to listen than yourselves."

"No, it does," Prasutagus said.

"Rome can be a friend and ally, King Prasutagus," Cadell said. "King Verica has found great support amongst the Romans. Even you are old enough to remember that Aedd Mawr was a widely respected ruler before the Catuvellauni took over Trinovantes lands."

Prasutagus nodded slowly.

"Indeed," Titus added. "What Cadell says is true. Rome extends its hand in friendship. We hope to establish many trade agreements and more with the Greater Iceni people. Our emperor is keen to reestablish all the treaties and agreements made by Caesar."

Which included the payment of tribute promised by our grandfathers but only paid in half or not at all by our people.

Prasutagus sat back in his seat. After a long moment, he asked, "What does King Verica ask of us?"

"For now, only that the Greater Iceni stay their hand in this conflict. We know Caratacus and Togodumnus are trying to raise allies to prevent King Verica from retaking his lands. All King Verica asks is that the Greater Iceni," Cadell said, and then looked at me, "and the *Northern* Iceni stay neutral in this conflict."

"As was the posture of your father when the Catuvellauni launched the attack on their neighbors under Cunobelinus, Caratacus's and Togodumnus's father," Druce added.

"And in time, Rome hopes to offer more to the Greater Iceni," Titus said.

Prasutagus nodded. "You have given us much to consider. And I do not like to make such decisions on an empty stomach. It is early still. Please," Prasutagus said, rising. He gestured to the table in the back where the morning meal had been laid out. "Will you join us?"

We made our way to the table at the back. Servants worked busily, pouring drinks and serving food. I caught Pix's gaze as I crossed the room. Her arms crossed on her chest, she shook her head ever so slightly.

Apparently, she trusted the Romans no more than I did.

We settled in at the table.

"Venta seems to be twice the size it was when I saw it last," Cadell told my husband as the servants filled his plate.

"My father labored hard to make Venta a hub for trade for the people of this region."

"I saw magnificent horses as we rode here, as well as at your horse market," Darius said.

"All the Iceni are horse people. We are adept at raising and riding horses," I replied.

The man smiled dismissively at me, then turned to Prasutagus. "I was surprised to see some Roman goods in your marketplace."

"The merchants of Londinium travel everywhere in the country," Cadell told his companion.

"There is a statue of a woman in your courtyard. Is that an ancestor?" Silvius asked Prasutagus.

"No," Prasutagus replied. "That is Epona, lady of horses, our patron goddess."

"I have heard this name in Gaul. This goddess is known there as well," Silvius said.

"Epona is widely worshipped by our people," I said, then added, "I don't think you are from Rome, Silvius. Where are your people from?"

"From the lands near the Black Sea, Queen Boudica."

"You are very far from home," I told him.

"As I am reminded with each mile I take. Your forests here are unlike any others I have ever seen."

"How so?"

He laughed, and then shook his head. "I should not say. You will find me superstitious."

"I live for superstition," I replied with a grin.

"The forests here have eyes, Queen Boudica."

At that, Darius laughed. "Silvius and half the legion were haunted by stories of druid curses and walking forests before we launched from Gaul. General Plautius put to rest such cowardice in our men. There is nothing to fear from trees."

"Tell that to Caesar," Pix quipped.

I gave her a stern look, reminding her to silence her tongue.

The Romans flicked their gazes toward her but said nothing.

"As I said, I am merely superstitious," Silvius replied, the other Romans nodding at him.

The Atrebates men looked less confident.

"It is good to be cautious of things you feel but don't understand," I told Silvius, holding his gaze.

"Yes. It is," he answered, meeting my look—both of us making our meaning plain.

"Tell me, Queen Boudica, will we find your brother, King Caturix, such an amiable host?" Titus asked, gesturing to the spread of food before him. "You Celts never water your wine. Your blood must be made of it. But I like it this way. And your meat is always well cooked."

"We thank you. Though, I dare say, you are unlikely to find my brother at all. Caturix is not in Oak Throne. With the passing of my father, he is traveling between farmsteads. I'm afraid any journey north would be pointless, but I am glad to pass along your message to my brother. I will see him as soon as he returns."

"I see," Cadell said with a frown. "So, he is not at Oak Throne."

"No, sir. But as a daughter of King Aesunos, I am pleased to relay your message. I'm sure the Northern Iceni and the Greater Iceni will be united in all of their thoughts, not just in marriage. When we are ready to reply, I am sure you will find us like-minded."

Cadell nodded. "I understand. Thank you, Queen Boudica. We will be eager to hear your reply."

With that, we finished the meal, the men complimenting the spread, and then the party prepared to depart. We returned once more to the square before the roundhouse. There, the Romans' and the Atrebates' horses stood waiting.

"King Verica will eagerly await the reply of the Northern and Greater Iceni," Cadell told us.

"You will hear from us soon," Prasutagus replied. "We send King Verica our greetings."

Titus smiled at Prasutagus. "General Plautius hopes to make your acquaintance one day very soon, King Prasutagus. The emperor will want to ensure all those kingdoms with which Caesar made alliances are safe in these troubled times. And, of course, we will want to revisit the promises made in Caesar's time."

Prasutagus simply nodded to him.

The man smiled but said nothing more.

With that, the men mounted their horses.

They were escorted back out of the city with Prasutagus's guards before—and behind—them.

As soon as they were out of sight, I turned to Pix.

"Follow them. I want to know where they go next."

She nodded, and then hurried off in the direction of the stables.

Prasutagus and I stood in silence for a long moment.

Riding hard, Pix rode past us and out of the king's courtyard, hurrying to catch up.

"I need to send word to Caturix. I hope I have not overstepped. Do you think they will ride north anyway?" I asked Prasutagus.

"No. I think Cadell understood your meaning. Ah, Boudica, every choice we make could alter the future of our people. How to proceed…"

I thought of Ula's words once more and her anger. Unite now or perish later. If it were only that easy.

Galvyn joined us.

"My king?" he asked.

"Increase the guards on the palisades around the city and the king's compound. Bring on more men if you must. Venta is now on curfew. The city will be closed from sundown to sunup."

"Yes, King Prasutagus."

"I want messengers sent to the chieftains. They must close their villages and be on alert."

"Yes, King Prasutagus."

"And Galvyn?"

"My king?"

"Artur does not go into the city alone."

"I understand," he said, then hurried away.

I looked up at my husband. "What do you think?"

"Ever get the feeling that no matter what choice you make, it is the wrong one?"

"Constantly."

"Then may the gods guide us, Boudica. Because I cannot see a path forward that does not end in pain."

CHAPTER 16

Back in the roundhouse, Prasutagus and I adjourned to the formal meeting chamber.

"I must send word to Bran and Caturix," I told him.

Prasutagus nodded. "We must speak to Caturix in person. Ask him to join us here in Venta, if you think he will."

"Of all my siblings, Caturix's mind is the one I understand the least, but I will impress upon him the urgency. The Northern Iceni who rode with us haven't yet left. I will send the messengers to my brothers then rejoin you," I told Prasutagus, then went in search of Davin, Cai, and the others.

I found the Northern Iceni warriors huddled together in the dining hall.

Cai rose when I entered. "Is it true, Boudica? The Romans? We did not see them, but everyone was talking."

I nodded. "Yes," I said, then gestured for them to sit

down.

"What do they want?" Cai asked, then paused. "I'm sorry. You are queen now, not Bran's little sister. It was wrong of me to ask."

"We are all still friends," I told them. "And I need you now. I must get word to Caturix and to Bran. Davin, take a party back north. Tell Bran the Romans have paid us a visit. They had originally intended to ride north to Oak Throne to speak to my father, but I believe I dissuaded them. If not, Bran must be on his guard. He must be ready to speak but promise nothing. That is the important part. He must promise nothing. Please, take half the men and go. Be wary, as you may meet the Romans on the road."

"I will take the path through Ogmios's farmstead. We can cross the river and cut them off, arriving in Oak Throne first," Davin said.

I nodded. "Very good," I said, then turned to Cai. "Will you go to Stonea?"

Cai nodded.

"I will take these men," Davin told Cai. "You take the rest."

Cai nodded.

"We should go at once," Davin told me.

"Be safe," I told them, then Davin and a handful of others quickly departed.

"Cai, please ask Caturix to come to Venta. We must respond to this threat as one. We should meet here to discuss."

"I understand," Cai replied.

"And tell Caturix... I did not reveal that he was at

Stonea. They believe his seat is still in Oak Throne but that he is traveling. If the Romans do not learn the Iceni have changed the king's seat, perhaps it is better for him."

"Crafty, Boudica," Cai said.

I shook my head. "Overprotectiveness. I would hide my brother in the mists."

At that, he chuckled.

"Repeat to no one what I have told you here. A path is not decided. It may still come to war."

At that, Cai and the others nodded.

"You can rely on me, assuming Pix hasn't taken my horse," Cai said.

"I watched her ride out. She has Saenunos's horse. Not a problem. He no longer needs it."

The others laughed and then departed, leaving Vian and me alone.

I turned to the girl. "What do you think?"

"I cannot say."

"Cannot or will not?"

"It's just that such things are so far beyond me. Days ago, my greatest concern was scrubbing pots."

"So it was, but that was then, and this is now. Now, tell me, what did you hear?"

"Well, I heard everything they did say. But I also heard what they didn't."

I gestured for her to go on.

"Even if you don't fight with the Catuvellauni, that doesn't mean our troubles are over. They were less than direct about their plans for the Trinovantes, and I got the impression that Rome would hold those lands for Aedd

Mawr, which would give them a foothold in this land, just as they did in Gaul. That's dangerous because the whole world knows Rome does not stop. More than once, they referenced the promises made to Julius Caesar. What promises were made to Caesar?"

"The Iceni—both Northern and Greater—promised to pay taxes and send slaves as tribute to Rome in exchange for peace."

"Did they?"

"The Northern Iceni did nothing. The Greater Iceni paid their taxes."

"Then there will be a reckoning for that lapse. Rome will be here in force. They may ask us to make good on those promises."

"Yes."

"Last time they warred here, they were defeated and left."

"Last time, they did not come at the side of one deposed king and in the name of another. King Verica is within his right to retake his crown, but…"

Vian nodded. "But this time, the Romans may try to stay, to expand their holdings."

"Unless we fight."

"Unless we fight," she repeated, her eyes narrowing as she thought it over. "What will you choose?"

"What would *you* choose?"

"Both choices could go terribly wrong."

"Yes."

"Then may the gods guide you to the right answer, Queen Boudica. Because even if you win, you may lose."

CHAPTER 17

Leaving Vian, I made my way back to the formal meeting room to find Artur alone therein.

"Did you see them?" I asked.

He nodded. "Their men wore skirts."

"So they did."

"And their hair..." Artur frowned. "They did not look like real men. They were strange."

"Their customs are very different from ours."

Just then, Nella rounded the corner.

"There you are," she said with exasperation. "I have been chasing you all over this hall," she said, making her way toward Artur. There was a thunder in her eyes I did not appreciate.

"Artur was just coming with me," I said, reaching out for the boy who took my hand.

"He was—what do you—he was supposed to—"

I silenced her with a look.

"Yes, Queen Boudica," she replied tersely, and then huffed off.

When she was gone, Artur let go of me.

"Artur, is everything all right? Was Nella—"

"Everything's fine, Queen Boudica."

"I am going to find Prasutagus. Would you like to join me?"

The boy hesitated a moment, then came along with me.

"What do the Romans want?" Artur asked.

"King Verica has returned from Rome with the Roman soldiers. He is here to recapture his throne."

"Does he want our help?"

"In a way."

"Does he want us to fight with them?"

"No. But he doesn't want us to fight against him either."

"King Antedios always said we should support our allies. That the Greater Iceni were only as good as our word. Are we allies with King Verica?"

"We are not."

"Are the Northern Iceni?"

"No, they are not either."

"Then, are we allies with King Caratacus and King Togodumnus?"

"That's...more complicated."

"Why?"

"Because sometimes people pretend to be our friends but aren't."

"And they were pretending?"

"Yes."

The boy grew silent for a long moment, and then said, "Ardra said *you* are pretending."

"Ardra said... Pretending at what?" I asked. My temper flared at once, but I reined it in, not wanting Artur to think he had upset me.

"To be my mother."

I paused, and then squatted down to meet the boy face to face. I saw a stranger in his green-and-gold hazel eyes— no doubt, a shadow of the mother he had lost. "Artur, I have no wish to replace your mother. I could not. No one can. I never knew her, but I am sure she was an extraordinary woman. I could never be her, but I can look after you as your mother would have wanted."

He studied my face. "Ardra said you will send me away when you have your own sons and that I shouldn't trust you."

"May the Great Mother hear my words... I swear I will never send you away from your home. You may trust me."

Artur looked skeptically at me. "All right, Queen Boudica."

"Just Boudica."

"All right, Boudica."

I smiled. "Good, now, let's go find your father," I said with a smile, but there was thunder in my heart. When I saw Ardra again, the young druid and I would have words.

ARTUR AND I ENTERED THE SMALL, PRIVATE MEETING CHAMBER where, not so long ago, Prasutagus had asked for my hand from my father. There, I found Vian and Prasutagus.

Prasutagus's smile went from Artur to me.

"Artur," he said.

"I... Boudica said I should come with her."

Prasutagus nodded to him. "Come," he said, gesturing to the boy. "Look here," he said, pointing to a map he had laid out on the table. On it, he had placed several wooden tokens.

"What are these?" Artur asked, lifting one of the tokens.

"They represent men," Prasutagus answered. "The ones with red paint are the Romans, white for Catuvellauni, yellow for Trinovantes, blue for Cantiaci, and black for Atrebates."

I joined them at the table, looking down at the likeness of the tribes on the map. Prasutagus was already tracking the movement of Rome's forces. If the tokens were accurate, the number of Roman soldiers was horrifying.

"There are so many of them," Artur said, looking at the Roman tokens.

"Yes," Prasutagus agreed. "Can you see where they are going?"

Artur studied the map. "Toward Camulodunum, some

of them. Others are coming up the Thames into Atrebates land. And here, these are in the Cantiaci's territory.

"That's right," Prasutagus replied.

"What are those?" Artur asked, pointing to other tokens sitting off to the side.

Prasutagus scooped up a handful of the tokens. "Greater Iceni," he said, setting the light green tokens in place in Venta. He then grabbed another handful. "And Northern Iceni," he added, placing the dark green tokens near Oak Throne. "As well as Regnenses and Coritani," he said, setting the other tokens on the board. "The rest for the tribes to the north and west."

Artur considered. "What will we do, Father? Will we join the Catuvellauni or King Verica?"

"Hmm," Prasutagus mused. "What would you do?"

"I…" The boy paused, then looked at the map. "I don't know. The Romans are strange. I don't trust them."

"Nor do I," Prasutagus said. "Nor does anyone."

"Except King Verica," Vian said.

"What King Verica expects from the Romans and what the Romans deliver may be very different things," Prasutagus said, adding, "Verica has been in Rome for many years. Perhaps he is more Roman than one of us, now."

"He changed his standard," I noted. "The raven of the Atrebates is gone. Now, he has a vine leaf on his standard."

"A Roman god?" Vian asked.

"Perhaps," Prasutagus replied. "I don't like this news that Aedd Mawr has sent Rome on his behalf."

"If we fight with the Catuvellauni, won't many Greater

Iceni die?" Artur asked as he knelt to look at the map, his hands on the table, his chin resting atop them.

"Yes," Prasutagus said.

"And the Catuvellauni cannot be trusted. Look what they did to the Atrebates and Trinovantes," Artur said.

Prasutagus set his hand on the boy's head. "That's right."

"What of the northern tribes? Beyond the Coritani. The Brigantes? The Parisii?" Vian asked.

"The northern tribes care little about the squabbles of southern kings," Prasutagus said.

"Unless the Romans do not stop with the Catuvellauni," I said, looking at the map. A terrible sense of the dread lay in my stomach. I had not forgotten Ula's words. No. Not *her* words. The words of the little people of the hollow hills. "If they don't stop, we will have sat by and done nothing."

At that, the room fell silent. The weight of that real possibility falling on us.

"Why not go and ask them?" Artur suggested.

"Ask who?" Prasutagus asked.

"The Romans. Go see their leaders. Ask them what they plan to do. If they lie, you will know it."

Prasutagus looked at me. "Not a bad idea. What do you think?"

"I *would* like to see those elephants," I told him with a grin.

Prasutagus lifted one of the Greater Iceni pegs and set it in the middle of a sea of Roman tokens. "Then let's go see some elephants."

CHAPTER 18

I t took the entire day before news reached us once more. First, it came in the form of Pix.

"Snaked along behind 'em. Ne'er did see me," she said as she slugged back an ale, wiping her mouth on her arm. "They had an argument about what to do. The Romans wanted to ride north anyway, but the Atrebates talked 'em out of it. They headed back south toward Trinovantes territory."

"Did you see anything else on the road?" I asked.

"Some people headed north into Greater Iceni lands. Looked like Trinovantes," she said.

"They're fleeing," I said, my heart feeling heavy.

Prasutagus nodded, and then turned to Galvyn. "Has there been any word from Divin?"

Galvyn shook his head. "Not yet, my king."

"Who is—" I began.

"He is the chieftain of Raven's Dell, the village closest

to the Trinovantes on our southern border," Prasutagus explained.

"Coming with their children, livestock, and all," Pix said.

"For all their talk of reestablishing rightful rulers, the Romans must have spooked them," Galvyn said.

Prasutagus nodded.

"No doubt the elephants," Pix said.

"Or the legions of men," I replied with a frown.

Late in the night, when the moon was high in the sky, a horn sounded announcing another rider. Prasutagus and I left the meeting room and went to the courtyard to find a rider hoisting the Northern Iceni flag. I recognized the man from Stonea.

"Pellinor," I said.

"Queen Boudica," he said, bowing to me. "King Prasutagus. King Caturix has sent me ahead. He, too, wishes for a meeting. He will ride first thing in the morning."

"Good," Prasutagus said, and then gestured to the man. "Come. Take your rest. It must have been a hard ride. You will be famished."

"Thank you, King Prasutagus."

Prasutagus and the man returned to the roundhouse, but I lingered a moment, watching as a groomsman led Pellinor's horse away.

"What is it?" Pix asked.

"Last time, when Caesar came, the answer of what to do must have been easy."

"Yer enemy is smart, Strawberry Queen. They found us divided. Now, they are the hammer on the wedge."

I sighed heavily. "Every decision feels like the wrong one. If we do not get involved, Rome could turn on us next. If we get involved, we risk the Iceni people."

"Come on," Pix said, putting her arm on my shoulder. "Time to forget yer troubles for the day. Nothing a good night of drinking and frolicking with your king won't cure."

"What about you?"

"Well, ye sent my handsome boy away. So, I suppose I'll have to find some way to amuse myself. Trying to convince Betha's daughter, Ronat, to try *new* things."

"Pix!"

"What? Got a kiss out of her. It's a start."

I shook my head.

"If ye don't like it, I can join ye and yer king instead. We'd have a merry time."

"I'm sure we would. But no."

"Sad."

I laughed. "Come on. Before you get any more wild ideas."

"Oh, these are me tame ideas. If I told you me wild ones, yer cheeks would be as red as your hair."

At that, we both laughed and headed inside.

THE DRUIDS RETURNED LATER THAT NIGHT, JUST AFTER THE evening meal.

"Is all well at the King's Wood?" Prasutagus asked.

"This whole country is stirred up like a hive of bees," Ansgar said. "But that is to be expected."

"It has been a long day. I think I will adjourn," Ardra said, giving Prasutagus and Ansgar a bow. She paused briefly to incline her head to me and then disappeared down the hall.

"Has Henwyn read the signs?" Prasutagus asked Ansgar, settling in the druid. "What do the gods say?"

I paused a moment, wanting to hear, but instead, I turned and followed Ardra.

I caught up with the girl just as she was about to enter her chamber. Surprised, she turned and looked at me.

"Queen Boudica, what can I do for you?"

"Inside," I told her, gesturing for her to enter the room.

She looked confused but entered, moving aside so I could join her.

I closed the door behind us.

"I honor our gods and have always revered our holy people, but I will not have you speaking to Artur behind me, no matter your station. You may be training as a druid, but that gives you no right to come between a child and his father's wife."

Ardra looked puzzled, her eyes wide. "I'm sorry, Queen Boudica. What do you mean?"

"Artur told me what you said. I only have the best intentions toward that child. He must see me as I am, an ally to him, not someone in competition with his mother's memory. I'm not. And you will not say such things to him again."

"I confess, Queen Boudica, I have no idea what you're talking about."

I studied her face. "You didn't speak of me to Artur?"

"No. Not at all. My duties lie in his education, nothing more. Why would I want to step between you? It is good you are here to care for Artur."

I frowned. Why would Artur lie? *Would* he lie? Perhaps, if only to test me.

"I swear by the Mother, I have said nothing against you," Ardra added.

"I have your word?"

"Of course," she said vehemently. "You may ask Ansgar. I am no liar. Maybe the boy is resisting your affections to test you."

"Very well. Say nothing of this to Artur. I will handle the matter."

"My queen," she said, bowing to me.

"I'm sorry to have infringed upon your privacy. Good night, Ardra."

"Good night, Queen Boudica."

With that, I departed. Someone was a liar here, either the druidess or the boy. I hated the idea that Artur had lied to me just to get a rise out of me, but I understood. I could be hard on my father when the mood suited me.

Sighing, I returned to my bedchamber.

Morfran sat sleeping on a new perch—someone must have installed it that day. He opened one eye to look at me when I entered. Not finding me of any interest, he went back to sleep.

I sat down on the side of the bed and pulled off my

boots.

It had been a very long day.

THAT NIGHT, NEITHER PRASUTAGUS NOR I COULD SLEEP. Despite longing for him, my mind was distracted. Thoughts of Rome, the Catuvellauni, my people, Artur, Ardra, my fight with Ula, Belenus's and Father's deaths, and everything else swirled like a tornado in my mind.

"You're still awake," Prasutagus whispered in the darkness.

I chuckled. "So are you. What are you thinking of?"

"Vercingetorix," he replied, referring to the Gaulish king who had stood against the Romans...and failed. "He rallied the Gauls against Rome, failed, and was taken to Rome in chains. After six years of imprisonment, they strangled him to death in the temple of one of their gods just for show. If he had found a different way... Aye, Boudica, I see no good way out of this," Prasutagus said.

"What did Ansgar say? Did Henwyn read the signs?"

"They consulted the goddess Brigid. The bees whisper...so many have come, so many warriors, and more to follow. Boudica, I will do whatever I can to keep you safe."

I grinned at him. "As I will for you."

Prasutagus pulled me into his arms and kissed me on the top of the head.

"You left the hall after Ardra," Prasutagus said. "Is

everything all right?"

"Yes. There was a misunderstanding between us. All is well now."

"I'm glad to hear it. Ardra has had a difficult life. She was abandoned by her family as a child. I don't know many details, but I do know the family farmstead burned. Afterward, all of the family moved west, leaving Ardra behind with the druids."

"Why? Why would they leave one child behind?"

"I don't know. Ardra is very bright, and at times, the gods speak through her. She has been a good tutor for Artur."

I nodded. "That is a terrible story. I'm glad she found her way to the druids."

"As am I."

Prasutagus nuzzled his face into my neck. "No matter what happens, Boudica, we are together. I'm glad."

"As am I."

I lay there in the darkness for a long time.

Soon, Prasutagus's arms grew heavy as sleep took him. His breathing shallowed.

Although it felt good to be in my lover's arms, rest still did not come easy for me.

His tale of Ardra's beginnings puzzled and worried me.

But that was not the only thought that plagued me.

Again and again, I replayed my argument with Ula.

I could still feel the sting of Ula's hand on my cheek.

But it was her words that stung more.

Her ominous warning echoed through my mind.

CHAPTER 19

I woke early the following day. The sun had barely risen, but I found myself in the stables checking on my spoiled boy.

Druda, it seemed, was faring better than I was. When I arrived, I found him dozing.

"Look at all this grain and hay," I said, patting the sleepy horse on his neck. "They will fatten you to the size of an ox." I grabbed some brushes and began working him down. A short time later, a girl with yellow hair appeared.

"Queen Boudicer," she said sweetly, mispronouncing my name. "Queen, we brush 'em horses every morning. You don't need to worry yourself. I was coming for him now."

"It's no trouble at all. I was just missing him. Who are you?"

"Isoldee," the girl replied.

"I am pleased to meet you, Isoldee. I'm sure Druda is in excellent hands, but you must be careful. He's very spoiled, and he will huff at you in annoyance if he doesn't get what he wants."

At that, Isoldee laughed. "I will watch for him, Queen."

It was then that a horn sounded from the gate of the king's compound.

"Someone's come," Isoldee said, looking over her shoulder. She rushed to the door and looked out. "Your people, Queen. I see the tree on the banner."

Setting the brush aside, I went to the door of the stables. From there, I spotted Caturix, the druid Einion, and a dozen warriors.

"They must have ridden in the dark to get here by now," Isoldee mused. "Let me go get the horses."

Isoldee and I walked across the green to meet with Caturix's party.

After he dismounted, Caturix met my gaze. "Boudica," he said, and then smiled lightly. "In the stables? Why am I not surprised?"

"Welcome returns," I told him, then turned to the Einion. "Wise one."

"It is good to see you again, Boudica."

"Did you ride all night?" I asked, eyeing my brother, who looked sleepless and road-weary. He had dark rings under his eyes, his boots were splattered with mud.

"Almost. I could not sleep. Nor could Einion. We decided not to wait."

"I'm glad. Prasutagus and I were no better. Come. I will find you something to eat."

I led the party inside. I was met by Galvyn, who looked

like he'd dressed hastily. "King Caturix," he said, bowing to my brother. "Please, won't you come?"

We all adjourned to the dining room. There, Galvyn poured the men mugs of ale. I could smell the scents of baking bread and frying meat from the back.

Prasutagus appeared a moment later, Artur at his side. "Caturix," he said in welcome.

"Prasutagus, well met. This is Einion, the druid of Stonea."

"I am pleased to meet you, wise father," Prasutagus said, raising his hands to his forehead in respect.

Caturix's gaze went to Artur.

"This is my son, Artur," Prasutagus said, introducing the boy.

"I...I did not know you had a son," Caturix replied in confusion.

Artur looked like he wanted to melt into the ground. The boy stared at his feet.

"His mother was Esu. His natural father died when he was very small. Artur, this is King Caturix of the Northern Iceni."

"King Caturix," Artur said, bowing. Then he whispered to Prasutagus, "May I go?"

Prasutagus nodded, and then patted the boy gently on the back.

He hurried off to the kitchens.

My heart felt sorry for the boy. He was Prasutagus's son in his heart, but by blood, he was not, and he knew that. Even though his foster father was king, he would have no claim to the Greater Iceni throne. If he was a bastard, perhaps he'd have a chance, but he was no blood relation to Prasutagus. No wonder he felt ill at ease about his situation here. But had Ardra flamed those fears, or had Artur lied to test me?

"Excuse me a moment," I said, following the child into the kitchens.

There, I found Betha and Ronat laboring hard over the fires.

"Take this and get it on the table," Betha told Newt, handing him a breadbasket.

The boy turned to go, nearly running into me. "I'm sorry, Queen Boudica."

"No matter," I replied, snatching a round of bread from the basket.

There was a small table at the side of the kitchen where the servants sat. There, I spotted Artur.

"We've got the pork frying, and Ronat is slicing cheese," Betha reassured me. "We'll have it all served in a few moments."

"I have no worries about that. I was chasing something else," I said, then grabbed a platter. Placing the bread thereon, I snatched up some cheese from the cutting board and then joined Betha. "A few slices, please," I said, gesturing to the boy with my eyes.

"He always hides when there are visitors," she whispered.

I nodded.

The cook set several slices of meat thereon. Pausing to pour a cup of milk, I went to Artur.

He looked up at me, confused.

"Queen Boudica?"

"Just Boudica," I reminded him, then set the plate and cup before him, then gently set my hand on his shoulder. "You are welcome to join us in the dining hall."

He shook his head.

"Hmm," I mused, and then snatched a slice of the cheese from his plate. I sat across from him. "Looks a fine bite. Is it sharp to the taste?"

He nodded. "It's better with bread," he told me, breaking off a hunk of the round on his plate. "Like this," he said, stuffing the cheese into the bread.

I modeled his actions.

He nodded. "Good," he said, and then took a bite.

I did the same. "You're right. Very fine."

The boy gave me a light smile but then looked away, as if he wasn't sure how he felt about smiling at me.

"Do you have enough there?" I asked. "I can bring you more of whatever you like."

"No. I'm all right. Thank you."

"All right," I said, rising. I set a gentle hand on his shoulder, giving him a light squeeze, and then departed.

Betha caught my gaze as I went, giving me an affirming nod.

I was just exiting the kitchen when I heard Ginerva's voice. "Who has come now? And at this hour!" she demanded.

"King Caturix," Nella told her.

"Hmm," the woman harrumphed as she entered the kitchens. When she spotted me, she scowled. "What are you doing in here? Esu is waiting for you! King Caturix is here!"

"I…" I began.

"Shall I fix a plate for you, Ginerva?" Betha asked. "Artur is here. You can join him. And there is still some of that orange marmalade."

"Very good," Ginerva said as she went to join Artur. "Esu needs to fire her new maid. All that girl does is loiter about like *she* is queen here."

"Go on, Queen Boudica, I will see to Ginerva," Nella told me.

"Very well," I said, making my way from the kitchens.

"Not as if she's any help with the family anyway," Nella muttered when she thought I was out of earshot.

"Mind your tongue," Betha told her harshly.

I frowned hard. Nella's attitude was so rude it was almost commonplace. Such women always seemed to have a mean spirit.

I returned to the hall to find that Vian, Ansgar, and Ardra had joined our company. No doubt, Pix was still asleep.

As we ate the morning meal, everyone chatted lightly, keeping the talk as pleasant as possible, Einion sharing that a two-headed calf had been born in Stonea.

"That is something," Ansgar said, a thoughtful expression.

"Is there meaning to it?" Vian asked. "An omen?"

"From one becomes two," Ansgar said simply, the druid Einion nodding.

Vian frowned. I couldn't help but sympathize with her

sentiment. Like Belenus, these druids riddled. That was why I always preferred Ula's way. She was direct. Sometimes, painfully so—literally.

"Do not worry yourself over the meaning," Ardra told Vian. "The ways of the druids are difficult for ordinary people to understand."

Vian shifted in her seat, the slight troubling her.

"Such signs are difficult for *all of us* to understand," Ansgar told the novice, giving her a scolding look.

Ardra shrugged. "As you say."

"And sometimes a two-headed calf is just a two-headed calf, is it not?" I asked, looking from Einion to Ansgar.

Einion laughed. "Indeed, it is."

"Even *ordinary* people can understand that," I added, then turned to my plate.

Prasutagus, sensing the tension, turned the conversation to the road conditions between Stonea and Venta.

I flicked my gaze toward Vian.

She gave me an appreciative glance.

After the meal was done, Prasutagus, Caturix, Ansgar, Einion, Ardra, Vian, and I removed to Prasutagus's private meeting chamber. Prasutagus called for Ewen, the chief of his warriors, to join us.

We gathered around the map, Prasutagus explaining to Caturix what we had learned of the Romans' movements.

I stood beside my brother, watching as he took in the information.

"I received another messenger from Togodumnus and Caratacus," Caturix told us. "They are convinced Rome will sweep over us all and urgently ask that the Northern Iceni rally our forces. They have sent messengers to the Coritani as well."

"What has been the Coritani's answer?" Prasutagus asked.

"They, too, have been visited by Rome. The triumvirate will abstain from the fight, as will their neighbors to the north, the Brigantes and the Parisii."

"The Cornovii?" Ansgar asked Caturix and Einion. "Any word?"

"We have not heard."

"Who has Caratacus and Togodumnus convinced to join them?" I asked.

"To the west, the Dobunni, Belgae, and Durotriges," Caturix told me.

"The Cantiaci are already resisting," Prasutagus shared.

"Leaving the Regnenses on the coast," I said.

"Who Caratacus and Togodumnus are now wooing to their side," Prasutagus added.

"The Regnenses have always been close with the Atrebates kings. Caratacus and Togodumnus may not find the support they expect," Ansgar said.

"Nor will they with the Northern Iceni. Caratacus and Togodumnus are complicit in my father's murder," Caturix said bitterly, but I saw the worry in his eyes. "What say you, Prasutagus?"

"I want to talk to Verica," my husband replied. "I say we pay him and his Romans a visit and see what we are up against. Will you ride with me, Caturix?"

Caturix, his eyes on the map, nodded.

"And you, Boudica?" Prasutagus asked, arching a playful eyebrow at me.

"Do you need to ask?"

"I shall come as well," Einion said.

"And I," Ansgar added, and then turned to Ardra. "You will stay here, continue young Artur's tutelage."

"But I—"

"You will stay," Ansgar told the girl.

"Yes, wise one," she said, her expression barely hiding her disappointment.

Ewen turned to Prasutagus. "Shall I prepare the men?"

My husband nodded.

My brother looked up from the map to me, his gaze meeting mine.

And for the first time in my memory, I saw fear in Caturix's eyes.

CHAPTER 20

We rode out within the hour. Prasutagus gathered an impressive band of warriors to ride along. While she looked terrified, Vian chose to come too.

"You asked me to join you to see, to advise you where I can. So, I will come and see," she said.

Pix punched her gently in the shoulder. "Ye have the old spirit in ye."

Vian gave her a gentle smile.

I joined Prasutagus, who was saying goodbye to Artur. "We will not be gone long," he told the boy.

"What if… What if they take you captive?" Artur asked.

"They will not. They want us as allies. It is in their best interest to treat us well."

"They could, though. And then march on to the Greater Iceni."

"They could, but they will not."

Artur still looked nervous.

"Will you do me a favor while I am gone, Artur?"

Puzzled, he looked at me.

"I need someone to exercise Morfran. Will you look after him while I'm away?"

"I… Yes, I can do that."

"Thank you."

Prasutagus ruffled the boy's dark hair, but still, the child scowled. "We will be back soon," Prasutagus told the boy once more.

At that, Artur nodded, then turned and ran off.

As Prasutagus and I rejoined the party, he sighed heavily.

"It is too much for him all at once," Prasutagus said.

"Yes. I can see that. Poor child."

"Thank you for making an effort with him."

"There is nothing to thank. He is a sweet but sad child. I only hope I can help heal his pain."

Prasutagus put his arm over my shoulder and kissed my head. "You are too good."

We rejoined the others, both of us mounting.

When I was settled on Druda, I turned to Caturix, meeting his gaze.

He didn't have to say anything. Both of our worlds had turned upside down in a few short months. It would have been impossible to imagine the two of us in this scenario a year ago. And yet, here we were.

"Ride out," Prasutagus called.

The standard-bearers, hoisting the running horse banner of the Greater Iceni and the tree banner of the

Northern Iceni, set off through the gates, the rest of us following behind them.

SINCE WE GOT A LATE START IN THE DAY, PRASUTAGUS suggested we take the road south to Raven's Dell to spend the night.

Caturix, who had barely slept the night before, agreed.

It was nearly dusk when we approached the forest village. The bannermen led us through a narrow valley sided by moss- and fern-covered rocks. Torches illuminated the path. On the hilltops above the dell, archers watched in the darkness. I could just make out their silhouetted forms. A horn sounded in the distance. And then again and again. We emerged from the valley into a dense forest dotted with small roundhouses and many, many people gathered around campfires. Warriors guarded the entrance to the village.

The crowd that had gathered in the village was enormous. It looked like a festival.

"What is…" I began, unsure what to ask.

"Trinovantes. Fleeing," Prasutagus said, "as Pix said."

A man pushed through the crowd. He had long, black hair and an equally long beard and mustache. He wore a simple tunic, but I spotted a fine sword and several daggers on his belt.

"Prasutagus," he called, spotting my husband.

Prasutagus turned back to us, gesturing for us to dismount.

"Divin," Prasutagus said, leaving his horse to join the man.

"By Taranis's chariot, I am glad to see you," the chieftain told him.

I dismounted, and then Caturix and I joined Prasutagus.

"Divin, this is King Caturix of the Northern Iceni. And my wife, Queen Boudica," Prasutagus said, introducing us. "This is Chieftain Divin."

"You are welcome in Raven's Dell, King Caturix, Queen Boudica. My wife and I saw you wed at Beltane, which now seems like a lifetime ago. Come," he said, gesturing behind him. "I was planning to send a man to Venta in the morning. As you can see, we have our hands full here. The Trinovantes are running from Rome. And there is someone you'll want to speak to," he told us, gesturing for us to join him.

Pix, Vian, the druids, and the warriors followed along behind us.

As we went, people called out to us.

"King Prasutagus. Peace, king. Protect us from the Romans."

"Queen Boudica, may the gods protect you."

And even to Caturix, they sent their prayers.

"King Caturix, bless you, King."

On their faces, I saw fear. As we passed, I could see that they carried all their earthly belongings.

I paused when a kitten jumped into my path.

"Kit," a little girl called, rushing toward the kitten.

"Child, come back. That is the queen and king," an old woman called.

I paused, scooping up the kitten. "Lost, little one?" I asked, scratching the kitten's ears.

The playful creature batted at my hands.

"Queen Boudica," the little girl said, staring at me with wide, blue eyes.

I gently handed the kitten back to her. "Have to watch that one. She's ready to run."

To my surprise, the girl burst into tears. "She's the only one I could catch! All the others ran off when it was time to go. She's looking for the rest of her family."

I knelt and pulled the girl into my arms, giving her a hug.

"She has you," I whispered in her ear. I pulled back and smoothed the child's hair away from her face, wiping her tears from her cheeks. "You are her family. Take good care of her, all right?"

The girl nodded.

"The Forest Lord and the Maiden will watch over the others. Don't fear for them," I said, then kissed the little girl on the forehead and rose.

An old woman had joined the girl. "Thank you, Queen Boudica," she said, her voice catching in her throat.

"May the Mother watch over you," I told the woman, reaching for her hand and gently squeezing it.

I let her go, and then rejoined the others.

"There are so many families," I said, looking around. "So many."

"And more on the road headed this way," Divin replied.

We wound down the path to the chieftain's round-house, which sat not far from a stream. A waterwheel turned nearby.

The chieftain opened the door, gesturing for us to come inside.

Within, we found a small but comfortable home, a fire burning at the center of the roundhouse. There was a small table on one side of the room. Toward the back was a sectioned-off area where the chieftain's family must have slept. Sitting on the benches before the fire were two priestesses.

They rose when we entered.

"King Prasutagus, King Caturix, Queen Boudica," Divin said, "these are the priestesses Mirim and Dynis of the Trinovantes holy site called Maiden Stones."

"Wise ones," Prasutagus said, lifting his hands in honor.

The priestesses wore long, pale-colored gowns, the hems trimmed with embroidered leaves and flowers. The younger of the pair, Mirim, had long, dark brown hair. Her face was heavily decorated with kohl. Beads, feathers, and shells adorned her hair. Dynis, the elder, was similarly adorned. She had braided her snow-white hair at the temples, pulling it back where it was affixed with a silver pin shaped like a man.

"Royal ones, we are glad to meet you," Dynis told us.

"Sit. Everyone, please sit," Divin said, and then

gestured to a teenage girl. "Brangaine, pour some ale for our guests. My daughter," he said, motioning to the girl.

Prasutagus smiled at him.

Our party joined the priestesses by the fire.

Divin's daughter worked quickly, passing out tankards of ale.

"Thank you, Brangaine," I told her.

"Queen Boudica," she said, her cheeks flushing red.

"You are riding south?" Divin asked Prasutagus.

Prasutagus nodded. "Yes. We will meet with King Verica and see these Romans for ourselves."

"Their forces are like flies on a carcass," Dynis said. "There are thousands of them. The Romans are making their way to Camulodunum where Togodumnus holds the city."

"Why have these people fled? Are the Romans attacking the Trinovantes people?" I asked.

"Some, in the confusion," Mirim answered. "Those loyal to Caratacus and Togodumnus are attempting to make a stand, but they are failing. Many Trinovantes are laying down their arms and letting the Romans pass."

"We have not forgotten our king, Aedd Mawr. Most of us are behind him, even if he returns at the side of the Romans. While many are afraid," Dynis said, gesturing outside, "others are in jubilation. We will be glad to be free of the Catuvellauni chains."

"Some people have fled to Maiden Stones for guidance or protection. Dynis and Mirim have been helping them here," Divin told us.

"Fear," Dynis said. "The people are fleeing in fear of

the unknown. When you see it, you will understand. The Romans march through the villages, thousands of thundering feet. The trees, the stones, the rivers all shudder. Many who feel it have fled north, away from the sound, no matter their loyalty to Aedd Mawr and his line."

"Has King Aedd Mawr come?" Mirim asked Prasutagus.

My husband shook his head. "They say he is too frail to make the trip."

Dynis pressed her closed hands against her lips. "This does not bode well."

Mirim shook her head.

"Does the king have a son?" Divin asked.

"His son is dead. But he does have a grandson," Prasutagus said.

"With a Roman mother," Mirim added, her tone revealing her disdain.

Prasutagus nodded.

"I am doing my best for all these refugees, King Prasutagus," Chieftain Divin told my husband. "But Raven's Dell is a small village."

"I will speak to the people in the morning. They are welcome in Venta and throughout Greater Iceni lands," Prasutagus said.

"And farther north into Northern Iceni territory," Caturix added. "They do not have to live in fear."

"Thank you, King Prasutagus, King Caturix," Dynis told them.

"I will send a rider back north and help with supplies," Prasutagus told Divin.

"I am grateful for that, King Prasutagus."

"Father," Brangaine said, setting her hand on her father's shoulder, "should I prepare a place for them to sleep?"

Divin paused. "We... we are wall to wall with people here. Perhaps we can put them—"

"We need no special accommodation, Chieftain Divin," I said. "Leave the walls for your elderly and ill. A fire ring will serve our party just as it serves the people."

Divin paused, then looked to Prasutagus, who nodded in agreement. His gaze then went to Caturix. "King Caturix?"

"As my sister says," he replied.

"Someplace close to the roundhouse. Will you see to it?" Divin asked his daughter.

Setting her pitcher aside, she nodded, and then went outside.

"Dynis," Ansgar said, turning to the priestess. "The others from your order? The other sacred sites. Has there been any word?"

Dynis shook her head. "Maiden Stones is secluded, hidden away from the fray. There has been no word from others yet."

Ansgar exhaled deeply. "We shall pray to the Mother to keep them safe."

"Have you heard anything else of the Romans' movements?" Caturix asked the priestesses.

"Only that their ships are making their way up the Thames."

"To Atrebates lands," Divin suggested with a nod.

"By dividing their massive forces, they can attack on multiple fronts. The Catuvellauni would not have enough men to fight that many wars, but the Romans do," Vian said.

"We try to reassure the people that the Romans have come at the behest of Aedd Mawr and Verica, that they are here to help. But even as I speak the words, I am not certain I believe them," Mirim said.

"We feel the same, Priestess, so we ride south," Prasutagus said.

"May Taranis watch over us," Ansgar said solemnly.

Brangaine returned a few moments later to let us know our campsite had been readied. A small fire burned. There was just enough space around it for our people. We spent the rest of the night in talks. Some of the Trinovantes who had seen the Romans joined us, sharing what they knew.

"As far as the eye could see, an army of glimmering armor. All dressed alike. Each man is outfitted with armor. Horses. Chariots. Carts. Thousands... There were thousands of them," one man said, his eyes sparkling with terror.

"That is a lot of men to fight," Divin said worriedly.

"And feed," Vian said, chewing her lip as she considered.

She made a good point. No doubt, the Romans had brought supplies with them, but they would also rely on the land—our land—to make up the gaps.

Prasutagus rose. "I'll... I'll be back," he said, and then disappeared into the crowd.

Ansgar, Vian, Divin, and the others sat talking while I sat in silence, my eyes on the fire.

I understood Prasutagus's need to move, to think. I, too, did not know what to believe.

"There is no winning this," Caturix said darkly. "No matter what side we choose, we lose. No one comes with that much force to aid a deposed king. Verica is not that charming."

"Our land is rich in resources. Just like those of the Gauls," I replied.

"What would Father do? Belenus?"

"Father and Belenus would choose whatever was best for the people. As our grandfather, Saenuvax, once did."

"That time, the Romans left."

"Yes."

Caturix met my gaze. "What will Prasutagus do?"

I had not known my husband long, yet at the same time, I had known him a hundred lifetimes. "He is a protector."

Caturix nodded. "May the gods be with us, Boudica. Especially when all choices feel like the wrong ones."

I frowned but said nothing more, keenly aware that the worries that pricked at Caturix's heart were the same as my own.

It was late in the night when the others lay down to rest. Prasutagus has not yet returned. Between my own restlessness and worry over Prasutagus, I rose.

"Take yer spear," Pix said, one eye open.

"Why?"

"Because I'm too tired to follow ye, so take yer spear and keep yerself out of it."

"Some guardian you are."

At that, Pix laughed, and then rolled over.

My gaze went briefly to Caturix. My brother had fallen asleep quickly. He grimaced in his sleep. It didn't take much imagination to understand what drove that look on his face.

Leaving the party—spear in hand—I made my way through the village. Everywhere I looked, people slept at makeshift camps before fires: children, the elderly, animals, mothers, and fathers. One small boy, perhaps no more than three years of age, hugged a baby goat to his chest as he slept.

As I walked the camp, I felt my anger rising—at Caratacus and Togodumnus, at Verica, at the Romans, at anyone who could not simply leave what was not theirs alone. The Trinovantes and Atrebates were entrenched in a war that would suck in everyone else like a whirlpool. From farmers to kings, all of our hands would be forced.

Ula's words rang in my head.

I trusted Ula.

I trusted the greenwood.

But the old ones of the hollow hills... Could you trust them? They played their own games, and they hated mankind. What if they lied simply to engineer mankind's doom? I would not put it past them. Yet, as I worked my way through the crowd, forcing myself to look at what Verica's revenge had already wrought, I could not help but think maybe there was something to what had been whispered in the mossy wood.

Fight now or lose later.

I swallowed hard, and then made my way to the river. There, in the moonlight, I saw someone standing beside the water. It didn't take me long to realize it was Prasutagus. His arms were raised to the sky. His words drifted softly on the wind.

Approaching slowly, I tried to keep my footfalls silent so I did not disturb him. He was speaking the language of the druids, a language I had heard many times before but did not know.

The wind blew through the trees.

"Queen of oak.

"Queen of stone.

"Champion of the greenwood.

"Protect us..."

Overhead, I heard the flutter of what sounded like a hundred birds. All at once, an unkindness of ravens lifted off from the branches. Cawing loudly, signaling what felt like their displeasure, they lifted off toward the moonlit sky.

I swooned, the birds' voices ringing in my ears. I closed my eyes. I felt their power in my chest. It stirred a strange sensation within me, as if I were one with them. It was almost as though I could lift up and join them. The feeling was so strong that I felt tugged forward.

My eyes popped open.

When they did, the world looked strange. I was still in

Raven's Dell, but the world had taken on an odd golden sheen. Everything was in hues of deep green and gold.

And there, at the side of the river, was not my husband but a woman dressed in armor. It wasn't her shield, sword, or fine leather armor that gave her identity away. Instead, it was her hair. Her red locks—not the color of mine and Prasutagus's fiery orange—the shade of red roses, fluttered in the breeze. She held out her arm, which had been painted with woad. A raven landed thereon. It squawked at me.

I shuddered.

This was no earth spirit appearing before me.

This was something entirely different.

The Morrigu, Lady of Battles.

"How now, queen of oak?" she asked, her voice sounding sarcastic. "What has brought you to my path?"

Realizing I'd been holding my breath, I exhaled deeply and then said, "Rome," my voice cushioned on my exhalation.

"Rome," she repeated. "Again, they come to make the land bleed. And what will you do, Boudica, daughter of Damara, granddaughter of Rian? What will *you* do about Rome?"

"I… I don't know."

"No? You *should* know. If you don't, it will all come to fire," she said with a laugh, her eyes flickering with flames.

"I will keep the Iceni safe. I will keep my people safe," I said resolutely.

"There. That is the spirit I know," she said, nodding as she stepped toward me. "Keep the Iceni safe. Good. Do that. Keep the Iceni safe. Keep the Trinovantes safe. Keep the Atrebates safe. Keep the Cantiaci safe. Keep the Regnenses safe. The Coritani, the Belgae, the Dubonni, the Parisii, the Silures, the druids on Mona, the maids of Avallach… Keep them all safe. Is *that* what you will do?" she asked, standing before me.

Her eyes flickered with flames.

"I…" I began, unsure what to say.

She grabbed my hand, which held my spear. She placed her hand over mine. Her touch felt like fire. "You must awaken that hard thing within you, Boudica. You must shake your warring spirit loose. The rivers, the valleys, the hills, the trees, the stones depend upon you. You must shake off this daydream and awaken that iron within you. Set the fire free, or it will be too late."

"What should I do?" I whispered.

The goddess leaned in close to my face. "Bring fire!"

Her breath was like a burning flame. I stepped back.

This time, I stumbled, landing on the ground below me.

Again, I was beside the river.

"Boudica," Prasutagus said, rushing to me. "Are you all right? I'm sorry, I didn't hear you approach."

"I'm…" I began, but I was *not* all right.

Prasutagus studied my face. "The shadow of the Otherworld lingers in your eyes. What happened?"

"A vision," I whispered.

Prasutagus nodded. "I was praying to Cernunnos to guide me."

"Did he?"

My husband nodded. "We must protect this land."

"Yes," I agreed.

He smoothed my hair away from my face. "What did you see?"

"The Morrigu," I whispered, knowing the meaning of my words. The elusive lady of battles never showed her face. She was a secretive goddess who only appeared when things became dire.

After a long moment, Prasutagus asked, "She gave a message?"

I nodded.

"What does she want of us?"

"Fire."

CHAPTER 21

We rose early the next morning and headed south. I was shaken by the vision of the Morrigu. All this time, the greenwood had been whispering to me. But the Morrigu was something else entirely. I had never seen the lady of battles in my visions before. Her words, coupled with those of Ula... Maybe I was wrong to resist supporting Caratacus and Togodumnus.

As we rode south, we passed several travelers headed north. They made their way toward Greater Iceni territory in carts, on horseback, and on foot. They bent low as we passed. One old woman in a wagon cried out to us.

"King Prasutagus," the old woman called, moaning. "King, where is it safe to go? Where can I take my family, my grandchildren?"

"Ride on to Venta," he told her. "Ride on there with my blessing, Grandmother."

"May Epona bless you, all of you," she said tearfully.

Pix clicked to her horse and reined in beside me.

"Do ye see it in their eyes?" she asked.

"I see fear," I replied.

"Look deeper. When ye do, ye will see them marching. It cast a shadow on their spirits. Ye will understand when ye see."

When we stopped to rest, Prasutagus sent three riders ahead to meet with the Romans and Verica to apprise them of our arrival.

"We may lose our heads the moment we set foot in that camp," Caturix said flatly as he warmed himself by the fire.

"That *would* make it easier for them to take Iceni lands," Prasutagus replied.

Caturix huffed a laugh.

"But it would whip up rebellion, would it not?" Vian asked. "They would not risk it. I would think the last thing they want is for the tribes to unite. United, we are a force to be reckoned with. As it was when Caesar came."

"Yes," Ansgar agreed. "Vian is right. But King Caturix is not wrong to be wary."

"None of it will matter once ye see," Pix said as she sat sharpening her knife.

Everyone turned to her.

Pix offered Caturix her whetstone. "Ye will be wanting this."

My brother frowned at her but said nothing.

That night, Prasutagus and I lay restless beside the fire, neither of us knowing what would come in the morning.

WHEN THE DAYBREAK CAME ONCE MORE, WE SET OFF AGAIN. This time, however, we were met on the road by our own men, accompanied by others carrying the banner of King Verica—and a group of Roman escorts. The men were well armored and rode fine horses.

"King Prasutagus, King Caturix," King Verica's man called. "We have come to escort you to General Plautius's encampment.

"Very well. Thank you," my husband replied.

I watched skeptically as the Romans fell into line in front of and behind our party.

Behind me, Pix cursed under her breath.

We trotted along the road behind the men, riding through a field leading to a peak. The long blades of grass, dotted with purple asters and red poppies, waved in the breeze. The air blowing from behind me was sweet.

"Boudica...

"Protect the greenwood...

"Protect the forests...

"Protect the stones..."

When we reached the crest of the knoll, I pulled my horse to a stop. Prasutagus halted alongside me.

The valley below was filled with soldiers—thousands and thousands of soldiers. Tents erected in neat rows rolled on for miles. Men worked busily, building fortifications all around the encampment. This was not a dozen warbands or a hundred or so men. This was an invasion. The Roman army stretched as far as the eye could see.

I could hear their voices on the wind, calling to one another as they worked. Their armor glimmered gold in the sunlight.

The priestess Dynis was right. Like flies on a carcass. They had swept in with a force like I had never seen before.

Pix reined her horse in beside mine, but she was uncharacteristically silent.

After a time, I turned to her. "Like before?"

"Nay, Strawberry Queen, nothing like before."

I did not ask her meaning. It was plain. When Caesar had come, he had done so sloppily and met with resistance that eventually sent him packing.

What filled the valley before me was no disorganized mess.

It was death.

PRASUTAGUS TURNED AND MET MY GAZE. "THEY ARE NOT here for us. Remember."

I nodded but felt less confident. That was what they said, but was that what they truly intended? How did Caratacus and Togodumnus think they would ever stand against such a force?

With help.

With *all* our help.

I cast a glance back at my brother.

Caturix stared steely-eyed at the camp, but his gaze gave away nothing.

I met my husband's eyes once more. He nodded to me, and then clicked to Raven. With that, we rode on.

We made our way toward the encampment. Watchtowers had been erected in intervals along the wall and at the gate. I marveled at how they had managed to accomplish so much in such a short time. The men on the gate called to one another, and soon, the gates swung open to reveal the encampment within.

A vast green space where men practiced arms, a row of smithies, tents for armorers, and more sat at the front. To one side, I saw a long row of pasture. When a strange animal sounded, its noise sounding like a trumpet, Pix's horse whinnied then shied sideways.

"Be easy now," Pix told the horse, and then leaned forward, whispering in its ear.

Tracking the source of the sound, I looked across the tops of the tents. In the distance, I spied the elephants.

"Look," Vian told Pix. "There."

"I see," Pix said, her voice stiff.

Soldiers paused their work as we rode past. In the distance, I saw several men digging a latrine. They had chains on their necks and had been bound together.

"Who are those men?" I called to King Verica's man.

The gentleman followed my gaze. "Trinovantes loyal to those bastard brothers, Queen Boudica."

My eyes wafted over the men. True, there were some fighters in the group, but I also saw men too old to lift a blade working alongside those too young to fight. These were not just captive warriors. This was slave-taking.

Making our way down the lane, we finally approached a large tent. A dozen Roman soldiers stood on each side of the tent flap.

A moment later, the man I presumed to be King Verica appeared. The torc on his neck gave him away, but otherwise, he was dressed in the Roman fashion—his hair had been cut short, and he wore no mustache or beard. He wore armor similar to the others but with a Celtic cape draped over his shoulders and clasped with a brooch in our style. Like the others, he wore a short tunic, revealing his legs.

His appearance must have taken Prasutagus by surprise.

My husband shifted in his saddle.

"King Prasutagus," the man called, going to my husband. "You've grown into an echo of your father."

"King Verica," Prasutagus replied politely, dismounting.

As he did so, my eyes went to the second man to step out of the tent.

Dressed in fine black leather, his buckles made of polished silver, a sword and dagger on his belt, he surveyed our party with the eyes of a wolf. The Roman had short, shaggy black hair, a muscular frame, and an ice-blue stare. When his gaze fell on me, he stilled.

My heart pounded in my chest.

I had seen him before.

Was that possible?

I *had* seen him before.

The vision the Dark Lady Andraste had shown me in Ula's cottage... It had been so misty, so unclear, but it was him.

He held my gaze, and then smiled.

The expression made my skin rise in goosebumps.

"That be a handsome killer," Pix whispered to Vian.

"Who? The king?"

"No. Not him."

I dismounted Druda, then turned and waited for Caturix.

"Please meet my queen. This is Boudica, daughter of King Aesunos," Prasutagus said, gesturing for me to join him and King Verica.

"I had heard the rumor that the Northern and Greater Iceni had finally joined their houses," King Verica said, bowing to me. "I am pleased to meet the daughter of King Aesunos. I was sorry to learn of his death."

"Thank you, King Verica," I said, then turned to Caturix. "My brother, King Caturix of the Northern Iceni."

"King Caturix. I return to our lands to find things much changed." King Verica's gaze went to the druids. "Wise ones," he said, bowing to them. King Verica looked behind him. "Let me introduce you to my dear friend, General Aulus Plautius, Emperor Claudius's most trusted soldier."

The black-haired man laughed lightly. "I cannot accept such flattery. I am merely pleased to serve my emperor. King Prasutagus," he said, giving my husband a brief nod.

"King Caturix," he added, greeting my brother in the same fashion. "And Queen Boudica, was it?"

"Yes," I said, willing my voice to be steady.

"A rare beauty," he said with a smile, holding my gaze a moment longer than he should have. "Come, let's have some wine to celebrate such a momentous occasion. It is not every day the kings of a foreign land come to me. It's far more often the other way around, and usually with a lot more bloodshed," he said with a laugh, then turned and headed into the tent.

"Come, my friends, there is much to discuss," King Verica said, gesturing for us to follow.

Prasutagus and Caturix went ahead.

Pix held my arm for a moment, pulling me back. "Watch ye. There is a shadow of the past on that one," she whispered.

"Shadow of the past?"

"Ye know what I mean. Even *I* sense it. Shrewd as a fox and vicious as a badger. Be careful. Ye understand?"

"Yes."

"Good," she said, and then let me go.

We entered the tent, joining King Verica and the general. Within, a man sat at a table, writing on parchment. He looked up at us. He was a man unlike any I had seen before, his skin a dark mahogany color, his eyes the color of chestnuts. He held my gaze, gave me a soft smile, and then inclined his head to me.

Another man, a brute of a warrior with a scar on his cheek, stepped in front of us. "Your arms, please."

I paused.

General Plautius smiled. "Just a precaution," he said. "We ask it of all our visitors."

King Verica laughed lightly. "The wine is worth it, my Iceni friends."

Frowning, I handed the man my spear.

The soldier turned to Pix.

"Ye will not be taking anything from me, Rome."

"Pix," I said, pleading with her with my eyes to be cooperative.

"I'll wait outside," she told me, then turned back.

"Mistress," the man said to Vian.

"I… I have nothing," she told him, her voice trembling.

When the soldier extended his hand for the crescent boline knives on the druid's belts, Prasutagus intervened. "Those are holy relics."

Uncertain, the man turned to the general.

"They are druids, Aulus," King Verica explained. "Those knives are for roots and herbs."

"Tell that to Caesar," General Plautius replied with a laugh. "Gentlemen," he said politely, gesturing for the druids to hand over their knives, "if you please. With my apologies to your gods."

Prasutagus moved to speak again, but Ansgar lifted his hand to stop him. "We honor the customs of all people," Ansgar said, removing the blade and handing it to the man, Einion doing the same.

With that, the general smiled widely, and then motioned for us to follow him.

Soldiers stood guard before a leather drape, separating the front of the tent from the rear. Verica and the general led us through to the back. On the other side, a fire burned cheerily, fine chairs set around a brazier. Everything had been draped with expensive-looking cloths made of silk and velvets. Two young boys dressed in the Roman fashion, wearing short tunics, their hair cut short, waited with flagons of wine. Also within, we once again found Titus Carassius and Silvis Hispanus, two of the Romans who had joined us in Venta.

"You will remember Titus Carassius and Silvis Hispanus," General Plautius said absently as he went to pour himself a goblet of wine.

"King Prasutagus," Titus said, bowing to my husband.

"King Prasutagus," Silvius echoed. He turned to me. "And Queen Boudica."

"My brother, King Caturix of the Northern Iceni," I said, introducing him.

"King Caturix," Silvius said politely.

Titus also gave Caturix a bow.

"Sit, sit," King Verica told us, motioning for the boys to serve the wine.

"Ah, Prasutagus, I am glad to see you here," King Verica told my husband with an exhausted huff as he sat. "I lamented the death of old Antedios. Such a steady hand at the helm of the Greater Iceni all these years. But as I reassured Aulus, his son is cut of the same cloth."

"And you are a learned man of your people, or so I understand," General Plautius said, eyeing Prasutagus closely. The general leaned against the table at the back of the room. "Druid taught. Is that right?"

Prasutagus nodded. "I am. It is important to know the

history of your people, your ancient ways. Knowledge of the past can guide your choices in the future."

"Well spoken," General Plautius said. "My tutors would appreciate those words. I wish I'd had your motivation to learn. My tutors whipped my fingers with rods when I was too stubborn to listen. I came by knowledge the hard way."

"And still do, many times," King Verica said with a laugh that the other Romans joined.

"Queen Boudica, we are pleased to see you again," Silvius said. "Was it not a difficult ride for you, traveling so far from Venta?"

"The Iceni are born in the saddle," King Verica said with a laugh.

"It was no difficulty," I told Silvius.

"I say," Titus added. "Your queens are certainly in the forefront here. What was the name of that stubborn beauty in the north?" he asked General Plautius.

"Cartimandua, Queen of the Brigantes."

"Cartimandua. I think she kept one of Marcus's balls as a souvenir of their conversation," King Verica said with a laugh, which the others joined.

The general smiled into his cup. "I was told to be wary of Britannia's queens, that they are all witches. What do you say to that, Queen Boudica?" he asked, gazing at me.

"I say that it is wise to be cautious when dealing with any unknown," I said, then paused. "Especially with redheads," I added with a grin.

At that, the others laughed, the general included.

"King Prasutagus, King Caturix," King Verica said,

shifting in his seat to find a more comfortable position for his ample frame. It was clear that he'd spent much of his time in Rome at the dinner table. "I am glad to see you both. Titus, Silvius, and Darius did not leave Venta with a clear impression regarding your plans for the Iceni during this conflict. Where do you stand? What are your thoughts? Tell us."

"They are...evolving," Prasutagus said.

"No doubt evolving quickly now that you have seen our forces," General Plautius said, motioning for the boys to pour everyone more wine.

When one of the boys came to me, I covered my cup with my hand and shook my head.

"And you, King Caturix, are your thoughts evolving?" General Plautius asked my brother as he swirled his wine in his cup.

Before he could answer, King Verica asked, "Aesunos's son, is it true you have wed to the Coritani?"

Caturix gave him a brief nod. "It is. My wife is the daughter of King Volisios."

"We find the east united," King Verica told the general.

"Well, that is either a very good thing or a very bad thing for you, King Verica. Now, tell us, which is it?" he asked, his gaze shifting from Prasutagus to Caturix, his smile faltering, replaced by the hard steel within him.

"That depends on Rome," I answered.

The general turned to me. He grinned slyly. "How so, Queen Boudica?"

"King Verica has come here to reclaim his throne. Rome

is his ally. The question remains, what will Rome do when that goal is accomplished?"

"Once we help King Verica defeat his enemies and regain his throne, Emperor Claudius would like to engage in friendly relations with all the kings in your land. As well, we'd like to help develop the small village of Londinium, establish more trade between our people. Many Romans are eager to learn more about your land and the business opportunities it affords. You have many goods here that Romans are eager to buy. And, I am sure, your own people are eager to trade and become part of the larger world."

"There is also the matter of tribute," Titus added, looking from Prasutagus to Caturix. "Your kings made arrangements for tribute with Caesar in exchange for his friendship. Not all of your kings have kept up their end of the bargain. We'd like to reestablish those relationships."

"Taxes," Caturix said sourly.

"Tribute," Titus corrected my brother.

General Plautius rose. "You are a coin pincher, Titus," he told the man. "We are men of action. Assuming the right conditions are met, I'm sure the tribute issue could be revisited."

"What conditions?" my brother asked.

"Nothing much," the general said, picking up a wine flagon and refilling Caturix's cup. "Simply do," he said as he poured, but then, he paused and tipped the bottle back, stopping the flow. "Nothing."

"We know Caratacus and Togodumnus are trying to gather allies," King Verica said. "Those whelps think they can hold on to what they have taken from Aedd Mawr and me. No. I will retake my throne and usher in a new era of prosperity for the Atrebates," King Verica said.

"Speaking of Aedd Mawr," Prasutagus said, "I was sorry to hear he was not well enough to cross the channel home once more."

"His grandson rides from Rome," King Verica told us. "He is green, but he will rule the Trinovantes well with the right advisers."

The general sat back in his seat and sipped his wine. "I understand your fears, my friends. When you see this impressive force, you must wonder what our intentions are. But we have not come to conquer. Rome wants trade. Rome wants wealth. Caesar went about everything the wrong way. Why enslave people when you can easily befriend them? Why excite everyone into a rebellion when you can coax them into friendship?" Grinning, he added, "For a small, annual tribute to the emperor, of course."

"And for protection," Titus added, waggling his finger at Prasutagus and Caturix, "against these Catuvellauni thugs!" he proclaimed, looking very self-satisfied while also revealing how unaware he was of the complicated nature of our relationship with our neighbors.

"I understand the difficult decision you face," General Plautius told us. "My advisers tell me that the Northern and Greater Iceni are fierce warriors. I have also heard you are noble, well-respected amongst the tribes. King Verica is due his throne. The Trinovantes also deserve their royal family restored. Rome is here to help and to bring prosperity. Roads. Innovations. Luxuries. Trade. That is what

Claudius wants to bring, not the sword—at least, not to his allies. I hope you will agree to be his allies. Then, we can all live in peace."

"It is a big world, my noble kings," Titus added. "We would have you join it."

"They speak the truth," King Verica added. "There is much wealth to be had, Prasutagus, Caturix. The Iceni could greatly benefit. I implore you to consider your people's future. I *will* retake my lands, and the Romans will see Aedd Mawr's family restored. I would be glad to have my neighbors, the Iceni, as allies when I am done."

"I think we've given them quite enough to think about. My people will prepare us something to eat. While I am a lowly soldier, I will do my best to host Rome's future friends," General Plautius said, then gestured for us to rise. "Come. Queen Boudica strikes me as the curious type. Let me show you something," he said, then led our party outside.

As we went, the general offered me his arm. "Have you seen my elephants, Queen Boudica?"

I hesitated a moment, then took his arm. "Only a glimpse."

"Such fantastic beasts. Wait until you see."

Walking beside him, I tried not to notice the feel of his arm on mine, the curve of his muscles. Why had Andraste shown me him? Did the general remember the vision, or was it one-sided? Refocusing, I asked, "How did they manage the crossing? Even horses are not easily persuaded to ride in a boat."

"Mahouts," Aulus replied.

"Mahouts? What are mahouts?"

"Trainers who care for the creatures. They know herbal remedies to keep the animals calm on the rough oceans. The elephants trust their mahouts. They will follow them anywhere."

"You speak as if the animals are intelligent."

"They are. You can read a lot from an animal, and a person, from their eyes. Do you agree?"

"I do."

"You will see. They may be hulking, but they are wise creatures."

The general escorted us around the tents and down the neatly aligned passageways. The soldiers stopped to watch as we passed. I eyed their armor and weapons. They were all similarly equipped, but the symbols on their shields were different.

"General Plautius, what do the symbols on the men's shields mean? I thought Rome's symbol was the eagle."

"The symbols represent their legions, Queen Boudica. The Hispania," he said, pointing, "the Valeria Victrix, and the Gemina."

"And how many men are in each legion?"

"Six thousand five hundred men."

As I calculated, I felt like someone had dropped a rock into the pit of my stomach.

"I see," I said.

The general studied my face. "Yes, I see you do."

Finally, we arrived at the stables. There, amongst the horses, were six creatures of immense size with wide ears and long noses.

"May the gods protect us," Vian whispered behind me.

"Sai," the general called to a thin, lithe man dressed in rags. The young man, with shaggy dark hair, came to stand before the general.

"General Plautius," he said, his eyes to the ground.

"This is Queen Boudica of the Greater Iceni. Take her to see the elephants."

"Yes, General."

"Carefully."

"Yes, General."

The boy looked up briefly at me. "Queen," he said, then motioning for me to follow him.

I cast a quick glance at Prasutagus, who merely smiled.

Caturix gave me that exasperated look he always gave me when he thought I was about to do something rash.

"You care for these animals?" I asked the boy.

"Yes, Queen."

"Where have they come from?"

"Far to the south, Queen. They—and I—were brought from there."

The boy led me to one of the animals. The great beast eyed me closely as I approached. To my surprise, I sensed a gentleness in the creature.

"Why, it's not ferocious at all."

"No, Queen. It is the man who rides them who is ferocious. They are loving, family animals."

The elephant reached out with its long nose and wrapped it around the boy's waist.

He chuckled lightly, and then tickled it. "You may touch him, Queen," the boy told me.

I did as the boy told me, gently touching the creature's leathery skin. The elephant unwound from the boy, then touched my face and smelled my hair.

"Such a long nose," I said, giggling.

"It is called a trunk, Queen."

"A trunk," I said, patting the creature. "Well, aren't you the most fascinating thing I have ever seen."

The boy gestured that we could step closer to the elephant. He set his hand on the animal's stomach and motioned for me to do the same.

"It is unfair to ask such creatures to engage in war," I whispered, my gaze on the eye of the gentle giant.

"Yes, Queen," the boy replied. "But Rome does not ask what is fair."

I met and held the boy's gaze.

After a moment, he smiled. "He likes you. Come," he said, then tapped the animal's thigh.

The elephant lowered itself to the ground.

The boy handed me the elephant's lead. "Go on. Climb up."

"What do I—"

"Step from his leg and then up. You won't hurt him. Hold on to the rope."

Grinning, I gripped the rope and eyed the elephant. After making a few calculations, I began my climb.

"Boudica," Caturix called, his brotherly side getting the better of him.

While I heard the disapproving tone in Caturix's voice, my brother should have known there was no use in trying to dissuade me. With the boy's help, I climbed up onto the creature's back.

Once I was seated, Sai called to the elephant, and the great creature stood once more.

I held on tightly. It was not unlike riding a horse—only five times a horse's size.

The creature turned its head, reaching back to touch my foot with its trunk. I gave it a gentle pat on the head.

General Plautius and King Verica laughed.

"You look very good atop a war elephant, Queen Boudica," General Plautius called to me.

"I have you where I want you now, Rome," I told him, making him laugh—and making Caturix scowl harder.

Prasutagus, however, was grinning at me.

I leaned forward toward the elephant's wide ear. "What a great, noble creature you are. So far from home, may Epona watch over you."

Sai led the elephant around the corral. It was strange to ride such a lumbering creature. But there, atop the giant, I got a magnificent view of the camp. Thousands. There were thousands of warriors. If we did not come to Caratacus's and Togodumnus's aid, they would quickly face defeat. As the elephant circled its pen, several of the other elephants reached out to gently touch him as he passed.

"They are fond of one another?" I asked Sai.

"Those are his brothers, Queen," Sai told me. "They are family. They are very intelligent creatures, and they care about one another. When one dies, the others mourn."

My heart ached, knowing that such creatures were used for war.

The mahout led the elephant in a circle and then back to where the others were waiting. Sai tapped on the elephant's side, and then the creature lowered himself to the ground so I could climb down more easily.

I dismounted then paused to pat the creature's head, meeting its eye. Yes, there was intelligence there, but also, great warmth.

"Thank you," I whispered to the elephant and then turned to Sai. "And thank you."

The boy bowed to me. "Queen."

"How was it?" General Plautius asked.

"A once-in-a-lifetime experience."

"Good thing your people believe in many lifetimes."

A young boy in servant's garb appeared. He whispered to Titus.

"Ah," the man exclaimed. "Our meal is ready."

"Very good. Shall we?" the general said, gesturing for us to return.

"King Caturix," Silvius said, falling in line beside my brother. "King Prasutagus," he added, pulling my husband into the conversation. "I wanted to ask you about these fine dogs I have seen…"

General Plautius fell in line beside me. "I think you liked that elephant, Queen Boudica."

"I did. I am a champion of all things of nature," I said. "Although I admit, I do not like to see them used for such purposes."

"And that fine dapple horse you rode in on, was he born to be your bearer?"

At that, I chuckled. "No."

"It is a wide world, Queen Boudica. In it are many wonders, including those elephants. I have traveled from the Rhine to the far south where there is only sand as far as the eye can see. Different gods. Different religions. Different appearances in people. But I have discovered a few universal truths."

"And those are?"

"Everywhere you go, men will fight for only three things."

"Which are?"

"Wealth, religion, and love."

"That's probably easy to discover if you bring war everywhere you go."

At that, the general laughed. "The women of Britannia's wit is as sharp as their spears. You are right, of course, but you'd never hear a Roman woman say so."

"Let me assure you, they are thinking it."

He chuckled. "You are quite unexpected, Queen Boudica."

"I am pleased to surprise you."

The general's eyes danced toward Prasutagus and Caturix. "Husband and brother… You have access to important ears. Tell me, what can Rome do to make the Iceni stay their hands in this battle?"

"The Greater and Northern Iceni are independent people. We want to stay that way."

"What of your future? What do you see for your people in the years to come? The world is growing. Would you have your people stay poor farmers or would you see their wealth increased?"

I raised an eyebrow at him. "We are a people of the land. We have no need for the material wealth you are trying to entice us with. Not everyone is tempted by wine, silks, and jewels."

He grinned at me. "If you don't value wine, silks, and jewels, perhaps learning will entice you. I speak ten languages and can write in five. I know the stories of many cultures. You have no need of jewels, but what of intellect, innovation, the mind? With a little help, your people, your cities, your farms could develop beyond your dreams. Or, you could reject such knowledge. But something tells me you wouldn't have your people be the most ignorant in all of Britannia when new knowledge is at your fingertips."

At that, I paused.

The general grinned. "Finally, I have found a way to make you speechless. My elephants could not do it, but my suggestion of learning has."

I grinned. "You are wrong, General."

"How so?"

"You have accidentally stumbled upon one of my weaknesses."

"Have I? What is it? You must tell me."

"My pride in my people."

The general laughed, then met and held my gaze. Once more, I found his blue eyes so startlingly familiar. Had it really been him in my vision? Why, Andraste? Why *this* man? "Don't worry, Queen Boudica," he said, his voice sounding sincere. "Your weaknesses are safe with me."

CHAPTER 22

W hen we returned to the tent, we found a massive feast spread out for us. The elaborate dishes, elegantly presented with herbs, mushrooms, and even flowers, surprised us all. Vian uttered a soft gasp.

We settled in at the table, the servants pouring wine for us.

"I am intrigued by this young woman who sits with your holy people. She was there in Venta as well. Are you a druid, lady?" Titus asked Vian.

Vian shifted nervously. "No, sir."

"Maid?"

"No, I…" Vian said, turning to me.

"Vian is my adviser," I explained.

"Adviser? A woman?"

"As with the Gauls, women have equal footing here in Britannia," General Plautius explained to Titus. "Naturally, a queen who works for the good of her people would have her own adviser. After all, not everyone is enticed by wines, silks, and jewels," he said, winking at me.

Titus laughed. "As you say, General. But I can't say I understand anyone who is not enticed by Bacchus's gifts," he said, and then took a drink of the wine, smacking his lips and exhaling loudly.

The general chuckled.

The Roman servants placed delicate portions of quail, legumes, honeycomb, bread, cheeses, tiny boiled eggs, and fish, covered in unique but nice-smelling sauces, on my plate. Across the table from me, I saw they had done the same for Vian. She stared at the food, but I could see her mind was busy. After a moment, she took a bite. She paused as she ate. I watched her brows arch and her expression change with each delicious mouthful. I couldn't help but sympathize with her. The aromatic food tasted better than any fare I had ever eaten before, the tastes of butter, honey, orange, lemon, heavy creams, and even floral flavors infusing the morsels.

"King Prasutagus," General Plautius said, turning to my husband. "I spoke with your wife on the importance of education and innovation."

Prasutagus glanced my way for a moment. And for the first time in my memory, I saw a flicker of something I didn't recognize. Was that mistrust? No. Not mistrust. Jealousy?

"Rome offers far more than wealth and wine," General Plautius continued. "We can help the Iceni develop in other ways," the general told my husband, then turned toward Caturix. "I know that deciding whether or not to join this battle with the usurpers Caratacus and Togo-dumnus is something you are weighing. That is why you are here, after all. To determine King Verica's plans, Rome's intent, and to see our numbers for yourself. You are calculating, just like the rest of us."

King Verica eyed Prasutagus and Caturix, his eyes going from them to the general.

"We have no qualms with King Verica, nor his plans to retake his throne. Nor do we have any issue with seeing Aedd Mawr's line reinstated in the Trinovantes lands. What Rome wants, however, is another matter," Prasutagus told the general.

"Prudent. Prudent," General Plautius agreed, popping a grape into his mouth. He chewed a moment, and then said, "What Rome wants is allies."

"For a price—taxation and slaves," Caturix said darkly.

"If the money is an issue for you, let me assuage that worry," General Plautius said. "Despite Titus's inclination to count every coin, the emperor has given me some leeway in how Rome approaches her old allies. Let's say we waive any outstanding debt for unpaid tribute or undelivered slaves. Instead, Rome counters with an offer to *fill* Iceni coffers as a token of gratitude for your neutrality in this conflict. And, going forward, Rome will expect a biannual—

albeit small—tribute in thanks for the benefits Rome provides the Iceni people."

"Benefits such as?" Caturix asked.

"Roads. Trade. Alliances. All things that will benefit both the Northern and Greater Iceni. My royal friends, you will find a variety of reactions to Rome's appearance here in Britannia. Queen Cartimandua has already set out her terms for tribute and trade. Soon, the Brigantes will begin enjoying the wealth of Rome. As will many others who come to us on friendly terms. It always goes better for those who agree to friendly relationships, does it not?" General Plautius asked Titus.

"Every time," the man agreed.

"Access to the growing world…that is what I offer. The days of Caesar are long behind us. For those who oppose us, I bring the sword. For my friends," he said, then lifting a goblet of wine, "I bring the world. But make no mistake," the general added, that stern tone reappearing, "those who fall to Rome become Rome. Our leaders become their leaders. Our coins become their coins. Our gods become their gods. Our allies, however, keep their gods, their coins, their leaders."

"And their heads," Titus added with a laugh that the general joined.

The general lifted his goblet to the man, both of them smiling.

"You have given us much to consider," Prasutagus said.

"But do consider it, King Prasutagus," King Verica said. "Imagine how we can reshape the east if we work together."

"Bah," General Plautius said, setting down his cup and lifting a ripe apple. "No more of this kind of talk. We have said our piece. Instead, you must tell me more about the hunting here. I have hunted the wide world, and everywhere has unique animals. Tell me, do you have wolves here? Bears?"

And with that, the conversations shifted.

Caturix stared into his plate, moving the food around as he considered.

Prasutagus, however, met my gaze. In my husband's expression, I saw that he was considering. Rome was making a generous offer. In exchange for doing nothing, for giving up the men who had plotted to kill my father, we could have opportunity and peace.

It wasn't a hard decision to make.

And yet...

Despite the vision and the strange sense of familiarity I felt toward General Plautius, there was something here I did not trust.

That mistrust was what lingered behind Prasutagus's eyes.

When the meal was done, Prasutagus signaled that he wished to go.

Catching Caturix's gaze, I relayed the sentiment.

My brother nodded.

"General Plautius, thank you for hosting us most hospitably," Prasutagus told the general.

"It is the will of the gods," General Plautius replied. "I would not offend Vesta, goddess of the hearth, by mistreating a guest."

"You have such a goddess?" I asked.

"One of many," the general replied. "Perhaps you would like to learn more of our gods, Queen Boudica."

"I would."

"Then let us talk more of them the next time we meet," he said, then motioned to his servants. "Their horses."

With that, we slowly made our way back outside. Our warriors, who had been resting in a tent nearby, joined us. Servants appeared, carrying our weapons. A young boy returned my spear, sword, and dagger. Once we were reequipped, we made our way to the camp entrance. There, our horses waited. Cai, Pix, and the others mounted. The druids and Vian joined them.

"I hope to hear from you soon, my brothers," King Verica told Caturix and Prasutagus. "And it is good to meet you, Queen Boudica. When all this is done, I will try to convince Aulus to send you an elephant."

At that, I smiled but said nothing. The elephant and its mahout had no place in our lands. As much as I relished the moment with the creature, I would prefer nothing more than to see it home.

"Fair travels," General Plautius told us. "May we all meet again as friends. And to assure that happens, I have something for you to consider," he told my brother and husband, slipping scrolls to them. "Read when you have a moment, and let me know your thoughts."

The men slipped the scrolls into their pockets, Caturix's brow flexing with confused annoyance as he did so. They mounted their horses.

"Queen Boudica," General Plautius said, making me pause. "It was a great pleasure to meet you. I hope we meet one another again under the right conditions."

"Then we must both endeavor to keep the conditions right, Rome."

"Indeed, Britannia," he said with a grin.

The general held my reins as I mounted Druda.

He gave me one last smile, then we turned and rode out of the camp.

As we did so, Pix reined in beside me.

"Watch, ye. The trap is laid," she said.

"Prasutagus and Caturix are not about to fall for Roman tricks."

"That wasn't the trap I was talking about."

CHAPTER 23

We rode away from the camp and north once more. Our guard was on alert as we made our way back into the forest.

Caturix reined his horse in beside Prasutagus, and the two talked in a low tone.

I frowned at being excluded from the conversation. It had not escaped my notice that the Romans had addressed matters of state importance with my brother and husband, ignoring me on such matters. Roman women, I understood, were expected to be docile and quiet. But I was not Roman, and King Verica knew that.

Yet, the general... General Plautius had shown what felt like too much interest in me. I could see in Prasutagus's eyes that he had not liked it. Perhaps I had been too quick to respond warmly to his—not flirtations—attentions. I wanted to take the measure of that man. Not the way men did, in the size of armies or sternness of one another's gaze, but to capture a glimpse of the general's spirit and, hopefully, make an assessment of his intentions.

And I had.

Rome was here to help King Verica. That much was clear.

But what was equally clear was that Rome was also here for itself. How far they would stretch their hand, I wasn't sure. But Caratacus and Togodumnus were in for a fight.

I didn't want Rome here.

I also didn't want to play ally to those conniving Catuvellauni brothers.

And something told me, of the two, the general was more honest, which was a horrifying thought.

"I saw ye atop that beast. Were ye not scared?" Pix asked me.

"No. Not of the animal. It is a gentle creature. It is coaxed to be ferocious, but that is not its nature."

"Unlike our people, who have a ferocious nature, but yer general is coaxing them to be tame."

I raised an eyebrow at him. "*My* general?"

"Familiar to ye, was he?"

"I... I don't know."

"Yes, ye do. A dangerous snare, that one. Always. Every time."

"Then we shouldn't trust him?"

"Hmm," Pix mused. "I didn't say *ye* should not trust him. But what is good for ye and what is good for our people may be two different things."

I nodded, and then grew silent.

We rode throughout the day until the sun grew low on the horizon. Finding a secluded glen, we set up camp for the night. As the others prepared the camp, I took Druda, Raven, and two other horses to the nearby stream for a drink.

As the beasts drank their fill, I crouched by the water, washing my hands and wetting the back of my neck. The early summer sun had me sweating. When I was done, I sat back and stared into the water. The waves wove around stones and trickled over the smallest of waterfalls. The floor of the stream was greenish brown, but you could see the variety in the colors of the rocks, some dark, some light. Some had a blue tint. Others were shot with quartz and other glimmering material that shimmered in the slants of sunlight cascading down from the leafy canopy overhead. On the water's surface was a reflection of the chartreuse leaves overhead. The breeze blew gently, carrying the scent of ferns, loam, and wildflowers. The water tinkled sweetly as it wove past.

I closed my eyes.

Great Andraste.

Guide me.

Help me.

I heard a giggle overhead. I recognized the soft sound, like a tiny silver bell.

Opening my eyes once more, I looked up. Blobs of fading sunlight shone into my eyes, but I could see their silhouettes on the tree branches. Tiny men and women looked down at me. When the leaves shifted, blocking out the sun, I could make out their red caps and clothes made of furs, feathers, and plant matter.

"The ancient goddess is a'weaving in riddles. Boudica. Boudica. Protect the forests. Protect the stones!"

I rose to get a better look. But then something came hurtling toward me.

"Banshees be cursed," I whispered, chiding myself for not expecting it.

I felt the item strike my head, right between my eyes, and then everything went black.

"Boudica. Boudica?" Prasutagus's voice called softly. I felt someone gently shake my shoulder.

I opened my eyes to find my husband looking down at me.

"Prasutagus?" I said, my hand drifting toward my forehead.

"Are you all right?"

"I..." I began, and then looked up into the branches of the trees. The piskies were gone. "Yes."

I looked up to see Caturix standing behind my husband.

"You fainted," my brother told me.

"Piskies," I whispered with annoyance, then moved to sit up. When I did so, I felt something tumble down my chest, landing on my lap. I paused a moment, finding a stone lying in my clothes. But it was not just any stone. Muted green in color, with streaks of silver cutting across it, the stone was shaped in the form of a snail shell.

I lifted it a moment, studying it.

"What is it?" Prasutagus asked.

I handed it to him.

He studied the stone. "Piskies?" he asked with a grin, then handed it back to me.

I slipped the stone into my tunic pocket, then rose, Prasutagus gently supporting me.

Downstream, Druda whinnied at me.

"Oh, now you're concerned?" I replied to which Druda blew air at me.

Caturix met my gaze. "All right?"

I nodded.

With that, my brother went to collect the horses.

"Come by the fire," Prasutagus said. "You look pale."

"The greenwood is whispering."

"Yes, I feel their eyes upon us. What are they whispering?"

"They are asking me to protect them."

"Come. I want to show you something."

We went beside the fire. There, we found the druids and Vian.

"Boudica," Ansgar said. "Are you all right? You look unwell."

"Just a momentary affliction. It will pass," I replied, then sat beside the fire.

Prasutagus pulled the scroll from his vest and handed it to me.

Caturix rejoined us as I read.

"Forty million sesterces," I said, reading the offer aloud. "That is... How much is that?" I asked, looking from Prasutagus to the druids.

"About sixty million of our own coins in value," Ansgar said.

"To be shared between the Northern and Greater Iceni," Caturix added.

Stunned, I stared at the letter. My mind quickly unfolded images of buildings, harbors, ships, roads, enough money to build Venta into something extraordinary.

"It is a fortune to be paid for doing nothing," Einion said.

"It's blood money," Caturix said tersely. "The Catuvellauni will pay for that *nothing* in blood."

"Do we care?" I asked my brother. "If things had gone differently, Saenunos would wear your crown. Already, our father is dead. Belenus is dead. The Catuvellauni had their hand in that. Think, Brother. Had Saenunos succeeded, do you think he would have let you live?"

My brother stared into the fire.

"It is a significant offer the general has made," Ansgar said. "And with it, forgiveness for tribute gone unpaid, slaves not sent. This letter is an alliance with Rome, as King Verica has made. We have all seen their forces. We do not have the men to drive that force back. I advise you, my kings, to accept Rome's offer."

"I don't trust General Plautius," Prasutagus said. "His

smiles are lies. There is more happening here than we can see."

"Prasutagus is right," Vian said, making everyone turn to her.

"Why do you say that, Vian?" I asked.

"Behind his secretary's desk was a map of Gaul. On it, I saw many tokens at the coast—symbols of men and ships. Maybe the board is old, but the Romans have many more forces in Gaul and many more ships. For what purpose?"

Prasutagus nodded. "General Plautius is like a faire illusionist, waving one hand to keep our eyes occupied while the other is busy pulling the real trick."

"And yet, such an amount," Ansgar said. "Think of what that money could mean to our people, my kings."

"Ne'er did I think I would hear one of our wise ones speaking on behalf of the eagle," Pix told Ansgar.

I turned to find her standing behind me.

"Yer brothers stood on the white cliffs calling to Taranis and Condatis to crush the Romans, now ye would open yer coffers and let them fill them? Are ye so easily bought, druid?"

A flash of anger crossed Ansgar's face, but he stifled it. "Emperor Claudius is not Caesar. Times are not the same. King Prasutagus and King Caturix have different choices before them."

"No," Pix said sternly. "If ye stick yer heads in the nooses now, don't be surprised when ye find yerselves hanging from them later," she retorted angrily, then turned and walked off into the darkness.

"Pix," I called to her, but she ignored me.

Caturix sighed heavily. "Boudica. What do you think?"

I inhaled deeply, and then let my breath out slowly. The truth was, I felt the weight of Pix's warning, and yet... "Our duty is to our people. To protect them. To keep them safe, and with them, the land, our ways, our people. As the general said, when Rome conquers, those lands become Rome. In that, he didn't lie. I won't see that happen to the Iceni."

I turned to Prasutagus, meeting his gaze.

"You are not wrong. My mind is one and the same," he said.

I turned to Caturix. "Brother?"

"Then we will stay our hands," Caturix said. "Let Caratacus and Togodumnus bleed. I won't have any more of my people suffer for their ambitions."

Prasutagus nodded. "Then we are agreed." He turned to Ansgar. "In the morning, you and Einion, if that pleases King Caturix, will ride with a party of soldiers back to their camp. Tell Rome we accept their offer."

Caturix nodded to Einion.

Prasutagus turned his gaze back toward the fire. "And may the Great Mother and the Forest Lord watch over us all."

CHAPTER 24

The ride north the following morning was a somber affair. A party of soldiers to protect them, the druids returned to King Verica and General Plautius with our answer as we rode back into Iceni territory. Obviously annoyed, Pix had spent the day riding alongside Vian and avoiding conversation with the rest of us.

I understood why she was angry.

In fact, I knew her sentiment would be shared by many.

Even I was unsure if we were making the right choice.

When we reached Raven's Dell that night, we were exhausted and emotionally spent.

Chieftain Divin asked us nothing, merely saw to our comfort. Still, the small village was filled with people fleeing the impending battles.

"In the morning, I will ride for Oak Throne. Please tell

Einion to ride on to Stonea. I will join him there after I talk to Bran," Caturix told Prasutagus and me.

"You are welcome to rest with us at Venta for a time if you like. But I understand," Prasutagus told him.

"Thank you for the offer," Caturix said.

When we lay down to rest that night, I became restless once more. I snuggled into Prasutagus's arms.

"You're awake," he whispered.

"As are you."

"My heart is ill at ease."

"As is mine."

"You are right, Boudica. Our job is to protect and nurture the people. I only worry that we are exchanging their safety now for something much worse later."

"You pluck the same worry from my heart."

"We will watch. If Rome—and Verica—do not make good on their promises, nothing is holding me from pushing back."

"Except twenty thousand troops and war elephants."

"I thought you liked those elephants."

"I did, but not what they are used for."

"And the general... What did you make of him?" Prasutagus asked, and this time, I heard an unfamiliar catch in his voice.

"He is silver-tongued."

"Yes."

"What is it?"

Prasutagus kissed my shoulder. "The old familiarity. The eye within me saw him in double. And in that vision, I could not tell if he was friend or foe or both."

Like me, Prasutagus had felt a familiarity with the general. I wasn't sure if that made me feel better or worse. "We will trust…for now. And at any sign of cracks in truth…"

"Let's only hope that they show before it's too late."

THE FOLLOWING DAY, I JOINED CATURIX AS HE PREPARED TO depart.

"Prasutagus and I will stay here in Raven's Dell until Ansgar and Einion return. We must help the chieftain with all of these people," I told Caturix.

"I will send word to the southernmost Fen folk as well. We, too, will do what we can to get the innocent people out of Rome's path."

I shook my head. "By Andraste, what a mess."

Caturix nodded in agreement and then mounted his horse.

"Everything has come unglued at once," Caturix muttered as he settled in. "Boudica, if you hear anything, promise you will send word. Father is gone. Belenus too. I trust Einion, but he is not them."

I met my brother's gaze. I didn't like seeing Caturix looking so uncertain.

"Caratacus and Togodumnus will reach out to you," I told my brother. "You must put them off."

"I will do more than put them off."

"Go slowly, Brother. Stonea is well-protected in the Fens, but we share a border with the Catuvellauni. Suppose they are successful at repelling Rome? Where will that leave us? We must teeter carefully on a string."

Caturix nodded. "Yes. You're right. As long as we keep the Iceni safe."

"As long as we keep the Iceni safe."

Caturix shifted in his saddle, his water pouch coming loose and falling to the ground.

I reached for it, and then rose, my head swimming. "Whoa," I said, grabbing my brother's leg to steady myself.

"Boudica?" Caturix asked.

"I'm all right. It's the heat," I said, handing the pouch to him.

My brother cocked an eyebrow at me but said nothing more.

"Wish Melusine well for me."

"Thank you, Sister."

Prasutagus joined us. "Brother... Safe journeys. I will send some men and see the druid Einion returns home safely."

"Thank you, Prasutagus."

"Be cautious on the road. There is no telling which of our neighbors have spies," Prasutagus said.

"Likely all of them," Caturix answered.

Prasutagus chuckled. "May Great Cernunnos watch over you."

"And you."

Caturix met my gaze one last time. "Be well, Sister," he

said, then waved to his men. Clicking to his horse, he rode off.

Prasutagus and I watched as Caturix and his party disappeared down the road.

My husband took my hand. "Don't worry for him."

"My brother is very able, strong, a good fighter. But…"

"We are all in a new world now, Boudica. We must learn to survive it."

"Yes," I said, then turned and looked back at the village of Raven's Dell, which was now swarming with Trinovantes. "Let's begin."

CHAPTER 25

Prasutagus, Chieftain Divin, and some of the men went to one end of the village to construct makeshift tents for the growing influx of people. Pix had gone with some others to help in the kitchens, preparing what food there was to be found for the swelling number of people. Vian and I stood at the entrance to Raven's Dell, watching as another party walked toward the village.

"Are they wrong to leave?" Vian asked. "The Roman general said they have come to retake the lands for King Aedd Mawr. Why are they fleeing?"

"They are afraid. The last time Rome came, they brought the sword. The people have no reason to expect otherwise this time."

Vian frowned. "Raven's Dell cannot host all of these people. They will soon run out of food. Perhaps…" She began, and then paused.

"Perhaps?"

"I still feel awkward giving suggestions to a queen."

I laughed. "That is a feeling you must outgrow."

"All right. Well, there are farmsteads between here and Venta. Surely, some of those can accommodate the families. And maybe Galvyn and I could organize other places for people. It seems to me most farmsteads are always in need of a hand, especially during summer season. And aren't there undeveloped lands in Greater Iceni territory, spaces for new farmsteads?"

I nodded. "All good ideas. You're right to ask. I will speak to Prasutagus."

Vian eyed the people coming up the road. "It would be good to know how many people are already here and how many new come in."

I grinned at her. "That sounds like a task you can manage."

"I will see to it."

"And I will take your suggestions to the king."

Leaving Vian, I made my way across the village to join Prasutagus. As I went, however, I encountered the priestesses from Maiden Stones once more.

"Wise ones," I said, puzzled to see the priestesses looking like they were preparing to go. "Can I... Are you leaving?"

"Queen Boudica," Mirim said. "Yes, we are leaving. Dynis will return to Maiden Stones. I am on my way to Mona."

"Mona?"

Mirim nodded to me. "They must be informed of the matters happening here."

"That is a very long journey. Please, let me get a horse for you."

She paused. "Very well."

Together, the three of us turned and made our way back toward the stables.

"You spoke to these Romans?" Dynis asked me.

"I did."

"What did you think, Queen Boudica?"

"King Verica was compelling. He is here solely for his lands."

"That's very good for the Atrebates, but what of the Trinovantes?" Dynis asked.

"Aedd Mawr is in Gaul. His grandson rides from Rome."

"So, we become Roman," Dynis said, a miserable tone in her voice.

While I wanted to reassure the priestess, she was not wrong. Her words mirrored my own fears. "In the least, the Trinovantes people have nothing to fear from Rome. Rome's war is with Caratacus and Togodumnus, not with the Trinovantes people."

"The Trinovantes will not have Boudica and Prasutagus watching over us. Instead, we will have a child puppet and his Roman mother looking to get rich off the labor of a people they do not know but claim to rule."

"Your druids... Someone should speak to the Romans on the people's behalf. General Plautius is not altogether unreasonable."

"We will watch and consider," Dynis said.

When we arrived at the stables, I asked one of the boys

to fetch a horse. "Can I send a guard with you?" I asked Mirim.

"No, Queen Boudica, I know the old roads. I will follow them unseen."

I paused. "My sister, Brenna, has just joined their order. Everything has come undone since she rode to the holy isle. May I send a very hard message with you?"

The priestess inclined her head to me.

"Brenna does not know our father and the druid Belenus have died, nor that my brother Caturix has taken the throne, unless news came to her through rumor. Our uncle Saenunos orchestrated our father's death with some support from the Catuvellauni brothers. Please, tell my sister that regardless of these hardships, we are all well. The people are safe. Caturix has taken the throne, and our other brother Bran has wed. The Northern Iceni are strong. She should not return to Oak Throne. She should stay and do her studies as she planned. Brenna will want to return to help, but there is nothing for her here. She should stay on Mona. Will you take this message to her?"

"Of course, Queen Boudica."

"Brenna *will* try to leave. Please, do what you can to convince her to stay on Mona."

The moment such news reached Brenna, she would be devastated and want to return. Perhaps, if the message came from a holy person, she would listen.

"I will try to convince her to stay," Mirim replied.

A boy returned with one of the horses. "Chieftain said to take this one. All saddled for you, wise one," he told the woman.

She set her hand on his head. "Thank you, child," she said, and then mounted.

Dynis came and stood beside her sister. "I will walk the road with you awhile."

Mirim nodded, and then turned to me. "My thanks, Queen Boudica. May the Great Mother keep you."

"And you. Both of you," I told them.

With that, the pair turned and made their way down the road, out of the village.

"Where are they going?" the boy asked.

I looked down at him, surprised by his free tongue. At the royal houses, the servants were taught not to ask questions. But this was not a royal house, and this boy was just that—a curious child.

I knelt beside him.

"The priestess walking will return to the Maiden Stones in Trinovantes territory. The other will ride to Mona."

"All the way to Mona?" he asked, his eyes wide.

"Yes."

"How will she get across to the island?"

"There is a ferry, or so I am told."

The child's brow scrunched up. "Is she going to Mona because she is afraid?"

I shook my head. "No. But our holy people must know what is happening here."

The boy looked at me. "Should I be afraid?"

I set my hand on his head, ruffling his hair. "No. This is Greater Iceni territory. I decree that we shall have no problems here," I told him with a grin.

At that, the child smiled.

I reached out for his hand, rising once more. Again, my head felt dizzy. I was under the sun too much and needed something to eat.

"Come," I told the boy. "The men are working hard building shelters. King Prasutagus will be thirsty. Will you help me take ale to them?"

The boy grinned at me. "Of course!"

And with that, the pair of us got to work—despite the gnawing ache of worry that lingered in my heart.

CHAPTER 26

T he boy and I collected pitchers of ale, enlisting the help of Pix and another young woman, and then headed in the direction of the working men.

"Does this mean you're speaking to me again?" I asked Pix, who worked alongside me, helping me pour drinks.

In the distance, I caught Prasutagus's eye. He, like many of the others, had removed his tunic and was working bare-chested under the hot sun. It was a fine sight to see. Apparently, my husband read my expression because he winked at me and gave me a knowing smile.

"I figure I am not ye and only know what *I* would do. I would fight. But if ye see a better way, I cannot argue with ye."

"Let's hope this is the better way," I said, feeling my own nervousness peek through.

"May the greenwood hear your words."

Leaving Pix, I took a tankard to my husband, who paused his work to join me.

Prasutagus was sweaty and dirty. He leaned on his shovel, catching his breath.

"My love," I said, handing him the drink.

"I swear you heard my wish for an ale and a rest," he said with a laugh. He caught my hand. "Bless your hands," he said, then took a long drink.

"The work is coming along well here," I said, eyeing the makeshift camp. "Vian had an idea," I said, and then relayed the girl's thoughts.

Prasutagus nodded. "Good. Yes. She is right," he said then swigged back the rest of the drink. "Let me send riders to the farmsteads. Already, I have sent word to Venta to ask for food. We can do more here," Prasutagus said, then eyed over the people.

"I spoke with the priestesses. Mirim is riding to Mona. Dynis is returning to Maiden Stones. They worry that without Aedd Mawr here, and his grandson little more than a puppet, they are not truly safe."

"They are not wrong to fear."

I looked up at my husband.

He sighed heavily. "Aye, Boudica, I, too, feel it. We can't protect everyone, but we *will* do good anywhere we are able."

I nodded.

"Come on, Wife. Find me a rain barrel. I need to dunk my head before putting on this tunic once more."

"Will a stream suffice?"

"Nature's bath... What more can I ask for?"

Prasutagus and I left the worksite and made our way to the brook. I sat beside the stream while Prasutagus washed his face and wiped the sweat from his body. I eyed his muscular form greedily, eyeing the markings on his skin. A flush went through my body, reminding me I was a new bride and very much in love with my husband.

Prasutagus paused and looked at me. "What is it?"

"I see a Stag King in the woods," I said with a sly smile.

Reaching out, he took my hand. "And I, a forest maiden with fiery red hair. Come, nymph."

Grinning, I took my husband's hand, and he led me into the forest. Overhead, the trees made a canopy of green. The summer sunlight shone down on us, making Prasutagus's red hair glimmer. We made our way to a secluded spot in a thicket of trees.

Assuring we were alone, Prasutagus gently pulled me toward him, pressing his lips against mine. I caught the light taste of ale on his lips. I wrapped my arms around him, feeling his sun-warmed skin. He leaned in close to me, pressing his body against mine. Amid all this chaos, I was again reminded of the intense love I felt for this man. My body ached for his touch. When he set his hand on my breast, I moaned.

Leaving his mouth, I kissed his salty neck, my hands roaming across his muscular back. Prasutagus caught the length of my skirt and pulled it up, his hand sliding up my thigh and squeezing my arse. Our wild kisses roved over one another. Then, I leaned in, undid the ties on his trousers, and latched my leg around his waist. Prasutagus moved toward me, and soon, we became one. My back against the wide oak, I looked up into the leaves as my husband and I made love.

I groaned with pleasure as my body rocked, feeling this man I adored.

Like the Maiden and the Forest Lord...

Husband and wife...

I closed my eyes, relishing the feel of my husband's touch.

Soon, we were brought to the pinnacle of pleasure. We rested in one another's arms for a long moment. Finally, the two of us pulled apart, making ourselves presentable once more.

Prasutagus wrapped me in his arms.

"I was so eager to begin my life with you," he whispered in my ear. "I never imagined it would begin like this."

"For my part in that—mine and my family's—I'm sorry."

"No. Not you. Nothing you could ever do would hurt me. To the south, the world burns... but all I care about is you, my family, our people. Nothing else matters."

I kissed my husband one more time. "Ansgar will come soon. Then, we can return to Venta."

Prasutagus nodded. "Yes, there is much work to be done," he said, then chuckled lightly. "But I did not lead you into these woods to talk of war," he added, kissing my forehead.

"And why did you lead me into these woods, King Prasutagus?"

"It was you who tempted me, nymph."

I laughed.

Prasutagus took my hand, and then sighed. "Let's hope Ansgar returns soon."

"And that Rome keeps her promises."

"May the gods hear your words."

We worked the rest of the day in the village helping the people, sending messengers, and doing whatever job needed to be done. Late that night, everyone gathered around the fires outside. Prasutagus and I sat with the chieftain Divin and his family, listening as one of their more colorful local residents recanted the tale of a magical donkey that turned into a mischief-making man at night. The story made the children laugh, a sound I was happy to hear.

Late that night, I curled up beside my husband and fell quickly to sleep.

It was just past dawn the next morning when the chieftain woke us.

"King Prasutagus, Queen Boudica," he said. "I am sorry to wake you. The druids have returned from the Roman encampment."

Prasutagus and I rose groggily. I dusted off the leaves and pine needles from my dress as the pair of us went to meet Ansgar and Einion.

"My king," Ansgar said, bowing deeply.

"Ansgar. It is early," Prasutagus said, a worried expression on his face.

"We rode throughout the night, my king. The Romans had men following us. We led them into the woods. There, they were turned around by the whispers of the greenwood."

"Were you threatened?" Prasutagus asked.

"No, my king, merely followed. But the fey things altered their path. We have not seen them since."

"Come, let us speak in private," Prasutagus said, leading the two men away from the others.

"I will see to something for them to eat and drink," the chieftain told us. "Join us in the roundhouse when you are ready."

Ansgar and Einion inclined their heads to the chieftain.

Prasutagus led us to a small bonfire nearby. In the light of the fire, I could see that the two men were weary.

"My brother has ridden on to Oak Throne," I told Einion. "He asks that you ride to Stonea."

"Very well. Thank you, Queen Boudica."

"First, you must take some rest," I told the druids. "The road has wearied you."

Einion nodded.

"We spoke to the general," Ansgar told Prasutagus and me. "We informed him that you have accepted the offer. He was pleased."

"Very pleased," Einion added. "I say, he can be a jovial man. Shrewd, no doubt, but he is cordial enough. He has guaranteed the money with these," the man said, producing two scrolls from his pocket. He handed one to

Prasutagus. "The actual coin is forthcoming. The general has promised it would be yours within a fortnight."

"What else did you see?" Prasutagus asked.

"The men are preparing to move out. There was talk of Togodumnus, but I cannot say more than that."

Prasutagus nodded. "So it begins."

"So it begins," Ansgar agreed.

Prasutagus set his hand on the druid's shoulder. "Get some rest, old friend. We will ride to Venta when you are ready."

"My king."

With that, the pair disappeared into the chieftain's house.

Prasutagus looked down at the scroll in his hands. "Soon, we will discover if General Plautius is a man of his word or not."

"Let's hope we don't learn to the contrary too late."

CHAPTER 27

After the druids had taken their rest, we prepared to leave for Venta. With our party assembled, we planned to head north once more.

"I will send more help," Prasutagus reassured Chieftain Divin. "Don't hesitate to ask for anything. And if you hear any news, send word right away."

"Yes, King Prasutagus," the chieftain replied. He turned to me. "I am sorry I could not make your acquaintance under more hospitable circumstances, Queen Boudica. I wish you both happiness in your marriage."

"Thank you, Chieftain," I told him, then mounted Druda.

We turned once more, heading north to the relative safety of Greater Iceni country.

I could only hope that the deal we had made kept it this way.

WE RETURNED TO VENTA TO FIND A CITY VERY MUCH ON edge. As Prasutagus had instructed, the guard had increased almost tenfold. As we rode into the city, the people cried out to Prasutagus and me.

"Are they coming, King? Are the Romans coming for us?"

"Queen Boudica, are we safe here?"

"King Prasutagus, what should we do?"

I looked at Prasutagus, who slowed Raven to a stop. Venta might be ten times the size of Oak Throne, but the people's fears were still the same.

"Gather before the gates to the king's house. I will address you all there. Be at peace, people of the Greater Iceni. Be at peace. You are safe."

With that, we rode ahead, a throng of people following behind us.

"What will you say?" I asked my husband.

"The truth, as best I can."

When we arrived at the king's house, we found the gates closed and the walls manned. As soon as we drew close, the gates opened to reveal Galvyn and a small contingent of servants waiting for us. Hiding amongst them, I spotted Artur. Morfran rested on the boy's arm.

I waved to the child.

He smiled softly, in his shy way. He whispered some-thing to the bird, then released the raven.

With a caw, the bird flew to me.

I extended my arm, Morfran landing thereon.

"I see you have been keeping busy," I told the bird who squawked at me.

Druda exhaled loudly in annoyance.

I chuckled. "Jealous."

We dismounted, joining Galvyn.

"My king," Galvyn said, bowing to Prasutagus. "Queen Boudica," he added, turning to me. "Welcome returns," he said, then eyed the crowd moving toward the roundhouse behind us.

"Inform the men," Prasutagus said. "I will speak to the people from the wall."

"Very good. And, my king," he said hesitantly, "there is a rider here. He arrived an hour past."

"Who?"

"From Caratacus and Togodumnus," he replied with a frown.

"Keep him in my meeting room until we are done," Prasutagus said, then turned to Ansgar. "Will you keep him busy until we can join you?"

The druid nodded. "Yes, my king," he said, then made his way into the house. Ardra stepped out of the crowd and followed along behind the druid.

Prasutagus turned to Artur. "There you are, my boy. Come and let me see you."

Artur went shyly to him. "Hello, Father."

"Have you been well?"

He nodded.

"Keeping busy with Boudica's bird, I see."

Artur smiled, his heavy brows lifting for a moment. "Yes. He is a very smart bird," he told me. "Father..." he began, then paused. "Never mind."

"What is it?"

"There have been many whispers of the Romans invading. Are they coming here?"

"No," Prasutagus said. "Boudica and I have spoken to the Romans. You will be safe. All the Greater Iceni will be safe."

"You spoke with them?" he asked, his eyes going wide.

Prasutagus nodded. "Yes."

"Remind me to tell you later of their elephants," I said, giving the boy a smile.

Morfran cawed at Artur.

"He likes you," I told the Artur. "Can you continue to watch over him for me in the weeks to come? There is much to attend to, and I am afraid I'll neglect him," I said, stroking the bird's feathers.

"If you wish it."

"I do."

"Then, okay."

"Thank you, Artur."

The child nodded and then looked behind us. "Why are all those people gathering?"

"We will speak to them about the Romans," Prasutagus said, then extended his hand to the child. "Come with us?"

"*Me?*"

"You are a member of this household. Let them see you."

"But Father," Artur began, then paused. "I'm not *really* your son."

"You are my family, Artur. The people will be reminded," he said, then turned to me. "All right with you?"

"Of course."

We made our way across the square and up the steps to the rampart. A throng of people had already assembled, with more coming from the city.

As soon as they spotted us, they began to call out.

"King Prasutagus, what is happening?"

"Are we in danger?"

"Are the Romans coming?"

"Should we flee?"

"Queen Boudica, should we go north?"

"What do we do, Queen?"

Two archers moved in on either side of Prasutagus and myself. Their arrows already nocked, they watched the crowds.

Pix slipped in, quiet as a fox, behind me.

Great Mother.

Lady of the greenwood and mother to us all.

Give us the right words to speak to the people.

"My people," Prasutagus called. "Greater Iceni. Peace. Peace. May the Great Mother and the Father God shine their blessings on you all."

"And you!"

"And you, King!"

"To you and your family, King Prasutagus."

An echo of voices called out prayers to us.

"My people, the rumors you have heard are true. Rome has returned to these shores," Prasutagus called, causing a murmur and cries of fear to echo through the crowd. "But they do not come as Caesar came. They do not come to conquer our people. They arrive at the side of King Verica of the Atrebates and on behalf of Aedd Mawr of the Trinovantes. They come at the side of those tribal kings who befriended Rome to regain what was lost to the Catuvellauni—their thrones, their lands. Boudica and I have spoken to Rome. While they come with a mighty force, they do not come for the Iceni—neither Greater nor Northern. They are not here for our lands or people. Rome returns to us in a different form. As a partner of trade. As a means to accessing the wealth beyond the channel into Gaul.

"A choice was laid before the Greater and Northern Iceni, and together with King Caturix of the Northern Iceni, we have chosen peace. We have chosen your safety and the safety of your families. I will not ask you to bleed for Catuvellauni ambitions, just as my father did not ask you to bleed when Cunobelinus, and later his sons, ousted Verica and the heirs of Aedd Mawr. This is not our fight. We will not make it so. And so doing, we will keep the sanctity and independence of *all* Iceni people. Our tribes are united in this decision. Neither Boudica nor I will ask for a drop of Iceni blood in a war that has nothing to do with us."

The crowd was silent then someone asked, "Will they not come anyway, King Prasutagus? As Caesar did?"

"Why come for us when they can bargain with us? We have many goods Rome wants—iron, silver, horses, hounds, and pretty brides," he said, making the crowd laugh. "Peace, diplomacy, and prosperity are the way forward for our people."

"You will not call us to arms, King?"

"No. But remember, we are Greater Iceni. Our general mistrust of *everyone* always serves us well," Prasutagus said, making the crowd laugh. "We will trust Rome's words with our hands on the hilts of our swords. But we will not fight. Not now. The battle is not ours, and we will not die for no reason."

"Let the Catuvellauni suffer their own fates. Greedy, blood-thirsty curs!" one of the men yelled, winning him a cheer from those around him.

"This is Cunobelinus's mess," another called in agreement. "Let his sons sort it out."

A murmur of agreement surrounded the speaker.

"Queen Boudica, what of the Trinovantes fleeing? So many have come," one woman called.

I stepped forward. "The Trinovantes people are innocent. Like forest creatures fleeing a woodland fire, they run toward any shelter. They flee because they do not know what will become of their tribe. Until their lands are settled once more, we will keep, shelter, and protect them like the Great Mother would wish—for we are all her people."

"These are our words," Prasutagus said. "You will see an increase of warriors in the cities during these uncertain times, and I advise all of you—be you a merchant, resident of this city, visiting farmer, or other—be vigilant. Be vigilant. Keep one hand open, offering friendship, but keep the other at the ready…just in case."

Prasutagus turned to me.

"May the Great Mother watch over us all," I said, but then felt a tremor go through my body, and a cold sensation ran from my head to my toes. I stepped closer to the rail and looked down at the crowd, eyeing them from one side to another. After a long moment, I added, "But if the time ever comes where the Mother must step aside, if war and fire ever come to us, may the Morrigu have mercy on our foes, for I will burn them all," I said then set Morfran loose. With a caw, the raven flew from my shoulder and out over the crowd.

I shuddered, feeling the chill pass from my body.

The crowd stared wide-eyed at me.

Confused, I stepped back. Clearing my throat, I added, "May the Great Mother protect us all. Blessed be."

"Blessed be," the crowd called in reply.

When I turned to look at Prasutagus, he, too, stared wide-eyed at me. "Boudica," he whispered.

"What is it?"

"Nothing. Just…nothing."

CHAPTER 28

With the business with the people done, Prasutagus and I turned to deal with the Catuvellauni.

"That was the easy conversation," Prasutagus said as we made our way back toward the roundhouse. "The next will be far more difficult."

"We will find the right words."

Galvyn joined us. "The man's name is Phelan. He is eager for an answer. Togodumnus and Caratacus are dug in somewhere, and Rome is on the move."

Prasutagus nodded. "He will not like our answer, but we will not be drawn into the conflict."

"What was decided with Rome?"

My husband handed the housecarl the scroll from the general. "Keep your eyes out for a party from Rome."

I watched Galvyn's eyes as they read over this dispatch. They went wide when he read the number. "Such a great sum."

"What they ask is great, so should be their thanks. Let's pray they are true to their word."

Galvyn nodded.

Pix drew in beside me. "What was that?"

"What was what?"

"Ye speaking for the Morrigu."

"I... The lady of battles chose those words herself."

"Ye must guard yerself against being an instrument for such a creature, goddess or no. Ye are a creature of the greenwood, Boudica. Do not be guided by dark things."

"I hear you," I told her, unsure what else to say. It was not as if I had called the goddess to me.

Prasutagus paused before we got to the door, looking down at Artur. "We must speak to the messenger now."

"I will go call for Morfran," he added, glancing up quickly at me.

"I am sure he will return soon."

Artur nodded, then ran off. Had the child been spooked?

Moreover, had I spooked myself? The Morrigu was a dark force. The lady of battles always wanted a fight, even when such tactics were not the most useful. There were other ways to win peace.

Turning, Prasutagus and I entered the roundhouse, making our way to the formal meeting chamber.

The man sitting at a table picking at a platter of food rose when we entered.

"King Prasutagus. Queen Boudica," he said, bowing.

"Please," Prasutagus said, waving for the man to sit.

Ansgar was already seated at the table. He nodded to

Prasutagus and me.

The Catuvellauni messenger signaled to a servant behind him that he was done with his meal. Ronat, who had been attending the man, cleared the plate, then set about serving ale.

Behind me, Pix gestured to the girl to bring her a cup.

The servant sucked in her lips, suppressing a laugh, then complied.

"We are sorry to make you wait," Prasutagus told the messenger. "Phelan, isn't it?"

"Yes, King Prasutagus. I am glad to see you returned. Kings Caratacus and Togodumnus are eager to hear from you."

Prasutagus nodded, then said, "When Cunobelinus, the kings' father, warred on Verica and Aedd Mawr, my father did not engage. He did not want bloodshed and tried to discourage Cunobelinus from aggression. They were friends, after all, but my father did not join him in their war against the Atrebates and Trinovantes. Now, still a friend of Caratacus and Togodumnus, I come as my father's son. The Greater Iceni and the Catuvellauni have always maintained alliances but have not shared arms. And, we will not do so this time either."

"But King Prasutagus—" the man began, but my husband raised his hand, interrupting him.

"Tell Caratacus and Togodumnus that the best way to prevent bloodshed is to speak to King Verica. We encourage diplomacy between the kings in an effort to save lives."

"You know Caratacus and Togodumnus will never

agree," the man replied waspishly.

"Then the Catuvellauni will fight Rome and the Trinovantes and Atrebates who seek to retake their lands. And many of your warriors will die. Rome's force is everything the bards sing of. I have seen them with my own eyes. Like grains of sand on a beach, their numbers are endless. I advise the kings to negotiate. They *must* negotiate, or your people will be decimated."

"Rome's numbers..." I added with a shake of the head, meeting the man's eyes. "Implore them to negotiate for the sake of your people."

The man rose. "I will take your message to my kings. But with all due respect, King Prasutagus and Queen Boudica, if we do not stand united now, Rome may turn that army on you when they are done. Who will be there to protect you then?" he said, then angrily snatched his gloves from the table and left the room.

Prasutagus motioned to the guards at the door to see him out.

We were silent for a long time when Ansgar finally said, "He is not wrong to ask the question."

"No. He isn't," Prasutagus agreed.

Feeling the tension in the room, I rose and went to the scrolls on the wall, fingering through them until I found the one I wanted. Taking the scroll with me, I unrolled it, revealing a map of Venta.

"Until we truly know the answer to the messenger's question, we have other things to consider. Rome has bought our allegiance and neutrality at a great cost. So," I said, gesturing to the map, "what do we spend it on first?"

WE SPENT THE REST OF THE DAY IN CONFERENCE UNTIL tiredness from the long ride began to wear on us.

"Queen Boudica," Galvyn said. "My niece has come to attend you. You look like you are ready to get some rest. May I call her now?"

"Yes, of course," I said.

"Thank you, Galvyn," Prasutagus said.

Galvyn departed.

I turned to Vian and Pix. "You both look like you could use a rest as well."

"If ye don't need me, I'm going to the tavern for a pint and a look around. Ye should come with me," Pix told Vian. "Ye haven't batted yer eye at any of these fine warriors yet. We need to keep looking for ye."

The girl laughed lightly. "No. But thank you for the offer."

Pix shrugged. "Suit yerself," she said, then departed.

"Queen Boudica," Vian said, curtseying to me, then left the meeting room.

"I will take this to your private meeting chamber," Ansgar said, rolling up the map. "And I will speak to the men in the village tomorrow. If Rome is true to her word, our city will soon rival Camulodunum."

"Thank you, my friend," Prasutagus said, clapping the druid on the shoulder as he left the room.

Soon, we found ourselves alone.

Prasutagus pulled me into his arms. "I think I will sleep well tonight."

"The same," I said, my head pressed against his chest, hearing the rhythmic beating of his heart. I inhaled deeply of his scent, relaxing into him for the moment.

However, the moment didn't last long. Soon, there was a knock on the door.

"Queen Boudica," Galvyn called.

Prasutagus and I separated.

Galvyn entered, a blonde-haired girl with golden braids tied up at the back of her neck, a face full of freckles, entering behind him. "My niece, Brita."

"Queen Boudica," the girl said, curtseying deeply.

"I am glad to meet you, Brita. I'm tired, smelly, my feet hurt, and I'm fairly sure there is tree bark in my hair. Care to give me a hand?"

At that, the girl laughed. "Of course, Queen Boudica. Shall we go to your chamber?"

I turned and looked back at my husband, who was smirking at me. No doubt, he remembered how that tree bark had gotten there. "I'll join you after a time," he said, then turned to Galvyn. "Have you seen Artur?"

"He is with Ardra on the wall."

Prasutagus gestured to indicate he would go after the boy.

"Very well," I told Brita, "let's see about that tree bark," I said, then we departed.

As we were leaving, I heard Prasutagus ask Galvyn, "How did Nella take the news?"

Galvyn laughed. "I suspect her being my niece will spare her the brunt of Nella's fury."

I glanced at Brita.

She raised and lowered her eyebrows.

"Have there been any problems?" I asked.

"Well," the girl began. "I did reorder your wardrobe to the way that made sense to me. I was advised on what I was doing wrong. Repeatedly."

I grinned. "If you are advised on anything again, you can simply reply that *I* am the *only one* permitted to advise you on anything—save the king himself."

At that, the girl grinned. "Thank you, Queen Boudica."

When we arrived in the bedchamber, I noted the girl had been faithful to her word. Many furniture pieces had been rearranged, and the room reorganized.

Setting my hands on my hips, I looked it over. "It looks good."

"You think so?"

I eyed the fresh-cut wildflowers on the table next to my bed and the wreath of dried flowers and herbs on the wall. "Your handiwork?" I asked, gesturing to the wreath.

The girl nodded. "I am very good with herbcraft. My father says that I can make anything grow. I'm partial to flowers."

I smiled. "Then we shall get along just fine," I replied. "Now, I am dying for a bath and a rest."

"I will see to it," Brita said, then got to work.

I sat down on my bed, pulling off my boots. My feet ached. My hands ached. But as much as I wanted to complain, I would not. Having seen the plight of the Trinovantes, complaining about belligerent servants and saddle sores seemed trivial.

Brita returned shortly after that and helped me with my bath. There really was tree bark in my hair, to both of our amusement.

"Do you have a large family?" I asked the girl as she worked.

"Besides my uncle, I have two brothers and my father. My brothers work with my father at a stall in the city."

"They are tradesmen?"

"Yes. We make saddles and tack for horses."

"And your mother?"

"She... She died three winters past."

"I am sorry to hear it. I lost my mother when I was very young. I know what it is like to live without that anchor."

"Yes, m'lady," she said, but her voice sounded strained.

"What is it?"

"My mother and I... My mother was not a soft-hearted woman."

"I see," I said. Much like my own father had been difficult, Brita, too, had suffered difficulties with her family.

"And your father?"

"A goodly, kind man. Like my uncle. My father wished me to marry, but I would rather find some skill for my hands than look for whatever husband might want me."

I laughed. "Then my hair is very grateful."

She laughed.

I glanced up at the wreath on the wall. It was nicely woven. "Do you do other such designs?"

"I do," the girl said affirmatively. "When you have time, I will show you."

After Brita helped me comb out and braid my long locks, I slipped into a nightdress.

"Can I bring you anything to eat?" the girl asked me. "You've barely had a thing all day."

I shook my head. "My stomach is uneasy. It's tied up in knots with everything going on. Maybe tomorrow will be better."

"All right. I will come in the morning after sunup to set out your things," Brita told me as she cleared the bathing cloths.

"Trousers," I said with a yawn, "and a tunic. I have much work to see to tomorrow."

"Very well, Queen Boudica."

"Thank you, Brita. Again, welcome. I am delighted to have you here."

"I am happy to be here, my queen."

The girl set about her work while I crawled into bed. In the morning, Prasutagus and I would survey the land to the north. For years, Prasutagus had wanted to extend the city. Now, he would have the funds to do so.

As I closed my eyes, my thoughts went to General Aulus Plautius. All our hopes were pinned on the truthfulness of his words.

That was a significant risk to take.

My mind went to the general's blue eyes once more, again feeling tugged by the deep sense of familiarity.

A soft voice whispered through my mind. *Beware, Boudica… Some people* never *change.*

CHAPTER 29

The next several weeks passed with all of us on edge. Word had come that the Romans had advanced deep into Cantiaci territory, seizing the capital of Durouernon. There were whispers that King Anarevitos had been killed in this fighting. We also learned they had chased Caratacus and Togodumnus from Camulodunum, recapturing the Trinovantes stronghold once more. Caratacus and Togodumnus had retreated, but we had not heard to where. After that, we had heard nothing. It felt like the waiting would never end. Prasutagus and I kept busy. Taking a team of workers along with us each day, we walked the city's outskirts to the north and east, planning the expansion of the city.

"It would be wise to consider how you want to organize your city," Vian suggested. "I remember one of the village elders telling a tale once of an island city from myth that was divided into rings as it rose up a great hill. One ring for the market, another for the temples, another for the people, and so on. They formed the city like this for defense and to tramp down those illnesses known to stew from markets and livestock. As your city grows, the merchants and traders will be bursting everywhere we look. You do not want traders mixing with the homes of the people."

"That is well thought," I said with a nod. "I remember that story."

Vian nodded. "I loved such old tales, imagining an island city."

"The druids on Mona share that story as well," Prasutagus added. "As well as the tale of Lyonesse and how the island fell when a mountain exploded, the survivors coming to our shores, building our ancient stone temples."

"Ye can wax poetic about stone temples all ye like, but yer mind should be on walls. It ne'er hurt to dig deeper trenches or build taller walls. Something elephant-proof, just in case," Pix said, giving me a wink.

I rolled my eyes at her.

We were sitting in the shade under a tree considering our plans, when Newt came running toward us.

Prasutagus rose to meet him.

"King Prasutagus, Queen Boudica...they...they sent me from the roundhouse."

"What is it, Newt?" Prasutagus asked.

"Romans, King Prasutagus. A party of them riding through the city now."

"Thank you, Newt. Catch your breath, then head back, and tell them we are coming."

The boy grinned. "I don't need to catch my breath.

That's why they sent me. I am faster than all the others in the house," he said, then turned and ran off.

I chuckled, watching as he sped away.

"Seems we have guests," Prasutagus said, offering his hand to help me stand.

I took his hand and then rose. Black spots swirled before my eyes. I reached out for Prasutagus, holding onto his arm as I nearly stumbled.

"Boudica?" he asked.

"I'm… I'm all right. Just dizzy for a moment."

"You keep having such spells," Prasutagus said, a worried expression on his face. "We should talk to Ansgar."

Pix laughed. "Ansgar will hardly be an expert on this matter."

"What do you mean?" I asked her.

"Can't ye see?" Pix asked me, then turned to Vian. "Ye see too, don't ye?"

The girl nodded, a grin on her face.

"What?" I asked.

"Would have thought her eating that fishy garum on her bread along with apple butter and bacon would have given it away," Pix told Vian, who grinned at me.

"Are you…" I began, realization washing over me. "Are you suggesting I'm with…with child?" I asked, then started counting the weeks since my last moonblood. I had not had a cycle since before Beltane. Could it be?

"Boudica?" Prasutagus asked.

"We'll be seeing a Strawberry Prince or Princess come winter for sure," Pix said, then scooped up our belongings.

"Best be getting back. Let's see if the general sent your coin or not. These buildings and walls won't pay for themselves. Come on, Vian," Pix said, gesturing for the girl to come with her.

Prasutagus and I stood alone under the oak tree.

"Could it be?" Prasutagus asked me.

"With everything going on, I hardly noticed. But I've been feeling off since Raven's Dell. I just thought it was the tension."

Prasutagus smiled widely, his eyes growing wet with tears. He pulled me close. "Boudica, how happy you have made me."

"I will need to speak to one of the healing women... just to be sure. I will make the trip to Oak Throne."

"We have such women here. I can—"

"No. For now, I will return to Oak Throne."

Prasutagus nodded. "Whatever makes you feel more comfortable. What strange days. I would never wish to live in times like these, but I am glad to find happiness in the middle of it all." His hand drifted to my stomach. "I *do* feel a roundness here."

"I thought I was enjoying Venta's good food too much."

"You have been, but I guessed it to be your normal appetite."

I laughed. "I don't know if I should laugh for joy or be embarrassed."

Prasutagus chuckled, then cradled my face in his hands. "Only joy. That is what we will have between us in this lifetime."

"Only this lifetime or all lifetimes?"

Prasutagus kissed me on my forehead. "May the gods hear our prayers and grant us our love again and again."

"So mote it be."

HAND IN HAND, WE RETURNED TO THE ROUNDHOUSE. THERE, we found a contingent of armed Roman soldiers waiting.

"Each time they come to Venta, their numbers multiply," Prasutagus said.

"Indeed," I replied in a low tone.

I scanned the party. There was no sign of the general, but I did spot Titus Carassius. He had changed from his armor, now wearing a Roman toga. He stepped down from his wagon to join us.

"King Prasutagus," he called politely, waving his fleshy arm. "I am pleased to meet you again, my friend."

"Titus Carassius," Prasutagus replied.

"And Queen Boudica. You are looking radiant today."

"Thank you."

"Shall we go inside? It was a long ride and has grown very hot," he said, mopping the sweat from the creases on his brow.

"Of course. Do come in," I said.

"Good. Very good..." Titus said, heading toward the door.

I managed to cut him off, opening the door to find Newt on the other side.

"We will need wine and food in the formal chamber," I told the boy. "Tell Betha it is the Romans."

The boy nodded and then ran off.

"I will say one good thing about your roundhouses, they do pinch off the heat," Titus told Prasutagus.

I hurried ahead of them to the formal meeting chamber to ensure it was ready. Opening the door, I found Nella and a very flustered-looking Ginerva.

"Queen Boudica," Nella said, frowning at me as if I had interrupted something.

"We have guests," I said. "I'm very sorry, but we will need to clear the room."

"I'm trying," Nella told me, exasperation in her voice.

"Come now, Ginerva. King Prasutagus needs the chamber," Nella told the woman.

"I told you, I am looking for Antedios!" the old woman answered waspishly. "I will not leave until he comes back from the hunt. Where is Esu? Why does she keep leaving me alone like this?" the old woman asked, then burst into tears.

At the other end of the hallway, I heard Prasutagus and Titus.

I went to Ginerva. "Ginerva," I said gently. "Have you met Brita? She is a new maid here."

"Whose maid?"

"Mine," I replied.

"Well, Prasutagus's sister should have a maid. Maybe

she can see to me as well. Nella always pulls my hair when she fixes it."

I had no doubt she did. "Let's see if we can find her," I said, taking the old woman's arm. "It is a fine day outside. Have you been out? Quite warm," I said, leading her away.

We exited the chamber just as Prasutagus and Titus came down the hall.

I gave my husband a knowing look, then led the old woman away, Nella following behind us.

Winding down the hallway, the old woman's arm linked in mine, we made our way to Brita's chamber.

"Brita is the niece of Galvyn," I told Ginerva. "She's a charming girl."

"Like my Esu," Ginerva said proudly. "And her boy. He's a sweet child, Boudica. You must look past his broodiness. That comes from his father, may he be cursed," the old woman said, spitting on the floor. "That man bruised and bloodied my poor daughter. I warned my husband it was a poor match. But my husband was little better. I saw to both of them in the end."

"Saw to both of them?"

"Fever root," Ginerva said with a grin. "Just a pinch mixed into their ale. Brings on a fever that looks like a normal bout of illness, but in the end, it makes their hearts stop like that," she said, then snapped her fingers.

Shocked, I looked back at Nella, who simply shrugged.

"He never beat Esu again after that," Ginerva said with a laugh. "And then, she married the king. How about that?"

"Remind me never to cross you, Ginerva," I said.

At that, the old woman laughed. "You brought me orange marmalade from the market. How could I ever be angry with you, Boudica?"

I was very sure that if her mind cleared too much, she might think otherwise.

I knocked on Brita's door. The girl opened it to reveal a small chamber. On the floor were spread many flowers, stones, and a mortar and pestle.

"Queen Boudica," she said, curtseying to me.

"Queen? Boudica is Esu's new maid," Ginerva said with annoyance. "What is your name, girl?"

"This is Brita," I said, "Galvyn's niece. Remember?"

"Yes. I remember. What are you working on here, girl?" Ginerva asked, entering Brita's chamber.

"Making paint," Brita said, looking at me in confusion.

"I'm very sorry. We have Roman guests, and Ginerva needed to be guided away. I couldn't think of anything else to distract her."

"Oh. Of course. It's no problem at all. I am happy to help Nella keep her busy."

"We will see to it now, Queen Boudica. You will want to see your guests settled," Nella told me.

"Thank you, Nella, Brita."

Brita smiled at me. "Of course," she said, then turned to Ginerva. "Look here, Ginerva. I am making blue paint from these stones," she told the old woman.

Nella nodded to me, then closed the door.

Smoothing down my tunic and pushing my hair back, I

made my way back to the meeting chamber. As I went, two thoughts warred in my mind.

Ginerva had murdered Esu's first husband *and* her own husband. Was she to be believed? Prasutagus said Esu's first marriage had not been good, but how bad had it truly been? If what Ginerva said was true, bad enough.

Pix's words were bouncing alongside the shocking news that Ginerva was a killer.

My hands drifted to my stomach.

Are you there, sweet one?

Was I truly pregnant?

I entered the chamber to find Prasutagus and Titus sitting together drinking wine. In fact, the Roman was already waving for Ronat to refill his cup. Behind him stood five guards, all of whom held heavy-looking chests.

I could see the burden of strain in their eyes, but they said nothing.

I slipped into a seat beside Prasutagus.

When Ronat moved to fill my cup, I waved her aside. How many times Ula had grumbled that children were born weak-witted if their parents drank too much wine and ale? I would not tempt the Great Mother.

"Water," I whispered to Ronat, who nodded to me.

Setting the wine flagon on the table, the girl quietly departed.

"Very good," Titus said, setting down his cup. "When you don't water it, the wine is quicker to help one relax." He turned to the men behind him, motioning for them to deposit their burdens on the table.

Once they had done so, Titus said, "Go rejoin the others outside."

The men said nothing, merely retreated, our guards along with them.

Titus rose. "It is a lucky day, Prasutagus. A lucky day, indeed. I bring a gift from the general. As agreed," he said, then opened the chests, revealing enormous amounts of coins.

Prasutagus and I both rose. The wealth before us was like nothing I had ever seen before. Gold—so much gold— enough to pay for our plans and so much more.

"Let's see how many pairs of earrings you can buy with that, Queen Boudica," Titus said with a laugh.

"A pair for every woman in Britannia, I would wager," I said with a laugh.

Titus chuckled. "The general didn't want to keep you waiting, but we had our own business to attend to. After a night's rest, I'll move on to Oak Throne to see your brother."

"You are most welcome to stay here with us in Venta," I said.

"Very good. Very good," he said, sitting back down. "It is all there, of course," he said, waving his hand at the chests. "*And*, I come with good news."

Prasutagus and I sat once more.

"News?" my husband asked.

"In addition to defeating King Anarevitos, who was killed in battle, and taking over the Cantiaci stronghold, the general has had success with the Catuvellauni. He pinched those Catuvellauni usurpers on the River Thames.

There, so-called King Togodumnus was killed in the fighting. The general is pursuing his brother."

I stilled, puzzled by the mixed emotions that washed over me. The news from the Cantiaci was, sadly, expected. But Togodumnus... I had disliked Togodumnus intensely. Nothing I had heard of him nor saw in him convinced me he was a good man. And yet, the idea the Romans had defeated him—killed him—left me with a feeling of disquiet. In such a short amount of time, two of our kings had fallen.

"Soon, we will have Togodumnus's brother. King Verica was very pleased, of course. He will be back in his own home very soon."

"The Catuvellauni brothers have a young sister. By all accounts, she is afflicted with madness. I hope that when Rome reaches Verulam, her condition will be kept in mind. She is innocent of her brothers' machinations. Perhaps she could be handed over to our holy people. Will you mention it to the general for me?" I asked.

"Of course, of course," Titus replied dismissively.

Prasutagus, noting Titus's lack of attention, prickled. "How the innocents of our royal houses are treated in defeat is a matter of importance to our people," Prasutagus told Titus. "We do not slaughter innocent women and children here, no matter the sins of their male kin. As my wife has mentioned, we would ask that Princess Imogen is treated with courtesy."

"I will see that Aulus hears your request, King Prasutagus," Titus said with more sincerity.

"It was my wife's request. I am merely echoing it."

Titus glanced at me. "Yes. Yes. I do forget that, like the Gauls, your women have an equal voice here. How curious."

"Is it so?" I asked, annoyance washing up in me. "I understand that among your gods, there are many powerful goddesses. Do they not have an equal footing to their male counterparts?"

"Of our heavenly gods, Jupiter is father and ruler to them all. All the other gods are below him, including his wife, Juno."

"I see," I replied.

Ronat returned a moment later with a jug of spring water in her hands. When she saw the gold on the table, she paused but said nothing, merely filled my cup. Thirsty, I downed the water.

Titus lifted his goblet and waggled it at her. "You need more servants in your hall, Prasutagus," he told my husband. "Your wife and guests go thirsty," he said with a laugh.

Prasutagus chuckled. "Well, now I have the money to afford them," he said, gesturing to the gold.

"Indeed, indeed," Titus replied. "I hope your kitchens are better staffed than your hall. I have spent days on the road surviving on boiled eggs and apples. Your people eat so simply. I have not adjusted to it yet."

"I hope we will be able to tease your palate with pleasing but humble foods," I said, then rose. "I shall see to your arrangements for the night and send Galvyn to assist with Rome's gift," I told the men.

Prasutagus nodded to me and then gave me a soft,

knowing smile. In the bloom of realizing our happy news, we had to deal with a bloated, self-important Roman. Was our whole marriage to be like this?

I gave the Roman a nod, then turned and left the room.

Togodumnus was dead, and the Greater Iceni were sitting on a pile of gold, more of which was headed to… "Oak Throne," I whispered, realization washing over me. I hurried down the hall, making my way to the family quarters. "Pix? Pix!"

"Queen Boudica? What is it?" Galvyn asked. "I'm sorry, my queen, I was just coming from King's Wood. I only now learned we have visitors."

"Rome has come. I'm looking for Pix."

"I saw her ride off toward town."

"Dammit," I cursed, then paused. "The Romans will spend the night. Please make sure that chambers are readied and the men comfortably lodged. Tell Ronat to spare no expense on the dinner. I will not have that bloated, arrogant man burping complaints about our food. I'll be back shortly."

"My queen?"

"I'm headed to the taverns. And if that Roman keeps talking, I might just stay there."

At that, Galvyn laughed. "If he keeps talking, I'll be by to join you!"

I FOUND PIX IN THE THIRD TAVERN I TRIED. THE PEOPLE seemed puzzled to find their queen randomly roaming the city, checking into taverns, even if Galvyn had insisted that I take two guards with me. In the third tavern, I found Pix engaging in a match of strength against a brute of a man.

"Pix," I said, joining her.

"Hush ye, Queen. I almost have him."

At that, I chuckled.

Around me, the people watched, looking from me to the match.

I stepped back, crossed my arms on my chest, and watched.

"Why do ye think ye can beat me?" Pix asked her bald-headed competitor.

"Why do *ye* talk like that?" the man replied with a laugh, then went back to straining once more.

Around them, the others chuckled. "To get ye confused, of course. But I could easily win this match."

"And how would you do that?"

"Distraction."

"If the queen cannot distract me, how could you do it?"

"Like this," Pix said, then pulled her tunic down, revealing her breast.

At that, the man broke, and Pix overpowered his hand.

"Winner! The queen's guard is the winner," the tavern owner called.

Pix scooped up the coin from the table.

"You're right. You did have an easy way of cheating," the man told her with a laugh.

"Me? A cheat? Ye hear that, Queen? Will ye not defend me?"

I shrugged. "You got yourself into this mess."

The man grinned at her. "The least you could do is give me a better look."

Pix eyed him up and down. "I would do that for ye, but I think Queen Boudica needs me now. Can I find ye here again?"

The man nodded.

"Good," Pix said, then leaned across the table, grabbed the man by his shirt collar, and kissed him. When she let him go, she gestured to me that she was ready to leave.

I shook my head. "Drinks for all. The gods know we all need one," I called to the tavern, earning me a loud cheer.

Passing some silver to the tapster, I followed Pix outside.

"Why do I get the feeling that I'm traveling?" she asked.

"The Romans will ride to Oak Throne tomorrow. Bran must be ready. Ride through the night."

"As ye like, Boudica. But the fey sent me here for ye, not for yer family."

"Make sure you complain next time you see them."

"And now that ye have a little one…"

"That is not certain."

"It is. Ye know it."

"Then finish the task and get back quickly. For me and my little one."

"Can I take Druda?"

"You most certainly *cannot* take Druda. Take

Saenunos's horse. You seem to favor that fancy beast. What have you called him, anyway?"

"Saenunos, of course."

At that, I laughed. "Anyway, don't complain about the trip. Cai is in Oak Throne."

"'Tis true," she said, then grinned. "All right, Strawberry Queen."

"Best be careful with all your gallivanting, or you could end up like me," I told her.

"With a wee one?"

I nodded.

"Sadly, no. Had a child once, came hard. The babe lived but a few hours. The priestesses said I would ne'er have another."

Suddenly, I felt sorry for my jest. "I'm sorry."

"Need not be. It is long past."

"I'm still sorry. Long past or not, I'm sad for your loss."

"I thank ye, but it was long ago."

"Long ago. For you, that is saying something," I said but put my hand on her shoulder all the same.

"Thank ye, Boudica," she said, patting my hand. She gave me a grateful smile, then we turned and made our way to the stables.

CHAPTER 30

After seeing Pix off, I rejoined Prasutagus and Titus. The news that Anarevitos and Togodumnus had been killed would shake our whole world.

Once more, I questioned myself.

Togodumnus, Caratacus, and Anarevitos had warred to keep their people safe. That plan had not worked. Would ours go any better?

I could hear Titus's voice in the meeting chamber long before I reached it. I paused before the door. Steeling myself, I entered the meeting chamber once more.

Prasutagus rose when I entered, forcing the Roman to do the same out of decorum.

"Queen Boudica," Titus said.

"Please, be at ease," I told the man.

"We were just discussing the architecture of our round-houses," Prasutagus said as I joined them.

"So we were. It is the same design I see all over your country—and in Gaul. It is a workable style, for certain. In Rome, we build with stone, and far more often, in square and rectangular designs."

"And how do you heat your houses?"

"We, too, have firepits but of a different design. Of course, the weather in Rome is far more moderate than here."

"And are you from Rome originally?" Prasutagus asked.

"I am, although a grandmother of mine came from the Thracian people. Of course, Thracians were barbarians, and the Romans sought to elevate them through alliances and rule. My father helped Rome in their campaigns against a rather brutal sect of Thracians, liberating his mother's people from tribal oppressors. I don't have the sword arm of my father, but I have been pleased to serve Rome in my own way."

Prasutagus smiled politely. "I am sure Rome is grateful for all of your family's contributions."

At that, Titus smiled. "You understand the Roman mind very well, King Prasutagus. Rome is a friend to those who are a friend to her," he said, gesturing to the chests.

A moment later, there was a knock on the door, and Galvyn appeared. "King Prasutagus, Master Titus's chamber is prepared."

"Master Titus," Titus said with a chuckle. "How quaint you people are." He rose, wobbling on his feet a moment, then righted himself. "I shall take my rest now."

"Anything you need, please just ask," King Prasutagus said.

"Sir," Galvyn said, gesturing for Titus to follow him.

Titus left the chamber, following behind the housecarl. "I say, how narrow these halls are," we heard him remark as he disappeared.

Prasutagus and I met one another's gaze, both of us shaking our heads.

"Where did you go?" Prasutagus asked.

"I sent Pix to Oak Throne."

"I thought as much."

"I'm not sure if word will reach Caturix in time. I was thinking that maybe I should ride north with Titus."

"That is regrettable."

"Yes, except I will see Ula while I am there...about the child."

Prasutagus smiled at me. "About the child."

"Our very rich child," I said, looking at the chests. "What do we do with it?" I asked.

"Spend it," Prasutagus replied.

"No. I mean, what do we do with it? Literally?"

At that, Prasutagus laughed. "Come with me," he said, taking my hand. When we exited, Prasutagus motioned to the guards at the door. "No one is allowed inside. Servant nor otherwise," he told them.

"Yes, King Prasutagus," they answered.

Prasutagus led me to our bedchamber, closing and locking the door behind us.

"This was my father's bedchamber before we moved

here," he said, then went to the side of the bed. "You will have to help me," he said, gesturing to the bed pole at the other end. "Toward the wall. Push on three," he said.

I grabbed the pole and braced myself.

"One, two, three."

At that, we gave the bed a hard shove. It moved aside to reveal nothing much, save a dusty cowhide underneath. Prasutagus pulled the hide away, revealing a wooden door underneath. He gestured for me to come.

Sticking his finger in a hole, he lifted the trap door, revealing a narrow flight of stairs leading to the darkness below.

Snagging a torch from the wall, Prasutagus lit it, then motioned for me to follow him.

We made our way down the narrow staircase and into the ground below.

"There was an ancient well here," Prasutagus explained. "It dried long ago. The first king of the Greater Iceni built his home above the dry well. At that time, this chamber and the main hall were the only rooms of the roundhouse. All of the Greater Iceni fit behind the walls of the king's compound. The king's house grew up around that original design. But the first king... He knew the value of having somewhere secret to hide. So, he created this space."

The walls of the narrow stairwell were made of stone. When we reached the bottom of the stairwell, Prasutagus lit a brazier, shedding light on the small space. We stood at the bottom of what was once a dry pool. The floor was made of smooth stone, and the walls were made of large rocks. There was just enough room for us to stand, but barely. But the shape of the place was less impressive than what it held—gold. A lot of it. Gold and silver coins, gemstones, cups, platters, and all manner of wealth.

"The Greater Iceni are not a poor tribe, but we have never seen wealth like the Romans gave us. You asked what we'll do with all that coin. Galvyn and I will move it here. No one else, not even Ansgar, knows the location of this hoard. No one but you, my wife."

I picked up one of the coins. On it was the face of Prasutagus's grandfather. "Does this mean I can order as many Roman-style dresses as I fancy?"

Prasutagus set his hand on my cheek. "It means you— and my son or daughter—will never want for anything. I will keep you safe, Boudica. Nothing means more to me than that."

I wrapped my arms around my husband, pressing my head to his chest. "We will have a child."

"We will have a child."

"Amid all this madness."

"A child born to match the times," he said, then paused. His voice deepened, taking on the tone of prophecy, as he added, "A child born of fire and blood who will wield the dagger of the shadowy one."

I pulled back, searching Prasutagus's face.

He looked dazed for a moment, then shook his head, clearing the vision away.

"Prasutagus?"

"Such a fiery one…" he whispered.

"You saw our child?"

"Yes, I think so. I saw a misty vale with needle-like mountains. And some strange, foreign place far away from here. And... and, our daughter."

"Daughter?"

"A daughter with a dagger made of flame."

CHAPTER 31

Thankfully, Titus spent the rest of the afternoon resting, allowing Prasutagus and I some time to come to terms with the Cantiaci's defeat and Togodumnus's death. We retreated to Prasutagus's small, private meeting chamber, Vian, Galvyn, and Ewen joining us.

"Our Roman guest is settled?" Prasutagus asked Galvyn.

"After some doing. He had a bath, and was rather annoyed to discover we had no young boys on hand to *attend* him," Galvyn said, shifting uncomfortably as his eyes darted toward Vian and me then away again. "He told us he will sleep until evening meal."

"I will be glad when he leaves this place," Vian said.

"So shall we all," Galvyn replied.

"But he comes with good information," Prasutagus said, standing before the map once more. He lifted a number of red tokens and placed them on the map.

"The Romans have now taken over Cantiaci territory. They hold Durouernon. They defeated Togodumnus and Caratacus at the Thames, where Togodumnus fell. And now, they push inland with King Verica, pursuing Caratacus."

"The Regnenses?" Ewen asked, touching the portion of the map on the shore to the south.

"No word," Prasutagus said.

"There is still no change in the north?"

"Not that I have head. Thus far, they are steering clear of the conflict."

We all stared at the map, well aware that the number of red tokens on the board had increased exponentially and were moving across the southeast of this land like a growing mold.

Apparently, I was not the only one who thought as much, because Prasutagus said, "If the Romans prove false to their word to the Greater Iceni, the north will rally behind us. A false word to one is a false word to all. All of us are watching. So, for now, we watch and wait."

SADLY, OUR GUEST WOKE LATER THAT EVENING WITH A ravenous appetite and in need of entertainment.

"I'm afraid we keep no entertainers on hand," Prasutagus told the man.

"And I was told you are musical people," Titus said in confusion.

"Well…" Prasutagus began.

"My king," Galvyn said. "Pardon the interruption, but my niece, Brita, is rather skilled with the mandolin. Shall I fetch her?"

Prasutagus nodded.

"There. Now. That is better. I say, Queen Boudica, such fine tarts," he said, lifting his fifth tart. "Homey food, to be certain, but a fine honey."

"Our cook sings to the bees," I told Titus. "She uses magic to charm them. They give her the best honey as a reward."

"Sings to the bees?" Titus asked, a confused expression on his face.

I nodded. "Indeed. Bees are sacred to our goddess, Brigid. Our ancient sects know all forms of bee magic. If you anger one of our cooks, she will send a hive of bees to sting you. So, I am very glad to hear you are enjoying the meal," I said, biting my lip so I didn't laugh. While the priestesses at the King's Wood did serve Brigid and her bees, I might have exaggerated Betha's influence on the creatures.

"Indeed," he replied. "Indeed, I am," he said, looking uncertain as to what to believe.

Brita returned a few moments later, her mandolin in hand. She curtseyed to Prasutagus and me. She gave the Roman a wary look, but curtseyed to him as well.

"We are sorry to bother you, Brita. But, perhaps, a song for our guest?" Prasutagus asked her.

Brita nodded. "Yes, my king," she said then sat.

Brita stroked the strings of her instrument then began her song, recanting the tale of the giants and maidens who danced in rings across our land until they became circles of stones.

When she was done, we all clapped.

"Such a sweet, lovely voice," Titus said, eyeing the girl in a manner I did not appreciate.

"Sir," she replied, bobbing a curtsey to him.

"Thank you, Brita," I told her. "It was very well done."

"I'm glad you enjoyed it, Queen Boudica," she said, smiling from Prasutagus to me.

"I'm told there is some island of yours where people are taught to sing and other such stuff. Is this true?" Titus asked, sucking the grease from his fingers.

Something within me stiffened.

"Just a school," Prasutagus said dismissively. "To learn instruments and such."

"You should send this lark there," Titus said. "She has far too sweet a voice to spend her life braiding hair and washing gowns," the man said, then tossed a bone on his plate. "I am well-fed, and this wine has made me tired. I will excuse myself," he said, rising. He waved for his attendant.

"Can we... Is there anything else we can do for you?" Prasutagus asked.

"No. No," he said then burped. "Yes, a very good dinner indeed. I wish you all a good night. More riding to be had in the morning, I'm afraid. I'll be off now," he said.

His attendant following along behind him, he disappeared once more.

"May I..." Brita asked, motioning as to whether or not she should go.

Prasutagus nodded to her. "Thank you again, Brita," he told the girl then turned to me. "I agree with Vian. I will thank the gods when he is gone," Prasutagus whispered to me.

My eyes followed the man. "Where he goes, so goes Rome. Now we can see what kind of guest we have invited."

"If the sons of soldiers turn to slovenly messes like him, we have made a grave mistake."

"Having met General Plautius, I am surprised to see such a man in his keeping."

"We do not know enough of how the Romans think, how their people are organized. We must do what we can to remedy the gaps in our knowledge."

I nodded.

A moment later, Artur appeared at the threshold of the dining hall.

"There you are," Prasutagus said, gesturing to the boy to join us. "Hiding from the Romans?" he asked as Artur came and sat beside us.

"I was with Ardra."

"And what were you and Ardra doing?"

For a brief moment, a strange expression crossed the boy's face but he quickly covered it. "Studying."

"Hmm," Prasutagus mused then asked, "Did you see the Roman?"

Artur nodded.

"And what did you see?"

"How can a man like that hold such rank to talk to kings?" Artur asked, a look of disgust on his face.

"Boudica and I were just questioning the same."

"Are they all like that?"

I shook my head. "No. When we rode south, we saw soldiers. General Plautius is a man of war. This Titus is something else. The soldiers are the Rome that people fear."

"Yes and no," Prasutagus said. "Men like Titus speak, and the soldiers move at his command. They are both to be feared."

"Yes, you're right," I said.

Artur looked down the table where Titus had left a heap of bones and mess at his table setting.

"Sit," Prasutagus said, fixing the boy a plate. "He hasn't eaten all the good meat."

"Must have overlooked it," I commented, making Artur smile.

"So, what were you and Ardra studying?" Prasutagus asked.

So, he had noticed the boy's hesitation too.

"I… The history of the Greater Iceni."

Prasutagus nodded slowly. "And did you learn anything new?"

"Only that your great-great-grandfather married a priestess from the King's Wood."

"That is true."

"Is it common for nobles to marry holy people?"

"My own mother was a priestess," I said. "She served at the Grove of Andraste."

"Is that so?" Artur asked, looking truly interested.

I nodded.

"I think it is a good thing. Our druids and priestesses are special people. They know a lot. That's why you know so much, Father. You are practically a druid."

"Only in part. But tonight, let us toast the King's Wood's goddess," Prasutagus said, filling mine and Artur's cups with water and handing a mug of ale to Galvyn. "To Brigid and her bees. May her legions of stingers protect us."

"To Brigid!" we all called.

CHAPTER 32

The following day, I made ready to ride north with Titus, his guard, and my own party of Greater Iceni warriors.

"It is quite kind of you to see us north," Titus said skeptically.

"I'm Northern Iceni," I told him. "I would see you safely through our lands to Oak Throne."

"I wish all your people were as wise and accommodating. If they had been so, the Cantiaci king might have kept his head."

"He had a reputation for losing it frequently anyway," I joked, my words not exactly matching my spirit. Even though Anarevitos's fury had a reputation, the fact that the Romans had dispatched the Cantiaci king still did not sit well with me. But from Rome's point of view, no doubt it had been an excellent motivator for the rest of us.

They weren't wrong.

After saying my goodbyes to Prasutagus and the others, we headed north.

"You must tell me about the Northern Iceni," Titus said. "What are your people like, Queen Boudica?" Titus asked, the two of us riding side by side.

"We are horse people, much like the Greater Iceni. But we are fishermen too. The Wash is to the north of us, a great inlet where many people fish and hunt oysters."

"Oysters? Oh, that is very good. I think I have heard of this Wash. A great gateway into your land, is it not?"

"It is."

"Far north, though. Do you suppose your brother will have some of these Northern Iceni oysters for us?"

"It is the season for them. I would expect it."

"And your people's pennant... a tree, I believe?"

"Yes. There is a great tree that sits at the heart of Oak Throne. It was there when the first king built his fort. And what of the general's legions? I noted their symbols and that they have different names. What earns the legions their distinctions?"

"That depends. Some are named after the lands from which they come. For example, General Plautius leads the Hispania.

"Then, those soldiers are not Roman?"

"Oh, they are Romans, of course, but from Hispania... where Rome now rules."

"I see. And the others?"

"Named after battles they have won, as in the case of the Valeria Victrix and the Geminia. Of course, this is not the first time the Geminia has been in Britannia. They came with Caesar as well. And then there is the Augusta."

I stilled then said, "Ah, yes. The Augusta."

I had not seen the Augusta amongst the general's men. Nor had he mentioned them.

"They should be crossing Ocean to the south as we speak, alongside Cogidubnus, the son of Verica. Such a fine young man. Have you met him?"

"No, I have not."

"Perhaps you will have the chance very soon. We will have Caratacus on the run. Legate Vespasian commands the Augusta. They are a powerful force. These Regnenses people… They seem partial to the Atrebates."

"Verica's father, Eppillus, made a power-sharing agreement between their tribes. They were one but separate. The Catuvellauni did not adhere as steadfastly to that agreement."

"They are friendly to Rome," Titus told me matter-of-factly. "They have been in regular contact with King Verica. These Catuvellauni brothers oscillated from threatening to wooing them. They would have none of it. No fear, Cogidubnus and Vespasian are coming. Soon, we will have that region well in hand. The emperor will be very pleased."

"Emperor Claudius seems very unlike Caesar."

Titus laughed. "You are right about that, Queen Boudica. Claudius knows you don't need to bash men on the rocks when talk works just as well."

"That is good for those willing to talk."

"So it is. That is why the general and the emperor get

along so well. Two like-minded men. Me too. We are all wit," he said with a flourish of his hand.

I gave him a smile but inwardly groaned.

The ride north took most of the day, especially with the cart and Titus's slow pace. But you could tell we were close when Druda began prancing and picking up his pace, eager to get home.

"Something in the air," Titus said, eyeing Druda.

"Oak Throne. This one knows he is close to a meal," I said, patting Druda's neck.

Soon, the fort appeared on the horizon.

I had never felt more relieved to see Oak Throne in my life.

When we rode toward the river, Titus perked up.

"What river is this?"

"The Stiffkey."

"And you engage in trade here?"

"We do. Oak Throne is the heart of the Northern Iceni. What trade there is to be had comes through the Stiffkey."

"That is very good. Very good indeed. King Caturix will do well to increase your..." He eyed the docks where two fishing vessels sat. "Well, to increase everything."

We crossed the river and then the earthen bridge leading to the gates of the city...which were closed.

"Boudica?" Ector called, a nervous tone in his voice.

"I am riding as an escort. Please open the gates."

The man hesitated a moment, then called below.

When the gates opened, I found the market quiet. The people were gone. The shops were closed. Almost no one was on the street save the Northern Iceni warriors.

"Cautious people," Titus said, mostly to himself. "A cautious people," he added, directing the comment at me.

"We have faced some internal strife of late, which resulted in my father's death," I said, seeing no risk in mentioning it. "It is a strange time for the Northern Iceni."

"Then I hope that they, like their princess, come to see the benefits of friendship with Rome."

I gave him a smile.

As we made our way through the market, I spotted Eiwyn, Phelan, and Birgit peering out from the doorway of Eiwyn's home. Birgit waved to me. I returned the gesture, then pointed to my pocket, letting them know I had something for them.

"Later," I mouthed to them.

The three of them nodded and smiled.

Watching from the doors to their homes, the people eyed the Romans suspiciously. This would be the first time they had seen the soldiers, gotten a glimpse of what had come to the south. And like us all, they were hesitant, fearful.

"Ah, here is your great tree," Titus said, eyeing the oak as we made our way to the roundhouse.

A wind blew across the fort, making the leaves quiver. From the glimmering green, a soft voice called:

"Boudica...

"Boudica...

"Stand with your shield before the greenwood.

"Boudica...

"Boudica...

"Stand with your shield before the stones..."

I shuddered lightly, my attention drawn beyond the tree to the narrow passage that led to Ula's cottage.

There was no sign of the woman.

We rode forward to the roundhouse. There, Bran and Bec waited, Bran's men gathered with him. There was no sign of Pix.

"I don't see your brother, Queen Boudica," Titus said, a hint of annoyance in his voice.

"But here is my other brother, Prince Bran," I said.

"Ah, I see," Titus said. "May the gods shine upon the house of the Northern Iceni and Prince Bran," Titus called.

"Well met, Rome," Bran answered. While he sounded cheerful, I knew him better. He felt anything but welcoming.

I dismounted Druda only to find Tadhg at my side.

"Boudica," he said, smiling at me.

I ruffled his hair. "Well met, Tadhg. Will you see to the horses?" I asked, handing him Druda's reins.

He nodded.

Titus's servant helped the man down.

I waited for him, casting a warning glance at my brother.

Once Titus was settled, I walked with the Roman to meet Bran and Bec.

"Titus Carassius, may I introduce my brother, Prince Bran, and his wife, Lady Bec. This is Titus Carassius, a representative of General Aulus Plautius."

"You are welcome in Oak Throne," Bec told the man with a curtsey.

"I say, Britannia has a fascinating variety of beautiful

women," Titus said, then turned his attention to Bran. "Prince. I am pleased to meet you. I was hoping to find King Caturix."

"The king had some matters to attend to which took longer than anticipated. We expect him tonight," Bec told the Roman. "But, please. Come inside. We have refreshment for you, and our housecarl will see to your men."

"Very good. Very good. It has been a long, hot ride," he said, mopping his face.

"This way, if you please," Bec said graciously.

Bran and I lingered a moment. Balfor joined us.

"Pix was here then away to Stonea with Cai," Bran whispered.

I nodded, then looked over my shoulder. The Roman soldiers stayed with the cart.

"Boudica," Bran said nervously.

"Pleasantry. All pleasantry. They are here to grow our alliance with Rome, nothing more."

"What can I do?" Balfor asked.

"See that their men have refreshment and plan to have a spoiled, pampered guest for the night."

He nodded, then headed off.

"And me?" Bran asked.

"Just be your charming self," I said, then motioned for him to follow me inside.

Within, I found Cidna working hard as she laid the table. Catching her glance for only a moment, I winked at her. But the woman was so busy shooting glances at the Romans, she paid me no mind. Once she and Albie had the platters laid out, she disappeared to the back.

"What a fine hall. Quaint. Rustic," Titus said, looking about. "Ah, here is the wine," he said, then looked around expectantly.

"Allow me," Bec said, then poured him a goblet.

"Wonderful," Titus said, then drank.

Bec gave me a wondering glance.

I merely shook my head.

At that, we all settled in at the table, eating and drinking, Bec making the usual inquiries—the weather, the number of travelers on the road, and so on—about our journey. The priestess amazed me. She proved to have the skills to match Rome's politicians.

After Titus finished the first flagon of wine, he asked for another. Cidna delivered two more bottles but glared at Titus when he wasn't looking. Wine was expensive, and in Oak Throne, not always easy to come by. Once his thirst was finally quenched, Titus's attention went to Bran's dogs lounging by the fire.

"What manner of dogs are those?" he asked my brother, gesturing to the two largest.

"They are mastiffs," my brother replied. "Do you like dogs, Titus?"

"Oh, indeed I do. We do a bit of gambling with them in Rome. Races and fighting. Such great dogs would be good in a ring with a bear."

"Fighting bears?" Bec said, unable to hide the shock in her voice.

"Oh, yes. Bears, lions, even... well, such a matter is not suitable for such a gentle lady," he said, giving Bec's hand a squeeze—and leaving traces of the grease from the boar he'd been eating thereon.

I watched as Bec nonchalantly wiped her hand on her skirt.

"Well," Bran said, looking to redirect the conversation. "We don't have such games here, but they are excellent hunting dogs. Do you hunt, sir?"

"Hunt? No. Well, I have never tried it. I'm afraid most of my meals come to my table already cooked with a nice bit of plum sauce on the side."

"Hunting is an honorable skill," Bran said. "Perhaps if you stay with us long enough, you will allow me to take you out and show you how we hunt with our dogs. It is a good sport," Bran said with an encouraging grin.

"I say," Titus said, turning to me. "Are all Iceni people so hospitable, Queen Boudica? I shall be sure to share with the emperor the great welcome I have found amongst your people—Greater and Northern Iceni alike. I feel like one of the family."

I smiled at him. "I'm glad to hear it."

"I cannot say I am interested in hunting," Titus told Bran. "But I do like those dogs. Are there any pups in the village? The general—you know him, Queen Boudica— will be very jealous when I return with such a fine dog."

"I shall inquire for you," Bran said.

"Very good. Very good. Thank you, Prince Bran. Well, we shall speak no more of dog fights, and instead, let me tell you of our fabulous colosseums. We have the greatest arenas in the world. And our gladiator battles... well, they are a sight to behold. Strong men from every land battle to show their strength. There have been many Gauls in the fighting rings. Strong fighters, much like your own people, I would suppose."

"Aside from such entertainments, do you play games of dice or cards?" Bec asked, leading Titus off on a less repugnant topic but one he seemed sure to know quite a lot about.

"Why, yes, Lady Bec," he said in pleased surprise. "Let me tell you about the best hand of cards I ever played," he began, then went on and on and on.

A simple "uh-huh" or "is that so" from my brother and Bec proved enough to keep him talking.

Distracted, Titus didn't see when Balfor appeared at the door. He waved to me.

"If you will excuse me a moment," I said, leaving the trio.

Titus waved absently as he explained to Bec the rules of his favorite card game.

"Boudica," Balfor said in a low tone. "The Roman soldiers are rather insistent we do not get close to the wagon. We would feed and water their mules, but they would not hear of it."

"Gold and silver," I whispered to the housecarl. "They are protecting a considerable sum of wealth. I will speak to Titus and suggest the chests be brought in tonight. He has arrived with gifts from Rome."

"Gifts of gold?"

I paused, suddenly feeling less than comfortable about the way the arrangement sounded. "We have agreed to stand aside in the conflict. Rome hopes to make a friend of the Iceni and sweetened the deal."

"Then it is a bribe."

"They frame it as a gift. But, yes, you could call it that."

"And Prasutagus and Caturix agreed?" he asked, unable to suppress the surprise in his voice.

"We have seen the forces to the south with our own eyes. Balfor, we must find a way to keep the Iceni out of this conflict, or we will be crushed. Already, the Cantiaci have fallen. King Anarevitos is dead. Those Trinovantes who were loyal to Togodumnus and Caratacus are battling for their lives. King Togodumnus was killed in the fighting."

"May the Mother be merciful," he swore in disbelief.

"Indeed, may she be. I have no wish to be a friend to Rome, but I'd rather seek a peaceful way to protect our people than die trying."

Balfor nodded. "I understand."

"Let me talk to the soldiers," I said then the two of us headed outside. I gestured for Balfor to stay back when I went to speak to the men.

The soldiers came to attention as I drew close.

"Soldiers," I said, pausing.

"Queen Boudica," their chief man replied.

"The Iceni are people of the horse, and it is a long ride from Venta to Oak Throne. Our goddess Epona will be much offended if we do not attend to your mules. I know what cargo you carry and your charge. Perhaps one of you would accompany me to the stables to retrieve feed and water for the animals."

The men shifted.

"Marcus will go," the leader finally said.

"Very good. Come, Marcus. You will find little in the barn to worry you," I said, gesturing for the man to follow me.

We went to the stables and around the back to the well. I turned the crank, sending the bucket down for fresh water.

Marcus stared off into the distance, a suspicious look on his face.

Beyond the walls, the forest was alive with night sounds. Frogs, birds, and other wild creatures called. A mist had risen up from the river, making the forest beyond a mix of mist, shadows, and darkness.

"Are you from Rome, Marcus?" I asked the soldier.

"I... No, Queen Boudica. But I am Roman."

"Where are you from?"

"Egypt, Queen Boudica."

"Egypt," I replied, unfamiliar with the place. "And do you have such forests in Egypt?"

"Nowhere has forests like Britannia," he said, looking off to the horizon once more. "Your trees speak here."

"And what do they say?" I asked.

The man, not expecting that answer, looked back at me. "Say?"

"Mm-hmm," I mused. "You said they speak. What have they said to you?"

"Not words, just a feeling."

I grinned. The greenwood was whispering.

"A feeling of what?"

"Darkness," he said, looking out at the horizon. "Before we crossed Ocean, some of the men mutinied. They would not come here where the trees walk, and people shift their forms. An isle of mages."

"And is that how you find us?" I asked, setting a full bucket aside and sending down another. "Have we proven as frightening as you thought?"

He turned and looked back at me, his gaze softening. He watched me as I cranked. "You should not be doing that work," he said, then joined me, gesturing that he wanted to take over.

I stepped aside, letting him work.

"No, Queen Boudica, *you* are not. But your forests..."

"You see, but I may have you precisely where I want you even now. Maybe I lured you here to push you down the well," I said, then sang a few notes into the well, the sound echoing back at me.

Marcus looked at me, wide-eyed.

"I jest, I jest," I said with a laugh.

He softened again, chuckling. "You are no witch, Queen Boudica."

"No. I'm not. But I will tell you, our forests here are ancient, and they *will* whisper. But if you mean them no harm, no harm will come to you."

Marcus filled the second bucket, then set it aside.

"Let's get the grain," I said, snagging the other bucket, then waved for the man to follow me into the stables. Therein, I paused at the grain bin to fill two containers.

Druda knickered at me. "No, this is not for you," I called back to him.

Marcus chuckled.

Our hands full, we made our way back toward the roundhouse.

"Thank you, Queen Boudica," Marcus said as we went.

"For what?"

"For having a care for the animals."

"It is a long ride in the sun. And what of your men? Have you eaten?"

"Your housecarl has seen to us."

I nodded. "Very good. Once the wagon is unloaded, hopefully, we can get the yokes off the creatures, and give them a rest. There is a pasture if there is time."

Marcus laughed a light laugh.

"What is it?"

"We were forced to ride north, Queen Boudica. I am ashamed to admit it. No one wanted to ride with Titus in such a small force into your wilderness. But instead of monsters, we find welcome."

"Remember what I have said," I told him. "That is my best advice to you."

When we rejoined the other men, their leader hurried to take the buckets from me. "Thank you, Queen Boudica."

"Of course. If anyone needs anything else, you need only ask," I said, then made my way back inside.

I found Titus amusing Bec and Bran—or, at least, they were playing the part of being amused—with a coin game.

Balfor was watching from the doorway.

He gestured to Bran with his chin.

I shook my head.

Both of us chuckled.

"Balfor, please ready the conference room. I will advise the Romans to bring in the chests."

"Very well, *Queen* Boudica."

I grinned at him.

"What? You wear it well, Princess," he told me.

I clapped him on the shoulder, then rejoined the others, watching as they played. Bran found himself the loser, again and again, Titus winning the game each time.

"Come, now," my brother said, sitting back. "You must tell me the trick of it. Already, I am five silvers short."

"Never, never," Titus said with a laugh. "It is all sleight of hand, Prince. Ah, here is Queen Boudica."

"Sir," I said gently. "Perhaps it would be wise to unload your cargo. The supplies will be safe in the roundhouse for the night. You have my word. Balfor will see to it. We will prepare a space. You can speak to my brother of it in the morning."

"Your word it is safe within the house, Queen Boudica?"

"Yes. You have my word."

Titus waved over his shoulder to his servant. "Tell the men what the queen has said, then come back. I'm going to bed."

The servant nodded, then ran off.

Bec rose. "Let me see you to your chamber."

Titus turned to Bran and me. "I wish you both a good night. I hope to see King Caturix in the morning."

"I am sure you will," Bran replied.

Titus followed Bec away.

As soon as he left the room, Bran's smile faded. "What an odious man," he whispered.

"You have no idea. But his lips are loose. I learned a lot."

"Such as?"

"The Romans as invading on two fronts. They sent a legion into Regnenses territory."

"By Andraste's toe," Bran cursed.

"Best stay in Andraste's good graces, Brother. No cursing her toe," I said, then sighed. "All right. I'll be back."

"Where are you going now?"

"To see someone far more cantankerous than that dark goddess."

CHAPTER 33

I slipped out of the roundhouse and made my way to Ula's cottage. Bending under the eave, I was about to knock when Ula called, "If you've come with your Roman friends, be off with you."

"I am here with a friend, I think. Not Roman. Greater Iceni. I was hoping you could confirm for me."

There was a ruckus inside, and a moment later, Ula appeared. She was chewing a bite of something. She eyed me up and down as she considered.

"Put a baby in your belly, did he?"

"I think so."

"Best come in," she said, then turned and went back inside, leaving the door open for me.

I slipped into the cottage, closing the door behind me.

Everything was as I'd left it, as if the changing world had no effect on the woman, whereas my whole life had been turned upside down.

"Lie down, then," she said, gesturing to her small cot

as she went to her bench and grabbed some herbs, throwing them in a pot.

"Are you well, Ula?"

"Best as I can be with your brother having bonfires and music every other night. He has half the village celebrating like its Midsummer every day."

"Isn't it good that they're merry, especially in these uncertain times?"

"Uncertain times. So say you, riding into Oak Throne with your Roman friends."

I frowned. "Ula, when we last spoke, there was tension between us. I hate that we left it like that. I am doing the best I can for the Iceni—all of the Iceni."

"Leading Caturix into whatever choices *you* make."

"I'm trying to protect us all."

Ula harrumphed, then set a pot full of herbs to brew.

"Lie back," she said, waggling her finger at me.

I did as she said, noting how uncomfortable her bed was. "No wonder you are prone to moods. Your bed is as lumpy as a turnip sack."

"I am sure you have a fine, big bed in Venta," she snipped at me.

"Why don't you come and see. I would be glad to have you in Venta."

"I doubt you'll listen to me any better there than you do here. Now, be still."

Ula lifted my tunic and then undid the top laces on my trousers, feeling my stomach with her rough hands.

"When did you bleed last?"

"Before Beltane."

She felt around, pressing gently. She nodded as she considered. After a time, she pulled her hands back. "Merry-begot from the feel of it. Should be here near Imbolc."

"Imbolc."

Ula nodded, then went back to her fire.

I sat up, redoing the laces on my pants and adjusting my tunic.

"Thank you, Ula."

She waved her hand dismissively and then stirred the pot hanging over the flames.

I took a seat on a bench opposite her.

Ula said nothing, merely worked.

"Prasutagus had a vision. He saw a girl child."

Ula stilled, then looked into the fire. Her eyes grew drowsy.

I knew the look. She was seeking her own vision in the fire.

"Child of flames... child of vengeance... where you fail, she will succeed," she intoned.

"Fail? Fail at what?"

Ula shook her head, clearing the vision. "It's no matter. The wheel is in motion now. There is nothing that can be done to stop it now. But that is the way of fate. Only the Dark Lady can alter one's course, and she plays her own game." Ula poured the liquid from her pot into a mug and handed it to me. "Drink."

"What is it?"

"Raspberry leaf and other herbs. It will strengthen your womb for that firebrand."

"Did you really see such a child?" I asked, looking back toward the fire. "Such—"

"Strength," Ula interrupted me. "Guile. That is what I saw."

I sipped the hot liquid.

Ula rose and went back to her table, grabbing a bowl. She sat down once more. Within, I saw small pieces of meat and carrots. It was a meager meal. As I watched her eat, I realized the truth. Ula was an old woman. Her time in this world was in its dusk. And like all old women, she felt the discomforts of age. Her meat was cut small so she could chew it more easily. Her carrots were cooked soft and heavy with herbs so she could taste it.

"Ula, in the days to come, you will ask Bran for help if you need anything. Food, firewood, coin. Whatever you need, you will not hesitate to ask for it."

"Don't get sentimental."

"I'm not. It's just..."

Ula paused and looked at me. "Just what?"

I grinned. "It's just that I won't be here to look after you. I don't like you being on your own."

At that, Ula laughed loudly, her tone telling me she found my words absurd. She rose and went back to the table. She began bundling herbs into a cloth satchel. "Drink one cup a day. When this is done, go find raspberry leaf at your markets or ask the druid. It won't be the same. My mix is better, but it will have to do," she said, then turned and handed me a bag.

"Thank you, Ula."

She nodded.

"I... Ula," I said, then paused, feeling the mixed emotions washing through me once more. "Ula, I know what the little people of the hollow hills said. I hear the whispers of the greenwood. But I can only see two choices before us with my own eyes: fight or make peace. King Togodumnus is dead. King Anarevitos of the Cantiaci is dead. The entire south is on fire. I have seen their forces. They are...horrifying, with more pouring into the south as we speak. In my heart, I *want* to fight. I do. I know what Caesar tried to do here." I shook my head. "Pix is angry with me. You are too. I'm trying to be practical, to protect everyone. This is the best way I see to do that. Tell me if I am wrong. There is no one in the world I trust more than you. Tell me."

Ula sat once more, a serious expression on her face. She gazed into the fire. "That is your job. To protect the Iceni," she said, nodding—to herself or to something she saw in the fire, I wasn't sure. After a long time, she gazed up at me. "We cannot stop a storm. I will not chide you, Boudica. You and your druid king are no fools. If what you have seen with your own eyes tells you this is the right step to protect the people, then take it."

"But the signs have been so dark."

"So they have. As you sit in the roundhouse drinking wine with Rome, the land bleeds."

I frowned, a wave of guilt washing over me. After a moment, I said, "Togodumnus and Caratacus had a hand in my father's death. I do not care if they bleed."

Ula nodded. "No. And you should not. But watch these Romans, Boudica. They *will* lie to you. Where you can, do what the greenwood bids of you. Turn your stubbornness on Rome."

I chuckled. "I cannot help but do so. It's my nature to turn it on everyone I meet."

Ula chuckled then sighed. "Life is not meant to be easy, Boudica. It's meant to have meaning. The gods will use you as they see fit, and no amount of tongue-lashing from me or that half-fey warrior woman of yours will change that."

"Yet something tells me you will get in your jibes all the same."

"Bah," Ula said with a laugh. After a moment, she pointed at my belly. "No wine or ale."

"I remembered."

"I would not have my firebrand coming out a halfwit."

"*Your* firebrand?"

Ula laughed.

"Are you telling me I should name her Ula?"

"No," Ula said with a chuckle.

I polished off the tonic and then went to the washing bucket. After scrubbing the cup, I set it aside to dry.

"Thank you, Ula. I should probably go back."

Ula waved her hand dismissively at me.

"Good night, Ula."

"Good night, Boudica," she replied.

Then, on second thought, I bent and kissed her cheek.

"Bah, get out of here," she said, wiping my kiss away with the back of her hand. "That wee babe has you sentimental. Be gone with you."

I laughed. "Good night," I said, then walked outside into the warm summer night.

The mist rising off the river caused a heavy fog bank to envelop the fort. I listened for any sound, any sign of Caturix's return, but it was quiet. A dog barked somewhere in the distance, followed by a baby's cry shortly thereafter. After that, there was nothing save the call of the birds and the croaking of toads.

My hand drifted to my stomach. "Firebrand, eh? Well, come Imbolc, we will see, my sweet, fiery one."

CHAPTER 34

I returned to the roundhouse to find everything quiet. Balfor met me in the main dining hall.

"Your guest is snoring. I can hear him through the door."

I rolled my eyes.

"And the chests are taken care of. I will stay awake waiting for Caturix."

"Thank you, Balfor. Please let me know if you need anything."

"Cidna fixed your room for you as best she could. Riona is at the grove."

"Is everything all right?"

"A bad toe that got worse. Red as a strawberry, it was. Lady Bec sent her on to Dôn after Riona and Ula had an argument."

I laughed. "I'm sorry I missed that."

"Getting waspish in her old age, Ula."

"Speaking of. Will you see to it she has a new bed? She

can have mine or Brenna's if needed. Fresh straw and new linens. She will complain. A lot. Blame me for insisting."

"As you wish, Boudica. I'll send the men to handle it."

"Coward."

Balfor laughed. "Give me all the Romans you want. I'd rather them than Ula's wrath."

At that, we both laughed.

"Good night, Balfor."

"Good night, Boudica."

I slipped down the hall to my familiar chamber. It felt strange to be there. Feeling exhausted, I lay down on my bed. My whole body ached with tiredness. I set my hands on my stomach as I drifted off to sleep, dreaming of the little one growing inside me.

I WOKE IN THE MIDDLE OF THE NIGHT TO THE SOUND OF someone else in the room with me. I opened my eyes to find Pix there.

"Pix," I said groggily.

"Go back to sleep. 'Tis not yet morning."

"Caturix?"

"Taking a rest before seeing your Romans."

"I should speak to him," I said, moving to sit up. My head swam for the effort.

"Be still. He isn't here anyway."

"Not here?"

"Not in the roundhouse."

"Then where—oh."

"Oh," Pix said with a laugh. "Then ye know where he is. Sleep, Strawberry Queen. There will be time to pander to yer Romans in the morning."

"They are not *my* Romans," I replied, unable to hide the annoyance in my voice.

"And yet here they are, under yer roof."

"I thought you said you had forgiven me."

"I have. But I will not let ye forget that yer making a mistake."

At that, I said nothing more. Pix plucked at the strings attached to the doubt in my heart. And they were louder—far louder—than I would have liked.

IT WAS MORNING WHEN I FELT SOMETHING WET SLIDING across my face. Confused, I scrunched up my brow and cracked open my eyes to find Nini staring at me, panting loudly.

Cidna laughed. "I bet Riona never woke you like that."

"And her breath smelled significantly better."

At that, we both laughed.

I sat up slowly.

"Did what I could with your clothes. Not much aside from shaking the wrinkles out of them," she said, gesturing to the gown. "Best I do for myself most days.

Didn't see any spots to scrub out, so I suppose you're good. Why'd Ula give you all that raspberry leaf?" Cidna asked, lifting the sack sitting on a bench near the bed.

"I guess I'll be needing it."

Cidna laughed. "Well, isn't that something? You hear that, Mad Pix? We'll be drowning in babies come winter."

Pix groaned, then rolled over.

"Drowning in babies? What do you mean?"

"You haven't heard yet? You aren't the only woman in this house drinking raspberry-leaf tea. Let me get some pork and eggs on for you, then. If your hunger is anything like Lady Bec's, I'll need a whole hog before it's done."

"Don't forget the Roman's appetite."

"Who can forget about that?" Cidna said, then disappeared.

I rose groggily and redressed in a clean, red tunic, brown leather trousers, and my leather vest. Leaving my spear leaning in the corner, I belted my sword and dagger, pulled on my boots, and headed back to the hall.

There, I found Bec tidying the dining room.

"The Mother's blessings this morning, Priestess," I told her.

"And to you, Princess."

At that, we both chuckled.

"I've recently become aware of a secret," I told Bec.

"Is that so?"

"That there will soon be a princess or prince in this house."

Bec paused. "How do you know? Ula?"

I shook my head. "Cidna."

Bec's brow furrowed.

"Don't be angry. She only told me because I will be bringing a princess of my own into this world."

"Boudica," Bec said excitedly, then set down her pitcher. She pulled me into a hug. "May the Great Mother be thanked for such blessings." She stepped back and studied me. "When?"

"Imbolc, or so Ula predicts. You?"

"Yule," Bec said, her cheeks growing red, revealing that her child had been conceived before she and Bran were wed. "Such strange times to bring a new life into this world. But all the same, I am grateful."

"As am I."

"I should go get Bran out of bed before the Roman wakes."

"I wouldn't expect Titus to wake until midmorning."

"Thank the gods," Bec replied with a laugh. "But let me get Bran all the same."

I sat down at the table, poured myself a water, and began nibbling on the bread.

"Psh," Cidna hissed, waving at me as she arrived with a fresh basket of bread. "That's from last night."

I didn't dare tell her I could hardly tell the difference.

"I'll take that to those soldiers. Here. Eat this. And I'll have Albie bring you some tea. Ah, here is our king. May the Shining Ones bless you this morning, King Caturix," Cidna said, giving my brother a curtsey.

"Cidna," he replied.

Cidna scooped up the basket of old bread, then disappeared to the back.

"Boudica," Caturix greeted me as he pulled off his gloves. "Well met."

"And you, Brother."

"Thank you for sending Pix."

"Of course."

"She talked my ear off from Stonea to Oak Throne, telling me why we were making bad decisions," he said, chuckling lightly to himself as he poured himself an ale. "She almost convinced me. Until I saw those chests."

"They are very convincing."

"Let's hope they are worth their weight in promises."

"May the gods hear your words, Brother," I said, lifting my cup to him.

"What news?"

I told my brother the news Titus had shared. The more I talked, the more Caturix scowled.

"They will have the whole of the south in their hands," he said darkly.

"Everything except our little corner of the world."

Caturix frowned, then leaned toward me. "The triumvirate has their doubts. Already, King Dumnocoveros and King Dumnovellaunus encourage Melusine's father to reconsider."

I frowned. If the north suddenly aligned against the Romans, we would be in trouble. "If they do, they will need to bring the Brigantes and Parisii along with them."

"They seek to drag me into the conflict with them."

"Do not, Brother."

"Despite Pix's best intentions and Volisios's wavering, I

have not forgotten whose hands have my father's blood on them."

Bran and Bec returned shortly after that, and the conversation turned to less stressful topics, such as sharing the news of all of the impending arrivals—including Melusine's.

"The future of the Iceni is unfolding all at once," Bec said. "May the gods be kind to us."

"And give us wisdom," Caturix added.

Titus rose shortly thereafter. After eating half a hog's worth of meat, he and Caturix disappeared into the meeting room, Bran along with him.

Bec, exhausted from dealing with Titus, went to lie down. I took the opportunity to make my way back into the village.

I had barely made it to the tree when the children found me.

"Boudica," Eiwyn called, waving to me as she, Birgit, and Phelan raced down the road toward me. "Boudica! Wait for us."

I stopped and let them catch up.

"Boudica," Eiwyn said, her eyes wide. "Were those Romans with you?"

"They were."

"Their men's legs were showing!" Eiwyn exclaimed. "They were wearing dresses," she said, then laughed hysterically.

"How can anyone be afraid of men who wear dresses into battle?" Birgit asked with a laugh.

"Didn't you see their fine weapons?" Phelan asked the

girls. "Dresses or not, they are warriors. What do they want here?"

"To speak to Bran and Caturix."

"Why? Will they make war here?" Phelan asked nervously.

I could see the shadows lingering behind his eyes. His father had died in Saenunos's coup. No doubt, the pain of war and loss was still fresh.

"No, the Northern and Greater Iceni will make peace with the Romans."

"Oh, that's good," Eiwyn said in relief. "They will leave us alone, then?"

"That is their promise."

"Are they liars?" Birgit asked. "My eldest sister Edwara makes many promises, but she is a liar."

"Time will tell," I replied. "Now, you must accept my apologies. How many times I have ridden from here to there and brought you nothing. I didn't forget this time," I said, reaching into my satchel. From within, I pulled out a sack of candied nuts. "They are roasted with maple syrup until they cook crispy. A merchant in Venta sells them. Will you share with the other children?"

"Of course," Eiwyn said. "Give them to me. I will round up the others."

"I'm glad to see you all," I said, hugging each one—a trick I always used to ensure they were all well-fed and not skin and bones. After I hugged Phelan, I held his shoulders. "Is your mother well? Do you need anything?"

"She is well enough."

"And the shop?"

"My uncle has taken over."

"Run on," I told Eiwyn and Birgit. "Phelan will catch up."

"Don't eat them without me," he called to the girls who sprinted away.

I dipped into my vest and pulled out a small bag of silver. I handed it to the boy. "Take this to your mother. Tell her it is a gift from me to her, and she is not to say no. If you need anything, ever, tell Bran and Bec. They will look after you."

"All right," Phelan said, putting the sack in his pocket.

"May Bright Bel watch over you," I said, kissing him on the forehead.

"And you, Boudica," he said, then ran off. "Eiwyn! Eiwyn! Wait for me."

I chuckled, hoping my silver made its way to Phelan's mother before it was lost from his pocket during his adventures.

Turning, I made my way through the village until I heard the familiar bleating of goats and a woman's voice as she chattered sweetly to them. Not long after, I caught the sound of an excited squeal. I made my way to Kennocha's house. Outside, I found Kennocha and Mara tending to the goats, Mara squatting as she petted a newborn.

"Boudica," Kennocha said, clapping her hands. "How good to see you. Look, Mara, Boudica is here."

"Dis. Dis," Mara told me, pointing at the baby goat. The child held onto the fence with one hand, her knees wobbling.

"Look at her stand!" I said happily.

"And walk, too," Kennocha said, bending. "Mara, come to me, my little princess."

"Dis. Dis," she told her mother, her words more of a spitty exhale than actual words.

"I see. Now, come. Show Boudica how you can walk."

At that, Mara left the side of the pen and walked on her wobbly legs to her mother. When she reached Kennocha, the woman scooped her up, setting a kiss on her cheek, then joined me.

"A good number born this summer," Kennocha said, pointing to the goats. "And those three were born yesterday. It will be a good market this year."

"You are well, then?"

She smiled lightly, her lips pulling with a light tremor in the corner. "Well enough. But today, we are happy. We had a visitor last night. What more can we ask for?"

"I'm glad," I said, tickling Mara's chin. "How big she is. And how sweet," I said, kissing her on her hand, making her laugh.

"Is all well in Venta?" Kennocha asked.

"With Prasutagus and my new home, all is well. As for the rest…"

Kennocha nodded. "There was much talk of the Romans who arrived yesterday. Who is that man?"

"A Roman politician. He came as a messenger from their general."

"Will war come here?"

"Not if we can help it. We are working hard to form alliances that will protect our sovereignty."

Kennocha nodded. "Many are worrying there will be a battle."

I took Mara from Kennocha's arms. "Not if we can help it. We would not see any more Iceni blood shed over other men's ambitions," I said, making faces at Mara as I spoke.

"Then may the gods watch over you and help you make the right choices."

"May the gods watch over us all. Especially, sweet little girls," I said, giving Mara one more kiss. Once more, I dipped into my satchel, pulling out a small soft toy for the child. Made in the likeness of a goat, but with soft rabbit fur, I had spotted the toy in the market. "Here you are, sweet Mara," I told Mara, handing her the gift.

"Boudica..." Kennocha chided me, but I silenced her with a look.

"Oooh," the girl said, rubbing it against her cheek again and again.

I grinned at Mara.

"Will you be in Oak Throne long?" Kennocha asked.

I shook my head. "If I can convince the Roman, we will leave before the midday meal. Speaking of which, I should go back." I stroked Mara's cheek once more. "She really is such a pretty thing. I see you in the shape of her chin. Maybe a little of Brenna in the cheeks. But the eyes and brow are all Caturix."

Kennocha smiled. "Yes, I thought the same. I wish you well, Boudica. And a safe journey home."

"Take care of your mother, little one," I told Mara, kissing her once more, before handing her back to her mother.

With that, I left them.

For the hundredth time, I wished things had been different. I wished Kennocha was at Caturix's side. Melusine was sweet and charming, but a practical voice, such as Kennocha's, would serve as an excellent guide to my brother right now. And married to Kennocha, I would not have to worry about the Coritani trying to influence Caturix's choices. Right now, the Northern and Greater Iceni were in agreement. What would happen if the Coritani truly decided to stand against Rome? Caturix, married to Melusine, would be stuck in the middle. I only hoped his hatred toward Caratacus and Togodumnus would carry him through. While I did wish things were different, I felt no ill will toward Melusine. She was not at fault. In fact, she had my pity. She deserved more than she got with my brother. As her father's daughter, she'd become a pawn—a fate Brenna and I had barely missed.

Turning, I made my way back to the roundhouse. With a bit of luck, I could convince Titus to return to the comforts of Venta sooner than later. And if I couldn't convince him, I was certain Cidna's cooking could.

Pasting on my best smile, I made my way back to the Romans.

CHAPTER 35

As luck would have it, by the time I returned to the roundhouse, I noticed that the Roman soldiers were already preparing to depart. Squelching the hesitation I felt, I joined them.

"Marcus," I called to the young man who had helped me with the mules last night. "Are you planning to leave?"

"Queen Boudica," he said, giving me a short bow. "Please direct your inquiry to Antonius," he said, gesturing to another in their party.

"I understand," I said, giving the man a soft smile that he returned with his eyes only.

I joined the soldier. "Soldier, are you preparing to return south?"

"Yes, Queen Boudica."

"Very well. I shall prepare to ride with you."

"Queen," he said, giving me a brief nod.

I made my way back inside. Within, I heard Titus and Bran laughing loudly.

"You should have seen the size of his nose," Titus was saying, his eyes wet with tears. "The entire theater erupted in laughter."

My gaze flicked to Bec, who was smiling politely.

Caturix had a strange expression on his face. I wasn't sure if he was suffering from stomach cramps or trying to look jovial.

"Oh, Queen Boudica, Queen Boudica," Titus said, wiping a tear from his eyes. "I was just telling Prince Bran about a play I watched in Rome. We have a great number of theaters. I always try to watch everything new. I will tell you all about it on the ride back to Venta. I am told we can reach the city today if we leave within the hour."

"So we can. I will make ready."

"Very good. Very good," Titus said.

"Let me help you," Bec told me, and the pair of us made our way back to my chamber.

"Where is Pix?" I asked, finding the chamber empty.

"I asked her to prepare your horses," she said, then groaned. "Ugh, that man. What vulgar things he shares in common company. I am glad Bran can keep him amused. I bit my tongue more than once."

"They are a different people, that is certain."

"Yes, they are," Bec replied tartly.

I quickly packed up my things and grabbed my spear.

"I hate to see you leave," Bec told me. "You've only just arrived. We haven't even had the chance to complain about our pregnancy ailments together yet."

"Dizziness," I said.

"Vomiting," Bec replied.

At that, we both chuckled.

"I hope to see you again soon. Under better conditions," Bec told me.

"And you...Priestess, Princess, and Sister."

"I like that. Sister."

"Sister," I said, then pulled her into a hug.

"Don't poke me with that thing," she said, moving my arm to tilt the spear away.

"Don't worry, Gaheris taught me where the pointy end was."

At that, Bec chuckled.

Together, we made our way back to the hall.

Titus was making his farewells to Bran and Caturix.

Cidna joined us, passing me a small satchel. "Romans are supplied. This is for you," she said.

"Why are you giving me mine separately. You didn't poison them, did you?"

"Crossed my mind," she told me with a laugh.

I kissed Cidna on the cheek and then bent to pat Nini. "Be a good girl," I told her, then turned back to my Roman guest.

"Come along, Queen Boudica. We are traveling more lightly now, but it's good if we waste no more time," the man told me.

I said nothing, merely followed along behind him.

Caturix gently took my arm. "Send word if you hear anything new, and I shall do the same."

I nodded.

Outside, I found Pix waiting. She lingered with Cai,

leaning against her horse as the pair chatted. Druda stood waiting for me.

Along with them was Moritasgus, the stablemaster. He waited with a basket at his feet.

"What is this?" Titus asked.

"I had Balfor make inquiries," Bran told the man. "There was a litter of pups in the village. They are ready to go. Please, choose whichever one you like. It is my gift to you."

Bec opened her mouth to speak but closed it.

"I say," Titus said, going to Moritasgus. "Thank you, Prince Bran! Thank you, indeed. What an excellent gift," he said, then looked over the puppies. "These small things shall become the great giants like you own?"

Bran nodded. "They do."

"They are very good dogs," Moritasgus told Titus. "They train up fast with the proper attention."

I joined Titus and Moritasgus, bending to look at the hamper full of puppies.

"You choose for me, Queen Boudica. You will know which to take," Titus told me.

My feelings were conflicted. "Hmm," I mused. "I think you should take a male. He will be loyal to you, go every-where you go. Everyone will be amazed to see him at your side. I am sure many will come to you for siring. If you treat him gently, he would be a good guard dog for you. And if he is treated with kindness, he will protect you with his life."

"Oh, excellent. Excellently thought, Queen Boudica. Yes, let me have one for just such a purpose. They will think I've returned from Britannia with a small pony at my side!"

I chuckled, then plucked a healthy-looking boy from the basket.

"And I will have this one," I said, lifting a sleepy, sweet-looking boy. "As a gift to the general. Will you take him to General Plautius for me?" I asked Titus.

"Indeed! He will be pleased with such a gift, Queen Boudica. Very pleased."

I stroked the sleeping pup's ear. "Sweet thing. And they are weened enough?" I asked Moritasgus.

Moritasgus nodded. "They are, but they would do better on a diet of soft meat for a time."

"You will see to that," Titus told his servant, then motioned for the boy to take the puppy I had chosen for Titus.

"Queen Boudica, shall I take the other one as well?" the servant asked, reaching out to me for the pup. When I met the servant's gaze, I felt relief. While Titus would pay the dog little attention aside from strutting about with him, his servant had tender eyes.

"No, I will hold him for a time. He's too sleepy to let him be jostled around in a wooden pen."

The young man nodded.

Moritasgus helped the servant attach the pup's carrier to the back of his horse while Titus made ready to depart.

Turning, I met Bran's gaze. "That was thoughtful of you."

"I'm trying a bit of your diplomacy, *Queen* Boudica. I only hope I am not sending the dog to a fighting ring."

"I think Boudica has nipped that inclination," Bec replied.

"I'm sure it will be worth more in bragging rights," I said, kissing the pup I held on the head. "I'm sorry it was a quick visit."

"Queen Boudica," Titus called, waving that he was ready to go.

"Here. I will hold him while you mount," Caturix said, reaching for the puppy.

We went to Druda, who eyed the puppy curiously while I slipped onto the horse. Pulling a scarf from my satchel, I fashioned a sling, then gestured for Caturix to hand the puppy up to me.

I settled it in like a baby.

Caturix laughed. "Some things never change. May Epona watch over you, Sister."

"And you."

With that, I turned to Pix, who gave Cai a surprisingly passionate kiss goodbye and then mounted her own horse. I gave Cai a small wave.

He returned the gesture bashfully.

I reined in beside Titus. "Ready?"

Titus chuckled when he saw the puppy. "What an unusual creature you are, Queen Boudica," he said, then turned to my brothers. "Be well, King Caturix, Prince Bran, Lady Bec. And thank you, Prince Bran," he called, then tapped his heels against his horse.

The guard moved off.

I gave my family one last wave, then followed.

Once more, we made our way through Oak Throne toward the gates.

When we neared the lane down which sat Ula's cottage, I spied the old woman sitting on a woodpile at a house at the end of the lane.

I lifted my hands to my forehead in respect.

She waved dismissively at me but gave me a warm glance and a nod all the same.

And with that, we left Oak Throne behind.

Me, an Iceni Princess and Queen, escorting the eagle through my lands.

CHAPTER 36

We arrived in Venta late that night. At the king's compound, Prasutagus and Galvyn greeted us.

"Welcome returns," King Prasutagus called, then joined me, giving me a hand. "And who is the passenger, my queen?" he asked, looking at the little pup who had fallen asleep once more.

"Bran gifted one to Titus. I selected this one to be sent as a gift to the general," I said, handing Prasutagus the sleepy puppy so I could get down.

"That was thoughtful of you," Prasutagus said, a jealous tone in his voice.

"The Romans have never seen dogs like ours before."

Prasutagus nodded. "It's a good idea. I am sure the general will appreciate the gesture."

The servants came to collect Druda and the others' horses.

Pix, who was carrying the other puppy under her arm, reached for the one Prasutagus held.

Titus's servant followed along behind her.

"I'll show this boy what to do so they don't die before they get where they're going. Come on, Rome," Pix told the boy, the pair of them disappearing with the pups.

"How did it go?" Prasutagus asked in a low tone.

"Caturix was late, but Bran kept Titus entertained."

Prasutagus laughed. "I was not thinking of the Romans. How did it go with the wise woman?" he asked, setting a gentle hand on my waist.

I grinned at him. "Imbolc," I said. "And all seems well."

"Good," Prasutagus replied.

"This one will be joined by one of Bran's and Bec's, as well as one of Caturix's and Melusine's."

"May the Great Mother be thanked. Is that so?"

I nodded. "We will make our prayers to her. In these uncertain days, the Mother still sheds her grace on us."

Behind us, Galvyn led Titus back into the roundhouse.

"We will be rid of him tomorrow," Prasutagus said.

"May the gods hear your words. There is other news," I said, then told my husband what Titus had revealed about a force sailing from Gaul with Verica's son and another Roman officer into Regnenses territory.

"The general said nothing of another force."

"Vian saw it on their maps. Naturally, they mistrust us. We mistrust them."

"That is true. Though I am sure, you will have the general won over in no time."

Again, I heard that hint of suspicion in Prasutagus's voice. "Jealousy is not flattering on you, Husband."

"Aye, Boudica. It's not you. It's just... I don't trust his *friendliness* toward you. I'm sorry. I truly am. Let's get you inside. You will be tired from the long ride, and here I am interrogating you. Not only do you suffer, but so does my tiny baby girl."

"A firebrand."

Prasutagus raised an eyebrow at me.

"Ula called her a firebrand, an avenger."

"Avenging what?"

"Maybe it is better if we don't know."

PRASUTAGUS AND I SPENT THE NIGHT ENTERTAINING TITUS, who seemed to have enjoyed Bran's company far more than ours. The man headed off to bed early with the intention to ride south at first light.

"I need to return to the general to report on the excellent reception I have received from both the Northern and Greater Iceni—and the great care Queen Boudica has bestowed upon me," he said, patting my hand. "Now, I must sleep off all this fine wine to be ready by morning," he'd said, then went to bed.

"I am glad he is done with our wine," Prasutagus told me. "Betha informed me this morning that we were down to our last two flagons. What is rare to us, he drank like water."

We both laughed.

"Queen Boudica," Brita said, curtseying as she entered the hall. "I have poured a bath for you if you are ready."

I looked to Prasutagus. "Go on," he told me. "I will check on Nella and Ginerva and discover what Ardra has done with Artur. I haven't seen the boy the whole day."

"Very well," I said, kissing my husband on the cheek, then followed the maid.

My bedchamber was lit with warm light from the braziers, the steam and herbs in the hot bath filling the room with a gentle perfume. I opened my satchel and handed Brita the bag of herbs therein. "Can you help me with a draft of this? Just one small spoonful of herbs in a small pot of water. I should drink a mug daily."

"Of course," Brita said, then got to work while I disrobed and slipped into the washing basin.

"Was everything all right while I was gone?"

"My uncle is helping me settle in. Artur and I spent some time with your bird. We moved Morfran's perch to Artur's chamber. He is very good with the creature."

"I'm glad to hear they like one another. I'm afraid I neglect Morfran."

"Artur is thrilled to look after him. The priestess Ardra... she is Artur's tutor?" Brita asked.

"Yes."

"She seems very protective of him."

"Why do you say that?"

"It's only... She didn't want to leave Artur alone with

me. When we were together, he seemed guarded in his speech. I don't know. It just struck me as strange."

"Perhaps she is protective of him due to Queen Esu's death."

"Yes, my uncle said the same."

"You mentioned it to Galvyn?" I asked, trying to read Brita's expression. Something must have struck her as odd since she'd brought it up to Galvyn and me.

"I did. As I said, it was probably nothing, it was just that her manner was so... Well, if I didn't know better, I would say she was acting like a jealous girlfriend," Brita said with a laugh. "How old is Artur?"

"Ten."

Brita shrugged. "The druids can be strange people. I don't know."

I frowned. "Something about her strikes me as off as well. You are not wrong to question, Brita. If you see anything else, don't hesitate to mention it."

"I'm sure it was nothing. Please, take your rest. Only the Mother knows what you have endured since you left."

"You don't want to know."

At that, Brita laughed. "Of that, I am certain."

I closed my eyes and let the water envelop me.

I must have drifted off to sleep because soon, I heard waves on the shore.

From the sound of the surf and the scent of the air, I knew I was at the Wash.

"Asleep again, Selkie?" Gaheris called sweetly.

I felt a strange ache in my stomach, a pain that I could not identify.

"You wore me out," I told him with a grin.

"With what?"

"All the frolicking."

"Your days of frolicking are over, Selkie," Gaheris replied, but there was a dark tone in his voice.

"Gaheris?" I asked, but when I opened my eyes, he was gone. Instead, I was lying on the beach as it looked after the incident, after he had died.

There was blood in the water. It rolled in crimson waves.

Overhead an eagle cried so loudly it made me shudder and then jump.

The water splashed, and I felt a pain in my side.

"Boudica," Brita said, taking my arm. "Be careful."

"What..."

"You fell asleep in the tub. I didn't have the heart to wake you."

"Oh," I replied, pulling my knees to my chest as I tried to shake the dream away.

"Bad dream?" Brita asked.

I nodded.

How beautifully the dream had started. For a moment, *just a moment*, Gaheris had been alive again.

"Your drink is ready. I don't know these herbs," Brita said, sniffing the mug before handing me the drink. The steaming liquid smelled sweet. I wrapped my hands around the mug, trying to warm them as a shudder went through my body.

"The water grew cool. Let me add some warm water to reheat it," Brita said.

I sipped the liquid as I stared at the wall, wishing the image of the bloody water away. Only when Brita returned with the warm water was I able to shake myself from the trance.

"It's raspberry leaf and other herbs. The king and I will welcome a child come Imbolc. Please, tell no one. Not yet."

"Queen Boudica! What welcome news. May the Great Mother bless you."

"Thank you, Brita."

"I am quite deft with the sewing needle. Don't worry. I will be able to make you new dresses as you...progress," she said with a giggle.

"Progress. I like that word," I said with a laugh.

Brita then worked on washing my hair while I scrubbed up. When I was done, Brita fixed my hair and then helped me from the bath. After I changed, I crawled into bed feeling exhausted. Who knew idle chatter could wear out a person?

"Rest, Queen Boudica. I'll see everything else is settled. Good night."

"Good night."

I lay there resting, my eyes open.

I did not want to dream again.

"Ah, Gaheris," I whispered into the darkness. "Why did you have to go?"

CHAPTER 37

I t's odd when you sleep so deeply that you are unaware of the passage of time. In what seemed like moments later, I felt Brita shake my shoulder.

"My queen? Queen Boudica? Prasutagus asked me to fetch you. The Romans are readying to leave."

"But it's night."

Brita laughed. "You slept the whole night, my queen. It is morning."

Confused, I sat up. Brita had laid out my clothes, leaving me the options between a deep blue dress or trousers and tunic. Sensing that I would not be riding or doing much of anything that day—feeling a deep weariness inside me—I settled on the dress.

I changed quickly into the blue gown.

Brita quickly pinned my hair up, adorning my locks with a gold horse hairpin.

When I was ready, I made my way to the dining hall but found it empty.

"They're outside," Newt told us. "I think they're leaving."

"Banshees be cursed," I whispered under my breath, then hurried to the courtyard.

There, I found the men loading up the mule wagon with some supplies. I saw many baskets filled with furs, cloths, silver trinkets, swords, and more. Titus, it seemed, was taking some of the Greater Iceni's finest goods back with him...including the pups. The soldiers had placed the wooden pen in the wagon.

"Fetch two blankets. Quickly," I told Brita, then went to Titus. Prasutagus stood with him. "Titus," I called politely. "You must forgive me. I'm afraid yesterday's long ride tired me more than I expected."

"It's still early, Queen Boudica. Still early. Prasutagus and I went to the market. So many goodly items for sale. But Rome never rests, so we must set off."

"Do you have everything you need?"

"Indeed. And your kitchens supplied the men with ample food for the trip."

"Then I wish you a safe journey. May your gods watch over you, and our gods give you safe passage."

At that, he laughed. "For that, I thank you. My men jump at every sound in the woods. They believe your forests are filled with cursed spirits and that your druids can cause their skin to turn inside out, fall off, or some other superstitious nonsense. I never listen to what the soldiers prattle on about. No. No. As I have told them, Britons are people no different from ourselves. They are people. Just different looks, different clothes, different languages. In the end, we are all just people. I know some in Rome think you all wild barbarians, but my father was a good soldier and a wit. He always taught me better. I do take after him," he said, then waved to his servant to help him mount.

Brita returned a moment later with the blankets.

"I wish you well, Queen Boudica, King Prasutagus. We shall see you again soon," Titus said, then waved to his soldiers to depart.

Hurrying, I turned and went to Marcus and the other men standing nearest the wagon.

"Soldiers," I said. "Please. The pups should have some shade overhead and something to sleep on in the pen. May I?" I asked, and not waiting for an answer, stepped onto the side of the wagon, getting closer to the pen, all while cursing the skirts of my dress.

"Queen Boudica," Marcus said, stepped closer, his arms outstretched in fear I would fall.

"Ah, here you are," I told the puppies. After arranging the pen so it was half-covered with the blanket, I nimbly opened it and slipped the blanket inside for them to sleep on. I gave them both a quick pat. "Be well, little ones. No bear fighting. May Epona watch over you," I said, then latched the pen once more and then moved to climb down.

This time, I held out my hand to Marcus. The soldier helped me down.

"Make sure they get water throughout the day, or they will perish on the road."

He grinned at me. "We will see to it, Queen Boudica."

"I have your promise?"

He nodded, then pulled back his hand and bowed to me.

"You men. Catch up," one of the Roman soldiers shouted to the men with the wagon.

"We must go," Marcus said.

I nodded, then stepped back. "Marcus... If the woods whisper to you, whisper back that you are a friend. The trees will listen."

He smiled at me, then the wagon pulled out, the soldiers walking along beside it.

"Will they walk all the way back to their camp?" a voice asked from beside me.

I turned to find Artur there. "Yes. Roman soldiers are used to walking far distances."

"They were very nice puppies."

"So they were. Shall I get you one the next time I go to Oak Throne?"

Artur considered a moment. "No. I'm happy to look after Morfran."

The bird, who had been resting on Artur's arm, squawked at the sound of his name.

"Smart bird," I said, stroking his feathers.

We watched until Titus's party left the king's compound. A contingent of Greater Iceni soldiers followed behind them, no doubt ensuring they left Venta unharried.

The gates swung closed once more.

Prasutagus stood at the center of the square watching them—and then watching the space they had just occupied. He stood there for a long time.

"What do you think he is thinking?" I asked Artur, gesturing to my husband.

Artur considered. "Prasutagus is a good king. He is thinking about his people and his family."

"Yes," I said. "He always has a care for us. No doubt you are right."

Morfran cawed then lifted off, flying in the direction that the Romans had taken. The bird disappeared over the wall and into the city.

"Queen Boudica," a soft voice said, joining us.

I turned to find the novice, Ardra.

"Ardra," I said.

She gave me a tight smile and then turned to Artur. "Come, Artur. We will walk to Arminghall this morning. We can stop by the King Stone, if you like," she told him with a bright smile.

"Have you asked the king's permission?" I inquired.

"I am a druid, Queen Boudica. Naturally, I can take Artur to the holy places. And the King Stone is one of Artur's favorite spots."

"You are a novice, Ardra, and Artur is Prasutagus's son."

"*Prasutagus's* son. I see. In that case, I will ask Artur's *father*," she said, then motioned to the boy. "Come, let's ask your parent."

With that, the pair departed.

I opened my mouth to speak but stopped short.

I had not meant it like that. Artur was my son now too. It was only that Prasutagus was particular about where Artur went during these strange times. He would not want

Artur wandering about, with or without a druid. I was not trying to say I wasn't his mother—I *was* his mother by marriage. Ardra had twisted my words, and in so doing, made sure that Artur felt that I didn't care for him, didn't see him as part of my family.

I watched as the pair approached Prasutagus.

Ardra spoke to my husband.

Beside her, Artur kicked at the stones on the ground. Even from this distance, I could see the pained expression on his face.

A few moments later, Artur and Ardra departed, exiting the gates of the king's compound. Ardra took Artur's hand. The two of them disappeared into the city.

Frustrated with the novice, I turned and went back inside.

I would have words with that girl when she returned—druid or not.

CHAPTER 38

L ater that night, when we gathered for the evening meal, I found Artur but not Ardra.

"Is Ardra not joining us this evening?" I asked Ansgar.

"Ardra will stay with the others at King's Wood for the next few days. Much work is to be done with the herb harvest, and my novice offered to help."

I turned to Artur. "Did you enjoy your visit to Arming-hall today?"

Artur nodded but didn't look up at me.

Prasutagus gave me a questioning look, but I said nothing more.

The meal passed with idle talk, mostly the others commenting on Titus's tableside manners, then we all departed.

It was not until later that night, when we were in the meeting room alone together, that Prasutagus asked, "Is anything the matter? At mealtime, I sensed some tension."

"Ardra..." I said. "I keep getting the sense she is trying to drive a wedge between Artur and me. Today, she twisted my words. I don't know. I don't trust her. I think there is more here than her being protective."

Prasutagus sat back in his seat as he considered. "I will speak to Artur."

"Thank you, my love," I told him.

Prasutagus took my hand and pulled me toward him. I sat down on his lap. "And how is our other wee one?" he asked, touching my stomach. "Your appetite matched that of my best warriors tonight."

I laughed. "I even held myself back for fear everyone else would go hungry."

Prasutagus and I both laughed.

"The others will see soon enough. Come Imbolc, the prince or princess of the Greater Iceni will be here."

"You're having a child?" a voice asked from the door.

We both turned to find Artur there. We must not have heard him over our laughter. Morfran, sitting on the boy's shoulder, cawed at us in annoyance.

"Artur," Prasutagus said with a smile. "Come. Join us. We have good news to share."

Artur stared at us. "You're having a child?"

"We are. Soon, you will have a younger brother or sister."

"No, I won't. I won't. You will have a child, and I will have no one," Artur said, then ran off.

I rose quickly. Prasutagus and I both hurried after him.

"Artur," Prasutagus called.

The front door of the roundhouse banged open and closed.

Prasutagus and I followed not far behind.

When we arrived, I saw Morfran flying off, but there was no sign of Artur.

"Which way did Artur go?" Prasutagus asked the guards.

"Toward the stables, King Prasutagus."

I moved to go that way, but Prasutagus stayed my arm. "Let me. I think it will go better if I go alone."

"Are you certain?"

He nodded.

I sighed heavily.

Prasutagus kissed me on the forehead, then went off in the direction of the stables.

Feeling miserable, I headed back inside and went to my bedchamber. That was the worst way for him to learn, especially after today. Ardra was poisoning the child against me. But learning like that had not helped anything.

Sighing, I lay down on the bed and closed my eyes.

I'm sorry, Esu. I'm trying. I'm really trying.

IT WAS LATE THAT NIGHT WHEN PRASUTAGUS RETURNED.

I had fallen asleep waiting for him.

He crept into the room quietly, but I woke all the same.

"I'm sorry," Prasutagus whispered. "I was trying not to make noise."

"No. It's all right. I was waiting for you. Did you find him?"

"I did."

"Is he... Is he all right?"

"As best as he can be. I think he is reassured that you and I having a child changes nothing between him and me. But Boudica...today, when he and Ardra went to Arminghall, what did you say, exactly?"

I knew it. "I asked Ardra if she had checked with you to ensure it was all right for Artur to go. I told her she should ask his father. Ardra made it sound like I was shoving him off, like he was nothing to me. I had not meant it like that at all. It's just that I know you are particular about where he goes. Especially now."

"Yes, you are right about that. I hesitated to let her take him," he said, then paused a long moment. "Boudica, you are welcome to make decisions for his care. I trust your judgment. I understand why you asked Ardra to consult me, but Artur did not see it like that."

"That is because of Ardra. There would have been no confusion had she not needled me on the topic. I didn't want to agree to something I knew you would be cautious about."

Prasutagus nodded. "Yes, it appears to have been a misunderstanding. I did try to calm Artur's worries. Perhaps, in a day or so, approach him once more."

I sighed heavily. Maybe my word choice had been

wrong, but my intention was not. I needed to be more careful. "All right."

"Don't think on it more. It was just a confusion. Rest, my sweet wife," he said, kissing me on the forehead. "I have something I forgot to attend to. I'll be back in a while."

"Anything I can help with?"

Prasutagus chuckled. "No. Not unless you want to join Galvyn and me in a discussion about the privy."

"Ah. Yes. Good night, then."

Prasutagus laughed. "Good night."

When I turned to sleep, I found rest hard to come by. Maybe I *had* chosen my words poorly. Perhaps Ardra was right to be protective of Artur. I needed to be more cautious of the child's feelings. Even a misplaced word could hurt. I knew that from my own experience. I turned in my bed, and turned, and turned. It felt like hours had passed. Finally, I got up.

Padding softly down the hall, I quietly opened the door to Artur's bedchamber. The boy was sleeping within. Morfran had tucked his head under his wing to sleep for the night. He peered at me with one beady eye but didn't make a sound.

The night air had grown cool.

Artur must have turned in his sleep, shedding off his coverlets. I pulled them across him once more.

"Thank you," he whispered sleepily.

"You're welcome, sweet boy," I said, gently rubbing his back.

He opened his eyes just a crack to look at me.

"Boudica..." he whispered.

I adjusted the covers once more, tucking him in. "You are dear to me, Artur. I am sorry for any misunderstanding," I said, then leaned down and placed a kiss on his head. "Good night."

"Good night," he whispered, and as he turned to sleep again, I saw a soft smile on his lips.

Feeling like a ton of stone had lifted from me, I turned and left his room and went back to bed.

And this time, I slept.

CHAPTER 39

The following weeks passed with a painful lack of news. Slowly, messengers began to arrive, reporting of Rome's advances. King Verica and the Roman forces were retaking the Atrebates' land, including the Atrebates' capital of Calleva Atrebatum, and pushing back against Catuvellauni resistance.

Caturix had received word from King Volisios. Caratacus had reached out to the triumvirate for support once more. For now, the Coritani declined. They saw what was happening and grew anxious about supporting the Catuvellauni king. With Anarevitos's and Togodumnus's heads on spikes, it was not hard to see how they came to that conclusion. Caratacus was rumored to have fled to the far reaches of Catuvellauni territory.

Soon, word came that the Romans were preparing for a final push to retake Camulodunum, the heart of Trinovantes territory.

"Something is happening," Prasutagus said, reading

the message he'd received. "The Roman Emperor is in Gaul with an impressive force, his own large guard. They are preparing to sail across the channel. The majority of the Roman forces are converging on Camulodunum."

"Why there?" I asked. "Why not in Calleva Atrebatum with King Verica?"

"Calleva Atrebatum is King Verica's and his son's. The Trinovantes capital belongs to a very absent Aedd Mawr."

"You think Rome will make Camulodunum their own?"

"Aedd Mawr's grandson is just a boy…who has been raised in Rome. Yes, that is exactly what I think. Camulodunum is Trinovantes. But in reality, it will be Rome in all but name."

Prasutagus tapped the scroll on the table as he considered.

I stared at the scroll as he tapped and considered. The Trinovantes were about to become Rome. What did that mean for their people? And for us?

"What do we do?" I asked, feeling my heart beating loudly in my chest.

After a long moment, Prasutagus turned to me. "We wait. We have given our word to the general and to Rome. Now, we must keep true to it. We wait."

The waiting did not take long. A month after Prasutagus heard the news of the Roman Emperor in Gaul, a winded Newt found us working in the fields to the north of the city, expanding what would soon be our new marketplace. There, Prasutagus worked with the men building a new corral for cattle while I sat on the back of

the wagon and tried—and failed—not to eat all the straw-
berries I had bought in the market for Prasutagus and me.
I was sitting, my hand on my rounding stomach, when
Newt arrived. He ran to Prasutagus.

Feeling sorry to have to get up, I took my strawberry
basket with me to see what was the matter.

"They are riding through the city toward the king's
house right now," the breathless boy said. "The guards
sent me."

"Thank you, Newt," Prasutagus told the boy.

Shirtless and covered in dirt and sweat, my husband
spoke briefly to the others before grabbing his tunic and
joining me.

"Do we know who?" I asked.

Prasutagus shook his head. We went to the wagon
where I'd been sitting. Prasutagus dipped a cloth into a
water bucket and washed his face and body before pulling
on his tunic.

"Hold out your hands," I said, then lifted a ladle of
water and poured it over his dirty fingers.

Prasutagus scrubbed the dirt away. By the look on his
face, I could tell that his mind was preoccupied. His brow
scrunched up, his eyebrows nearly meeting.

"Sometimes, I think you may be Artur's father," I said.
"No one can scowl as much as that boy. And yet..."

Prasutagus looked up at me and gave me a soft smile.
"I'm sorry. It's just... I sense a problem about to unfold,
and I am not eager to hear about it. I'd much rather spend
the rest of the day digging fence post holes and watching
my strawberry queen eat berries. By the by, your lips..."

"Red? That's good. They will think I've taken on the Roman fashion and painted my face."

"You? Never. War symbols in woad, I'd believe. But not coloring your lips."

We both chuckled.

"Shall we take the wagon? Do you feel all right to walk?" Prasutagus asked, his hand on my rounding belly.

"I'm fine. Let's go see what's the matter."

Prasutagus and I left the others and made our way through the city. I was not surprised when Pix popped up, joining us.

"Where have you been?" I asked.

"Mind yer own business, Queen."

"You are my business."

Pix rolled her eyes at me but said nothing more.

When we arrived at the king's house, we found the gate open. The stable hands were there, helping twenty or more soldiers water their horses.

"Multiplying again," Prasutagus whispered to me.

I nodded.

Galvyn hurried across the yard to join us.

"My king. Three important visitors. Ansgar escorted them to the formal meeting room. We are giving ale to the soldiers, but they will not come inside to rest."

I frowned.

"Who has come?" Prasutagus asked.

"I don't know them, King Prasutagus. Their banner is not familiar to me."

Nor was it to me. A winged-horse banner fluttered in the breeze.

"Another legion kept secret?" Prasutagus asked me.

I shook my head, uncertain.

"Very well. Let's go in," Prasutagus said, gesturing for Galvyn to lead the way.

I smoothed my dress and tried to tidy up my wild hair as we headed to the meeting chamber.

"Leave it be," Pix scolded me.

We found three well-armored Roman soldiers waiting for us when we entered the chamber. I did not recognize them.

Ansgar rose when we entered. "King Prasutagus and Queen Boudica," he introduced.

The men, looking confused for a moment, rose.

The eldest, a silver-haired man with a hawkish smile, a large nose, and dark eyes, spoke first. "King Prasutagus," he said, bowing to my husband. "Queen Boudica," he said, acknowledging me. "I am Felix Arixis Isatis, legate of Rome. I have been sent by General Plautius and the emperor himself. My companions, Atticus Julius Scato and Drusus Titus Flamininus.

"Gentlemen," Prasutagus said. "My apologies for not having met you here. I had work that needed to be attended to in the fields. You will find me," he gestured to his clothes, "in such a state as a result."

"There is no shame in hard work," Felix said.

"Please, take your rest," Prasutagus said, gesturing to their seats.

"Queen Boudica," Felix said, turning to me as he sat. "I am pleased to meet you, lady. Rumor of your fire-red hair was not an overstatement."

I chuckled. "Is such a color uncommon in Rome?"

"Not unheard of but uncommon. What was it Aulus called her?" Felix asked one of the other men.

"The rose of Britannia," Atticus answered.

"The rose of Britannia. Yes, that was it. That is how you are known amongst us, Queen Boudica."

At that, I chuckled as I tried to ignore the flutter in my stomach that the flattery—and its source—evoked in me. "All roses have thorns, gentlemen. Remember that," I said with a wink, making all the men chuckle.

Ronat appeared, filling our drinks.

"I trust you had a safe journey here," Prasutagus told the men.

"Not without the usual complications, but we are here nonetheless," Felix said but did not elaborate.

"And sent by the emperor himself," Prasutagus said, sipping his ale. "And to what honor do we owe the emperor's attention?"

"Emperor Claudius is in Camulodunum, now safely under Rome's protection, the Catuvellauni invaders ousted or dead. The emperor has tasked us with ensuring that you, and the other client kings of Britannia, come to Camulodunum by the full moon."

"For what purpose?" Prasutagus asked.

"The emperor is keen to meet his new allies, of course. And to affirm all agreements between the rulers of Britannia and himself," Felix explained.

"All the kings?" I asked.

"And queens, where appropriate," Felix added.

"Next, we ride to Stonea to meet with King Caturix. We

are fortunate to have a Briton guide who knows the Fens to help us find the way to the king's new seat. I am sure it is quite a change for him living on the moors but having grown up in Oak Throne. King Caturix is your brother, Queen Boudica, is that correct?" Felix asked.

"He is." *They know. How do they know?*

"Very good. It is always good to see a solid alliance between those kingdoms who are also allies of Rome. Tucked away in this small corner of your country, you are quite exposed to the whims of your neighbors. It is important to have good neighbors."

"Speaking of neighbors, has there been any news of Caratacus?" Prasutagus asked.

"He is hiding in the woods in the western part of the Catuvellauni territory, ambushing our soldiers, running half-baked campaigns designed at an attempt to terrorize our men," Felix said with a laugh. "But Legate Vespasian has him on the run. We will have him in no time." Felix gestured to the other men to finish their drinks and get ready to go.

"Will you... Can we not offer you rest for the night, gentlemen? We have plenty of room, and Titus Carassius says we have excellent wine. I can see to your accommodations," I offered, trying to hide the nervous tremor in my voice.

"Titus Carassius finds the wine good wherever he goes," Atticus said with a laugh.

"That he does," Felix agreed. "No, Queen Boudica, but we thank you for the offer. We are under orders from the emperor himself to ensure all of his client kings arrive in

Camulodunum by the full moon. We have much ground to cover. We will take our leave now," he said, then rose.

Squelching my emotions, I simply rose, Prasutagus doing the same.

"We are sorry to see you leave so soon," Prasutagus said. "May we refresh your supplies?"

"We have it all well in hand, King Prasutagus, but we thank you. Titus Carassius did have one thing right, the Iceni are very obliging. Let's hope we find King Caturix the same," he said, then motioned for the men to follow him from the room.

We escorted the men outside, Ansgar following behind us. Seeing their superiors arrive, the soldiers began to mount their horses.

I took Prasutagus's arm, standing beside my husband as the men prepared to leave.

"King Prasutagus. Queen Boudica. Camulodunum by the full moon. That is the emperor's order. I trust we understand one another?" Felix said.

"We will be there," Prasutagus replied.

"Very good," the Roman answered, then clicked to his horse and rode off, the other two men bowing to us before the entire party rode away.

We watched as they departed.

"Order. That's a funny word to use with your allies," Ansgar said.

"Client kings. That is what Felix said. Client kings, as Caesar called us," Prasutagus replied.

"May the gods protect us when we begin hearing echoes of Caesar," Ansgar said.

CHAPTER 40

As the moon grew toward fullness, word started coming from the Trinovantes. The Romans were building, and building, and building around Camulodunum. Those people who had lived in the city were displaced, moving to farmsteads or villages away from the ancient seat of the Trinovantes.

"The place is swimming with Romans," Madogh, one of Prasutagus's spies, informed us.

Prasutagus had a vast network of people watching the Romans' movements from the north, in Brigantes territory, and south into Gaul.

"They're moving their forces around. With the arrival of the emperor, there are many Romans in Camulodunum. But there is a considerable force also stationed in Calleva Atrebatum with Verica and his son, Cogidubnus. Another Roman, Legate Vespasian, leads those men."

"I confess, their titles confuse me," I told Prasutagus and Madogh.

"The general is in command of the entire operation," Madogh explained. "Each of the Roman's legions—groups of soldiers—are controlled by a legate, such as this Vespasian. He is a man of some importance in Rome. Their soldiers have ranks amongst them. Under the legate, there is a chief centurion and regular centurions. These men are higher-caliber warriors. Under them are the legionnaires, common soldiers, and under those are the auxiliary cohorts. And they have other roles for their people, such as camp prefects who manage their camps, surgeons, quarter-masters, secretaries, such as Narcissus, who attends the general, tribunes such as Titus Carassius, who is a senior tribune. These are their administrators and politicians. The Romans are highly organized, with precise numbers of centurions, legionnaires, and so on."

"And I have been calling everyone sir," I said, making Madogh and Prasutagus chuckle.

"It is good if we learn their ranks. We should know who to talk to, who is in charge, who has influence over whom," Prasutagus said.

Madogh nodded. "If you can win the general to your side and earn his ear, that is all you need."

Prasutagus nodded. "Let's hope Boudica's gift to the general helps pave the way."

"Whatever it takes," Madogh said.

I looked back at the map. "What are they building in Camulodunum?" I asked.

"Walls, buildings, roads, ditches. It would be easier to ask what they aren't building. They are felling trees every-where for their projects."

"How are the people?"

"Many have left Camulodunum, but not all. Some were glad to see the arrival of Rome on behalf of Aedd Mawr. The Catuvellauni were invaders. Yet, the Trinovantes king has not come, nor his grandson. At least, not yet. Broc has sailed to Gaul. Perhaps he will learn more." Madogh tapped the map on the site of Camulodunum. "They worked quickly erecting a massive, rectangular-shaped house—two stories in height—in preparation for the emperor's arrival...with the help of Catuvellauni captives."

"Slaves?" Prasutagus asked.

Madogh nodded.

"Where is Maiden Stones in relation to Camulodunum?" I asked Prasutagus.

"Here. Along this tributary to the north."

"It sits in an ancient forest, Queen Boudica," Madogh told me. "Not a far ride from the village of Dunmagni."

"The Roman general. Where is he?"

"He was west with Verica until recently. He returned to Camulodunum shortly before the emperor's arrival."

"Did you see him? The Roman emperor?"

Madogh nodded. "He rode into Camulodunum on a war elephant, a great band of musicians before him playing horns and drums. The Roman soldiers lined up all along the road to greet him, calling and cheering. He arrived with his own guard, heavily armored. The general gave a speech, declaring..." he said, then paused.

"Declaring?" Prasutagus asked.

"Declaring Emperor Claudius had defeated Britannia,

that Claudius had finished what Caesar started. That we were a conquered people. And that soon, the Briton kings would come to kneel to the emperor in defeat."

Prasutagus turned and looked at me. "Not quite how it was presented to us, was it?"

"No, it was not."

"There are many ships in the harbor near Camulodunum, including the emperor's fleet, with more coming in each day. The Romans have built up the old roads to and from the harbor, clearing trees and the like. They come with wagons, horses, mules, and more goods than a person can ever imagine."

"If they are doing so much construction, they must be bringing in a workforce. The Catuvellauni captives alone cannot complete such tasks on so grand a scale."

Madogh nodded. "Many men, of all shapes and sizes."

"Like spiders building after a storm, weaving quickly, spinning webs all across our land," Prasutagus said in a hollow voice, staring at the map below him. After a long moment, Prasutagus shook his head. "Anything else?"

"Not that I saw, save... I did see some of their holy people. Veiled women, not so unlike the priestesses of Avallach, have arrived. As well, they have brought their robed priests. They are constructing a temple."

"To what god?" I asked.

"I don't know, but I do know *where* they are building it. That detail has the Trinovantes people upset."

"Where?" Prasutagus asked.

"Over the current site of the temple to Camulos, patron god of the Trinovantes."

I stared at the man. "Over it?"

He nodded.

"No one has said anything to…" I stared, then paused.
"No. There is no one to speak on the Trinovantes' behalf."

"The druids tried. The Romans were not interested.
The site has a well. That is all they cared about."

"It is an offense to the gods," I said.

Prasutagus stared at the map. "As Rome defeats our
people, their gods defeat our gods."

Neither Madogh nor I said anything.

After a moment, Prasutagus nodded, then clapped
Madogh on the back. "Thank you, Madogh. The work you
do for us is dangerous. My thanks will never be enough. I
hope my silver will suffice. Get your rest, please. You are
welcome to stay here tonight."

"If it is all the same to you, King Prasutagus, I will go
and see my sister and nephews in the city."

"Then I thank you for your services," Prasutagus said,
handing the man a weighty coin pouch.

"I will return to Camulodunum within the week."

Prasutagus nodded. "Very good. You will find us there
soon enough."

"Not on your knees, I hope, King Prasutagus?" he
asked with half a laugh.

"Decidedly, no," Prasutagus replied.

"Stay safe, Madogh," I told him.

"And you, Queen Boudica," the man replied, then
departed.

After he had gone, Prasutagus stood staring at the map.
"I will use some of the Roman's silver and build a great

smithy. I will expand our iron and silver-mining operations."

"And what will we be making?"

"Coins, to grow our own wealth and increase our trade. As for the iron... swords. Lots of swords."

CATURIX AND MELUSINE ARRIVED IN VENTA A FEW DAYS later. Melusine looked ripe with pregnancy, a round belly protruding from her tall, lean frame. She looked regal.

"Boudica," she called from the wagon, giving me a wave.

Caturix helped her down, the pair joining us.

Melusine embraced me. "Boudica, how good to see you," she said, then leaned back, looking me over. "How good to see both of you!"

I laughed. "And both of you as well," I said, setting my hands on her stomach. "Are you well?"

She nodded.

I turned to Caturix. "Welcome, Brother."

He gave me a light smile.

"Won't you all come inside?" Prasutagus said, gesturing.

"One moment," Melusine said, fetching a basket from the wagon. "I have brought sweets for ancient Ginerva. We had a very mad but fun conversation about them the last time I was here. Is she still…" Melusine said, then trailed off, not wanting to ask if the old woman was still alive.

"Alive. But the same," Prasutagus said.

Across the square, I spotted Artur watching our party. I gestured for him to come, but the boy shook his head and disappeared around the back of the roundhouse, Morfran taking off from a nearby tree, flying after him.

Still hesitant.

The child had experienced nothing but change in the past year. His home had become my home. And with it came my family and a future he had not asked for. And now, a new baby. A blood child of Prasutagus. I understood his pain, but he did not let me close enough to help him heal it or be with him to go through it. Besides Prasutagus, only one person got close to Artur—Ardra. While Ardra had done nothing to cross me again, the novice kept her distance. And she was rarely far from Artur.

"Ah, here is Ansgar," Melusine called cheerfully, greeting the druid. "Well met, wise one."

Caturix fell into step with me.

"Are you well, Boudica?" he asked. "The child?"

"No problems."

He nodded. "I am relieved to hear it."

Why was he worried? "Is all well with—"

"Yes, all is well."

As usual, Caturix opened up just long enough for a person to peek inside, only to close up once more. I would speak to Melusine myself since my brother was not feeling forthcoming.

"I half expected King Volisios to ride with you," I told my brother.

Caturix shook his head. "The triumvirate is sailing. Dumnocoveros and Dumnovellaunus are quite certain we are walking into a trap."

"Could be. If they poison us all at once, it will make taking over much easier."

"Boudica," Caturix chided me.

"They will not. It would cause a revolt. The only reason they succeeded where Caesar failed is because Caratacus and Togodumnus overreached. Little would have united us behind them. But such an affront as murdering us all… well, we are prideful people, even if we are too prideful to admit it. Wound that vanity too deeply, and they would have all the tribes rallying against them."

Caturix smirked at me. "You sound like our father."

"I'll take that as a compliment."

"As intended."

Within, the servants hurried, preparing food and drink for Melusine and Caturix.

Nella and Ginerva appeared from the back.

"Queen Melusine," Nella said politely, smiling widely as she curtsied. "I am very pleased to see you again. And look at you! Bright as a spring lark and round as an apple."

"Thank you, Nella. And here is sweet Ginerva," Melusine called.

"Queen Enid," Ginerva called, mistaking Melusine for Prasutagus's mother. "You've done your hair differently."

"I've done everything differently," Melusine said with

a good-natured laugh. "Look what I have for you," she said, handing the basket to the old woman.

Ginerva looked within. "Oh, all my favorites. Come, Nella. Where is my grandson? We will find him and share these. Thank you, kind lady."

"My pleasure," Melusine said.

"I saw Artur making his way toward the goat pens," I told Nella.

She gave me a curt nod. "Come along, Ginerva."

And with that, the pair departed, Ginerva chatting happily about the sweets Melusine—Queen Enid—had brought for her.

"She is so delightful. I am certain she was a spitfire in her youth. That tongue of hers is sharp," Melusine said with a grin.

She has no idea.

"She reduced me down, making me feel like a poor farmer when I asked to wed Esu. I was fortunate my father and Ansgar were there to speak on my behalf," Prasutagus said with a laugh.

"It's too bad all parents don't test their children's suitors in such a manner. I got lucky," Melusine told Caturix with a smile, which my brother returned.

We settled in at the table, Pix appearing from the kitchens with a mug of ale and a round of bread in her hand.

"Well met," she told Caturix. "Not Madelaine," she said to Melusine.

"Mad Pix," Melusine replied with a giggle.

Pix joined us at the table.

"What news?" Caturix asked.

Prasutagus relayed what Madogh had shared with us.

"And you?" I asked Caturix.

"My Roman visitors needled me about moving the Northern Iceni's seat to Venta, but I convinced them it wasn't a matter of concern. As for the other news, Caratacus got a messenger through. He is with the Dobunni and asks for my help."

"And your response?" I asked.

"As before," Caturix said with a shrug. "Though if Emperor Claudius thinks I will come and surrender myself to him, he is quite mistaken."

"You should prepare yourselves to make some gestures of supplication," Ansgar said. "Men like the emperor are not bothered with the nuances of how peace is won. General Plautius is the mastermind behind that. The emperor only sees the result, which, in his mind, is a defeated, peaceful, and capitulating Britannia, as they call us. Have you surrendered or allied yourself? They may be one and the same to the emperor."

Prasutagus turned to me. "Prideful people," he said knowingly. "This may be a problem."

"We will know soon enough."

"If it were up to me, I'd knife the emperor the moment I got close," Pix said, causing everyone to turn and look at her. "What? I've been alive far longer than the rest of ye. I would not regret the death it would earn me."

"And what about what would happen to the rest of us?" I asked.

Pix grinned. "That's the only problem. And I do mean the *only* problem."

"Well, let's remember to temper our moods when we get there," Ansgar told her. "We want Rome to think of the Iceni as friends. This is the path we have started down. Now, we must follow it."

Pix sighed loudly. "In the end, all of ye will tell me I was right."

No one said a word.

Because we all knew there was an excellent chance Pix would have the last laugh.

CHAPTER 41

We spent the rest of the night enjoying one another's company and sharing updates on construction underway in Stonea, Oak Throne, Venta, and Raven's Dell. We may not have liked Rome's presence, but Rome's money was easily spent.

Before heading off to bed, I stopped in to check on Artur.

I was about to knock on the door when I heard another voice inside with Artur in his chamber.

"Of course, they may be killed," a woman said in a whisper.

"Why would they be killed?" Artur replied, his voice sounding nervous and upset.

"You cannot trust these Romans. But would you really be so sad to see her dead? After all, she has come to take everything from you. She hates you. You can see it in her eyes."

"But she seems—"

"She's is a liar. Don't forget that. Everything she does is pretend. She is the reason you suffer. You will see, when her child is born, you will be cast aside. But don't worry, Artur. Many women die in childbed. It happens all the time. But, if she and her child *were* to die, you would be Prasutagus's only child and heir once more."

"But if something bad happens to—"

"You need not worry. Once you're a little older, you'll understand better. When you're king, we will wed. You will be king, and I will be your queen. Like we have always dreamed of. You, my husband, and me, your special friend..." the voice whispered.

I opened the door to find Ardra sitting at Artur's bedside. She leaned close to him, her hand under his coverlets and on his body. She snatched it quickly away, then pulled it to her chest, adjusting her gown as she sat up. But not before I caught the briefest glimpse of her naked breast.

"Queen Boudica," she said nervously. "You startled me."

Stunned by her words and what I had seen, I stood staring. Had she left her dress gaping to allure the boy? What was she doing? Had she touched him... Where... He was just a child, even if he was nearing an age when boys noticed such things. How old had Gaheris been when he stopped trying to slip frogs down my tunic and instead tried to see what was inside?

A dark shadow passed over my heart. Rage made my hands shake.

"Out," I told her.

"Queen Boud—"

"Out," I said again, this time sternly.

When the girl moved past me, I grabbed her arm hard. "You will get out of this house. You are no longer welcome here."

She met my gaze. "That is not for you to decide, *Queen* Boudica."

"I *have* decided, you venomous snake. You will leave. Now."

"But, Boudica," Artur protested, getting out of bed. "She is my special friend."

I met Ardra's gaze.

"You see, I am his *special* friend," she whispered to me with a smile.

"You are a humiliation to the gods you serve and the house you stand in." I yanked her toward me so I could whisper in her ear. "If the boy was not here, you would be in a puddle of blood on the floor already. Out. Now."

"Very well," she said, then turned and looked at Artur. "You know where to find me."

Galvyn appeared in the hall just then. "Boudica? Is anything the matter?"

I jerked the girl's arm hard. "You will have no further contact with that boy. Do you understand me?" I said, giving her a hard shake. "If I see you near him again, you will find your heart on the end of my spear."

"Calm, Queen Boudica. I'm going," she told me with a smirk, then pushed by.

"But, Boudica…" Artur protested.

I turned to Galvyn. "Where is Ansgar?"

"In the village."

"Send for Pix. She will escort this girl back to King's Wood where she will stay until Prasutagus and I return." I turned to Ardra. "We will speak to Henwyn, tell her what you have said and done here. She can decide what to do with you."

At that, Ardra paled.

Galvyn turned and hurried away.

Shaken, the boy rose from his bed. "Boudica."

"Artur, this girl is no friend to you. She is a liar. Please believe me."

"But she's the only one here who understands me!" Artur protested.

I met Ardra's gaze and gave her a fierce look. Her plot was unraveling. She had misused the child. And her words... had she been plotting to murder me?

"No, Artur."

"But I love her! I will marry her!"

Prasutagus appeared a moment later. "Boudica, what's the matter?"

At that opportunity, Ardra grinned at me and then turned to Prasutagus. "King Prasutagus," she wailed tearfully. "You must intervene for me. Queen Boudica is mistaken. I have done nothing wrong here. I was trying to comfort Artur. He is so upset about the new baby. I just... Queen Boudica has thrown me from the house."

Prasutagus looked confused. His gaze went from the priestess to me.

"She has taken advantage of our Artur's innocence and fragility," I told my husband. "And she whispered of ill intent toward me. Pix will escort her back to King's Wood. When we return, I will speak to Henwyn, and there will be a reckoning.

"No. She is mistaken! Please, send for Ansgar. He will defend me. King Prasutagus, I have been with you since before sweet Queen Esu died. You know I have been nothing but loyal and good to your son. Queen Boudica misunderstood me. Please," Ardra pleaded.

Prasutagus looked confused. His gaze drifted to Artur. The child stood in his chamber, tears on his cheeks.

Prasutagus turned back to me. "Boudica? Maybe there has been some misunderstanding?"

The fact that he hesitated wounded my heart and filled me with fury.

Beside me, the snake smiled.

"Please, Father," Artur pleaded. "Ardra is my friend. Boudica is wrong."

"I am not wrong, Artur. I am so very sorry, but you don't understand," I said, then turned to Prasutagus. "Prasutagus..."

Pix appeared a moment later, an apple in her hand. Galvyn stood just behind her.

"What's this, then?" Pix asked.

"Ardra must return to King's Wood tonight. Make sure she gets there. Tell the Priestess Henwyn that the girl has offended this house and that she will be dealt with upon our return."

"Queen Boudica," Ardra began weepily once more.

"You will go to King's Wood, or I will take you to the

prison with the other criminals waiting to be handed over to Rome. Silence your tongue," I snapped at her.

At that, the girl said nothing more.

I gestured to Pix. "Take her there directly. Ansgar can deliver her things later."

"And here I thought I'd get a good night's sleep. I told ye that priestess was no good," Pix told Prasutagus, then took Ardra by the arm and led her away.

Weeping, Artur slammed his door shut.

Galvyn and Prasutagus stood in the hallway looking utterly confused.

"Boudica, what has happened?" Prasutagus asked, looking bewildered.

Still smarting from his hesitation, I willed myself to be calm. "Ardra has been poisoning Artur against me. She has been whispering to him that he will be king—"

"That is not a crime for banishment. Maybe she—" Prasutagus began, but I cut him off.

"And that she will be his queen. She suggested that I might die in childbirth, speaking in a manner that suggested she could hurry that along. How, exactly, did Esu pass?" I asked then shook my head. "All this time, she has been whispering to him. I warned you. And I believe she acted in a manner she should not in order to win his trust. In a manner…" I began, struggling for words, "that previewed their intimate life as man and wife. If not more. If not worse."

"By Cernunnos," Prasutagus whispered. "In my own house."

I looked at Artur's door. "He doesn't understand. She convinced him that their bond is special."

Prasutagus's face washed with anger and grief. "Already, I have failed the duty Esu left me. I..." he said, then went to Artur's door and knocked. "Artur?"

"Go away," the boy answered.

"Go in anyway," Galvyn told Prasutagus. "You must discover the depth of the betrayal. He needs you, even if he doesn't know it."

Prasutagus entered the chamber, closing the door behind him.

"Ardra always had Queen Esu's ear. I always thought her too ambitious, but I never expected she would sink to such levels," Galvyn said.

I simply nodded.

"Nella will not be pleased. She is fond of Ardra."

"Then the girl has done well forming an army around her."

Understanding, Galvyn nodded. "Enemies within and without. You never know what form they will take."

"Yes."

"Aye, Boudica," Galvyn said. "Don't let yourself get so upset. Especially not in your condition. Please, take your rest. She's gone. Thank the gods."

I stared at Artur's door. More than anything, I wanted to go inside. But within, I heard a tense conversation underway. I would be no help there.

Not knowing what to do, I gave Galvyn a grateful nod, then went to my bedchamber.

Within, I sat down on the side of my bed.

Brita had already packed my things for the trip to Camulodunum. They sat waiting—along with Prasutagus's—by the door. How could we leave now? Emperor or not, how could we just go with this mess? Was Ardra planning to murder me? As a druid, she could easily poison me and no one would ever know. If I died, Artur *would* have been Prasutagus's heir. Was that her plan, to drive a wedge between Artur and me to make it easier for her to eliminate me so she could one day be queen? I shuddered, realizing that while my attention had been fixed on Rome, a killer was in my house. A killer...and worse. Artur...

Shaken, I was still sitting at the side of the bed when Prasutagus returned much later.

"Boudica," he said, surprised. "You're still awake."

"Only now have my hands stopped shaking."

Prasutagus sat down beside me. After a long time, he said, "It appears she was laying a trap, but it had not yet come to the worst. I never prepared Artur for the snares that come with rank. All around you, people will try to maneuver you, and women will try to use you. I didn't think I would have to warn him of such things, at least not yet. I've made a grave mistake. You mistrusted her from the start. I am sorry I didn't listen to you. I'm sorry I doubted."

"I think she was plotting to kill me," I said, then shook my head. "How can we leave now?"

Prasutagus sighed heavily. "Galvyn promised to keep the boy beside him at all times while we are gone. He will teach him the duties of a housecarl, so he knows how the house is run—at least, that is what Galvyn will tell him.

Galvyn will keep him distracted and won't let him out of his sight."

"Good. Yes, that will be good."

"Boudica," Prasutagus said, taking my hand. "I am sorry I hesitated. I replay that moment in my mind, the look on your face. I will *never* doubt you again."

"Good," I said again, then moved to lie down, my heart still pattering with anger.

Prasutagus rose and helped me to bed, covering me.

He then came and lay alongside me.

Neither of us slept, including the little one inside me, whom I felt fluttering.

After a time, Prasutagus said, "There are serpents everywhere we step. We must be careful."

"Yes," I replied simply, closing my eyes. "Yes."

CHAPTER 42

I t was late in the night when I felt someone shake my shoulder. I woke to find Pix mere inches from my face.

"Ye have slobber on yer face," she told me.

"I'm exhausted and pregnant," I told her, then sat up slowly and quietly so as not to wake Prasutagus. "Is it done?"

Pix nodded. "Priestess Henwyn said she will wait for your word. She was furious with the girl. I told her not to believe a word from that girl's mouth. I told her ye had good reason to send her away. Did ye?"

"I did."

"Plotting to kill ye?"

"I think so."

"And *bending* Artur to her?"

"She was."

"Ye should have killed her."

"If Artur had not been standing right there, I would have."

"Good. I am glad to know ye have it in ye."

I nodded. "Thank you, Pix."

"Strawberry Queen," she said, then grinned. "'Tis late, shall I snuggle in between ye?"

Chuckling, I shook my head. "No. There are already three of us taking up this bed."

"And to think, all I do for ye," she said with a grin. "I'll see ye at sunup then," she whispered, then left the room.

I lay back down, setting my hand on my round stomach.

My nerves got the better of me as I started to think of everything that could go wrong in Camulodunum. Willing my mind to be silent, I simply prayed.

Great Mother, in the days that come, watch over me. Watch over my unborn child. My family. And Artur. Protect us. Protect us from all those who wish to harm us—seen and unseen.

"As I do for you, so you must do for me..."

It felt like the blink of an eye when Brita called sweetly, waking me.

I sat up to find Prasutagus missing.

"The king?"

"Gone. He was dressed and off early this morning. He

asked me to let you sleep until the latest possible moment."

"And you? Are you ready to go?"

Brita gestured to her riding outfit, a tunic and trousers. She then rolled up the bottom of her pants to reveal a dagger sticking out of the top of her boot. "A gift from my uncle. Just in case."

"It's good to be prepared. Brita, if you feel nervous or uncertain, you don't have to come."

"No, I will see to you and Queen Melusine. It is an honor to be able to attend you both, even if in such strange circumstances," she said as she laid out my riding clothes. "Queen Boudica..." she began, then paused. "No. Never mind."

"What is it?"

"It's just... there was talk amongst the servants this morning that the priestess Ardra was sent from the house in the middle of the night."

"She was."

"Good," Brita replied. "I never liked her. Because she is a holy person, I tried to give her my respect, but she always made snide comments about you. It wasn't proper, and I told her so—often. Sometimes, I think she said those things just to upset me... Anyway, good riddance. I'm only sad that young Artur will be upset."

"May the Great Mother protect us from the likes of her."

"So mote it be," Brita said, then looked at me. "Now, let's see to that hair."

WHEN BRITA WAS DONE, I JOINED THE OTHERS IN THE DINING room.

Prasutagus and Caturix were missing.

"They've gone to ready the party," Melusine told me. "I say, this is lovely clotted cream. I haven't had a single good bite of anything in Stonea. The water there makes everything taste strange," she told me. "Either that or my taste is off."

I chuckled. "We will blame Stonea, of course."

Melusine and I quickly finished our morning meals and then went outside. There, we found the party busily preparing for the ride to Camulodunum.

I heard a caw overhead and then spotted Morfran headed my way. I held out my arm to receive him, then scanned the square for Artur. The boy had come from the stables with Galvyn. He was staring at me, an angry expression on his face.

"They say that even Queen Cartimandua will come," Melusine said, not noticing I was distracted. "I'm curious to see her. They say she is quite ruthless but rules her people well."

When Morfran landed, Melusine jumped.

"Boudica, leave it to you," she said with a laugh.

Artur glared at me once more and then disappeared into the crowd of people.

"Go on to the boy. To Artur. Artur," I told Morfran.

"Boudica? Everything all right?" Melusine asked, studying my face.

"It's...nothing. Just some small tensions with Artur."

"Sweet, shy boy. I always see him peeping. This has been a hard year for him."

"So it has."

"You will find a way with him, Boudica," she said, setting her hand on my shoulder.

A moment later, Prasutagus joined us.

"We have Druda ready," Prasutagus told me. "But if you prefer a wagon or chariot..."

I shook my head. "I trust Druda to get me there safely."

"Whenever you are ready, then," he told me.

"Ready?" I asked Melusine.

"Equal parts terrified and excited," Melusine admitted with a smile. "But I am glad to ride."

With that, the two of us mounted, Prasutagus helping me onto Druda, then checking my stirrups and straps once more. "Settled in okay?"

"Yes. I'm well. Prasutagus, how is Artur?"

"Sulking and silent. It will take some time for him to understand what game Ardra was playing. We spoke at length last night. She wove quite a tapestry of lies. It will take time to unravel them."

Ewen joined us. "My king, everyone is accounted for in both parties. We are ready to ride."

Prasutagus nodded. "Thank you, Ewen. I will speak to Galvyn, then join you. Make ready to depart."

Ewen rejoined the other warriors, then pulled his horn

and let out a long call. The party made ready to ride. Morfran screeched in protest. I followed the sound, spotting Artur beside Galvyn.

Pix rode up beside me, mounted on a horse that looked very similar to Raven.

"Who is this?" I asked.

"Nightshade," Pix said, the horse's ears pricking at her name. "She's Raven's offspring. Boys in the barn say she's too temperamental to ride, but I told them to give her to me. She prances too much, but she's fond of Druda," she said, motioning to how the mare was nosing my boy.

"Nightshade," I said with a grin. "You don't look the poisoning type," I added, reaching out to touch her, but the horse's ears flattened.

"Oh, the boys be not wrong. She hates everyone. But I spoke the old tongue to her so she is fine with me."

I laughed. "Then speak it on my part. I won't have some feisty mare kicking me out of spite."

"Do ye hear?" Pix asked the horse, whose ears flicked back toward me. "I'll see to her attitude with ye, Strawberry Queen."

I turned in my seat to find Vian and Brita behind me. Vian was riding Pix's old horse—Saenunos.

"Gave him to Vian, did you?"

"Well, I didn't think Saenunos would want to miss out."

I rolled my eyes and then shook my head.

"Ready?" I asked the girls.

They nodded.

A moment later, I saw Prasutagus mount. He turned in his saddle and motioned for me to join him.

Clicking to Druda, I joined Prasutagus, Nightshade whinnying in protest behind us.

"Calm ye," Pix told her. "That stallion carries a queen. Ye cannot boss him."

I joined Prasutagus. With Melusine and Caturix riding behind us, and a guard of Northern Iceni and Greater Iceni warriors following, we made our way out of the gates of the king's compound and into the city of Venta once more.

"May Epona watch over us and all we leave behind," Prasutagus said as we passed through the gate.

"And may the Morrigu stand guard," I added.

CHAPTER 43

T he ride would take several days. I spent much time talking with the others, including Caturix. Our father's death, and the truth about Kennocha and Mara, had brought us closer than we'd ever been before, even if Caturix was still prone to moods.

We'd been riding together, talking of the Romans' visit to Stonea, when Caturix said, "Their eyes were deep with suspicions and questions about moving my seat from Oak Throne to Stonea."

"How did you explain it to them?" I asked.

He looked over his shoulder. Melusine was deep in conversation with Brita and Vian. "I told them that I have a mistress in Oak Throne and would not have her cross paths with my wife."

I stared at Caturix. "What did they say?"

"They laughed, and laughed, and laughed, and asked nothing more."

I sighed. "At least you don't have to worry about that anymore. Sadly, they now know the path to Stonea."

"Perhaps. The mist is alive there. They may not find the way a second time. Guide or not."

"Let's hope they find little reason to look."

The journey took three days. Sick of being on horseback, which was saying something for me, I was both relieved and unnerved when we neared the ancient seat of the Trinovantes.

Passing by charred farmsteads, we soon encountered large parties of men working, cutting down trees, and clearing land. From the looks of their clothes, they were Catuvellauni. They wore the iron of slaves on their necks. Armored Romans oversaw the men as they worked, whips ready in their hands. So many trees had been felled. A forest of lifeless stumps had been left behind.

I felt a ball form in the pit of my stomach.

At the forest's edge, we found ourselves at the top of a valley. In the distance, we saw what had become of Camulodunum. Rows of perfectly aligned tents that seemed to go on for miles filled the valley. A vast trench had been dug all around the encampment. And along with it, protective palisades. Beyond the encampment sat the ancient city. The Romans were fortifying and extending the old walls. From this height, we could see that many of the roundhouses inside the walls were gone. Instead, we saw many buildings built in a square or rectangular shape. A massive building at one end of the city. Everywhere we looked, we saw signs of construction.

Three riders carrying the banners of Rome, the golden

eagle glinting in the sunlight, raced from the encampment toward us.

Prasutagus nodded to me, and the pair of us rode to the front of our party, Melusine and Caturix following behind us.

"Hold where you are," a Roman called when he reached us. "Identify yourselves."

"I am King Prasutagus of the Greater Iceni. This is my wife, Queen Boudica," Prasutagus replied.

"King Caturix and Queen Melusine of the Northern Iceni," Caturix called.

"You are expected. Follow us," the man said, motioning for us to ride behind them.

I glanced at Prasutagus.

He raised and lowered his eyebrows but said nothing.

The Romans led us down the road away from the army's encampment.

As we approached the city, we saw slaves working, extending the trenches that surrounded the city and reshaping them into rectangles. Wooden palisades were being replaced by stone walls.

"By the Forest Lord, the city will be ten times its size when they are done," Prasutagus said.

"I'm sure Aedd Mawr's grandson will be grateful."

Prasutagus gave me a knowing look.

We rode toward the city gate. Roman soldiers manned the walls and the towers.

"Open," our escort called in a loud voice.

The gates of the city swung open, revealing a foreign scene. Individuals of all shapes and sizes wore Roman togas, armor, or gowns as they made their way down the rows. I could see that many were servants or slaves who had been brought from abroad, their appearances unique. Along with them, I also saw the Trinovantes. To my surprise, the Romans vastly outnumbered the tribespeople. Several of the Trinovantes stopped to watch as we passed.

Despite all the changes, some things remained decidedly not Roman—the smithy, the market, and many of the vendors' stalls. But elsewhere, the city was being reshaped.

The soldiers led us down a long street toward an impressive two-story building. The building hosted an open balcony on the second floor, its design unlike anything I had ever seen before. I was studying the structure when General Plautius suddenly appeared on the balcony. When he saw us, he smiled and then raised his hand in greeting.

Turning to a servant beside him, he said something to the man who went running off.

The general gestured that he was coming to greet us, then disappeared.

The Romans came to a halt before the grand building. From within, I heard the sounds of music and laughter. A fleet of servants rushed out to help us.

Prasutagus slipped off Raven and then came to help me down.

"I will help Brita and Vian," Prasutagus said, then disappeared.

A moment later, the general appeared on the steps leading up to the massive building. Alongside him was a black dog, its feet so large the pup nearly tripped over them.

"My friends, the Iceni," General Plautius called, his arms wide as he came to greet us.

I stepped forward to meet him. "General Plautius."

"Queen Boudica. Come now, you must call me Aulus."

"And I hear I am called the rose of Britannia."

At that, Aulus grinned at me, his eyes sparkling. "I only report what I see," the general replied.

I bent to greet the puppy. The silly thing ran to me, rewarding my welcome with a lick on the cheek. "I see this one found his way to you."

"I'm glad to have the chance to thank you. It was very thoughtful, Queen Boudica."

"If you are Aulus, then I'm just Boudica," I said, looking up at him.

"Thank you, Boudica," he said, holding my gaze a moment longer than he should have. He bent to pat the puppy. "I'm told he'll grow into a giant."

"He will."

"Titus told us how you wore the pup in a sling to keep him comforted," Aulus said with a laugh.

"Well, he is Northern Iceni, after all. I had to look after him. And what have you named him?"

"Victory."

I raised an eyebrow at him. Did he have any way of knowing that was the meaning of the name Boudica?

Aulus winked at me but said nothing more.

Caturix and Melusine joined me.

Giving the puppy one last scratch, I rose.

"Ah, King Caturix," Aulus said, giving my brother a short bow.

"General Plautius, this is my wife, Queen Melusine. Melusine, this is General Aulus Plautius."

"General," Melusine said.

"I believe your father is expected. The Coritani kings are coming by sea, I understand?"

"Yes, General. That is correct."

"Well, we shall keep a watch for them. And here is King Prasutagus. Well met, friend."

"General Plautius."

Aulus's eyes looked over the rest of the party. "You are all welcome, my friends. We have accommodations for you in that building," Aulus said, gesturing to one of the Roman-built rectangular buildings. "Behind your quarters are one of the roundhouses from the old city. Your men can stay there. That said, you must understand that I have to ask for your weapons," Aulus said, gesturing to some Roman soldiers. "Don't worry. They will be looked after and returned to you when you depart."

The men waited for Prasutagus's word.

I could see the struggle on my husband's face.

After a moment, he said, "Very well," then gestured to the others.

Caturix followed suit, motioning to the Northern Iceni men.

"Even you, Boudica," Aulus told me. "We can't have any thorns here."

I laughed lightly and then handed over my weapons to the Romans. As my spear left my hand, a memory of

Gaheris flashed through my mind: his smiling face as he handed the weapon to me, him showing me how to wield it, the smells of the sun and sea.

Shuddering lightly, I let the spear go.

Instantly, I felt deep regret, deeper than anything beyond fear or anxiety of being disarmed, something far more profound.

"Boudica...

"Protect the land.

"Protect the oaks.

"Protect the stones."

"Very well. The emperor will receive you now, and on the evening of the full moon, we shall have a formal ceremony welcoming you all. I trust you have come with gifts?"

My heart dropped to my feet. I turned to Prasutagus.

"Yes," he said.

Aulus's eyes turned to Caturix.

My brother nodded to him.

"All right, now..." he said, eyeing over the party. "Just the royals and the druid. My men will see to the rest of you. Now, don't look nervous. There is good wine and good food to be had."

I looked back at Pix, who was frowning. She pushed her way to the front.

"Only those I said," Aulus told her, then eyed her carefully.

"I, too, am a druid. I will come along with ye."

Aulus held Pix's gaze. "There are a hundred men in

that room who will see you dead before you get within ten feet of the emperor."

"Oh, ye misunderstand me. I only want to see what *this* Roman emperor looks like."

"*This* emperor?"

"Aye, to see if he looks like Julius Caesar."

Aulus raised an eyebrow at her. "He decidedly does not."

"She will cause no trouble," I reassured Aulus. "You have my word."

"Well, if I have your word," Aulus said, giving me a smile, then turned and headed back up the steps. "Come along, my friends." The puppy trotted along behind him.

I looked back at Vian and Brita. Vian gestured that she was all right and for me to go on.

Turning, I followed along behind Aulus.

"Prasutagus...the gift?"

"I have seen to it," he said.

I turned back to Pix. "Mind your manners."

"As long as they mind theirs," she told me.

We climbed the steps, following behind the general. Braziers hung outside the wood doors. The building had been painted with whitewash, the columns painted a golden color.

The doors opened to reveal a large, open meeting chamber with a vaulted ceiling. On the second floor, spectators looked down at us. There were many Romans, but I also spotted our own people amongst them, although the faces were unfamiliar to me. Of those faces, I noticed a young woman standing on the balcony. She wore a deep blue dress adorned with silver thread. Her raven-black hair was pulled back at the temples. She had been watching me. When I met her gaze, she smiled and inclined her head to me.

I returned the gesture, then looked back to the massive chamber. Seated on the dais was the man I guessed to be the emperor. He wore gloriously white robes trimmed with purple, a deep purple cloak draped over his shoulder and pinned with a golden broach. On his head, he wore a ring of leaves made of gold. He had a head of thick, silver hair. His bangs were cut short on his forehead. He had a long nose with a bulbous end.

The musicians playing at the other end of the hall grew silent when we entered.

Aulus paused and spoke to a young man by the door.

The man, dressed in a toga, stepped forward to introduce us: "King Prasutagus and Queen Boudica of the Greater Iceni. King Caturix and Queen Melusine of the Northern Iceni. And their druid priests."

The emperor motioned for us to come forward.

"Rex Prasutagus, Regina Boudica," he said, gesturing to Prasutagus and me.

Prasutagus bowed deeply. Taking his cue, I curtsied.

When we rose, the emperor eyed me over, then turned to Aulus and said something in a language I did not know.

Aulus laughed lightly, then nodded.

The emperor then motioned behind us.

Prasutagus and I stepped aside.

"King Caturix and Queen Melusine of the Northern Iceni," Aulus told the emperor.

"Rex, Regina," the emperor said. "Your women are all very tall," he added, rising. He went to Melusine, who towered over him by a foot. "And beautiful," he added, taking a lock of Melusine's curling, golden hair into his hand.

Caturix turned a hundred shades of red. Only once had he looked like that before, right before he'd beaten another boy for calling him a coward when we were children.

"Emperor," Melusine said with a stiff smile. "I come with a gift for you," she said, holding out a box. The emperor had to take a step back and let go of Melusine's hair.

The emperor waved for a young attendant to take the box for him and open it.

Within was a beautiful dagger. The hilt was made of gold and encrusted with abalone and jewels. The craftsmanship on the hilt was divine and very clearly made by Melusine's hand.

"Ah," the emperor said, "what a treasure." He lifted the weapon from the box and felt its weight. "Fine craftsmanship."

"I am glad it pleases you, Emperor Claudius. It is my own handiwork."

At that, the emperor paused. "You, Regina?"

"Yes, Emperor Claudius. Do you like it?"

"I do. I do, indeed," he said, then set it back in the box then motioned for the boy to take it away.

"A woman smith," he said to Aulus.

Aulus lifted his eyebrows and merely shrugged.

"We have a gift as well, Emperor," Prasutagus said, motioning for Ansgar to pass him a box.

Once more, the young servant came forward to collect the box, which he then took to the emperor. Within was a fortune in raw amber.

The emperor's eyes sparkled. "A treasure."

"A gift to show our appreciation for our alliance and our hopes for goodwill and ongoing good relations in the future."

The emperor nodded. "I look forward to many more years of positive relations with the Iceni," he said, then waved the box aside. With that, he gestured to the musicians who sparked up a tune once more, then went back to sit on the dais.

Aulus rejoined us. "Well, with that done, you will want to refresh yourselves and redress before dinner. The servants will escort you to your lodgings, and I will see you when you are ready."

"Thank you, General," Caturix said.

The general nodded to him, then met Pix's eye once more. "Well done," he told her.

"What do ye mean?"

"I know restraint when I see it," he told her with a wink.

"Will you come with me?" a servant said, gesturing for us to follow.

As we turned to follow the servant from the room, someone called out to us. "King Prasutagus, Queen Boudica!"

I turned to see Titus there.

He waved to us. "You will join me for dice later, Queen Boudica. Say you will."

I nodded to him.

At that, he laughed, then waved for us to go on.

We exited the massive building and walked down the lane to one of the houses nearby. The servant entered before us, motioning for us to come inside. Therein, we found a central room with some comfortable, cushioned chairs, a long table, and a brazier. The sleeping areas were tucked away behind rich silk drapes.

"I will fetch your servants," the boy said, leaving us standing in the opulent, unfamiliar space.

The fire in one of the braziers cracked loudly.

"The old ones whisper," Ansgar said, voicing the ominous feeling we all felt.

"They are asking what ye are doing here," Pix said, frowning.

"I wish I knew," Prasutagus said, staring at the fire.

CHAPTER 44

Brita helped me change into a new, deep green gown the girl had fashioned for me. The beautiful dress was made of Roman silks that she had purchased in the market. Brita had embroidered the neckline with gold- and bronze-colored thread in knot design. She combed down my wild locks, braiding them back from the temples and adorning them with a golden horse pin. The length of my hair she forced into a twisted curl that lay on my chest. When she was done, I was looking as fashionable and ladylike as ever. Riona would have been proud.

"Like a new leaf in spring," Prasutagus said.

"You are looking very fine yourself," I told him, adjusting the ties on his tunic.

We returned to the common area to discover that the servants had laid out wine, baked goods, sweets, and fruits. They had just set out the last of it when I rejoined the others.

"What is all this?" Melusine asked, looking over the food. She had changed into a golden-colored gown. "I thought we were to dine with the others?"

"This is not your meal. These foods are just for your comfort....in case you have hunger before dinner," the servant explained, looking confused.

Pix—who had decidedly not redressed—picked up a morsel and popped it into her mouth. "Strange," Pix said as she chewed. "What be these?" she asked, pointing to the platter from which she'd gotten her food.

"Dried dates," the servant said.

"They look like bugs. Taste good, though."

The servant grinned, then came to the table. Pointing, he identified the other foods: apricots, grapes, plums, nuts, and more.

Melusine grabbed a small cake off a tray. She took a bite, then went and sank into a nearby seat. "I don't know what this is, but I'm in love with it."

"It is a honey, pistachio, and rosewater cake, Regina," the servant told her.

"Were I not already married, I would wed this cake."

"I will try not to be offended," Caturix told his wife, chuckling.

"Wine, King Prasutagus," the man said, offering him a cup.

My husband took the drink.

Ansgar did the same.

The druid did not drink often. I could see from his expression that the situation had unnerved him.

Brita, who had been busy setting out my things, joined us.

"By the Great Mother, it looks like a faerie feast."

"Nay," Pix said, her mouth full of food. "There be five times more at a faerie feast. These foods be less dangerous, but only by a little."

"Please, try something," I told the girl.

"You must try this," Melusine said, pointing to the cake she was eating.

Vian circled the table, nibbling small bites as she examined everything thereon, lifting pots and smelling them.

A few moments later, we heard the soldiers come to attention outside our building. The door opened to reveal Aulus.

"Ah, good," he said. "I was just coming to see if you were ready. Shall we?" he said, gesturing for us to join him.

"We will return soon," I told Brita and Vian. "You can feel free to rejoin our warriors if you feel more comfortable."

Vian gave me a brave smile. "We will be fine, Queen Boudica."

Leaving the women behind, we made our way back.

"You must tell me where all those marvelous pieces of amber came from, King Prasutagus," Aulus said with a smile.

"The sea," my husband replied. "Some years, amber pieces will wash up on the coast during the winter. It doesn't happen every year, but when my father was young, many pieces came ashore."

"The emperor was very pleased. And with the dagger," he told Caturix and Melusine. "Tell me, Queen Melusine. Is it true? Did you make the piece yourself?"

"I did, General."

"And where did you learn such skills? Are all women trained in smithcraft?"

"No," Melusine replied. "It is not common, even amongst our people, but I taught myself jewel craft. From there, I began to work with other metals."

"Your wife has talented hands," Aulus told Caturix.

Caturix gave him a weak smile.

We followed the general back to the massive structure. From within, we heard the sounds of music. "There will be music and talk for a time still," Aulus explained. "The meal will come afterward. Eat and drink, my Iceni friends. You are very welcome here."

At that, the general left us and returned to the emperor.

It was Titus who found us first. "Queen Boudica," he said with a grin. "I am happy to see you again. And you too, of course, King Prasutagus. Come. I would like you to meet someone special," he said, then pulled me away.

I looked back at Prasutagus, who raised and lowered his eyebrows at me but did not save me from only the gods knew what fate.

I was surprised when the Roman led me to the dark-haired woman I had seen earlier.

"Queen Boudica, I would like you to meet Queen Cartimandua of the Brigantes. I told everyone I would be sure you met so we could see you side by side, some of the fairest women in all of Britannia. That was, of course, before I spotted Queen Melusine. Let me fetch her too," he said, then dawdled off.

Queen Cartimandua was stunningly beautiful. She had deep blue eyes that matched the shade of her dress. Around her neck, she wore a silver torc with blue stones.

"Queen Boudica," Queen Cartimandua said politely. "I am pleased to make your acquaintance."

"And you, Queen Cartimandua."

"Carti, please," she said, then glanced about the room. "The Romans are looking at us," she said, then turned back to me. "Shall we pose for them or act as if we do not see them?"

"Or both."

"What do you make of Roman Camulodunum?" Cartimandua—Carti—asked me.

"I'm quite sure I prefer old Camulodunum," I replied. "The Romans are very industrious. So much building in so short a time."

"Yes," Cartimandua said simply, then sipped her wine. "You are not drinking," she said, waving for a servant to come. She lifted a goblet from the tray and handed it to me.

"I…" I began but did not know what to say. "I cannot."

"I see," she said. "You are with child."

"A wisewoman I trust told me it was bad for the child."

"Then you have good advisers around you, Queen Boudica. You don't need to drink; simply hold your goblet and smile. The more they drink, the more they talk. If you don't drink, you will be able to listen better. How is your Latin?"

"I understand enough."

"Get a tutor. Become fluent."

Titus and Melusine joined us. "Britannia's finest treasures," Titus said, pleased with himself. "My emperor," Titus called, capturing Claudius's attention. "I give you the true prize of Britannia. Gold, ruby, and onyx!"

At that, several people laughed.

The emperor inclined his head to us.

Cartimandua returned the gesture by lifting her drink in toast to the man.

"It is a fine bouquet of flowers you have collected here," Aulus told Titus. "If you will excuse me, I will borrow Queen Boudica for a moment," he said, then offered me his arm.

Titus waved Aulus away.

"Queen Cartimandua, do you know Queen Melusine, daughter of King Volisios of the Coritani?" Titus was asking Melusine as Aulus led me away.

"I think you saved me from some unwelcome parading," I told Aulus. "But I'm sorry to have left Melusine and Cartimandua behind."

"The dinner will be served soon. Don't worry, even Titus forgets a beauty then."

I looked across the room, trying to spot Prasutagus, but he was on the other side of the room with a group of men I didn't know.

"Regnenses," Aulus said, reading my expression.

"I understand a considerable Roman force entered the land through Regnenses territory."

"So it did. And now, King Verica has his throne. We expect to see the king tomorrow."

"And how many others?"

"Well, some people are still sorting out their priorities, so we shall see. Do you mind?" he asked me, gesturing to the stairs leading upward.

I shook my head. Grabbing the length of my dress, I went with the general up the steps and then toward the front of the building. He motioned for some soldiers to open the door that led to the terrace.

"I wanted you to have a good view," he said, leading me to the rail.

As I looked over the city, I could see the roads and buildings under construction.

"Some will come to Camulodunum and see Rome taking over—doing away with how things have been done in the past, changing things, tearing down old things. And they will be afraid. But not someone like you. When you look at this, what do you see?"

I chewed the inside of my cheek for a moment, then said, "Change."

"Yes," Aulus said, tapping his fist against the rail. "Development. Advancement. Change. With Rome comes new inventions, new ideas, new people," he said, eyeing me over. "New people," he repeated once more, then smiled at me. "You must help your people see this world as a world of change—for the better."

"I will endeavor to do my best…when I am certain of it myself."

"Ah, then I have just the thing to remind you," he said,

then reached into his vest, pulling out a small packet. He opened it to reveal a necklace. "It is a small gesture of my gratitude for sending me that fine dog. However, I also hope it reminds you that unfamiliar things are not necessarily bad things."

The necklace was made of linking rings of gold. At the center was a medallion shaped to look like an elephant with green gemstone eyes.

"May I?" he asked, lifting the necklace.

"I..." I said, hesitating. "It's an overly generous gift, Aulus."

"Nonsense," Aulus said, stepping behind me. He gently moved my hair aside. "I want you to always remember Rome fondly," he said as he lay the necklace on my neck.

I felt his hands gently touching my skin, the warmth of his flesh on mine, the soft feeling as his thumb gently grazed the back of my neck. My stomach quaked with nerves.

"Like ivory," he whispered. "Rose petals and ivory."

I felt annoyed with myself when my skin rose in gooseflesh. I trembled. "I..."

"There," Aulus said, finishing the clasp and stepping back. He looked me over. "The gems on the charm match the color of your gown. Very lovely."

I touched the necklace. "I don't know what to say."

"Thank you will suffice," he said with a soft laugh, his gaze holding mine.

"Thank you."

"You're welcome. We have many fine things in Rome,

Queen Boudica. I am happy to bring you just a small piece, as you brought something to me. Now, shall we find your husband?"

"Y-yes."

With that, we returned back downstairs. I was not surprised to find Pix at the bottom of the steps. With one leg against the wall, she stood nursing a goblet.

"Ye were missed," she told me, gesturing with her chin across the room to Prasutagus, then turned her attention to Aulus. "*Ye* were not," she told him with a stern glare.

Aulus paused. "I do not know your dialect, maid. What tribe are you from?"

At that, Pix just laughed and walked away.

"Boudica," Prasutagus said, joining us. "I wondered where you had gone."

"I was looking at the city from the balcony. It is quite a sight, all of the construction."

"I told your queen that while some eyes might see what we are doing here and worry, from a bird's-eye view, there is a beauty to the improvements we are making to the city. She needed to see it with her own eyes."

"I see," Prasutagus said stiffly, his eyes going to the necklace.

Aulus followed his gaze. "Your wife gifted me with my fine Northern Iceni dog. I wanted to repay her kindness with a reminder of her memorable ride. Do you like it, King Prasutagus?"

"It is a good likeness of the creature."

"We've had crafters come from the continent. Everyone is eager to do business here. Assuming you have more of them, those ambers of yours will fetch you a fine fortune, King Prasutagus. As will the metals on your land. I see much wealth in the Greater Iceni's future. In fact, I will have to visit you after we capture the fugitive Caratacus. Has there been any whisper of his whereabouts?"

"None that I have heard," Prasutagus said.

Aulus nodded, and I could see in his eyes that he did not believe Prasutagus. "Well, I will ask around. Lovely Queen Cartimandua may have heard something, and she is company that is quite easy on the eyes. Don't you think, Prasutagus?"

"My eyes seek nothing beyond my wife."

"Quite a loyal husband you have, Queen Boudica. You even command his eyes," Aulus said with a grin, then drifted off.

"Silver-tonged," Prasutagus said, his gaze following the general, then turned to me. "Are you all right?"

"Yes, just...confused. I feel like a wild thing caught in a snare. I would chew my foot off but don't know what good it would do me. I'm sorry, Prasutagus."

"Don't apologize. You're not at fault here," he said, but his voice betrayed that he felt differently. "Don't trust him, Boudica."

"I am struggling to find the path between courtesy and danger," I replied.

"As are we all," he said, his gaze going to Cartimandua and Aulus.

The Brigantes queen was smiling nicely and laughed at something Aulus said, but her eyes were sharp as ever. She leaned forward and whispered something in Aulus's ear that made him pause. After a moment, he inclined his head to her and then departed. As he walked away, I noticed his jaw was tightly clenched.

Prasutagus scanned the chamber. "This room is full of predators."

"And what are we, husband?"

"We are Epona's children. Wild mares and stallions. We will outrun them all."

CHAPTER 45

I t was not long thereafter that the servants arrived, quickly setting up the dining table for the feast. Soon, a bell was rung and the music grew quiet.

Emperor Claudius rose from his seat on the dais and went to the table, taking the seat at the very end. Only when he was seated did the servants gesture for us to join him at the table. I sat with Pix on one side of me, Prasutagus on the other. Across the table from me I found Ansgar, Melusine, and Caturix. Farther up the table, I noted the Brigantes queen speaking to a man I didn't know. He was one of us by the looks of him, a large golden torc on his neck.

The emperor rose. "Britons and friends, I welcome you to the site of my great conquest. Tonight, we will feast and celebrate my accomplishment. Where Julius Caesar failed, I have succeeded. And in doing so, I've brought you all here as my allies, part of our great empire, and soon client kings of Rome. Let us thank Ceres for these foods. We thank

Bacchus for this fine wine. And we cannot forget Mithras for our great success here in the wild lands of Britannia. Let us feast," he said then clapped his hands once.

From behind us came a fleet of servants who placed platter upon platter on the table before us. Roasted birds, pigs, and even a massive stag served as centerpieces on the table. Along with the meat were eggs, oysters, fish, and more. Fruits and vegetables served in unrecognizable ways filled the table. A platter of roasted mushrooms and herbs slathered in a golden yellow sauce was set before me. The aroma alone was enough to make my mouth water.

A servant appeared from behind me, filling my plate with neat portions of food, covered in delicate sauces.

"More of that quail," Pix told the young man serving her. "More," she said when it was not enough. "More again. Ye are not paying for it from yer own coin," Pix added, making the servant crack a smile as he finally placed a generous portion of food on the plate.

When my attendant finally set my plate down before me, I was puzzled. The food thereon was barely enough to feed a child. I looked down the table to the place where two Roman women were seated—and there were only two in the whole company. Their plates were also similarly scantily filled.

Melusine leaned forward, whispering to me over the mushrooms and a roasted swan—whose feathers adorned the carcass—to ask, "Boudica, is this all we get to eat?"

I nodded then gestured to the Roman women down the table.

Melusine followed my gaze then frowned.

Caturix waved to a servant. "My wife is pregnant. Fill her plate properly. Like mine," he said.

"If you have any of that rose and pistachio cake, I'll have that," Melusine told the man.

The servant looked confused but did as they asked.

"Ne'er worry, my Strawberry Queen," Pix told me. "I won't stand on decorum for these Romans. If ye need a bite more, take it from me."

Musicians sparked up once more, playing harps and lutes in a gentle manner.

My gaze went to them, and for a brief moment, I felt Brenna's absence most viscerally. I closed my eyes, thinking of my sister. I swooned in my seat. My head felt dizzy. It seemed to me I could see a small roundhouse, a fire burning at the very center. It was warm and cozy. There was a spinning wheel and a weaving frame on the other side of the room. I looked down at my hands, seeing a lyre sitting therein.

Brenna? I whispered in my mind.

"Boudica?" the reply came in alarm. *"Boudica? Oh, Boudica. Our father. Belenus. Sister, are you safe?"*

I am safe. But… see what I see. See what is before me. You will not believe your eyes.

Feeling a strange sense of double vision, I looked around the room.

A feeling, not words, met me in reply. The sensation of my sister was so intense, and that of her confusion and worry.

"Brenna," Caturix said, the name bubbling out of him unbidden.

"Brother..."

But then, I shuddered, and the sense of Brenna faded.

"Boudica," Prasutagus said, taking my arm. "Boudica, are you all right?"

I stared at Caturix. "Brenna."

"What's happening? Is Brenna all right," Caturix asked, moving to rise.

I lifted my hand, stopping him. "Yes. I think so. I saw her. No. I saw what she saw, and likewise. She's safe."

"Is this the first time this has happened?" Ansgar asked.

I suddenly wished I were anywhere else but seated at a Roman table. "No. Once, when we were children, Brenna fell and twisted her ankle so badly she couldn't walk. I saw what she saw, felt what she felt. That was how we found her. She was alone by the river where she'd been collecting stones."

"The sight has always been strong in Boudica," Caturix told the druid. "She is our mother's daughter."

I swallowed hard, touched by the compliment. I gave my brother a smile.

"What prompted the vision?" Ansgar asked.

"The music," I said, gesturing to the musicians. "They reminded me of Brenna."

"Well, I hope ye didn't show her yer tiny bites on that plate," Pix said, "or she would not believe ye to be her sister."

At that, the others chuckled.

I gave the others a reassuring smile. "I'm all right now. I promise."

"Let us cheer your missing sister," Melusine said, lifting her cup. "To Brenna."

"To Brenna," we all answered, lifting our cups.

The others turned back to their plates. Down the table, however, I felt eyes upon me.

I turned to find Queen Cartimandua looking at me.

She gave me a soft smile then lifted her hands to her forehead in the familiar gesture of respect given to druids and those close to the gods. Then, she turned back to her meal.

I looked down at the goblet of wine in my hands. The liquid therein rippled from the quake in my hands. For a moment, it reminded me of the sea...red with blood.

Great Mother...

Epona...

Watch over my sister. May Rome never touch her where she shelters.

THE ROMANS LINGERED LONG AT THE TABLE, DEVOURING course after course. Pix was the only one of our party able to keep pace. After a time, the food was taken away, the tables cleared, and the musicians played on.

Aulus rejoined our party. "How did you enjoy the meal?"

"It was delicious," Melusine said politely. "So many new flavors."

Aulus smiled. "We always eat well at the emperor's table. I'm afraid I'll be back to soldier's rations after he departs."

"General Aulus," Melusine said, "when we arrived, I saw some veiled women in Roman dress, but they are not in attendance here."

"They are priestesses of our goddess, Minerva," Aulus explained. "We shall build many great temples here, including to Minerva. The priestesses have come to minister to our people and help us plan the temples."

"What need do the Trinovantes have for Roman gods?" Ansgar asked, his voice more waspish than I had ever heard it before.

Aulus smiled and placed his hand on the druid's shoulder. "King Diras would have his mother's gods honored here."

"King Diras?" Prasutagus asked.

"Sadly, ancient Aedd Mawr has passed. King Diras, Aedd Mawr's grandson, arrived from Gaul this morning. He and his mother are resting. They will join us tomorrow."

"Is it true what we have heard, that the shrine to the Trinovantes patron, Camulos, has been replaced by a temple to a Roman god?" Ansgar asked.

Aulus smiled. "That is a question for the praefectus of Camulodunum. But do not fear, my friend. Rome honors all gods. Your people will be able to worship as they wish.

But, so too will any Romans who come here for trade…or for your lovely weather," he said with a knowing laugh.

Ansgar, decidedly, did not laugh.

"You said the priestesses were helping in the planning of the temples?" I asked. "I don't see many women in honorary positions amongst the Romans. Are your priestesses held in different esteem?" I asked.

"Minerva is a goddess of wisdom, Queen Boudica. It would be foolish of us to disregard the words of her priestesses. Would you like to meet them?"

"I would," I replied.

"Then, I will make the introductions tomorrow."

"General," Melusine said gently. "I must ask your guidance. I am quite weary. You have, no doubt, noticed my condition," she said, gesturing to her stomach. "It was a long ride, and I am quite tired. Is it considered rude for us to depart?"

"Not at all. The emperor has already retired. Please, feel free to take your rest whenever you wish. My felicitations to you and King Caturix."

"Thank you, General," Caturix said.

"We shall join you," Prasutagus told Melusine and Caturix. "Good evening, General."

"King Prasutagus," he said, giving my husband a polite nod. "Queen Boudica," he added, then turned to Pix. "Well done, warrior maiden. With no blades on you, you got through the night without incident."

Pix grinned at him. "Don't need a blade to have an incident," Pix replied. "I can kill a man with me bootlace just as easily as I can with a dagger. Sleep well, Rome," she said, clapping him hard on the shoulder.

At that, we turned to depart.

"I see you like him as much as I do," Prasutagus told Pix as we walked down the steps and back to our lodgings.

"Neither of us hates him enough," Pix replied.

Prasutagus harrumphed but said nothing more.

I fingered the elephant pendant on my neck. Whatever deeper instinct moved Prasutagus and Pix to mistrust Aulus, I didn't share it. The truth was, the emotion he evoked in me was far more dangerous and one I had no place feeling. I let go of the medallion. I trusted my loyalty. Prasutagus had my heart. Nothing would ever change that.

Yet still, I glanced over my shoulder as we left.

Aulus stood where we'd left him, silhouetted by the light pouring from the door to the hall.

He met my gaze, giving me a soft smile.

His expression evoked a smile in return. It came unbidden. But it came all the same.

Turning back, I followed my husband back to our lodgings. As I did so, I chided myself: *Boudica, what are you thinking?*

CHAPTER 46

That night, as we made ready to sleep, I sat down at the side of the bed and removed the necklace the general had given me.

Prasutagus took it from my hand. "Gold," he said, lifting it. "An expensive piece."

"He said it was a thanks for the pup and to help me remember the beauty of Rome."

"He is full of false flattery."

"I won't wear it again."

"No. Wear it tomorrow. But guard yourself against him, Boudica. I know you well, but he is playing some game with you. I cannot see the shape of it," Prasutagus said then sighed. "He sparks an old familiarity in me. I don't understand it."

"Yes. I feel the same."

"We live many different lives. The druids on Mona explained that while we often return life after life alongside those we love, other spirits rest in the Otherworld for many lifetimes, only rejoining when they are healed enough to come again. I don't know. There is no reason for the general to feel familiar to me, but he does. To you too?"

I nodded.

Prasutagus sighed heavily then lay back. After a moment, he sneezed loudly.

I giggled. "May Epona bless you. Are you all right?"

"The coverlets are soaked in rose smell. It's enough to suffocate a person. Didn't you notice?"

"I rather like it."

"I feel like I'm being strangled by a flower garden."

I laughed then lay down beside him. "Did you meet Queen Cartimandua?"

"No. I didn't have the opportunity."

"She's a clever one."

"They say her mother was shrewd and merciless. Perhaps mother and daughter are not so different."

I sighed heavily. "I will be glad when this is done."

"May Epona hear your prayers."

Neither of us slept well that night. When I did finally sleep, I was plagued by dreams. I saw the city of Camulodunum, but bigger than it was now. The place looked more like a festival than a city, teeming with Romans and their temples to their foreign gods. The rage I felt within me upon seeing it made my hands shake. And then there was fire. So much fire.

I woke with a jolt.

"Boudica," Prasutagus said gently. "I was about to wake you. The Coritani have come. King Volisios is in the antechamber with Melusine and Caturix. May I go get Brita?"

"It's still night," I whispered.

Prasutagus laughed. "No, my love. It is morning."

"Oh."

"Are you all right?"

"Dream. A dark one."

"You are full of omens these days."

"I will go see the general's priestesses. Do you suppose they read omens?"

"I am sure they do, but I'd guess you won't like what they say. Let me go get Brita. I'll be back in a moment."

I sat up slowly, then went to a small stand and washed my face. Brita appeared a few moments later to help me dress. Pulling my hair back in braids from the temples, she then helped me dress in a bright red gown.

"Shall I get the horse pendant necklace?"

I shook my head. "That," I told her, pointing to the necklace on the table.

Brita gasped when she lifted it. "What is this? Is this all gold?"

"A gift," I said off-handedly, struggling with the annoyance I felt within myself. Mostly, I was angry with myself for that brief flutter of something I should not have felt because of Aulus's touch, and for that glance between us. The general *was* toying with me. Did he think he could win my favor by flirting with me? Had he used the same silver tongue on Cartimandua? No, she would have seen through him. How had I fallen into the trap?

But a voice, a feeling, deep within me whispered the

answer. *Aulus, though he is Roman, is not new to me. I recognize the spirit within him.* As Prasutagus said, we lived many lives, and this was not the first I had encountered him. That was why I had seen him in my vision in Ula's cottage. But what shape our past lives had taken, I didn't know. But for better or worse, Aulus was no stranger to me.

"It is a very fine piece. This creature…"

"One of their war elephants."

"Do they have them here in Camulodunum?"

"Not that I have seen," I said. "How was it last night? Were you and Vian all right here?"

"After we ate, we joined our warriors. Though they spent most of the night griping about being disarmed, we made the best of it. We were housed in one of the old roundhouses. I think the previous tenants left in a hurry. Many of their personal belongings were left behind. One of the warriors said that King Aedd Mawr's roundhouse was torn down to build the building you were in last night."

"King Aedd Mawr is dead. I suppose that building is the new king's house."

"Is the new king of the Trinovantes here?"

"He arrived yesterday. We will meet him today. They say he is young and has a Roman mother."

"Then he is a Roman."

"Yes."

"Back in Venta, many people whispered about your decision to ally with the Romans," Brita said in a low voice. "But I see now with my own eyes your reasons why.

It was a wise choice, Queen Boudica. Not that my opinion matters much."

"It matters far more than you think," I told her.

Brita placed the necklace on me. "Thank you. Now, you are ready."

Outside, I heard the sound of trumpets.

"Someone new has come," Brita said.

"Shall we go see?"

She nodded, and we left the bedchamber, joining the others in the main room. There, I found Prasutagus, Caturix, Melusine, Vian, and King Volisios.

King Volisios turned to me. "Queen Boudica, it is good to see you again."

"King Volisios. I trust your journey went well."

He nodded.

"And the other kings of the Coritani?"

"They are outside."

The door opened, Pix joining us. "It be the Parisii," she said. "Rode up from the harbor. Nearly had a skirmish at the gate when they were asked to disarm."

"I can't say the thought hadn't occurred to me as well," King Volisios said.

"Who be ye?" Pix asked him.

"Father, this is Boudica's..."

"Guard," Pix said.

"Guard," Melusine repeated. "Her name is Pix. Pix, this is my father, King Volisios."

"Why do ye share the kingship with two others?" Pix asked him.

Melusine laughed nervously.

King Volisios studied Pix a moment, then said, "Well, aren't you interesting."

"Oh, King, ye have no idea," she told him with a wink.

At that, Volisios chuckled lightly.

Melusine coughed uncomfortably then said, "I'm sure we are wanted in the grand hall."

At that same moment, there was a knock on the door.

Pix answered it. "What do ye want?"

"I... They are wanted," the attendant said, gesturing to the rest of us.

I went to Prasutagus. He glanced briefly at the necklace but said nothing.

"Let's get this done," Caturix said sourly. "I am ready to go home."

"May the gods grant your prayers," Melusine agreed.

I went to Vian. "All well?"

She nodded. "My eyes are bulging at everything I see," she said then laughed.

"If you need anything, don't hesitate to find us."

She nodded.

I returned to Prasutagus and the two of us followed the others from the house. A servant led us toward the main building. There, we found other Celtic kings and queens waiting outside. The doors to the main hall were closed.

The Parisii, a man with a thick neck ring and his wife, were complaining bitterly about being left to wait outside after they had traveled all that way.

When we joined the others, I went to Queen Cartimandua.

"Good morning," I told her.

She inclined her head to me. "Queen Boudica."

"This is my husband, King Prasutagus."

Cartimandua gave him a soft smile. "King."

"Well met," he told her.

I scanned the square. "What is happening?"

"I am told the emperor will receive our pledges of fidelity momentarily."

"A ceremony?"

"We are to become Romans. Haven't you heard?"

Prasutagus huffed a laugh.

Cartimandua smiled lightly but said nothing more.

After a short wait, Titus appeared from within.

"Good morning, all," he called. "This morning, we will formally make our pledges of eternal friendship and alliance between your peoples and Rome. When you are called, please come forth and offer your pledge as instructed."

"What are we pledging?" the man I'd seen seated beside Cartimandua at dinner last night asked.

"King Abandinus of the Dobunni," Cartimandua whispered to Prasutagus and me.

"Merely friendship and allegiance," Titus said with a dismissive wave of the hand, then turned to go back inside.

"He drinks better than he lies," Cartimandua noted.

"Regina Cartimandua," a servant called, gesturing for the queen to go forward.

On the other side of the square, the Parisii king hissed

at Cartimandua. Clearly, there was no love lost between them, but Cartimandua paid him no mind.

Instead, the queen motioned for her men to line up behind her then climbed the stairs.

"Regina Cartimandua of the Brigantes," the herald called.

The queen entered the chamber, the doors closing behind her.

"I hope they take her head." The Parisii king then spat on the ground.

"Legate Vespasian told us to ride here or watch our cities burn," Abandinus of the Dobunni told us. "And now, the Romans are camped on our borders. They do not want us, they want Caratacus, who has brought this disaster upon us all. May the gods curse him."

"Where is King Verica?" King Volisios asked.

"Within," a stranger dressed in Regnenses garb replied brusquely.

"Rex Prasutagus and Regina Boudica," the herald called.

I looked up at my husband who nodded to me.

I turned back to Caturix.

He gave me a reassuring glance.

Taking my husband's arm, we climbed the steps. The doors swung open to us. Within stood all the Romans who had, the night before, looked drunk on wine and were keen to chat and befriend us. Now, the place was as silent as a funeral. Emperor Claudius stood at the front of the room. Nearby stood King Verica. Along with them was a young boy I didn't know. He was dressed in

Roman garb. I guessed him to be Diras, King of the Trinovantes. He was little older than Artur. Beside him stood a golden-haired woman dressed in the Roman fashion.

A man sat with a quill and parchment, making note of the event.

Queen Cartimandua, her contingent of men behind her, stood to the side with a placid smile on her face, her fingers laced together before her.

"Rex Prasutagus, Regina Boudica of the Greater Iceni," a herald standing near the emperor called in a clear voice than rang throughout the hall. "Emperor Claudius stands before you to accept your submission. In so doing, you become client kings of Rome, Romans in your own right, and sovereign rulers of the Greater Iceni. None may wage war against you nor take what is yours. As Roman citizens, you are entitled to the rights and protections of Rome. Come forward and make your promises," he said then waved us to walk forward.

Submission.

Submission?

But I remembered what Ansgar had said. The druid had anticipated this.

Prasutagus clenched his jaw so hard I thought it might break, but he gently held my arm and led me forward to the emperor.

Emperor Claudius met Prasutagus's gaze. "Rex Prasutagus. My friend. I have heard nothing but good words about the friendship and hospitality of the Greater Iceni. Please, kneel."

For a moment, I thought Prasutagus would resist, but he turned to me and offered me his hand.

We both knelt.

My heart beat hard in my chest, my temper boiling.

For the people.

We will accept this disgrace for our people.

To keep them safe.

To keep them from being drawn into war.

To use our influence to be the shield between them and Rome.

Emperor Claudius went first to Prasutagus. "Rex Prasutagus, I accept your submission and bid you rise as a Roman and friend," he said then turned to me. "Regina Boudica, I accept your submission and bid you rise as a Roman and friend," he said, gently touching my head.

Prasutagus extended his arm to me, helping me rise.

For a brief moment, I met his gaze. Within it, I saw the same wash of rage and despair that boiled in me.

"Please, stand with the others," one of the Roman officials said, motioning for us to stand beside Cartimandua.

Saying nothing more, we went and stood beside the Brigantes queen.

I tried to catch her gaze, to read her reaction to the entire affair, but she looked straightforward and said nothing.

The herald disappeared to the back to fetch another of our people.

When he did so, I glanced at Aulus.

The general had been staring at me.

He gave me a soft, encouraging smile, suggesting I had done well, then looked toward the back of the hall.

"Rex Caturix and Regina Melusine of the Northern Iceni."

A moment later, my brother entered, Melusine on his arm. Melusine looked scared and uncertain. As soon as she spotted me, she met my gaze.

I gave her reassuring smile.

Caturix, on the other hand, looked... I had only seen him look like that once before. When we were young, he had forgotten that my father had asked him to fetch some horses from a nearby farmstead. So busy helping the others work at reinforcing a section of the bridge damaged in flood, he'd forgotten all about it. I remembered how he'd stood there, covered in mud, as father screamed at him about being lax on his duties. When my patience wore out and I spoke up for my brother, my father had grown silent and said nothing more. But that look...frustration, sadness, and buried rage. My brother had the same look on his face now. But this time, nothing I could say would save him.

"Rex Caturix, Regina Melusine of the Northern Iceni," the herald began once more. "Emperor Claudius stands before you to accept your submission. In so doing, you become client kings of Rome, Romans in your own right, and sovereign rulers of the Northern Iceni. None may wage war against you nor seek to take what is yours. As Roman citizens, you are entitled to the rights and protections of Rome. Come forward and make your oaths."

Caturix's face twisted, his cheeks burning red.

As we had done, Caturix and Melusine knelt before the emperor who accepted their *submission*.

When it was done, they both rose and came to join us, Caturix practically choking on his rage.

After my brother, the Coritani triumvirate was brought forth.

They, too, were asked for their submission.

And like us, they swallowed their pride, knelt, and became Romans. The sense of shame, anger, and sadness was palpable. Togodumnus had never submitted. Neither had Anarevitos. Both had died for their pride. As a result, their men, women, and children were dying under Roman swords.

When I thought of the people of Venta and Oak Throne, of Stonea and Frog's Hollow, when I envisioned them being slaughtered, their homes burned by Rome, I swallowed my pride.

I would stand here feeling shame.

I would stand here feeling anger.

I would let sadness sweep through me.

For them.

That was what it meant to be queen.

I would sacrifice myself so they could live.

Urien of the Regnenses was called forth next. The Regnenses had long been friendly to the Atrebates. Now that news had come the Regnenses had opened the door to Roman Legate Vespasian, there was no doubt of their loyalty.

Urien made his oath then joined us in the line.

After him came the Dobunni king, who also submitted.

The Parisii were the last to join us. When they were

escorted within, a small contingent of Roman guards also entered behind them.

Once more, the herald called them forward.

"What is this *submission*," King Ruith said angrily, his nostrils flaring. "We have agreed to no such thing."

At that, the emperor paused and looked to Aulus.

"King Ruith, Rome extends its hand and protection to all those willing to accept it. In becoming a citizen of Rome, the Parisii will enjoy considerable benefits. Situated on the coast, the potential for your people, the future growth of your tribe, is exponential... *if* you kneel and accept the friendship of Rome."

"I kneel to no one," the man said defiantly.

In the back of the room, the soldiers pulled their swords, but Aulus gestured for them to be still.

"I was afraid you might say that," Aulus said. Swishing his open hands as if weighing something, he added, "On the one hand, you may keep your pride intact, but lose your lands. The Brigantes will have no qualms with ruling your people and enjoying the benefits of trade. On the other hand, you may kneel and accept the emperor's blessings and rise a recognized and protected client king of Rome."

King Ruith turned to his queen. The pair of them exchanged heated words in a language I did not understand. After a terse debate, the queen knelt. She pulled on her husband's tunic.

Reluctantly, King Ruith kneeled.

Once more, Claudius repeated his words. "Rex Ruith, I accept your submission and bid you rise as a Roman and friend. Regina Cailleacha, I accept your submission and bid you rise as a Roman and friend," he said, gently touching her head.

Emperor Claudius smiled. "I accept the submission of you, the eleven great rulers of Britannia. You have risen again as Romans. Welcome."

CHAPTER 47

Once the ceremony had concluded, the Romans clapped politely. The woman I presumed to be King Diras's mother elbowed him to participate. He had been fighting to keep his eyes open through the entire ceremony. I studied the young man. There was a vacantness to his gaze. This was no king.

A servant called for music and wine.

Once more, the room descended into cheer and frivolity.

The emperor sat, and the room exhaled.

The doors of the hall opened once more.

The moment they did, King Ruith and his wife turned and left the room.

"You quite nearly increased your land holding, Carti," I told Queen Cartimandua.

She gave me a light smile. "The day is not over yet," she said, making me laugh. Leaving me, she went to fetch a goblet of wine. Despite her placid expression, this time, she drank.

"I am glad Ansgar prepared us," I told Prasutagus.

"Many feelings of pride were damaged today on behalf of the people."

"Let's hope the people understand."

Prasutagus laughed lightly. "That is the thing, isn't it? They don't always understand."

A strange feeling held the room. The other tribal kings, feeling defeated and humiliated, wanted nothing more than to leave. The Romans, on the other hand, had grown even friendlier. In fact, a group of important-looking men, impressed by Prasutagus's amber, came to draw my husband into a conversation.

At the same moment, Aulus and King Diras's mother joined me.

"Queen Boudica, this is Julia Vitellius, mother of King Diras. I told Julia of your interest in our priestesses of Minerva."

"Newly arrived myself, I also hoped to visit our priestesses. When Aulus mentioned our similar interests... If you are free, we can go together," Julia told me. The king's mother was a handsome woman who was quite young to be a mother of a boy the king's age. She had curling golden hair and wore heavy eye makeup, her lips painted red. Long gold earrings hung from her earlobes.

"Yes. Thank you, Julia."

I turned to say something to Prasutagus, but he must have been keeping an ear on the conversation. He nodded to me.

"This way," Aulus said, gesturing for us to follow him.

The general led us from the building and down a side street. As we went, we passed many buildings under construction.

"Don't let the noise bother you, Julia. Before you know it, your new city will be glimmering from one end to the other. From your bedroom window, you'll look out on fields of flowers," Aulus told the woman.

"You talk like a poet, Aulus," the woman chided him.

"I shall take that as a compliment."

"Fields of flowers... More likely, Claudius's next *colonia*."

Aulus laughed.

"What's a *colonia*?" I asked.

"A place where old Roman soldiers go to get fat and die," Julia said with a sardonic grin.

"Here we are," Aulus said, approaching a roundhouse. Not far from it, the construction of a massive building was underway. "This will be Minerva's new home," Aulus said, gesturing to another towering building with columns at the front. "But for now..." he added, gesturing to a nearby roundhouse.

"In this barbarian hut?" Julia asked, sneering.

"Houses of such design are common in Britannia," I told the woman, trying to hide my annoyance with the woman's superior attitude. I reminded myself to be patient, that she was an outsider.

"I see," Julia said.

Aulus knocked. A moment later, a woman in a white gown, a veil over her head, appeared.

"Priestess Valeria, may I present Julia Vitellius, mother of King Diras, and Queen Boudica of the Iceni," Aulus said.

I could just make out the priestess's dark hair and the shadow of her face under her veil.

"May Bright Minerva shine on you both. Come," she said, gesturing for us to enter.

Julia picked up the hem of her skirt, then ducked as she entered.

I cast a look at Aulus, who gave me an encouraging glance, then went within.

Inside, the roundhouse had been cleared of any trace of the family who once lived there. On the back wall stood a stone effigy of a woman. Around her had been placed flowers and leaves. A brazier burned at her feet.

"You are welcome to our small shrine of Minerva," the priestess told us.

"I have come with a donation for the goddess," Julia said, handing the woman a coin pouch.

"We thank you and look forward to many more visits by the king's mother."

Julia nodded to the priestess, then went to the statue—presumably of Minerva—and knelt on the furs laid out there.

May the gods forbid she get her knees dirty.

I looked up into the rafters of the roundhouse. I could see the blue sky overhead in the gap in the roof. On the beams, I noted the carvings of leaves, acorns, stags, and an image of our Great Mother Goddess. Even here, the land taken by foreign gods, our goddess remained.

"Queen Boudica, are the lands of the Iceni far from here?" the priestess asked me.

"The Trinovantes and the Greater Iceni share a border to your north," I said.

"The general introduced you as Iceni…"

"The Iceni are two people, the Greater Iceni and the Northern Iceni. I am the daughter of the late king of the Northern Iceni and the wife of King Prasutagus of the Greater Iceni."

"Twice royal," the priestess said. Even from behind her veil, I could see she was looking at me expectantly.

"Right," I said, pulling a silver bracelet off my wrist. I handed it to the woman.

"The Goddess Minerva thanks you."

I highly doubt that.

"Minerva… What is your goddess a patron of?" I asked.

"She is a goddess of wisdom, trade, and war."

I looked back at the statue. The goddess stood with a spear in one hand, a branch in the other, and an owl on her shoulder. "That is a wide variety of skills."

"Are they, though?" the priestess asked. "One must be wise in making war or keeping the peace. In a way, it is all a matter of trade—lives for words for freedom. I suspect you can understand that."

I was surprised by the priestess's words. Perhaps I had judged her outstretched hand too harshly. Where I had judged Julia for her ignorance of our ways, I had shown my own ignorance.

"Yes, you are right."

"You are welcome to visit the temple of Minerva any time, Queen Boudica. This is just a temporary home for our goddess. Very soon, we will have a grand temple. We are always ready to share the goddess's teachings."

"Thank you, Priestess."

She bowed to me.

A moment later, Julia rose, then turned to me.

I nodded to her that I was done.

"Once all these proceedings are finished, I will return to speak more with you," Julia told the priestess.

"We look forward to that."

With that, Julia and I turned to depart. We ducked under the eaves of the roundhouse and outside once more. There, we found the general waiting.

"Julia, a messenger came for you. Your son requests your presence."

She arched an eyebrow at him. "Is that so? Very well. Queen Boudica," she said, then set off in a hurry.

"Scurry, scurry. We are all scurrying through life, aren't we?"

"Something tells me you never scurry, Aulus."

"Oh, I have been known to do so from time to time," he said, gesturing for us to walk on. "You must tell me what the others thought of the ceremony."

"The *submission* ceremony?"

Aulus shrugged, raising his hands in tandem.

"I am sure you can guess. We are all waiting to see if Rome keeps its promises or if it will grow too greedy, as it has done everywhere else."

It had not escaped my notice that Aulus was leading us

back to the meeting hall in a round-about fashion. As we went, however, we passed another construction site. Here, I noted, was a spring. Set to the side of the construction was a wooden totem. The face of Camulos was carved on the ancient tree trunk. The effigy had been moved aside like an inconvenience.

I paused, then stepped toward the image of the god, gently setting my hand on his face.

"I know why your men fear our gods," I told Aulus.

"Why is that?"

"Because when you walk into our holy places, no one holds out a hand for coin," I said, looking back at him. "Our gods speak to us."

"And what is old Camulos saying?"

I looked back at the face carved in the tree, then closed my eyes.

After a long moment, I saw Camulodunum in flames. Massive flames shot up from all the Roman buildings. But the effigy stood unburned.

"He says that if you do not find him a proper place in his city, it will burn."

"What will burn?"

"Camulodunum. All of it. You said the king wanted to honor his mother's gods. What about his people's gods? His father's and grandfather's gods?" I looked at the construction of the new temple nearby. "You have made a mistake here, Aulus. In defiling the shrine, you lose the confidence in people who are otherwise willing to give that Roman boy a chance. Show them that Rome cares about their world. Find a place for Camulos. Someplace where the people can still honor him. In so doing, the king —and Rome—will benefit. Perhaps, in time, the people will come to believe in King Diras...*and Rome.*"

"I thank you for the advice, and I will share it with the king. Rome is patient. The people will come to us in time. That said, it is hard not to be eager to expedite that process when you see something beautiful, something desirable. You want to reach out and take it. But if it is meant to be, it will eventually fall into your hand. And if not, there is no harm in holding it precious anyway."

"Do you believe in fate, General?"

"I do not. I like to believe I am the driver of my own destiny. Otherwise, my achievements are not mine. They are the gods'. And grand as they might be, I work hard for my rewards."

"Then your gods do not help you... not even Minerva in all her wisdom?"

"Perhaps they guide us, maybe even shuffle the cards in my favor, but it is up to me to know how to play the hand."

"And when you die? Our people believe the spirit lives many lifetimes, that we return to the Otherworld for a time, only to be reborn once more."

"When I die, I will join my ancestors in the Under-world, or maybe, if I am lucky, make my way to Elysium with other noble spirits."

"Then, there is no returning?"

"No."

"I see," I said, but in a way, I did not see. If Aulus

didn't believe we returned to this world again, how did I feel such a kinship with him?

I stroked the cheek of Camulos one last time, then raised my hands to my brow in respect. Afterward, we turned and made our way back to the meeting hall.

"Speaking of cards, Titus tells me your brother, Prince Bran, is rather deft at coin and card games. Shall we go see if there is a hand underway?" Aulus asked.

"I didn't take you for a card player."

"Then you must watch me carefully. Already, I have deceived you."

I chuckled. "Don't be so sure about that, Rome. I have what my people call the second sight. Your mind is as clear as the sky to me."

Aulus grinned at me. "It wasn't my mind I was worried about."

"I see."

"Of course. You have the second sight, Britannia. I expect no less."

CHAPTER 48

W e spent the rest of the night engaging in what felt like frivolity in the midst of war. The Romans sat reveling over their triumph in Britannia, leaving the rest of us feeling awkward and uncertain. I didn't blame the Parisii king and his wife for leaving. They came only to ensure they would not be invaded. The Dobunni apparently held the same opinion because they, too, disappeared from the festivities before I even had a chance to speak to them.

That deep pride was problematic.

Prasutagus took a different approach. Having made a positive impression on the first group of gentlemen he'd met, he was quickly introduced to other influential men. I watched with pride as my husband took a difficult situation and turned it into an advantage. Listening when I could, I heard Prasutagus making trade deals, inquiring about the sale of goods, learning more about where he could increase our wealth.

Having escaped Titus, who found a replacement for me in Melusine, I watched those gathered—Roman and Celt alike—trying to determine the players.

As I did, Queen Cartimandua stepped to my side.

"Prasutagus is doing well," she said, her eyes watching Prasutagus laugh with a group of men who had been introduced as senators, Roman politicians of some sort.

"He is."

"I understand he was trained in Mona."

"Yes, until his duties as prince outweighed his inclinations as a druid."

"Yet the druid's teachings serve him well here. He is wise to use this disaster to his advantage. As a man, the Romans listen to him."

I turned to her. "And not to you?"

She smiled lightly. "I must play a different game. But one that is effective all the same."

I smiled at her, feeling a sense of admiration.

"I wish you well, Queen Boudica," she said, giving me a smile, then drifted away.

"If there is one person more dangerous than the emperor in this room, it's Queen Cartimandua," a voice said from behind me.

I turned to find Aulus there.

"Are you saying your emperor is dangerous?"

"Of course. All men in power are dangerous when they wish to be."

"And women too."

"And women too. So, when do the Iceni depart Camulodunum?"

"In the morning."

"You will be missed."

"Good."

"Good?"

"If I am missed, I have played my role well."

Aulus laughed. "You are too honest to play a role. Who you are in this hall is who you are everywhere you go."

"You think you know me that well, General Plautius?"

"It is my business to read people."

"I thought your business was war."

"I am good at war. Yes. But to win wars, you must read people. I have been reading all night."

"Very well. Tell me what you have read."

Aulus grinned then stepped closer to me, his voice low. "The Dobunni will prove false on their words by the next full moon. And despite their words to the contrary, they know where Caratacus is hiding. The Coritani are split in their choices, but King Volisios is the shrewdest of them. He will convince the others to see the benefits Rome brings. If Rome can prove its use to them quickly enough, they will remain loyal. The Regnenses are allied to the Atrebates and hate the Catuvellauni. They are trustworthy. As for the Atrebates, King Verica uses his relationship with Rome to his advantage."

"Has he been effective thus far?"

"Soon, there will be no Catuvellauni, only Atrebates to your west."

"I see..."

"The Parisii are like the Coritani. Silver will silence

their tongues. If not, Cartimandua will gladly invade their lands and behead their king," he said with a knowing grin.

"And the Iceni?"

"Your brother waits for Prasutagus's cue on which way to turn. Now, do not protest," he said when he saw me open my mouth to speak. "He is not wrong to do so. You are wed to the smartest king in the room, Queen Boudica. King Prasutagus will use his intelligence to make a place for the Greater Iceni in the Roman Empire. You have married well."

"I'd rather say Prasutagus married well."

He laughed lightly. "Ah, but that is a given. I'm sure many men envy what the king has won," he said, gently setting his hand on my back.

I shifted sideways, removing his touch. "They may envy all they like, but my heart belongs to Prasutagus."

"I have no doubt you are fiercely loyal to those you love, Queen Boudica. In that, your rosy hair betrays you. They say those with such hair are fierce beyond reason—in all things."

"So we are. Which is why Prasutagus and I find one another so well matched."

"And, no doubt, why you were fearless enough to ride atop a war elephant when even the bravest of my men will not dare."

"Perhaps they fear the chaffing of their thighs."

At that, Aulus laughed loudly. "Perhaps. Perhaps."

It was then that Prasutagus left the senators and joined us.

"Have you wooed everyone to your side, King Prasutagus?" Aulus asked.

"One must take the opportunities where they are presented, when they are welcomed."

At that, Aulus laughed lightly. "Let me go and see if I can inspire the Coritani to the same conclusion," Aulus said, giving us a short bow, then left.

"I will be glad when this is done," Prasutagus said. "My head aches."

"And mine."

"Let's make our presence felt a bit longer then depart," Prasutagus suggested.

I nodded.

It was then that I felt another's eyes on me. Julia, seated beside King Diras, waved to Prasutagus and me.

We crossed the room to join her.

"King Prasutagus, Queen Boudica. Come, sit beside me," she said, gesturing for us to be seated near her.

"Queen Boudica tells me you are my nearest neighbors to the north," Julia told Prasutagus.

"That is right, Lady Julia."

Julia turned to her son. "Diras, this is King Prasutagus. He rules the Greater Iceni."

Diras looked at us. His eyes had a childlike glow. "Hello."

"We are pleased to meet you, King Diras. I was a great admirer of your grandfather. I am sorry to learn he passed."

Diras looked at his mother. "Who?"

"King Aedd Mawr."

"Who?"

"Your grandfather."

"Oh. He died?"

"He did."

"Oh."

Julia gave us a light smile, brushing off her son's confusion. "I am pleased to have a good alliance with such strong and trustworthy people to the north. May I call upon you if we ever need anything? All around me, I see Rome. But Rome does not always see things as others do."

"The Trinovantes are always welcome in Greater Iceni territory," Prasutagus told her.

Julia smiled at us. "Thank you. Something tells me that one day, I may be glad of that."

It was late in the night when I finally caught Caturix's gaze. My brother looked exhausted but was trying to cover his misery. When our eyes met, I signaled that we should go.

Caturix caught Melusine's attention, and the pair joined us.

"We should bid good night to the emperor," Prasutagus said, "if they will permit it."

Caturix nodded.

Leading the way, Prasutagus approached the emperor cautiously, pausing before the guards could signal for him to do so. One of the attendants caught the emperor's attention and whispered in the man's ear.

Emperor Claudius motioned for us to come forward.

"We would bid you good night and ask your permission to take our leave in the morning," Prasutagus said politely, bowing to the man.

"My friend, King Prasutagus of the Greater Iceni. I grant you leave and wish you a good night as well. And you, King Caturix, and your lovely wives."

"We thank you, Emperor Claudius," Caturix said.

The man waved his hand dismissively to us, then returned to his conversation with another Roman seated nearby.

I turned to Julia and King Diras.

"King Diras," I said. "Lady Julia."

"We wish you well, Iceni," Julia said.

With that, we turned to leave the hall.

Behind me, I heard King Diras ask, "Where are they going?"

"Home," Julia told him.

"To Rome?"

"No, love. To their home in the north."

"Oh."

As we went, I caught Cartimandua's gaze.

She inclined her head to me.

I returned the gesture, then we left the hall.

I passed a look over my shoulder as we departed.

Aulus was not there.

CHAPTER 49

Exhausted, Prasutagus and I made our way to bed. My husband pulled me into his arms, kissing my shoulder and setting his hands on my stomach. "How is my little one handling all this Roman food and talk?"

"I haven't felt hungry the whole time we've been here, come to think of it."

"Melusine seems to be quite the opposite. In fact, she looks far less pale than she did some days ago, even with the grueling pace of it all," Prasutagus said.

"She said nothing tastes right in Stonea."

"Hmm," Prasutagus mused. "She should speak to a midwife. Maybe something she is eating in Stonea is off-putting to the little one," Prasutagus said, feeling my stomach. "Under the folds of your gown, this little one is hiding. No one else can tell, but when I look closely, I see her there."

"She's excellent at subterfuge. None save Cartimandua seem to have noticed."

"Men do not always have an eye for such things," Prasutagus said, then paused. He exhaled heavily, then said, "I will be glad to be home."

"From what I can see, you have done well here, Husband."

"Yes, I have met many important people and talked more these last days than I have the last year. Some of that silver from Rome will need to go for building ships."

"I am certain you will make it work. And whatever I can do to help, you need only ask."

"Good, because I will need all of our minds together on this. The future of the Greater Iceni is a bright one, provided we can keep the peace."

"Then may the gods be with us."

"May the gods be with us."

WE WOKE AT DAWN THE FOLLOWING DAY AND PREPARED to go.

"I ne'er been so glad to leave a place since I crawled into that mound to run away from the Romans the first time," Pix said as she fixed the saddle on Nightshade. The horse pranced with annoyance. "Aye, ye…" Pix said, then whispered to the horse in a low tone. The words I did catch, I didn't understand. Soon, the horse settled.

"What did you say to her?" I asked.

"I just let her know she was going home. T'was enough to quiet her."

The rest of our party prepared to ride out. It was a strange, silent morning. The only sound that could be heard was that of the soldiers in the camp.

I patted Druda on the neck. "Let's be done with it," I told him, then mounted, Prasutagus at my side, watching out for me.

He stayed with me until I settled in and then went to mount Raven.

I glanced back at Melusine. "Are you all right? Are you sure you don't want a wagon?"

"Not at all. I feel better than I have for days. Perhaps the last of the morning sickness has finally passed."

I smiled at her. "Very well," I said, then coaxed Druda to join Prasutagus.

"I asked this morning," Prasutagus said. "They have our weapons at the gate."

The Iceni gathered, and we rode down the lane toward the city's gate. There, we were met by a contingent of soldiers.

"King Prasutagus," one of the men greeted us. "We invite your party to retrieve your weapons."

The others dismounted, reclaiming swords, daggers, and spears. Pix brought mine. I slipped my weapons onto my belt, my spear on my back.

"Better to see ye like this rather than draped in Roman gold," she told me.

"One must play the part."

"Be careful. Play too often, and it can change from playing to being."

I frowned, but said nothing more.

Once we were all armored, we prepared to ride off once more.

The gates before us opened.

I scanned quickly around the compound, surprised there was no sign of Aulus.

But then, I caught myself.

Did it matter? Why did I care?

Playing and being.

Pix was right.

I knew better than to care. Being who I truly was meant far more to me than whatever strange echoes of the past remained between Aulus and me. They meant nothing to the life I had now.

Prasutagus reached out for me, taking my hand. "Come, my queen. Let's go home."

THE RIDE NORTH PASSED UNEVENTFULLY. WHEN WE REACHED the southernmost Iceni border, Caturix and his party made their own plans to head northwest, back toward Stonea.

"We will stay in touch," Prasutagus reassured Caturix. "In the meantime, may the Great Mother and Forest Lord watch over you."

"And you," Caturix replied, then turned to me. "Sister, I wish you and your little one well."

"Thank you, Caturix."

I took Melusine's hand. "Perhaps you will have someone new in your arms when I see you next," I told her.

Melusine laughed. "And you as well."

"Be well, Sister."

"You too."

With that, our parties separated. We made our way back toward Venta.

IT WAS A LONG RIDE, BUT WE ARRIVED JUST BEFORE DUSK ON the third night.

Road-weary, I slipped from the saddle the moment we reached the king's house, dreaming of a hot bath and my bed.

Instead, we were met by a very flustered Galvyn.

"King Prasutagus," he said. "Queen Boudica, welcome returns."

"Galvyn, what is it?" Prasutagus asked.

"My king," Galvyn said. "I...I hate to greet you with such news. It's Artur."

"What's happened?"

"My king, the boy... The boy is missing."

"When?"

"He disappeared just after you left."

Prasutagus turned and looked at me.

Pix, who was trying to settle Nightshade, joined us.

"I see yer face. What is the matter?"

"Artur has gone missing," I told her.

"We have combed the city for him. We have everyone looking."

"The King's Wood?" Prasutagus asked.

"He isn't there. And the priestess Ardra is gone as well."

"She's taken the boy," I whispered.

Ansgar, Brita, and Vian, sensing a problem, joined us.

"What has happened?" Ansgar asked.

Galvyn relayed the issue.

"Did ye ask Nella where she may be? Two snakes in the same den, those two," Pix said.

"She swears she knows nothing," Galvyn said.

"I'll speak to her again," Pix said, then moved to go.

"No," I told her. "You and I will go again to King's Wood."

Prasutagus looked pale. "The docks. Has anyone gone to the docks?"

Galvyn looked horrified. "No, my king, I hadn't thought of it. You don't think... No, he wouldn't do that."

Prasutagus turned to me. "I will ride there now."

I nodded. "We will talk to Henwyn again."

"Vian and I will join the others searching here," Brita said.

I nodded to her.

"Go easy," Prasutagus told me. "It has already been too much riding for you and the little one."

"Don't worry. Pix will chide me endlessly if I do not."

"I know. That's the only reason I'm letting you go," he said with a soft smile, kissing me again. He then slipped back on his horse and rode off, three of his warriors riding along. Galloping from the king's compound, dust kicked up behind them.

"By the Mother, I didn't think of the docks," Galvyn said once more.

"We will find him," Ansgar said, then turned and headed inside.

I mounted Druda once more.

Pix reined in Nightshade.

"Be careful, Queen Boudica," Galvyn told me.

I nodded to him, then Pix and I rode out.

We hurried through the city and beyond, making our way to the small village where the holy people lived. Much like the Grove of Andraste, the druids at King's Wood kept to themselves and lived independently.

We rode down the lane, past the fields where the great Beltane celebration had taken place. I eyed the King Stone at the top of the hill, remembering the beautiful moments Prasutagus and I had shared there. Passing the henge, we crossed over a bridge at the River Tas and then made our way down the road toward the small village that sat off the road in the forest.

When we arrived, we found a large roundhouse at the center of the farmstead. Neatly organized gardens, storage sheds, and animal pens circled the main building. Even in the gathering darkness, I recognized the priestess Henwyn. She was cutting herbs in the garden.

When she spotted us, she wiped her hands on her apron.

Pix and I dismounted, tying the horses to a post.

"Queen Boudica," she said, bowing to me.

"We have just returned from Camulodunum to the news that Artur is missing," I said. "Galvyn said they have already inquired here, but I hoped you could speak more to what happened with Ardra since we departed."

"Aye, Queen Boudica, you cannot know how sorry I was to hear this news. We had such hopes for Ardra. As Ansgar's novice, we thought she'd left those dark tendencies within her behind. We were horrified to learn they'd lied buried all along. Ardra left the night she was brought to us. We thought she ran off to escape punishment. We never thought there would be more to it."

"Her family... Would she try to follow them wherever they went?"

Henwyn shifted uncomfortably.

"What is it?" I asked.

"Her family did not abandon her, Queen Boudica."

"Then what happened?" I asked.

"The whole family died in a fire, save Ardra."

"The whole family?" I asked.

Henwyn nodded. "The house burned. No one else survived. Ardra... She was just a girl when it happened. She never realized the possible consequences of her actions. There had been an argument... Ardra made a tragic mistake."

"Are you saying she lit the fire? Ardra murdered her family?" I asked, aghast.

"She was just a child. She didn't realize what she had done."

"She killed them," I said.

"And it didn't occur to ye that a murderess had no place in the king's house?" Pix asked, anger punctuating her voice.

"As I said, we thought that the gods had healed that side of her. She was very young when it happened, and she showed no further signs that she was dangerous. Ardra was a devoted student. That is why Ansgar took her on as a novice."

"Banshees be cursed," I said, gaping as I looked at Pix.

"Where be her old home?" Pix asked.

"Follow the River Tas from Arminghall. The ruins of the farmstead sit along the river."

Pix turned to me.

I nodded. "Let's go."

"Queen Boudica. Again, our deepest apologies to you and King Prasutagus. We never thought..." Henwyn said, shaking her head. "I tried to search for the girl the old way, but the gods did not permit me to see where she had gone. I'm sorry."

In an effort to steady myself, I took a deep breath, then said, "You cannot control the will of the gods. I only hope that for Artur's sake, we are not too late."

"I will pray to Brigid," Henwyn told me.

I nodded then mounted Druda.

With that, Pix and I set off again, returning to the river.

"How could Artur just go off like that?" I asked Pix. "How could he do that to his father?"

"And ye never disobeyed yer father, not even for love?"

"What does he know of love? He is just a child."

"He's the plaything of another with ill-intent. No matter how smart a person may be, they can easily fall into that trap," she said, giving me a look.

"And what does that look mean?"

"It means ye best watch that Roman general."

"What is there to watch? He didn't even come to see us off. There is nothing there."

"Did ye expect him to?"

"I… Well…"

"He plays the same game as Ardra, but he is a fox where she is a hammer."

"When I find her, I will hammer her."

"Unless I beat ye to it, Strawberry Queen," Pix replied.

We followed the river south. As we went, a light rain started pattering.

"Keep under the trees. We would not have ye getting sick as thanks for yer efforts."

Pix and I rode under the shelter of the green leaves as we made our way south. Overhead, the sky grew dark and began to rumble.

"She has displeased Taranis," Pix said. "We will find the boy."

"I hope you're right."

We rode more than an hour south when the trees thinned, giving up their shelter. The rain was coming done in earnest now, but we were close. In the distance, however, I spotted a finger of smoke curling into the sky.

"There," I said, then clicked to Druda.

Trotting ahead, we made our way to the charred remains of a roundhouse and barn.

Pix motioned for us to pause and dismount away from the buildings. Leaving the horses, we kept low as we made our way toward the ruins.

It was pouring. The rain had soaked through my tunic to my skin.

Creeping, Pix led the way. I followed behind her, astounded to see the deftness with which she moved, making no sound. I pulled my spear from my back.

Within the ruins, we heard the sound of movement. A pot clattered, followed by the sound of someone cursing.

Pix took the moment of distraction to rush the room. I followed quickly behind her.

When I turned the corner, I found Pix holding Ardra with a knife to her throat. Underneath the charred remains of the roof, a small fire burned. A pot had turned over, a broth of root vegetables and fish spilled on the floor.

"Where he be?" Pix asked, holding the girl tighter.

The girl's nostrils flared angrily. "I will tell *ye* nothing."

"This is not Venta, and I have no qualms about letting her slice your throat," I hissed at Ardra. "I am Northern Iceni, girl. Now, where is he?"

"Not here."

"Then where is he?"

"He ran off," Ardra said with a laugh.

I glared at her. "Artur?" I called. "Artur?" I yelled over

the rain and then began searching the ruins of the building, looking for any sign of the boy. I saw a satchel and bedroll in a dry corner, but there was only enough gear for one person.

Ardra laughed. "Do you really think he would come to you? There is no one he hates more than you, Boudica. I made sure of that."

Fury ripped through me. "Where has he gone? What happened?"

"We had an argument. He disagreed with me and ran off."

"What did you say?"

"Does it matter?"

"Where did he go?"

Ardra laughed. "I neither know nor care anymore."

"How long ago?" I asked.

Ardra shrugged.

"All this mess is your doing. He is a child!"

"I had that boy right where I wanted him until you showed up. Had Prasutagus not remarried, Artur would have been king and I would have been queen! But you had to come around, ruining everything, you and that bastard in your belly. It's your fault, Boudica, for coming where you were not wanted."

"Were you planning to kill me? Me and my child?" I asked, holding the girl's gaze.

She smiled at me.

"Let me cut her throat," Pix said.

For a moment, I considered it, then said, "No. She is useless. If Artur left her, he has seen through her game.

The druids have abandoned her. Let her find her own way in this world. The gods will sort her out."

"Go back to the filth where ye belong," Pix said, pushing Ardra to the floor and then moved to rejoin me.

But Ardra was quick. Pulling an unseen knife from her belt, Ardra jumped up and rushed toward Pix.

Moving unconsciously, I gripped my spear, then lunged.

Everything happened like time had slowed.

Pix turned, but it was already done.

My spear tip had met its mark, stabbing the girl in the heart.

Ardra stood for a moment, her eyes wide.

The knife in her hand clattered to the floor.

Then, she dropped.

Overhead, the sky rumbled, lightning cracking.

I could see the reflection of it in Ardra's lifeless eyes.

I yanked my spear away, shaking the blood off.

Pix and I stood there for a long moment. Finally, Pix asked, "What do we do with her?"

"Our chief concern is Artur. Let the wolves have her."

Pix nodded. "Fair enough."

"How can we find him in this weather? Can we track him at all?"

Pix paused. "Not like this. I can try me other form, see if me fox nose is better."

"I'll go by horse, retrace our steps, see if there is any sign of him. I will meet you at Arminghall. Maybe we missed him. Maybe he went there to pray to the gods."

Pix nodded, then hurried from the ruins and out of sight.

"May your ancestors take pity on you," I told Ardra, then hurried back to the horses. I eyed Nightshade. "I'm not Pix, but you best comport yourself," I told her, attaching a lead rope to her bridle. I mounted Druda. "Tell your girl to behave," I told my horse, then we set off.

Nightshade resisted at first, pulling on the rope until it made my hands burn from holding the line, but eventually, she relented.

We made our way back into the forest.

The rain was still coming down in buckets, making it hard to see and increasing my frustration.

My heart was beating so hard that I could barely think. That girl had lured Artur from the house, for what? Only to quarrel with him and send him off in a rainstorm? What had she said or done to make him run away? Where would he go? Given what I knew now, I knew I should be glad he was still alive.

I rode back to the henge. When I arrived, Druda and I rode toward the entrance of the sacred site.

"Artur?" I called. "Artur!"

But there was nothing. No one was there.

I dismounted and went into the stones.

The feeling of magic around me made my skin rise in goosebumps.

I went to the altar at the center of the shrine. Closing my eyes, I set my hand on the stone.

"You gods who watch this place... Great Epona, Sacred

Cernunnos, Wise Brigid, you creatures of the greenwood who whisper to me, help me find that boy."

I waited for a moment, hoping for some vision, some sign, but there was only silence.

The rain slowed to a patter. And a moment later, it stopped altogether.

"Artur?" I called, but there was no sign of him.

Feeling furious and miserable, with an ache in my groin and lower back, I leaned against the altar stone.

I closed my eyes once more.

Please be with me.

Please help me.

Esu... Esu... Can you see me? Help me find your son.

"Artur," I whispered.

A moment later, I heard a familiar squawk. I looked up to find Morfran sitting on the top of one of the standing stones. The bird shook himself, flinging the dampness from his feathers.

"Morfran," I whispered. "Morfran, where is Artur? Artur. Artur," I called the bird.

He whistled, a sound he often made when he wanted me to follow, then flew off.

I watched as he flew to a stand of trees nearby.

Leaving Druda and Nightshade, I followed after him.

I was soaked to the bone, and my whole body ached. It had been a long ride, and my pregnant body wanted no more of it. But I would not stop now.

When I made it to the stand of trees, I looked around, but there was no sign of the boy.

"Artur? Artur!"

Overhead, Morfran squawked at me, then flew off to the hillside nearby, landing on the King Stone.

Hurrying, I made my way up the hill that led to the King Stone. In my haste, I had forgotten that it would be slippery. Sliding and falling on my knees, again and again, I pushed my way to the top of the hill.

There, sitting with his back pressed against the stone, I found the huddling child.

"Artur," I said, rushing to him. I dropped to my knees. "Are you hurt? Artur, you are soaked through. Are you injured?"

The boy looked pale as milk. He met my eyes. Giant tears rolled down his cheeks. "B-Boudica," he whimpered then flung himself toward me, wrapping his arms around me.

I hugged the boy close to me, pulling him tight and kissing him on the head. "It's all right," I whispered. "I've got you now. It's all right."

He moaned lightly, then wept.

I held him for a long time, letting him release all of his feelings. Poor child. What machinations he had suffered.

When he finally exhaled deeply, I pulled back and wiped away the last of his tears. I met his gaze and held it. "Let's go home, hmm?"

He nodded.

We rose and moved to go back down the hill. "Be careful. It's slippery," I told him.

"Ye hold on to me," Pix said from behind us, making us jump. "Sorry, young prince, I didn't mean to scare ye.

Boudica, ye best hold on to me. I would not have ye and yer little one tumbling."

I didn't ask her where she'd come from. I knew well enough.

I nodded, then took Pix's arm.

Going carefully, we returned to the horses. Pix helped Artur mount in front of me.

"Boudica," Artur whispered. "Thank you for finding me."

"My sweet boy, I will always find you. You are my son," I told him, holding him close to me, then we made our way back to Venta.

CHAPTER 50

By the time we returned to the roundhouse, the ache in my back and groin had increased, and the cool breeze and rain had my skin rising in gooseflesh.

"Artur," Prasutagus said, rushing across the square to meet us. He lifted the boy from Druda as if he weighed nothing and pulled him close. "Are you all right?"

"Yes, Father."

"Where were you?"

"I... I made a mistake."

"Ye best get the boy and yer wife inside. Neither should be out in the night air a moment more," Pix said, passing off Nightshade and coming to me. "Ye don't look well, Boudica."

"It's nothing. I just need a warm bath."

Pix held her hands out to me and helped me to the ground. But the moment my feet touched the earth, my head felt dizzy, and I saw spots before my eyes.

"Pix," I said, reaching for her.

Then everything went black.

As I walked barefoot in the fog along an unfamiliar seashore, my vision was fuzzy. In the distance, gulls sounded. The water lapped against the pebbled beach. My ears felt stuffed and rang like something too loud had been struck too close. I looked down to find myself wearing a simple off-white shift like the priestesses wore.

I lifted one of my hands. It was covered in blood.

Ahead of me, I saw fire.

Something was burning.

No...not something. Many things were burning...boats in the water. There were so many boats in the water. And half of them were on fire. Like the dragons of legend, the fire-belching ships still made their way toward the shore.

Terror held my heart.

A flaming arrow flew over my head.

I turned.

The wind blew, making my auburn locks stick to my face.

I looked toward the dune above me to see warriors racing toward the shore.

One of the men in a druid's robes screamed and rushed forward, an ax in his hand, only to be hit by flaming arrows.

I moved to grab my spear with my other hand. But when I lifted it, I held a lyre.

And then I realized it was not my hand at all.

"Brenna," I said with a gasp, sitting up.

I woke to find myself in bed in the king's roundhouse.

"Easy, Boudica. Easy," Prasutagus said gently, then turned to Brita. "Fetch Ariadne. Tell her Boudica's awake."

Brita nodded and then rushed from the room.

"What happened?" I asked, confused.

"You fainted. Pix said you were caught in the heavy rain. Your skin was frozen. There was no time to fetch a priestess, so I called the midwife from the village. She said you had some bleeding. How are you feeling? Any pain?"

"The baby," I said, suddenly stricken with panic. I touched my stomach.

"The midwife was worried at first, but your womb was comforted after some rest. How are you feeling now?"

"My throat and head ache. And my lower back."

"You took some fever. You've been sleeping for more than a day."

"Artur?"

"He's still upset, but he's intact. Pix told me what happened. Boudica, thank the gods you all came away unscathed. To think I let that dangerous girl stay in my house, even after you warned me. I am so sorry."

"Please, don't apologize. She manipulated you all."

"I nearly lost my son, wife, and unborn child because of my foolishness. And I chided you in Camulodunum for over-trusting. I am truly sorry."

"Say nothing more," I said. "As long as Artur is well."

"He took a little fever from the rain, the same as you. He is resting. I know he will be relieved to hear you are all right. He wept when he heard our child was in danger."

"I must go to him," I said, moving to get out of bed.

"You will do no such thing," Prasutagus told me with a laugh. "Lie back and rest. Once the midwife sees you, I will feel much better."

I leaned back into my pillows.

"I will put on a pot of these herbs Ula sent. I know some of them myself, but not all. The midwife said it was a wise and well-mixed blend."

"Thank you," I said, my eyes closing. I shivered lightly, the dream returning to me once more. "I dreamt of Brenna."

"Yes, you have spoken her name in your sleep."

"I saw danger. I must send a messenger to Mona, ensure she is well."

"I will see to it."

"Thank you," I said, then drifted back to sleep once more.

When I opened my eyes again, I found a tall, dark-haired woman, her brow tattooed with markings of the moon phases, looking back at me.

"Temperature is still up," the woman said. I realized then that she had her hand on my forehead. "But her blood is strong," she said, letting go of my wrist. She met my gaze. "And, she is awake," she said, giving me a light smile. "Good evening, Queen Boudica. I am Ariadne, a midwife here in Venta."

"My child…"

"The bleeding has stopped for now, but you must rest. Your wisewoman in Oak Throne gave you a strong draft. Keep drinking it, along with some other brews I have left for you here, and you will recover in a few days. The ride strained the child, but the rain caused a fever and made your throat raw. With some rest, you will recover from both."

"Thank you, Ariadne. And Artur?"

"Also recovering. He is a strong boy. He will be well in no time. Children always recover quickly. Pregnant women must take their time. No riding. You must take a wagon for the remainder of your pregnancy. Do you understand?"

"I do, but my horse will not."

At that, the midwife chuckled, then rose. "I will come back in the morning to check on you once more, but you may call upon me if there is any need, no matter the time," Ariadne told Prasutagus and me.

"Thank you, Ariadne," I told her.

"You have our deepest gratitude," Prasutagus echoed.

"It is nothing, my king. I am glad to be of service. I will return tomorrow to check on the queen," she told Prasutagus, then turned to me. "Rest, Your Majesty," she said, then departed.

"Prasutagus," I whispered, a torrent of emotions within me.

"Rest and get well, my sweet wife," he said, setting a kiss on my forehead, then whispered, "You are everything to me."

CHAPTER 51

I spent the next several days in bed, mostly sleeping. Ariadne returned to check on the child and me and declared all danger had passed. On the third day, Artur came to see me.

"Boudica," he said sheepishly.

Prasutagus stood behind him, his hand on the boy's shoulder. "You have both been asking to see one another. Artur beat you to wellness."

I sat up slowly, still feeling weary from the fever and with a mild ache in my lower back.

"Artur," I said, gesturing for him to sit beside me. "Come. How are you? Are you feeling all right?"

"Much better," he said. "My throat doesn't hurt at all anymore."

"Very good," I said, stroking his dark hair. While Artur was tall for his age, I could see he was very much still a child in these moments. "Morfran will be glad to have you back to take him out."

"Pix has been exercising him, but she says they don't like one another. She told me I had to get well faster before he pecked her or she cooked him," Artur said with a flicker of a smile.

I chuckled. "Then, I am glad you are well."

"Boudica, I—"

Taking his hand, I shook my head. "We will say nothing more if it."

"It's just...if something happened to you or your baby because of me..."

"I am only glad nothing happened to *you* that cannot mend in time."

"It is my fault. I am sorry."

"It was *Ardra's* fault. You do not need to apologize."

"So I have told him," Prasutagus added.

I squeezed his hand. "No one blames you. We all make mistakes, Artur. All of us. That is how we learn. That is how we grow. And that is how we discover who deserves our trust and love and who does not."

At that, Artur nodded.

A moment later, a coughing fit took me, and I let the boy go.

Prasutagus fetched a mug of warm, honeyed herbs. Once the coughing passed, he handed it to me.

I sipped, relishing the feeling of the warm liquid on my raw throat.

"We should let Boudica rest now," Prasutagus told Artur. "Ariadne said you are still likely to drive up that fever if you exert yourself too much," he told me. "Please get some sleep. I will come to check on you again."

I nodded, sipped the brew once more, and then lay back down.

The following days passed in a haze of sleeping and eating, with Ariadne checking on me. Pix and Prasutagus both came to keep me company, Ariadne banishing the others so as not to risk them catching the fever. So far, it seemed only myself and Artur had taken ill.

Two weeks later, I finally felt well enough to get out of bed. With Ariadne's approval, I was allowed to go outside for some fresh air. The fever had gone, and the ache in my throat receded. The pain in my lower back had relaxed to a dull pinch.

That morning, I went outside to the garden behind the king's house and sat braiding ropes of garlic with Betha, Ronat, Brita, Nella, and Ginerva. Ginerva amused us with tales of her wild youth. None of them knew if they were true or not, but if so, apparently, the woman had her pick of lovers. We had been out there most of the morning, when Newt appeared.

"Queen Boudica, a rider from the Northern Iceni," the boy told me.

Leaving my work aside, I rose, relieved not to feel any pain.

"Thank you, Queen Boudica. Those are excellent braids," Betha told me.

"I'm only sorry it's not the Romans, today. I would charm them with my nicely perfumed hands," I said with a laugh, waggling my fingers and making the others laugh.

Leaving them, I went around the side of the house to

find a rider there. I recognized the man from Caturix's household.

"Oran," I called to him, wiping my hands on my apron.

"Queen Boudica," he said. "A message for you from the king."

"Shall I get King Prasutagus or—"

"The message is more for you, lady," he said, a grim expression on his face.

"What is it?"

"I bring bad news, and I am sorry for it, but your brother thought you should know that Queen Melusine grew ill shortly after returning from Camulodunum. Her child... their child was lost. The queen is recovering. Caturix said not to worry, she is expected to make a full recovery, but the child could not be saved."

"Ah, by the Great Mother, what sorrowful news. I am sorry that you are the bearer of it. Please, come inside. It is a long ride in the late summer heat."

"Thank you, Queen Boudica."

With that, I led the man into the main dining hall. A servant hurried along to bring food and drink for the man.

"Is there any other news from my brother?"

Oran shook his head. "No, Queen Boudica. There has been no news of Caratacus or the Romans. King Caturix asked me to share that as well."

I nodded, feeling a deep sorrow stick in my heart.

"Did Melusine have a fever, per chance?"

Oran shook his head. "I don't know much, Queen Boudica, but I know she had some stomach pains about a week after they returned. It was not long after the child was lost. Another mother in the village also lost a little one. The druid Einion fears something is wrong with the waters in the village well but isn't certain. They started digging a new well."

I nodded. "What sad news. May the Mother comfort them both. Rest, Oran. We will see a place readied for you to stay the night," I said, gesturing to a servant to attend to it.

Feeling upset, I turned to leave the roundhouse once more. By the time I got outside, tears pricked the corners of my eyes.

"Ah, Melusine, Caturix..." I whispered, tears sliding down my cheeks as I mourned their loss. I went to the effigy of Epona before the roundhouse, setting my hands on those of the horse mother. "Great Epona, bring comfort to my brother and his wife. Whatever your will, so may it be. But please, go gently. Go gently."

I knew Caturix would blame himself. His guilt over the way things had gone with Kennocha and Mara would weigh on him. Caturix would believe himself punished, and I had no way of undoing that. I felt great sorrow for my brother, knowing his hidden pain. And Melusine... what could I do but weep for her?

I placed my hand gently on my stomach, knowing how close I had come to the same fate with my little firebrand...

Sorcha.

"Sorcha," I whispered.

In response, the baby moved and kicked.

I smiled, wiping the tears from my cheek. "Oh, dear Sorcha, what a blessing you are."

CHAPTER 52

The remainder of the summer passed quietly, and soon, the leaves began to turn as autumn, and the harvest came upon us once more.

"I will help the men with the wheat harvest," Prasutagus told me. "The Romans are eager to purchase anything we do not need. And I am eager to sell to them."

In our small corner of the world, the threat of Rome retreated as the Roman soldiers moved west in search of Caratacus and to root out any remaining opposition to Rome's *friendship*.

That friendship had purchased the Greater Iceni new docks in Yarmouth and boats to sail from them. For weeks now, Prasutagus had been riding back and forth from Venta to the mouth of the Yare. While I was eager to see the improvements, Melusine's tragedy made for a powerful warning for me. Instead of gallivanting across the countryside as I wished to do, I stayed in Venta.

The news was slow in coming, but Prasutagus's spies

had learned that Rome was pushing west into Cornovii *and* Dobunni territories. The Dobunni, it seemed, had been sheltering Caratacus. Aulus was chasing the bands of warriors Caratacus had convinced to fight with him. Everywhere the former king of the Catuvellauni went, Rome followed. Caratacus was no friend to anyone. To save his own ill-gotten gains, he had drawn the entire south into a war.

Word also came that Roman Legate Vespasian had toppled several major forts along the coast and west, including Maiden Castle, the seat of the Durotriges. All along the southern coast, Rome took charge, including taking control of the valuable mines that dotted the lands.

In Venta, the evidence of the war was seen in other ways. Many Trinovantes moved into the territory. Along with the displaced, we also saw increased numbers of Romans in the city—traders, not soldiers. Merchants arrived with unusual wares, journeying deeper into our land than ever before. And rumor had it that the shanty town of Londinium was growing by leaps and bounds.

"Ansgar spoke with Henwyn today. We will hold the Mabon festival in the wheat fields outside the city once the harvest is done, thanking the gods for the bounty. We will invite everyone to come. We will make our offerings and prayers to the gods in thanks for the harvest. With everything in so much upheaval, I have neglected the holy duties my father always performed. I hope we can make amends."

"I think they will forgive you for spending that time preventing them from being pulled into a war."

"I can only hope."

Lying down, Prasutagus pulled me close to him, nuzzling my neck and kissing my shoulder. "I feel the chill of winter in the air."

"That's only your own icy feet that you feel."

"I slipped into the stream today. My boots have been wet all day," Prasutagus said with a laugh.

I chuckled.

Prasutagus sighed. "I am expecting the Romans to come soon, anyway. I was informed they will come twice a year for their tribute. The first of those visits should happen any time now."

"It's unsettling to have so many Romans about."

Prasutagus nodded. "More unsettling is the news that some of our men have gone to join the Roman army. As have many Trinovantes. Rome offers a rich wage and a promise of land upon retirement for those who earn it."

"Land where?"

"That is the question, isn't it?" Prasutagus set his hands on my round stomach and kissed it. "How is my Sorcha?"

"She is hungry today."

"Her or Boudica?"

"Or both. I am competing with Ginerva by complaining about my cravings. All day, I have been dreaming of a raspberry tart Lynet baked one Midsummer. I will go into the market tomorrow to see what I can find."

"Send Ronat. You don't need to go for yourself."

"No. But I want to."

"Very well. Just make sure Pix goes along with you."

"All right."

"There was news from Camulodunum."

"What news?"

"King Diras and Julia will return to Rome before winter breaks."

"Who will rule there in their place?"

"General Aulus is expected to pull his forces back before the depth of winter."

"Then the Trinovantes truly are Rome now."

"Yes."

"And King Verica? Any word of him?"

"Only that he and his son have comfortably settled into their lands once more."

"What of Imogen, the sister of Caratacus and Togodumnus? Was there ever any news of her?"

"No. It is whispered that Caratacus had her moved. I'd guess she is on Mona."

"Yes. That would be the safest place for her," I said, then paused. "The Romans keep pushing west."

"Yes."

"They would have no interest in Mona, would they?"

"I cannot see what a holy island would matter to them as long as Caratacus does not hide there. Even he would not betray the druids like that."

I frowned.

"I can feel your frown, even in the dark," Prasutagus said. "What is it?"

"It's just the vision I had. Brenna..."

"Yet the messenger you sent found your sister doing well."

"Yes. But still. I don't know."

"I think, sometimes, we see the past. Or maybe even the future. Not our future but further, to lives we have yet to live. Who is to say? But Brenna is safe, and the Romans still fear the druids. They have not forgotten what happened when Caesar came."

"I hope you are right," I said, entwining his fingers in mine. "I hope you are right."

THE FOLLOWING DAY, I WENT TO THE MARKET ALONG WITH Pix, Vian, and Brita.

"So many strange wares," Brita said, lifting a pot of some sort of cream from a vendor's table and smelling it. "Roses," she said, her nose crinkling.

"That is cream for your face, handmaiden," a young, handsome vendor told her. "It came all the way from Rome. All the ladies in Rome put that on their faces to keep their skin smooth," the man said.

Brita put it back down. "I have no need of such ointments."

"No, certainly you do not, in the bud of your beauty as you are," he told her, making Brita blush.

But Brita was right. Amongst the man's goods were many items I had not seen before. "Where have you found all these things?" I asked.

"Londinium, Queen Boudica. Wares are coming in by the boatload. They are eager to trade for our goods. You should go see, my queen. Glass and other ornaments for the home the likes of which we have nothing here in our lands."

"I am content with what I have."

"You may change your mind when you go that way. Eddard traded for cloth, fine silks and wools like the Roman ladies wear. Stolas, that's what their dresses are called. And togas for the men. Dresses for their men! Have you seen?"

"I have. But you best be careful, merchant. Those men in dresses have tongues sharper than swords. Watch yourself."

He laughed. "Thank you for the advice, Queen Boudica."

I winked at him then we went on our way.

"Does no one have raspberries?" I complained, my hand on my stomach. "They can keep their Roman perfumes and silks. I would trade the world for a bucket full of raspberries, leaves, bees, bugs, and all."

At that, the others laughed.

Vian paused along the way, stopping to examine a strange device made with beads connected to a frame.

Brita, her eye taken by the cloth the vendor had mentioned, moved on.

"Queen Boudica," Brita called, waving for me to come.

"Why don't I buy some cloth to make you a stola," I told Pix, biting my bottom lip, so I didn't laugh. I wanted to see what she would say.

"What do I be needing a dress for?"

"Variety."

"Ye can keep yer variety. When it comes time to run, ye will be happier in trousers. And faster."

"As you say."

"Look," Brita said, holding out a bolt of indigo-blue cloth. "Oh, you must have a dress made like this. We can save it for after the child is born."

I eyed the fabric. Brita was right. It was a lovely shade, and the material was soft and light, perfect for summer.

"Very well," I said, then turned to the vendor. "We will have it. And that one," I said, pointing to another bolt of deep green which would look lovely on Bec.

"Excellent, Queen Boudica. There is some thread here spun with silver," he added, opening a box so we could look.

I nodded. "Yes. That too," I told him, then paid the man his fee.

Vian caught up with us, the bead board in her hands.

"What be that?" Pix asked. "A toy for the wee one?"

"The man told me it is called an abacus," Vian said. "It is used in counting to help perform calculations. A bit like the use of staves. I thought, perhaps, I might be able to assist Prasutagus and Ansgar in some of their planning with the use of this."

Pix took it from Vian's hand, shaking it, making the beads switch back and forth. "Looks like it makes music."

Vian took it back from her. "Decidedly not."

As I scanned the market, I finally spotted a woman selling fruits. "There," I said, pointing.

With that, the four of us went to the woman.

"Queen Boudica," the woman said, bowing to me.

"Please tell me you have raspberries," I said.

She chuckled. "I think the queen's child is giving her longings."

"So she is."

"She, is it?"

I chuckled. "Time will tell."

"Well, she is in luck. These are the last of them. Had to fight the blackbirds for them," she said, hoisting a bucket.

I dipped into my coin pouch to pay the woman.

"So many new vendors," the woman said, her eyes on the market. "Many things from afar."

I nodded. "There are."

"And rumors along with them," she added nonchalantly as she prepared the fruits.

"Such as?" I asked.

"That the Romans have marched on the Dobunni, burning villages and taking hostages as they search for King Caratacus."

I paused. "Yes, I have heard the same."

"Then it is true?"

"As far as I know."

"'Tis a pity about the people. I hardly think the Dobunni people know where the king is hiding, and certainly not the women and children being loaded into ships in Londinium."

"No, very certainly not."

"These are strange days. That is all that can be said. Strange days and strange bedfellows, but I would not see my family on a slave ship set for Gaul. And I know it was you and the king who kept us clear of that," she said with a nod. "Some blueberries for the king," she added, handing me another basket. "He used to snitch them from my stall when he was a boy."

I chuckled. "Who can I tell him the gift is from?"

"Orda."

"I thank you, Orda."

"The Mother's blessings upon you, Queen Boudica. You and your little one."

Pix took the baskets from my hand. "Let me carry these for ye."

"That is not an excuse to eat them."

"Nay, I would not think of it," she said, her mouth already full of blueberries.

The others chuckled.

"It's too hot," Brita complained. "Perhaps that is enough walking today, Queen Boudica."

It wasn't hot. I knew Brita was using it as an excuse to make me return, but I didn't complain. "Yes. Let's go back. All I can think about is getting those raspberries to Betha," I said. "Assuming Pix leaves us any."

"I like the blueberries better anyway," she mumbled.

"Those are for Prasutagus."

"He'll ne'er know how many there were before they go to him."

"Pix!" I complained.

"Don't worry, Boudica," Vian said. "I am already counting how much she is eating," she added, gesturing to her board.

At that, Pix laughed. "Ye best be careful, or I'll shake that instrument of yers."

Vian shot Pix a dark glance, making Pix chuckle.

With that, we turned and headed back to the king's house. As we went, the merry party turned quiet.

Finally, Vian asked, "Are the Romans really taking slaves from the common people?"

"They had Catuvellauni and Cantiaci working with chains on their necks in Camulodunum," Pix said. "Didn't ye see them?"

"I did, I just… I thought perhaps they'd been warriors who resisted. But women and children?" Vian said sadly.

"May the gods watch over all the Iceni and spare us from that fate," Brita said, speaking the words we were all thinking.

CHAPTER 53

The days passed, and soon, the autumnal equinox was upon us. Due to Prasutagus's careful planning and Vian's calculations, Venta was well stocked with grain for the winter. We also made a deal with a Roman envoy from Camulodunum to sell our extra grain to the Romans to help shore up the gaps to feed their soldiers. I had mixed feeling about the sale. More and more, news was coming from the west and south of Rome's brutality as they marched.

It was becoming painfully clear that those leaders who opposed or betrayed Rome had opened the door for the Romans to do as they wished.

Villages were burning.

People were being taken hostage.

My heart ached, and I wondered what I could possibly do to stop the flow of violence.

But I was just one person.

What could one person do in the face of such a tremendous force?

With no answer to that question, I turned my attention to what I did have control over, the well-being of the Greater Iceni.

When Mabon arrived, we prepared for a festival that would draw hundreds of people. Poles had been erected, garlands of autumn flowers and vines strung between them. Sunflowers decorated the square. Bonfires had been lit, and barrels of apple cider and ale had been readied for the revelers, along with deer and boar roasting over the fires.

At the king's house, we spent days weaving dolls made of wheat for people to take back to their homes to decorate their doors and offer thanks to Brigid and the Mother Goddess for a good harvest. We had also worked nonstop baking apple tarts and preparing hand pies for the festival.

"Ye be too slow," Pix told Brita, pushing what had to be her twentieth hand pie toward Ronat for baking.

"She may be slow, but look at her art," Vian told Pix.

We all paused to look at Brita's handiwork. She had crafted a true-to-life sunflower on the top of her apple tart.

"It's beautiful," I told Brita. "Don't let Pix chide you."

"Will taste the same going down whether it looks like a flower or has simple dough on the top," Pix replied.

"You could put a little flourish into it," Nella told Pix.

"Blind as I am, my crimp is better than yours," Ginerva added, pointing at Pix's hand pie.

I grinned at them as I sat cutting out simple stars and moons to adorn the top of my pies and taking yet another bite of apple dipped in honey. The child didn't want me to work at all, only eat apples.

Pix sighed, then pulled back the last pie she'd made and began crimping the dough around the edges. "I shall adorn it for ye, but it still makes no difference to the stomach."

"But the Great Mother will be grateful you made it easier on the eyes. It's a simple kitchen charm," Brita told Pix.

"My knives have a better purpose than kitchen work," Pix told Brita with a wink, making us chuckle.

On the day of the festival, Brita helped me slip into a new gown. The girl had fashioned me a dark blue frock, trimming it with embroidery of sunflowers. My belly had outgrown the generous waists of my other gowns. This was my first proper pregnancy dress, designed with room to grow. I stroked my stomach, admiring my bulging belly. My pregnancy had become very pronounced, but I was glad. I wanted the Greater Iceni to see that life continued on.

Once we were ready, Brita and I made our way to the fields.

There, I found Pix and the others setting out the food, preparing the drinks, and placing the baskets of straw dolls.

Pix and Prasutagus joined us.

"Well, Harvest Queen. Ye be a fair sight. But ye forgot yer crown," Pix said, setting a wheat crown on my head. "Now ye be the picture of the Mother. Let the people see ye like that."

I turned to Prasutagus, who grinned at me.

"She's right. Now, you look perfect," Prasutagus said.

"Are you saying I didn't look perfect before?"

Prasutagus grinned at me.

It was late afternoon when the druids and priestesses arrived. They came by wagon, four women, three men, all of whom lived at the small farmstead in King's Wood.

"Priestess Henwyn," Prasutagus said, helping the elder priestess from the wagon. "You are most welcome."

"King Prasutagus," she said with a smile. "It is good to see you," she said, finding her footing. She patted his cheek. "You look well. Marriage to the Northern Iceni agrees with you."

Prasutagus smiled. "Thank you, Priestess."

"Queen Boudica," she said, turning to me. "Dressed for Mabon, I see. How lovely. And this little one," she said, setting her hands on my stomach. "Are you well, my queen? We heard you had a passing sickness after that business with Ardra."

"I am well, as is the child."

"Very good," she said, then looked to Prasutagus. "You did not call us to attend the queen."

"You must forgive me. There was no time. Ariadne saw to her."

"Must all your queens forsake druids and sworn priestesses for your village midwife?" she asked with a sly, but not angry, smile.

Prasutagus laughed lightly but said nothing more.

"Henwyn," Ansgar called. "It is good to see you in Venta."

"It is good to be asked," she replied, giving Prasutagus a knowing glance before joining the druid.

I turned to Prasutagus.

"Ariadne was a friend of Esu's. They grew up together in the village. Ariadne learned midwifery from her mother, who delivered Artur. That was how I knew her. But that is also why I trusted her with you and our child."

"I see."

"I'm sorry I didn't mention it before."

"Never feel sorry for having lived a life before me," I told him.

"You are too good," Prasutagus said, taking my hand and kissing my fingers.

"Only to those who deserve it," I replied.

Prasutagus chuckled.

Subconsciously, my free hand went to the amulet I wore under my dress, my fingers gently feeling the shape of the frog medallion.

Prasutagus and I lived lives before one another that would never be forgotten.

Gaheris…

Gaheris…

It is harvest season once more…

The crowd grew as the sun dipped low on the horizon. The sounds of pipes, flutes, and drums filled the air. Soon, everyone gathered at the center of the field where the druids waited. At the heart of the wheat field, one shaft of grain remained. A spiral of stones led to the single shaft.

As the sun dipped toward the horizon, Ansgar

collected Prasutagus and me to perform the final rite of the harvest season.

I eyed the crowd, spotting Artur with Pix, Brita, and Vian.

I gave the boy a soft smile that he returned.

Prasutagus and I joined the druids.

The last rays of sunlight burned down to glowing orange and deep pink, then faded into the dark blue of night. The crowd gathered around.

One of the druids lifted a carnyx, sounding the instrument.

The sound of the horn echoed across the field, silencing those who had come to listen.

Henwyn nodded to Prasutagus, who stepped forward.

"Greater Iceni," he called. "People of Venta, and those of you who have come to us from tribes beyond our borders, welcome. Tonight, we will thank the Great Mother and the Year King for the abundance they have bestowed upon us this harvest season. Raise your hands in prayer. May the Great Mother hear our thanks."

We all raised our hands.

"Great Mother, we thank you for your bounty," Prasutagus called.

"Great Mother, we thank you for your bounty," we echoed.

"Year King, we thank you for your gift of life," Prasutagus intoned.

"Year King, we thank you for your gift of life."

Henwyn gestured to me and then handed me a pitcher.

"May the earth be thanked for its generous bounty.

May the trees be thanked for the nuts, berries, and wood they provide. May the bushes and fields be thanked for their plentiful harvest. I pour this ale in your name as a symbol of all you have given us, returning it back to you," I said, tipping the pitcher and pouring the ale to the ground.

Ansgar stepped forward. "Tonight, we shall release the Year King," he said, gesturing to the single shaft of grain remaining. "As the Mother nourishes, the Year King provides life. But his year has come to an end. May the Year King's spirit be released so he may rejoin us in the spring, giving the Mother life once more." Ansgar handed Prasutagus a silver crescent boline knife.

Prasutagus knelt before the shaft of grain. "May the Year King, the Father, be thanked for the bounty brought to this land. And may his life force protect us this long winter. With great thanks," he said, then cut the last shaft of grain.

Rising, he handed it to Henwyn.

The priestess lifted it above her head for all to see. "The wheel has turned. The year has passed. The harvest is done. The Mother sleeps, and the Year King is dead. We shall meet him again in the spring when day and night are equal once more."

Henwyn turned to me.

"Greater Iceni, I thank you all for your hard work in these days of harvest," I began, but a soft murmur from the back of the crowd made me pause. I looked to find General Plautius and two Roman soldiers there. The general nodded politely to the others, his helmet under his arm, as he made his way through the crowd, finally pausing as he came to the front. The Roman met my gaze, giving me a soft smile.

"People of the Greater Iceni," I called in a loud voice, drawing their attention away from the unexpected visitors to myself. "We stand here in this field from which we have taken a bountiful harvest. Although these times have brought great uncertainty to our lands, the gods smile upon all the Iceni people. The Great Mother and her Year King be thanked. Tonight, the Year King dies so we may thrive and grow. May the Lord and Lady and all the greenwood be thanked. And may all of you be blessed in their name. Blessed be."

I caught the general's gaze once more. He lifted an eyebrow at me, giving me that same half-smile.

"Blessed be," the crowd answered.

Prasutagus stepped forward. "Come, my friends. The last shaft of grain has been cut. Now, let's celebrate! We are all friends here. There is cider, meat, and music to be enjoyed. Let us celebrate a year of hard work and bounty hard-won!" Prasutagus gestured to the musicians who played once more.

Prasutagus turned his back to the crowd, giving me a knowing look, then handed the knife back to Ansgar.

"Be sure the people eat, and don't worry. Boudica and I will see to our unexpected guests," Prasutagus told Ansgar.

Taking the knife, Ansgar nodded to him.

Prasutagus turned to me, taking my hand, then the pair of us went to meet the general.

"General Plautius, this is an unexpected surprise," Prasutagus said.

"King Prasutagus," Aulus said, giving him a bow. "Queen Boudica. I was on my way back to Camulodunum when I decided to make a detour to see how my friends, the Greater Iceni, were faring."

"You are most welcome," Prasutagus said politely.

"You have found us during the equinox celebration of Mabon," I explained.

"You are looking every bit a fertility goddess, Queen Boudica. A new development?" he asked, eyeing my round stomach.

"Not so new, General," I replied with a laugh. "And temporary, per the common course."

"I wish you both great felicitations," Aulus said, smiling at us both.

"Are you married, General?" Prasutagus asked.

"Actually, my title is Governor now. And no, I am not. I'm afraid I spend too much time in the saddle for it."

"Perhaps, one day, you will find a woman who convinces you to climb down," I teased.

Aulus laughed. "If such a woman exists, I look forward to meeting her."

"Governor, is it?" Prasutagus asked.

Aulus nodded.

"What does such a title imply?" I asked.

"That the emperor saw fit to put me in charge of all of Rome's interests here in Britannia."

"I see. Well, you have our congratulations. Come," Prasutagus said, gesturing to the festival area. "We have much food and drink. It will be good for the Greater Iceni people to see you are mortals after all."

Aulus gestured to his soldiers to follow along, and we all joined the festival.

Pix brought me a flagon of cider. "For ye after that nice speech," she told me, then eyed Aulus. "What do ye want, Rome?"

"Peace, Maiden. I am only here for a drink and a pie."

At that, Pix laughed. "And a fox only wants feathers for his pillow from the hen house," she told him, then looked to me. "Watch him," she said, then departed.

"Here," I said, handing my cup to Aulus as I gathered more for the rest of us. "Shall we toast?" I asked.

Prasutagus nodded to me.

"Then, to bountiful harvests," I said, lifting my mug.

"To bountiful harvests," the others replied, all of us clicking our cups.

After the soldiers drank, Aulus turned and said something to them in a language I didn't recognize. The men took their mugs and stepped a bit back, away from the crush of the crowd.

"I don't want your people to think we're interfering," he said offhandedly in explanation.

"King Prasutagus," Henwyn said, joining us. "We are ready for the first cut of meat, if you will."

Prasutagus nodded. "Priestess Henwyn, may I introduce Governor Plautius."

Henwyn nodded to him. "You are welcome here on this holy night, Roman."

"I am pleased to earn that invitation," Aulus said politely.

Henwyn gestured for Prasutagus to go with her.

"If you will excuse me," Prasutagus told Aulus. "It's tradition. I'll rejoin you shortly."

Aulus gave him a polite nod.

Prasutagus took my hand, giving it a light squeeze, then let me go.

"Something to eat?" I asked Aulus, who nodded.

We went to the long table where the pies were laid out.

"Now, you must tell me what to try," Aulus said, looking over the bounty.

I scanned the table, recognizing Brita's beautiful handiwork. "These," I said, gesturing to one of the beautiful pies. "These lovely pies were made by my maid."

"It is fine work. Your maid...the pies were made by your household?"

"Most of them."

"And by you?"

I chucked. "Yes, but—"

"You must show me your work."

"All right," I said, leading him down the row until I found the hand pie decorated with stars. "This is one of mine."

Grinning, Aulus lifted it and took a bite.

"It's apples, honey, and nuts," I explained. "I confess, I think I ate as much as I baked."

Aulus's eyebrows shot up. "Quite good. It reminds me of my mother's cooking. She was a homey baker as well."

"You flatter," I told him.

"Never. Ask anyone who knows me."

"Then I must consider myself a special case."

"Of that, I can assure you, Queen Boudica."

The music began in earnest, and the people lined up to dance together. Three big circles had formed, everyone linking arms.

Henwyn rejoined us. "Queen Boudica, Governor Plautius. Come. Join the dancing. You and your men, Governor. Come, you will enjoy yourselves."

"Are you certain, Priestess?" Aulus asked.

"Always," Henwyn replied, her eyes twinkling.

Aulus grinned. "Do all Iceni women know their minds so well?"

"Of course. Don't Roman women?" I asked.

Aulus laughed. "Not at all," he said, then motioned for his men to join him. "And you, Queen Boudica? Will you join in the dancing?"

"I am afraid this one forbids it," I said, setting my hand on my stomach.

"Then it must be a girl. She already knows her mind," Aulus replied with a wink, then turned to Henwyn. "Priestess, lead on," he told her.

With that, the Romans set their helmets aside and joined the others. Henwyn entered the dancing circle, lining the Romans up with priestesses as partners.

The fiddles played, the pipes called, drums beat, and the dance began again.

The strange tension that had fallen over the crowd since the arrival of the Romans began to dissipate.

Prasutagus joined me once more. With him, he had a

platter of meat. "You *can't* dance, my May Queen, but you *can* eat. I brought you one of the best cuts."

I took the platter from him and then sat on one of the makeshift benches.

"The eagle dances amongst the horse people. Did you ever think you would see such a sight?" I asked.

"No. And now, we must determine why he is really here," Prasutagus replied.

"You don't believe it was a courtesy visit?"

"With him, nothing is done without calculation."

"Hmm," I mused, then popped a bite of venison in my mouth, chewing as I considered. "Then let's get him a hard cider. And another. And another. By the time we are done, perhaps we can ply an honest answer from him."

At that, Prasutagus chuckled, then took a bite for himself. "May Quert," he said, referring to the Ogham name for apple, "hear your prayers."

CHAPTER 54

I t was late in the evening when we finally retired to the roundhouse, Aulus joining us. I was exhausted but far too interested in what Aulus had to say to excuse myself.

We adjourned to the dining hall, where Ronat served mugs of honeyed herbs that Aulus studied for a moment before drinking.

"So, you must tell us, Governor, why are you here?" Prasutagus said.

Aulus smiled, then leaned forward to set down his cup. "I like you, Prasutagus. Always honest and to the point. That is what I told the emperor about you, that he will find no better ally than King Prasutagus. So, let *me* be honest. I did not want to go to Caturix due to his...entanglements. I thought, perhaps, it was better to come to the two of you. There are whispers that the Coritani have been sending help to Caratacus. In fact, word that the Catuvellauni king —*former* king—has spoken to the triumvirate."

"This is the first I have heard of it," Prasutagus said in all honesty.

I nodded.

"We know the Greater Iceni are with us, that you share our vision. You see Rome as we wish to be seen—as a friend and ally. But Caratacus continues to seed discontent. And I fear your brother," Aulus said, turning to me, "may be pulled into duplicity."

"I know King Volisios shares his opinions with my brother from time to time, but Caturix is his own man, and he will do what is best for the Northern Iceni. There is no love lost between Caratacus and us."

"Yes, I have heard some details about your uncle, Boudica. They say he was responsible for your father's death—aided by Caratacus and Togodumnus."

I willed my face not to betray my emotions. "Yes," I said stiffly.

"I hoped the sentiment was as deep as I guessed. But I ask you to speak to Caturix, ensure he continues to see things our way for all our good. I would not want to inter-vene in Northern Iceni business, especially not with Boudica as such a strong ally to Rome."

"You won't need to," I said. "Never. If there is ever a matter with the Northern Iceni that Caturix is unable or unwilling to solve, I implore you—I implore Rome—to please speak with us, with me. The Northern Iceni are my people."

"I have yet to meet Prince Bran, though Titus speaks well and frequently of him. I will have to make a trip to Oak Throne one day."

"We would be happy to accompany you. Since you have been honest, allow me the same," I said, flicking a quick glance at Prasutagus. "We, too, have heard rumors. We've heard that many innocent people have fallen into harm's way, women and children captured or killed, innocent people being enslaved, all along the coast."

Aulus nodded. Lifting his mug, he sat back once more. "Legate Vespasian has a heavier hand and a less diplomatic way of maneuvering in foreign lands. This is part of the reason the emperor has changed my title to Governor. Now that I wield the title, I wield the power. I have heard of what you speak, Queen Boudica. In fact, I have just ridden from the coast where Vespasian and I discussed a more native-friendly stance, such as we enjoy here. I believe he understood my philosophy, and you will hear fewer rumors going forward. But you must remember, Queen Boudica, war is war. Do not be surprised when there are casualties."

"I understand."

"It is a bloody business. If only the tribes would remember we came here on the request of King Verica and the late Aedd Mawr, as allies, not enemies."

"I'm afraid you have Julius Caesar to thank for the temperature of your welcome," Prasutagus told him.

Aulus laughed. "Indeed."

I shifted uncomfortably in my seat. As much as I wanted to stay, everything hurt, and my eyelids were drooping. On top of that, I felt a flicker of frustration with Caturix. What was he doing? Feeling miserable, I rose. "I must apologize," I said. "My feet ache, and the child has had enough for one night. I must bid you good night."

Aulus stood. "Good night, Queen Boudica. Many thanks for including me in your revels this evening."

I nodded to him, then turned to Prasutagus, who rose to kiss me on the cheek, whispering, "I will join you after a time."

With that, I left the men and made my way to my bedchamber. When I opened the door, Brita peered out from her chamber. "Boudica?"

"I can see myself to bed. Rest. You danced the night away," I told her.

With a yawn, she nodded, then turned and closed the door, going back to bed.

In the chamber, I pulled off my boots—giggling at the newfound difficulty of reaching them over my stomach—and slipped off my dress. Washing up, I went to grab a bed gown from my wardrobe. When I pulled the shift off a shelf, a small leather pouch came along with it, the contents falling to the floor.

I kneeled down to find a coin—*the* coin.

I lowered myself to the floor and sat holding the Menapii coin in my hands.

Setting it up with one finger, I spun the coin. It twisted in quick circles until it wobbled and fell over. I lifted it again and again, spinning it over and over, my finger stopping the whirling with a click. Again and again, I turned the coin. As I watched it, my eyelids grew heavy, and my gaze softened.

The whirling sound made my head buzz, and soon, I saw a wheel.

The image was blurry at first, but with each spin of the coin, it grew clearer.

It was the wheel of a chariot. It raced across a field filled with long grass, the wheels twirling like the coin. I could hear the horses' rigging and the sound of their heavy breathing as they raced onward toward...toward...

Spin.

Click.

Spin.

Click.

Toward Camulodunum. But not the city as I knew it. It was massive, with huge walls and structures both within and outside the city. Roman pennants fluttered over the walls— no sign remaining that this was a Trinovantes city. Around me, I heard horses, chariots, and voices calling, screaming.

Spin.

Click.

Spin.

Click.

When I looked behind me, I saw warriors. Thousands of warriors.

And they all followed *me*.

"Boudica...

"Protect the trees...

"Protect the stones...

"Protect the greenwood...

"Protect us all!"

Sometime later, I woke, shivering, on the floor. Chiding myself, I pulled on my shift, then bent and picked up the coin, slipping it back into the leather pouch and securing it on the shelf where I kept it safe.

Padding across the cold stones, I slipped into bed, pulling the coverlets to my neck. The vision of what I had seen plagued me.

"Gaheris," I whispered as I slipped back off to sleep. "Gaheris, watch over me."

CHAPTER 55

I t was well after sunup when I woke the following morning. Even though it was my rumbling stomach that had awakened me, it was thoughts of Caturix that first popped into my mind. If Aulus was right, if Volisios was bending Caturix's ear, something must be done. It was clear what happened when Rome marked one as an enemy. I would not have my brother drag the Northern Iceni into a war that had nothing to do with our people.

Dressing quickly, I pulled my hair back into a bun and went out to see what I had missed.

When I arrived in the dining hall, I found only Vian and Artur. The pair sat side by side, Vian showing Artur how the bead board worked.

"You see, if we count the bushels of straw in such a manner, we will be able to easily keep a tally," Vian was explaining.

I smiled at them. "Good morning."

"Good morning," Artur and Vian replied in tandem, making both of them chuckle.

"King Prasutagus and the Romans left early this morning to look at the construction," Vian told me.

"Hmm," I mused. "Very well. Let me go see if Betha has any pies left."

"Boudica," Vian said with a light chuckle.

"Want one?"

She shook her head.

I slipped into the back of the house to the kitchen. I found the place empty, but there was a basket of pies and a few leftover straw dolls on the counter. Taking one of each and wrapping the pie in a cloth, I headed out back to find Nella and Ginerva seated in the herb garden.

"Look at Esu's maid. How fat she has grown," Ginerva said, shooting me a scolding look.

Nella shook her head. "Good morning, Boudica," she said, not altogether icily. Since the issue with Artur and Ardra, Nella had warmed considerably toward me. It seems she had decided to tolerate me. It was the best I could hope for.

Leaving them, I walked down the path, away from the compound, and was going to the stables to have my morning meal with Druda when I saw Prasutagus and Aulus. The Romans were preparing to leave.

I joined them.

"Ah, Queen Boudica," Aulus said. "I am glad to be able to say farewell."

"You're leaving already?"

Aulus nodded. "I'm afraid with the pending departure

of King Diras and Julia, I am needed in Camulodunum, but Prasutagus was kind enough to show me what Rome's money purchased. I will share the news with the other kings. Hopefully, they can make such wise investments in their lands."

"We thank you for your visit. Prasutagus and I will see to the other matter we discussed," I replied.

"Naturally," Aulus said, then mounted his horse.

"Governor," I said, going to him. "Here, you must take these tokens with you. This, to keep you nourished," I told him, handing him the pie.

He lifted it to his nose and breathed in the scent. "My thanks," he said with a grin.

"And this, to remember Britannia's gods."

He took the straw doll and attached it to his saddle. "I feel honored," he said, then slipped the pie into his saddlebag.

With that, I stepped back and linked my arm with Prasutagus's.

"Safe journeys," Prasutagus told him.

"Be well, King Prasutagus, Queen Boudica," he said, then clicked to his horse, his soldiers following him.

"Well?" I asked Prasutagus after the gates closed behind Aulus.

"I will ride for Stonea," Prasutagus said.

"That bad?"

"I must ensure that Caturix doesn't fall into a Coritani mess."

"Be clear with Caturix. He admires you. He will listen if you put things in a way he understands."

"Put things in a way he understands... like gifts of pies and straw dolls?"

"Precisely."

Prasutagus pulled me close and kissed me on my head. "You would give those Roman senators a run for their money, my queen."

"Let's hope I never have a reason to try."

Two weeks after Aulus's appearance in Venta, Prasutagus and a small band of warriors rode out for Stonea. Artur and I watched from the wall of the king's compound as they rode through the city and beyond.

"When will he be back?" Artur asked me.

"Soon, I hope," I said with a shiver. "I smell the snow in the air. Do you?"

Artur laughed. "No. It is too soon for snow."

"Is it? I thought of a soup my old cook used to make on the first snowy day. I was craving it all morning."

"Then you are wishing for snow because you want the soup."

"Who would wish such a thing?"

Artur laughed. "You."

"Well, perhaps I can convince Betha to make something either way. Come on, you can help me. She's much more easily convinced by your pleading eyes than mine."

"Boudica," Artur said with a laugh, then took my hand. We walked across the green to the king's house.

I sensed a lightness in the boy I had not felt in weeks.

And with that, I gave thanks. The dark clouds seemed to be finally behind him.

MY SENSE THAT THE SNOW WOULD SOON ARRIVE WAS NOT wrong. A cool winter wind blew across Venta in the days after Prasutagus's departure. And soon, the first flurries of snow followed.

Vian stood in the doorway of the roundhouse, glaring miserably at the snowflakes falling down.

"I hate it," she said affirmatively.

"Why?" Artur asked.

"I don't like being cold. I hate it when the sun disappears for days. I spend the whole winter by the fire."

"At least in Venta, there will be things to entertain you," I said.

"Yes, at least there is that."

Pix, on the other hand, stood staring up at the sky. "I ne'er did see such white snow," she said, watching as the flakes fell down, melting when they landed on her face. "Spent too many years without the winter. I did forget its beauty."

"You can have it," Vian said. "That's enough for me already," she said, then turned and headed back inside.

Pulling a shawl around Artur and me, I led us outside, joining Pix.

"I hope Father returns before the weather turns hard," Artur said.

I nodded. "As do I."

The boy stared down the road as if he were trying to see Prasutagus in Stonea.

"Those Romans will freeze their naked legs off in this weather," Pix said with a grin. "What do ye say, Artur? Do you want a tunic to your knees? You can dance around in the snow with your legs bare for the world to see," Pix said, then did a jig.

At that, Artur laughed. "I'd rather die than wear such nonsense."

"Their legs are exposed in battle," Pix said, then pulled her sword. "Drop onto a knee and slice," she said, making the move. "The shin bone is hard, but the muscle at the back...cut that, and it will down a man. Where be your sword anyway, little prince?"

"Well, I..."

"Hmm," Pix mused. "Prasutagus coddled ye. Or was it yer mother? That will not do. Go on and get your cloak and meet me in the stables. I shall show ye the sword while your father is busy. And in the spring, with a wee babe strapped to her chest, Boudica will show ye the spear."

At that, I laughed.

Without waiting for a second invitation, Artur ran back to the house.

Pix turned to me. "Do ye think Prasutagus will mind?"

I shook my head. "It is overdue."

"So it be. I'll keep him busy this winter, Strawberry Queen, so ye can attend to the other on the way," Pix said, clapping me on the shoulder as she headed off to the stables.

Alone, I held out my hand.

Fat snowflakes fell therein, melting in the warmth of my palm.

"Lady Epona, Great Mother, keep Prasutagus safe, and see him home safely through this first blush of winter. And watch over all the Iceni people."

CHAPTER 56

Not long after Prasutagus's return from Stonea, winter began in earnest. Despite the difficult weather, I was glad Prasutagus had made the trip. As it turned out, Aulus was right. The Coritani had been whispering to Caturix.

"Mostly, it is just talk. Caturix was firm with King Volisios about his disinterest in helping Caratacus. That said, your brother did not like to hear that the Romans know the Coritani are edgy."

"The Romans have spies everywhere."

Prasutagus nodded. "So I told him."

"Speaking of… What have *we* heard these days?"

"Things are growing quiet with the weather shifting. When winter arrives in earnest, the Romans will hunker down."

"Good."

Prasutagus nodded. "Let's only hope Caratacus doesn't use the quiet to his advantage."

"May the Mother blanket us all in the quiet of winter."

As it turned out, the weather was on the side of peace. For the first time in people's memories, snow fell deep before Samhain.

"There are still more trees to clear on the eastern slope of the Tay," Prasutagus told me as he prepared to head out one morning. "With the winter coming in so early and strong, we will need the extra firewood. I will be back by nightfall."

I kissed my husband and let him go. As I settled in by the fire in the great house, my thoughts drifted to Oak Throne and Ula. I hoped Bran and Bec would keep an eye on her this winter. Soon, the snow would become too deep for the horses to easily pass, and the rivers would freeze. It would be spring before I had news of Oak Throne. Maybe there would be a gap in the weather to get a messenger—and some silver—through to Ula. I knew the old woman well enough to know that she would never ask for help.

I set my hands on my stomach. The little one within me rolled. "Like the snow, do you? Well, seems you are in the minority. Four months to go, little firebrand. We will see what you think of this world soon enough."

The snow driving everyone inside, the weeks began to pass slowly. Samhain came and went, and soon, it was nearly Yule. I hated that I hadn't heard anything from Bran and Bec. Each day, anxiety crept up in me as I wondered how Bec had fared. Had her child been born? Was she all right? The tragedy Melusine experienced left me feeling nervous.

"Ye have worn a groove in the stones," Pix told me one afternoon as I paced back and forth across the hall.

"I'm worried about Bec," I said, then paused. Checking to make sure we were alone, I looked at Pix. "Why don't you go to Oak Throne?"

"Snow be too high to ride."

"I'm not talking about riding. The King Stone…"

"And where do ye think I can pop out?"

"In the mossy wood or at the Grove of Andraste. Could you do it?"

Pix considered. "'Tis not without risk. That mossy wood be crawling with dark things. I dare not chance that place."

"But it could be done."

"Aye."

I paced once more.

"Ye have enough to worry about here," Pix told me. "Ne'er mind what they are doing to the north. And Bec has that old witch of yours and a grove of priestesses to look after her. Ne'er you mind her. Worry about yerself."

Pix was right. Bec was in Ula's care, and Dôn was not far away. There was nothing to worry about. Ula would grump and grumble, but Bran and Bec's child would be born safely. Come spring, I would travel north.

News trickled in slowly, but it seemed that the Roman advance to the west had also ground to a stop. Nothing, however, could stop the building in Camulodunum. With the frames of buildings constructed in the fall, they were finishing the interiors in the winter. News also came from Raven's Dell that another Trinovantes village had been taken over by the Romans, the residents sent wandering in the dead of winter for shelter.

"I am weary of problems of Rome's making, and my body aches from chopping wood all day," Prasutagus said as he sat beside me in the meeting room.

"Shall I have Brita draw a bath?"

"And freeze afterward? No, Queen Boudica, you will have to keep me warm this night. I can feel the fire coming off my little one. Do you hear me, little firebrand?" he asked my belly.

"That is *my* stomach's flames you feel. Every bite of bread I eat sets my stomach afire these days."

"What, child, you cannot let your mother have a bite of bread? Shame on you."

At that, the babe twisted and turned.

"She hears you," I said with a laugh, "and does not like to be chided."

Prasutagus laughed. "I'm sorry, sweet one," he said. "Speaking of children, let me go see Artur before he falls asleep. Unless Pix has worn him thin already."

"They are keeping one another entertained."

"I am grateful to her. Vian has taught him much as well. Ansgar, too, has taken to instructing him in Latin. He is eager to learn."

"He is a bright boy."

Prasutagus nodded slowly, his gaze growing glossy. "He takes after his mother. She was very wise," he said, then paused, lost in his memories for a long moment. With a sad sigh, he rose. "I'll join you soon," he said, then departed.

I stayed a moment longer to put away my sewing. Riona would have been proud to see me embroidering the little dresses and gowns Brita was making. I was not as good a hand at it as the maid, but I could stitch a fair row of leaves.

Taking the sewing basket with me, I was making my way to my bedchamber when I heard sobbing coming from Ginerva's room.

I paused, then knocked on the door. "Ginerva?" I called. "It's Boudica. May I come?"

She did not reply, merely wept.

"Ginerva?" I called again. Worried, I pushed open the door. When I entered, I found her room dimly lit. The old woman lay in her bed, her long, silver hair unbraided. Her rheumy eyes were red from crying, her cheeks wet with tears. "Ginerva? What is it? Are you ill?"

"No, dear girl. No. It's just... I remembered."

"Remembered?" I asked, sitting down on the side of her bed.

"That my Esu is gone," she said with a sad moan.

I took her hand. "Yes. I am very sorry for it. I didn't know your daughter, but I have heard many good stories about her. It is almost as if I knew her," I said, and when I did so, an image of the woman formed in my mind, a sweet girl with curly dark hair and a smattering of freckles on her nose and cheeks, her eyes the same color as Artur's. Esu seemed to be on everyone's mind tonight.

Ginerva squeezed my hand. "You are good to her son. I know that. You are good to my grandson."

"I try very hard. And I will always do so."

She took my hand and gripped it tightly. "Promise me. Promise me you will always look after him."

"Ginerva?"

"Promise me," she said, giving my hand a hard squeeze.

"I promise it," I said, then pulled her covers up. "Are you warm enough? Can I bring you another coverlet?"

"I am settled here. Thank you, Boudica. Thank you for caring for my family. Thank you and Prasutagus, who treats me no different than he would his own blood," she said, then closed her eyes. "I will be glad when the darkness and confusion are done," she whispered. "It is too much to bear." She squeezed my hand once more, then let me go.

Rising, I kissed her cheek, then added another log to her fire. Closing the door slowly behind me, I slipped from the room.

WHEN WE WOKE THE FOLLOWING DAY, GINERVA WAS GONE.

CHAPTER 57

We took Ginerva by wagon to the nemeton. Near the stone altar at the heart of the henge, a pyre had been prepared to send her to the gods.

Light snow fell on Ginerva's body. Nella had dressed her beautifully with a stunning pale pink gown, the ancient woman's hair in braids like a maiden, leaves and winter berries in her hair. The fat snowflakes added to her adornment. I sensed the Mother Goddess there with us, reminding us that death was not an end but a beginning.

"May the Crone see Ginerva on this final passage into the Otherworld," Henwyn, dressed in a heavy fur, called as she lifted her hands to the heavens. "May the Mother embrace her as she begins a journey to a new life. May the Maiden ease her passage back to us when it is time for her to be born again."

Artur stood before Prasutagus and me. Though he tried not to cry, tears trailed down his cheeks.

This year had been too much for the child.

I set a loving hand on his shoulder.

When he leaned back toward me, I wrapped my arms around him.

"May all her ancestors welcome her as she returns to the place where we both begin and end," Ansgar called. "For life is but a never-ending circle. Ginerva, take your rest, then return to us once more."

Henwyn took a torch, then motioned for Artur to come forward.

The child hesitated.

"Shall we go with you?" I asked him, flicking my eyes to Prasutagus, who nodded.

The boy inhaled deeply, then said, "No. I will go."

Artur went to the priestess and took the torch. He paused before his grandmother—his last blood relative— whispering to her, then set the pyre aflame. When he was done, he handed the torch back to Henwyn and then stood as witness.

We stood in silence as Ginerva passed on to the Otherworld.

After the flames burned down, we loaded into the wagons to return once more to the king's house.

Back in the roundhouse, a small feast had been laid out. We ate, each person who knew Ginerva sharing stories of her, but a somber feeling filled the air.

Nella excused herself, her eyes wet with unshed tears.

Artur said nothing, merely disappeared midway through the meal.

"Should I go after him?" I asked Prasutagus.

Pix rose. "I'll go. I'll take him to the stable to thrash it out on a straw dummy."

"Are you sure?" I asked, looking at Prasutagus.

Pix paused. "King?" she added, looking for Prasutagus's permission.

He nodded, and Pix disappeared.

Ansgar sighed. "It is always sad to lose someone, but I remember her before she was lost to her memories. It is better this way."

At that, Prasutagus nodded. "Yes. I would not want such a fate."

"Nor I," Ansgar agreed.

"May the Dark Lady give us all a good death," I added.

Ansgar nodded. "May the Morrigu hear your prayer."

IN THE WEEKS FOLLOWING GINERVA'S DEATH, MY CHILD BEGAN to squirm mercilessly. Ariadne told me I had another month to go, but it was hard to believe. I was chronically uncomfortable.

Everything at Venta grew quiet as winter pressed on, and for long moments, I could easily forget that Rome was even a part of our world. However, the quiet was punctuated early one winter morning when a rider appeared from Yarmouth.

"King Prasutagus," the breathless man told us. "Fire. A building caught fire in the village. We're trying to save the supply sheds, docks, and ships, but half the village is gone."

Prasutagus paled, seeing a whole season's worth of work evaporating before his eyes. He turned to Galvyn. "Round up the men. We will take as many as we can. Let's hope there is something left by the time we get there."

"What caused the blaze? Does anyone know?" I asked.

"Accident, Queen Boudica. We had moved some oil imports to a building in the village. They got too close to a fire. The place went up like a torch."

I gasped.

Prasutagus turned to me. "I must go at once."

"I will go to the kitchens and prepare some supplies," I said, then hurried back into the house.

In the kitchen, Betha, Ronat, and I hurriedly prepared food for the men, stuffing everything into sacks. By the time we returned to the square, Prasutagus was already on Raven.

I handed him a satchel.

"I will be gone for a few days," he told me. "But if there is news of our child, don't hesitate to send a rider."

"Be safe," I told him. "May the gods go with you. Remember, everything can be rebuilt. Do not risk yourself."

Prasutagus gave me a grateful smile, then leaned down and kissed my forehead. "My May Queen," he said, a loving expression on his face, then he and the other men turned and rode off.

My heart sank as I watched him go.

"So much of his trade goods are stored in Yarmouth,

waiting to send to Gaul in spring," Vian said. "If it is a total loss… It will be a devastating financial blow to us."

"What can be done?" I asked Vian,

Her brow furrowed. "I…" she began, then looked back at the roundhouse. "I need to look at some things," she said, then turned and disappeared.

Leaving her, I went to the stables.

Druda was outside, his head hanging over the fence. He whinnied when he saw me, complaining that he had been left behind while Raven and the others set out on their adventure.

"I hear you, I hear you," I told him.

I stroked his face, then wrapped my arms around his neck, feeling his long winter coat. "I'm sorry," I told him. "That is one adventure we must miss."

Druda huffed with frustration.

"Don't worry, come spring, you will have two riders to carry."

Annoyed with me, Druda bopped the side of my head with his nose, then turned to rejoin the other poor, pitiful horses who'd been left behind, including Nightshade and Saenunos.

I made my way back to the roundhouse, my mind waffling between thoughts of the fire, my worries for Prasutagus, the potential financial implications, and wondering if Betha had any more bacon left from breakfast.

In the kitchens, I found Betha, Ronat, and Newt just settling in for their morning meal. All of them were talking about the news from Yarmouth. They paused when they saw me.

"My queen," Betha said, rising when I entered. "Did you need anything?"

"Please, don't let me disturb you. I just..." I said, my eyes going toward the platter filled with cooked eggs, meat, and bread at the center of their table.

Ronat laughed. "Come along, Queen Boudica. There is room on the bench beside Newt."

"I'll get you a plate," Betha said with a laugh.

I settled in with them. "I feel terrible. I'm taking your food."

"You are the queen," Newt said, looking confused. "All this food is *yours*."

"Betha cooked this for *you*. But maybe just a bit of bacon. And one round of bread. And maybe just a bite of eggs."

Betha laughed.

"My mother always makes extra in case Pix comes looking, which she usually does. There is plenty here, my queen," Ronat told me.

Reassured, I filled my plate and sat eating while Ronat and Betha discussed the fire and how easily the Roman oils caught flame.

"They smell sweet but are quick to burn," Betha said. "I hope the king finds something left when he arrives."

Betha, Ronat, and Newt quickly finished their meals, leaving me to linger over what was left, when Pix arrived.

"What's this?" Pix asked, mock annoyance on her face. "Did ye give me share to Boudica?"

Betha chuckled. "The queen has found out your secret."

Pix sat down and started filling her plate with what was left, including taking the round of bread from my plate and breaking it in half, taking half for herself.

"Hey," I protested. "I'm feeding two."

"And I missed a hundred years' worth of meals. Who has more to complain over?"

Ronat laughed. "You always say the wildest things, Pix."

"That I do," Pix told her with a wink.

Feeling over-full after my second morning meal, I headed off to bed to lie down for an hour or two, only to wake up once more just before evening dinner. I was beginning to like this lifestyle. For once, I felt very queenly.

The evening passed quietly. Pix took Artur out for training once more while Brita resumed working on sewing a gown for Bec. As for me, I vacillated between worrying about Prasutagus, pacing with my hands pressed against my lower back, and wanting to sleep. The latter finally won out.

"I'm going back to bed," I told Brita.

"Best get your rest now. Babes are easier to care for in the womb than without. And that little one will give you little rest on this side of things," she said with a laugh.

Chuckling, I made my way back to my bedchamber.

As I settled in, my thoughts went to Prasutagus.

"Great Epona, watch over him. And protect the Greater

Iceni. Don't let our hard work come to nothing," I prayed, then drifted off to sleep.

That night, I dreamed.

I was in a dense forest, a place that reminded me of the mossy wood, but I had never been there before. Great oak trees reached toward the sky. Amongst the trees were stones, jutting up from thick banks of ferns, faces carved thereon. The stones sat in a spiral. On them were carved the ancient symbols of our people: the double-disc, the mirror and comb, the crescent and the rod, signs whose meaning was known only to our holy people. Beyond the circle of stones was a small village nestled in the woods. I could not see it clearly through the trees, but I heard the giggling laughter of maidens echoing from the place.

"Boudica...

"Boudica...

"Protect the trees.

"Protect the stones.

"Protect the greenwood."

The image changed, and the forest faded to winter. Smoke billowed from the little village, the trees were cut to stumps, and the stones toppled. Blood marred the white snow.

"Boudica.

"Boudica!"

Overcome with terror, I woke with a start.

I jumped when I heard a knock on the door. "Boudica. Boudica?"

I rose, pulling my cloak around me, then went to the door. I opened it to find Ansgar on the other side.

"Ansgar, what is it?"

"I am sorry to wake you so early, my queen. But you must come at once."

"Prasutagus?"

Ansgar shook his head. "No. No word from the king. A rider," he replied, looking upset.

Slipping on a pair of simple slippers, I went to the main dining hall where Galvyn waited. I was surprised to find a priestess there. She wore a dark purple cloak, her golden hair pulled back in a bun. Snow still clung to her boots and shoulders.

"Boudica, this is Arian, a priestess from Maiden Stones."

"Queen Boudica," she said, bowing.

"Priestess, what are you—" I began, then stopped, my dream coming back to me. "The stones," I whispered.

"Queen Boudica, we urgently need your help."

"What has happened?"

"This autumn, the Romans began cutting trees in the forest not far from Maiden Stones. They have left us in peace, so we did not protest, but they have returned and penetrated into our sacred woods. Brigantia, our high priestess, and a Roman soldier had harsh words. They would not listen. They started cutting trees at the edge of our forest and taking stones. These are ancient stones, Queen Boudica. Many caves and barrows in the forest around Maiden Stones are entrances to the hollow hills or burial chambers of our ancestors. It is even said the first Trinovantes king is buried there. The Romans are gathering with sleds and teams of horses not far from our grove. It is clear they will soon begin work in earnest. Brigantia went to Camulodunum to appeal to Governor Plautius, but he would not see her. No one is listening to us. It is a sacred place. King Diras is gone. We did not know where else to turn. The priestess Dynis remembered your kind words to her when you met in Raven's Dell. She sent me here to plead for your help."

I felt like someone had dropped a rock in the pit of my stomach.

Arian looked at my swollen belly. "But you are... Perhaps King Prasutagus..."

"He is away," I said, turning to Ansgar.

Pix stepped beside me. When had she gotten there? "Have Druda and Nightshade saddled," she told Galvyn.

"The queen cannot go," Galvyn protested. "Would you have the next ruler of the Greater Iceni born on the road?"

"Would *ye* have our ancient stones laid as flagstones in a Roman hall?" Pix replied waspishly.

I turned to Ansgar. "I dreamt of this. The greenwood called me. I *must* go. Governor Plautius may not listen to the Trinovantes people, but he will listen to me."

"Let me go, Queen Boudica," Ansgar said. "I can ride to Camulodunum."

I shook my head. "I need you here in Venta. With Prasutagus gone, you must stay here in case the people need you."

Galvyn protested once more. "But Ariadne said—"

"That it will be a month before the child is born. Druda is sure of foot, and we will go slowly, but I must go."

"Boudica," Ansgar protested.

"Wise one," Arian told Ansgar, "if the queen does not come to speak on our behalf, there is nothing to stop these Romans. We have heard rumors from the west of other shrines defiled, the priestesses taken captive, or worse. You are safe here in Venta, venerable one. You have not seen. You do not know. We have no one to protect us. If Queen Boudica does not come, it will be the end of Maiden Stones and its priestesses."

"Queen Boudica, if anything happens to you... at least let me arrange a wagon," Galvyn said.

"The snow is too deep," Arian said. "But there are paths we can take where the horses can make it through. Epona is with us."

"I trust Druda," I told Galvyn. "Have him readied."

"Let us send a guard, at least," Ansgar said.

"All the men have gone with Prasutagus. Pix is enough," I replied, then turned to Arian. "I will join you in a moment."

"Queen Boudica," she said, tears coming to her eyes. "Thank you. We didn't know who else to turn to, but Dynis was sure you would come. And then...the greenwood whispered. We only hoped."

"I will come. Governor Plautius *will* speak to me."

CHAPTER 58

D ruda looked very pleased with himself to be saddled and ready to ride once more.

"Queen Boudica," Galvyn began. I could feel that he wanted to dissuade me once more, but he relented. Sighing, he said, "Let me help you up."

With that, the housecarl helped me hoist my far-too-bounteous self onto my horse.

Druda shifted as he adjusted to my weight.

"Druda will get me there safely," I told Galvyn. "And I will go slow."

"I will send a messenger to Prasutagus," Ansgar said. "Surely, the governor will hear you, but we cannot let the king go without knowing where you are."

"Very well. But I insist you tell Prasutagus not to worry and not to come. I will see to this matter. He must attend to the harbor."

Galvyn frowned. "Very well."

Nightshade pranced under Pix, the mare seemingly

unsure if she wanted to buck, bolt, or simply run. But once more, Pix whispered to her, and she settled.

I turned to Arian. "I'm ready."

The priestess nodded, then clicked to her horse, and we set off, riding out of the king's compound and into the city.

Overhead, Morfran called.

I turned back to see Artur on the wall.

I waved to him.

He returned the gesture.

The doors to the king's compound swung shut, and we set off through the city. Already, I could feel the slight discomfort of being in the saddle, but I knew Druda would not let me down.

We made our way out of Venta and onto the road south.

As we did, I said a quiet prayer.

"Epona, Great Mother, you creatures of the greenwood, get me there safely." The wind blew, causing the snow around me to swirl as it danced across the road and into the field nearby. As it did so, the white flakes seemed to gather for just a moment to form the figure of a woman with a flowing gown and long hair. The snowy silhouette formed for just a moment. It gave me a graceful wave before the wind pulled the image apart once more.

THE RIDE WAS SLOW GOING. DRUDA SEEMED TO SENSE HE needed to be extra careful with his rider, but still, I felt every bump and turn. The discomfort was worse than I had anticipated.

Arian reined her horse beside mine.

Behind us, Pix was singing to Nightshade in a language I did not know nor understand, but the mare looked happy and was settled, which was all that mattered.

"I am sorry to ask you to come in such a state," Arian told me. "We had not heard you were with child."

"It is not you who asks but the gods."

"All the same, I can see you are uncomfortable. I only hope you can convince the Romans where we have failed. I will take you to Maiden Stones. You can rest there then ride to Camulodunum thereafter if the Romans are not still encamped by our forest."

"The governor would not see the high priestess?"

Arian shook her head.

"Did he say why not?"

"No explanation was given. She was merely sent away."

"In Venta, you said there has been word from the west of shrines defiled."

Arian nodded. "Legate Vespasian, the Roman commander leading the forces there...they say he is cruel, that he has no respect for our gods."

I frowned. "It seems I have several things to discuss with the governor."

"If only someone can get through to them. I had heard the Romans did not defile the holy places of the lands they conquered. But that does not seem to be the case. I can only hope we reach Maiden Stones before the damage is done. The sacred spiral... Queen Boudica, how can the gods permit this?"

"I don't know, but I can say this, the Romans are either very brave or very stupid to take stones from the little people of the hollow hills. They may find them far less forgiving than our warriors."

Arian nodded. "May the little people curse them."

We rode throughout the day and into the night. To say that I was uncomfortable would have been a gross understatement. We stopped in a pine glade to camp for the night. When Pix helped me off my horse, I could not suppress a groan.

"Boudica?" Pix asked worriedly.

"My back aches, nothing more. It's all the sitting astride."

"I shall fix ye a place to sleep."

I nodded, then went to help Arian build a fire.

It was not long later that we had a small fire burning. Pix had laid out the furs so I could rest. The three of us sat huddled around the small flames, warming ourselves.

Tired from the long ride and carrying my heavy burden, I soon lay down to rest.

Pix covered me, then slipped in behind me, wrapping her arms around me.

"It was not wise for ye to come, but I know why ye did it," she told me.

"Let's hope Prasutagus feels the same way."

"He will chide ye, I am sure. But I can comfort ye," she

said, then gently held my breast. "By the Mother, 'tis big as a melon in summer!"

"And aches like a boil. Off," I said, pushing her hand away.

Pix chuckled. "I will get ye yet, Strawberry Queen."

I laughed lightly, then quickly fell asleep.

It seemed like no time later when Arian gently shook my shoulder. "Queen Boudica. The sun is coming up. We should go."

I nodded. "Yes. I'm coming."

Druda, who was still dozing, snorted at me when I fastened the saddle once more. "Stop complaining. You wanted to be ridden. This is what you get." But in my heart, I did feel bad for him. The snow was deep, and I was heavier than before. Plus, I could feel he was being cautious. This was not the fun race down the Wash he'd hoped for.

Once we were packed up, Pix helped me back up on the horse. This time, I felt the ache in my groin, followed by a sharp pinch.

I winced lightly.

"Boudica," Pix said warningly.

"Say nothing."

As soon as Arian was ready, we set off once more.

There was no denying the ache this time. As we rode, I grew increasingly uncomfortable, with pains rolling across my back. It was dusk when Arian turned in her saddle.

"Just there," she said, gesturing to a puff of smoke coming up through the woods in the valley below.

"And there?" I asked, gesturing to two similar spirals in the distance.

"The Romans."

I frowned, then followed the priestess into the valley.

We made our way toward the little village I had seen in my dreams. Beyond it, I spotted the spiral of stones. From the other side of the woods, their voices carried on the breeze, and I heard harsh masculine voices.

Arian led us toward the village. A woman with sweeping black hair wearing a heavy wool cape appeared from the small roundhouse when we arrived. Alongside her was Dynis, the white-haired priestess I'd met in Raven's Dell.

"Queen Boudica," Dynis said, coming forward. "You are as round as the Mother herself!" she said, looking shocked. "You should not have ridden from Venta."

"Where are the Romans?" I asked.

"But you..." Dynis began, but the other priestess lifted her hand to silence her.

"Queen Boudica, I am Brigantia, High Priestess of Maiden Stones. The Romans are on the other side of the glade. They have started cutting the sacred trees and taking the ancient stones. They told us to leave this village, or they would burn it and send us to Gaul in chains."

"Lead me to them," I told Arian.

Brigantia nodded to Arian. She and Dynis then handed torches to Arian, Pix, and me. Arian led us through the woods. I tried to ignore the rippling aches across my back and in my groin. I equally attempted to ignore the fact that my trousers were wet.

It was very possible I would birth this child on Druda's back. But my presence would mean nothing if I stopped now.

Arian led us through the woods.

As we went, we passed the spiral of stones.

"Maiden Stones," Arian said, "sacred to the goddess in all her forms."

I cast my glance toward the stones, spotting movement therein.

A girl.

A young girl peered out at me from behind one of the stones.

I opened my mouth to call out but stopped short when I saw the otherworldly twinkle in the girl's eyes.

"Boudica...

"The greenwood calls..."

Firming my resolve, I faced forward.

Arian led us to the other side of the forest. Soon, I could hear the men's voices and smell the scent of campfire smoke. At the forest's edge, I saw that three large trees had already been taken.

But more.

In the gathering darkness, from the stones and barrows, I felt eyes upon me.

The little people of the hollow hills were watching.

Pulling my spear from my back, I turned to Pix and Arian.

"Wait here," I said, then pushed ahead of the priestess toward the camp.

On the other side of the forest, four tents had been

erected. A sleigh, suitable for carrying heavy materials on snow, but not a design I was familiar with, sat loaded down with logs. At least a dozen men were sitting by the fire. They ate, a boar roasting on a spit before them. Planted in the ground nearby was the eagle, the crimson pennant fluttering in the breeze. At a smaller tent not far away sat another dozen or so men, irons clapped around their necks. They huddled by a small fire. Two rough-looking watchmen stood nearby, drinking ale and keeping an eye on the slaves.

I swallowed hard, pushing down both the momentary flicker of fear and the swell of pain within me.

They could kill me.

They could murder me where I stood—and start a war with all the Iceni.

No.

That would not happen.

I would make them listen.

I led Druda from the treeline and rode directly toward the Roman soldiers.

Spotting me, they came to alert, the soldier in charge coming to the front. With my spear in one hand, the torch in the other, I approached them without hesitation. The wind blew softly, making the torchlight flutter in the breeze. My hair blew around my shoulders.

"Hold, woman," the man called to me.

But I did not hold. Tapping Druda with my ankles, I edged him forward.

"Hold, I said," the man said, setting his hand on his sword.

"It is you who should hold, Roman. Stay your hand as if your life depends upon it because it does. I am Boudica, Queen of the Greater Iceni, sister of King Caturix of the Northern Iceni, and you are trespassing on sacred land."

"Queen Boudica..." the man began, stepping toward me.

"Hold, Roman," I said, my voice booming across the camp. How many times I had watched Dôn use the same trick, pulling a cloak of power from the Otherworld about her. Now, I felt it on me. I used it, making myself seem taller, more imposing, my voice louder. I pointed my spear at him. "Hold before the Great Goddess whose lands you defile. Stay your hand before the Maiden. Cower before the Crone. Hold, Roman, where you are not wanted, lest you risk the fury of our gods."

Another soldier standing behind the lead officer frowned at me and then whispered something to the man.

The lead soldier gestured for him to be silent.

Behind them, the captives rose.

"Rome, you tread where you are not wanted. Not a single tree, nor leaf, nor stone will be further corrupted by your touch. You will come no closer, or you will feel the curse of these woods upon you. You will stay your hand in this sacred place or feel the wrath of the gods. Each night you linger here, the ancient people of the hollow hills will creep forth and claim one of you. They will drag you into the mountains and devour you. This land has many eyes, and this night, all of them watch you.

"Go to Camulodunum. Go to your governor. Tell him Queen Boudica has come. Tell him that I stand between this sacred place and Rome. Britannia permits Rome to come no closer. Tell him this. I will not trade words with you who defile this place. Go and tell your governor that I await his answer. And I warn you… Leave this place tonight, or the forest will claim one of you."

The soldier held my gaze, then bowed to me. "Queen Boudica," he said.

I turned Druda, then rode back into the woods, rejoining Pix and Arian.

"Queen Boudica," Arian said, her eyes wide in awe.

"The governor will come," I told her.

"How do you know?"

"Because Rome will always come to Britannia," I said, my head feeling dizzy, my body wracked with pain. "Now, get me to your priestesses. The child is coming."

CHAPTER 59

The next few hours passed in a blur. We returned to the house of the priestesses, where Pix helped me down from Druda and then led me inside. Within, I found five young priestesses, Dynis, and their high priestess, Brigantia, waiting.

The pain in my groin was excruciating, and my knees had gone weak.

"Pix," I whimpered, hanging on to her.

"Queen Boudica is in labor," Arian told Brigantia.

"The Romans?" the high priestess replied.

"Oh, they got an earful. They will stay their hand. Boudica put a fear of the gods in them," Pix said with a laugh.

"Come, Queen Boudica," Brigantia said, gesturing for me to follow her.

"Ah, Great Queen, why did you agree to come when you were near your time?" Dynis asked.

"The gods called me," I said through gritted teeth. "I

dreamed of this place. Ah, gods, is it supposed to hurt this much?"

At that, Brigantia chuckled. "I am afraid so, Queen Boudica."

"Girls, you know what to do," Dynis said, clapping her hands. "Let's prepare for the queen's child."

As Pix led me to bed, I heard one of the girls whisper, "Is that really her? The Queen of the Greater Iceni?"

"Look at her," another answered. "Have you ever seen anyone look more like a queen than her?"

The priestesses led me to the bedchamber just off the main room, hidden behind a curtain. They lay me down on the bed, then Arian quickly began pulling off my boots, Brigantia loosening the ties on my trousers.

"Everything is wet with birthing fluids. How long have you had your laboring contractions?" Brigantia asked me.

"Since yesterday," I said, then clutched the coverlets. "Aye, gods."

"Lay back, Queen Boudica," Arian told me. "Brigantia will see how far you have to go."

I lay back while the others helped me remove my trousers. I closed my eyes, smelling the scents of burning sage and other herbs in the air. Suddenly, I wished Ula was there. Everything would have been okay if Ula had been there. The whole room felt too hot. I felt like someone was standing on my lower back. The pain in my groin made my moonblood aches dull in comparison.

I shifted uncomfortably as Brigantia examined me. "You are coming just in time. Another hour and this child would have been born on the road," Brigantia told me.

"Let's prepare something for the pain. Your womb is nearly ready, Queen Boudica. Your child will be here soon."

Pix sat on the bed beside me. She took my hand. "Sometimes, ye be too stubborn."

"I only hope Aulus will listen."

"Ne'er fear. He will listen to ye," Pix replied. "The only question be, for what price."

One of the young priestesses brought me a steaming cup of something that smelled of mushrooms and other herbs. The taste was horrid, but I forced it down all the same. When the birth pains came once more, it was all I could do to keep the liquid in my stomach.

Brigantia helped me shift into a long, simple gown.

"Rest," she told me. "The herbs will help dull the pain."

Soon, I grew dizzy, and the bed began to feel like it was spinning. Time slowed. While the birthing pains still had me, the ache from them was lessened. The young priestesses came and went. I watched them through the opening-and-closing curtain. The roundhouse seemed to house them all. It was a cozy place, bunches of herbs hanging from the rafters overhead. Two long tables sat at the center of the room, one for eating and one for working.

My mind slowed as I watched them. The scene seemed so familiar to me. With Mirim, who had gone to Mona, there were nine priestesses in the house. Nine sacred maidens... My mother had lived such a life. I might have as well if things had gone differently.

Gaheris...

"Queen Boudica," Brigantia said. "It is time to make ready now."

"But Gaheris is not here," I complained, feeling confused.

"Your babe does not care who is here. It is coming now."

Pix sat beside me, helping me sit up. "Ye squeeze me as ye need," she said, taking my hand.

"Queen Boudica, your child will come now. You must push when I say."

"But Gaheris," I whispered.

"He be with ye. Don't worry about him," Pix told me.

"Now," Brigantia called.

And then, I pushed. Again and again, I did as the priestess told me, pushing with all of my might. The pain made my head feel light. Everything slowed. I felt confused and desperate for it to be done. But I did as the priestess bid me and pushed.

"Push. Push. The child is coming now," Brigantia called.

I grunted and strained and soon felt the child come.

I collapsed backward onto the bed.

A moment later, I heard cries.

"Here she is. Here she is. Princess of the Greater Iceni, born here at the sacred shrine of the goddess. Be blessed, sweet girl. Be blessed by the Maiden. How strong she is. Listen to her," Brigantia called as the priestesses worked quickly, cleaning the child and me up.

The baby wailed loudly.

"Let me help you sit," Pix said, adjusting me in the bed.

Wrapping the child in a cloth, they handed her to me.

"Ah, Sorcha," I said. "Welcome to the world, little firebrand."

"She heard yer speech and had to come to see what all the fuss was about," Pix said, touching the child's cheek.

"Oh, Pix. Prasutagus missed it," I said, suddenly aware I had called for Gaheris, not Prasutagus, in my pain.

"He would have missed it either way," Pix said.

"All the same," I said, then stroked the child's face. She had a full head of dark, amber-colored hair and sweet little lips puckered in annoyance. She flexed her brow and fussed in my arms, whining and struggling.

"Perhaps try to feed her, Queen Boudica. It will calm her."

Feeling uncertain, I adjusted the neck on the gown and set the child to breast. She latched on with a tight pinch, making me wince and Brigantia laugh. "That is a fiery passion for the world. May she sustain it."

I stroked the child's cheek as she nursed. "Mad at me already, Sorcha?" I asked with a laugh.

"She didn't want to be born in the saddle," Pix told me with a grin.

I chuckled.

After the child had finished, Brigantia came to me and said, "Let me take her now. I will lay her to rest. You must sleep, noble queen. The laboring was hard. We will watch over her and wake you when it's time to feed her again."

"I...yes..." I said, then lay back. "Pix..."

"I'm here. I'll keep an eye on ye both."

Feeling reassured, I lay back and closed my eyes.

Before I could even think of it, I fell off to sleep.

The priestesses woke me several times throughout the night to attend to my tiny daughter. I was thoroughly exhausted but wanted nothing more than to hold and look at my child. She was such a tiny thing but so fierce. She wailed when she hungered, indignant to be kept waiting.

A firebrand, indeed.

Early the following day, Sorcha woke me with her tiny cries. Pix rose from the chair where she had been sleeping and lifted the baby from her cradle, handing her to me. I set the child to breast and then slipped my finger into her tiny hand. As the baby nursed, she flexed and relaxed her fingers over mine.

"How tiny she is," I said, stroking her hair. "Such a small thing."

"Like dropping a boulder into a small pool, that is how tiny she will feel in yer life," Pix said with a laugh.

On the other side of the curtains, the young priestesses hovered about, curious to see.

"Girls," I called. "Please, do not be shy. Come and meet Princess Sorcha," I called to them.

I heard one of them confirm with Dynis that they were *really* allowed, then they entered the chamber. The girls ranged in age from twelve to twenty, all of them similarly dressed in heavy wool robes that were off-white in color but had lovely flowers and leaves embroidered on the necklines, sleeves, and hems.

There were squeals of delight as the girls eagerly looked at the child.

"She's so sweet," one girl said.

"Her hair is dark red. See how it shimmers like firelight. She will look like you, Queen Boudica," another added.

"King Prasutagus has red hair too! I saw him once. It's true," said another.

"The goddess will bless her, Queen Boudica," a maiden told me.

I chuckled, feeling happy to have the girls so close.

The rest of the day passed with a mix of sleep and feeding. My body ached, but Brigantia reassured me that I would feel much better soon.

"It was a clean birth, Queen Boudica. And hardly any bleeding thereafter. Someone has been taking good care of you in Venta. The priestesses of the nemeton, perhaps?" Brigantia asked.

"Henwyn is a great asset to us, but I must attribute credit where it is due. My health is the handiwork of Venta's midwife and a cranky hedge witch in Oak Throne."

Brigantia laughed. "Then may the Mother bless them both."

Pix disappeared that morning, returning later smelling of snow, the cold air still clinging to her. "They be gone. No sign of anyone anywhere. They left the wood they did cut and the stones."

"But not the slaves."

"No, not those."

I frowned.

"Perhaps the little people of the hollow hills took the Romans," Pix said.

"If they did, I would be glad."

"Ye and me both," Pix said, then reached down to lift Sorcha from my arms. "And what of ye, firebrand? Shall I teach ye how to charm the creatures of the hollow hills and speak the old tongue?"

"You could teach me."

"Ye have enough to worry about. But this one... I will see to her."

We rested that afternoon and evening. I was lucky the child would sleep for many hours at a stretch, leaving me time to eat and sleep. Time passed in a blur. I was half dozing, Sorcha in my arms, the following morning when there was a knock on the door to the priestesses' house. Several of the young priestesses had come to sit with us, telling me about their work at the stones and listening to Pix's wild stories. The sound of a heavy fist on the door brought everyone to silence.

Pix rose at once, pulling her sword.

Brigantia gestured for her to wait. Leaving us, the high priestess went to the main chamber of the house. I could hear the clatter and scrape as the door opened.

After that, I heard Brigantia's voice and that of a deep, male baritone.

A few moments later, Brigantia returned.

"Queen Boudica, you have a visitor," Brigantia told me, then turned to the priestesses. "Girls, get your cloaks. Dynis and Arian will take you to the herb-drying hut."

The priestesses disappeared, quickly hurrying to get ready and then depart.

"Should I—" I said, moving to rise when Brigantia

waved for me to stay settled. "Stay abed, Queen Boudica," she said, pulling up my covers and smoothing back my hair. "You may be a queen, but you are still a woman fresh from childbirth. All men should understand that. I will be in the outer room if you need me."

I nodded.

Pix stood at the side of my bed.

Brigantia went to the curtain and pulled it aside.

"She will see you now," she told the visitor.

A moment later, Aulus appeared. His face changed as he took in the scene, his hard look softening.

"Boudica," he said gently.

"Aulus," I said, feeling strangely relieved by his presence.

"Britannia has summoned me. Rome is here."

CHAPTER 60

"P lease, sit," I told Aulus, gesturing to a chair by the bed.

Brigantia disappeared through the curtain.

Aulus met Pix's gaze as he entered, raising and lowering his eyebrows at her.

"My men returned to Camulodunum with a wild tale," Aulus said as he sat. "A goddess with hair made of flames rode from the darkness of the forest, her stomach as round as honorable Juno, and she cursed them for defiling sacred ground. Of course, they were half spooked by the forest already, seeing strange things and hearing voices in the wind. But the arrival of such a spirit, a flaming goddess demanding the presence of Rome, was enough to snip their balls and send them running back to Camulodunum."

"I'm glad I got their attention."

"And mine," he said with a laugh, then looked at the tiny bundle in my hands. "And who do we have here?"

"Sorcha, say hello to Governor Plautius," I said, gently moving aside the blankets so Aulus could see the child.

He smiled at her. "It is good to meet you, Princess Sorcha. So, are you the one who inspired your mother to terrorize my men?"

"I'm afraid that was your doing."

"*Me?*"

I gave Aulus a reproachful look.

He nodded, lifting his hands. "In my defense, my men told me there were excellent, wide trees and good stones to be found here, so I sent them about their business and didn't question."

"And when the high priestess of this place came to Camulodunum to protest?"

"The priestess came to Camulodunum?"

"So she did," I said. "And she was told you would not see her."

"This is the first time I am hearing of it."

Was he telling the truth or not? I was not certain. "Aulus, this is a sacred place. It is a special place for women. The forest itself is ancient. And the circle of stones, which you no doubt passed, have been here for thousands of years. You cannot touch this place. Surely, you understand. Amongst the Romans, do you have a sacred maiden goddess, a guardian of the girls and all wild things of nature?"

Aulus bobbed his head from side to side. "There is Vesta, the virgin goddess who is a patron to all Romans. And Diana, lady of the moon and forest."

"This place is called Maiden Stones. It is one of the

oldest shrines in our land. This forest and these stones are not for the taking."

"I heard quite a lot about your forests when my men returned to Camulodunum. In fact, they returned one short. The soldiers said the red-haired goddess told them they would be devoured by the woods if they stayed. And one of them has been, it seems. Or perhaps he met with a different fate," he said, glancing back at Pix with an arched eyebrow.

"'Twas not me, Rome. Ye of all people should know to fear the hollow hills," Pix said.

Aulus's brow flexed, then he turned back to me, looking for clarification.

"There are dark, ancient things in this land. These are the things that drove Julius Caesar from our shores. Look to your own stories. You will find such creatures there. This place is also their place, the little people of the hollow hills, and they do not welcome strangers here—as I warned your men."

Aulus stared at me for a long moment as he considered.

His eyes were so blue. Like the sky on a winter's day.

"I will tell the men to leave this place in peace," he said, then took my hand, surprising me. "Will that please you?"

My heart pounded in my chest. "It will," I said, then cleared my throat nervously.

"Warrior maiden, your queen needs something warm to drink," Aulus said, not looking back at Pix.

Pix flicked her gaze to me.

I nodded to her.

With a roll of her eyes, Pix departed.

"What else will please you?" Aulus asked once she had gone.

"You must leave *all* the sacred places in peace. There are rumors of this Roman, Legate Vespasian, terrorizing our priests and holy sites. You must put a stop to it. Whatever you discussed with him before winter, he has not kept his word. You must make him. The people will stand beside those tribes who have allied with Rome if they think we have made the right choice, but such actions against our holy people are causing rumblings. You will spark a rebellion and drive people to Caratacus's side."

"If I do that, if I put a stop to it, that will please you?"

"Yes."

"I will see to it."

"King Diras should have a druid adviser in Camulodunum," I said.

Aulus gave me a knowing look. "Boudica…"

"I *know* he is a puppet. You do not need to browbeat me. *You* need a druid adviser to help you understand the people and make your goals unfold easier."

"What does my success get you, Queen Boudica? Why do you care?"

Protects the stones. Protects the trees. "You are not here to butcher our people. Helping you see what we value protects our gods and way of life."

"You would protect your gods?" Aulus asked with a laugh, which I joined.

I was increasingly aware that he had not let go of my hand.

"You wouldn't protect yours?"

Aulus grinned. "And what can I expect in exchange for taking all of your good advice?"

"Besides a peaceful Britannia? What do you want?"

"Ah, that is easily explained but not easily achieved," he said, his gaze lingering on mine.

My heart slammed in my chest. No. I mean, he couldn't really be thinking that, could he? All of this talk between us was just...play. Wasn't it? Surely he knew I meant nothing by it.

"Here ye be," Pix said, entering with two mugs in her hands.

I snatched my hand away from Aulus to reach out for the mug.

Pix frowned at me, but handed me the drink.

I turned away from Aulus, feeling the weight of his words. I shifted my gaze toward Sorcha as I sipped.

"And for ye, Rome. 'Tis not poisoned," she told him, handing him a mug.

Aulus cocked an eyebrow at her then took a sip. "Ouch," he hissed.

"But 'tis hot," Pix added with a grin.

Aulus glared at her.

Sorcha began to fuss a little. I set the drink aside then rocked the baby gently.

"Where is King Prasutagus?" Aulus asked.

"He was away when the priestess arrived to ask for help," I replied.

"You know, King Diras may not like the Greater Iceni interfering in Trinovantes' affairs. He might take that as an infringement on his lands," Aulus told me with a baiting grin.

It was my turn to give him a browbeating. "Then it is a good thing you are there to explain it to him."

Aulus chuckled. "Very well, Queen Boudica. I will see to these matters."

"Thank you, Aulus," I said, and I truly meant it. "It means much to me that you are willing to listen."

"Perhaps, too willing," Aulus said with a laugh. "They would not recognize me in Pannonia."

"Pannonia?"

"In my youth, I was stationed at a wild frontier in the southeast where two fierce tribes near the river Danube continually warred with one another. It took seven legions to get that mess under control. But in the end, we won. Most likely, because I was *not* willing to listen."

Chuckling, I shook my head.

Aulus eyed Sorcha. "May I?" he asked.

I nodded, then sat up, carefully handing the baby to him.

He took Sorcha gently. "Sorcha, is it? What is the meaning of that name?"

"It means bright...shining. Like the sun. She is our firebrand."

Aulus smiled at the baby. "Hello, Princess," he said, staring at her for a long moment. Finally, Aulus looked up at me and said, "Why don't you come back with me to Camulodunum? This place is small and not really suited to meet your needs. I can see you and the princess settled comfortably within the hour. You can ride north to Venta once you have recovered."

"I thank you for the invitation, but I cannot. The holy women here...this is their purpose, to care for women, mothers. I cannot insult them by forsaking them."

"We have such priestesses of our own. I can more easily see to your care in Camulodunum," he said, then looked around the room, unable to hide the disgust on his face, "in trappings far more suitable for a queen."

"Aulus, thank you for the generous offer, but—"

"I would see you comfortable, Boudica. Not resting after your birth in a common bed with tattered linens. You are a queen. You should be treated as such," he said, then gently handed Sorcha back to me.

Pix shifted as if she wanted to say something and struggled not to intervene.

I understood what Aulus was saying. From his perspective, our people's ways were primitive. I understood this, but I disagreed.

"Aulus, I—"

"I will return to Camulodunum and have a cart prepared. I can come back for you before nightfall. We can send a rider to Prasutagus when we get to Camulodunum to let him know you are well."

"But, I—"

Aulus had just risen to go when we heard a knock on the door once more.

I heard a shuffle as Brigantia rose and then opened the door. A moment later, I caught her exchange of soft words with someone, followed by footsteps.

Pix moved to the side of my bed, her hand on her sword. To my surprise, Aulus also moved, positioning himself between the doorway and me, his hand on his dagger.

"Just here," Brigantia said, then pushed the curtains aside.

There was a strange moment of tension where no one said anything, then I heard a familiar voice.

"Governor Plautius," Prasutagus said stiffly.

"King Prasutagus. Welcome. Welcome. Come, see what you will discover here," Aulus said, stepping aside. When he did so, I saw a strange expression wash over his face. He smothered a mix of rage and sadness rolled into one in a single instant. The result was an odd, glossy look in his eyes as he smiled down at me.

"Boudica," Prasutagus said, coming to me. He placed his hands on my cheeks and kissed the top of my head.

"Your hands are cold," I said with a giggle.

"Alas, I am sorry. Since I got word from Venta, I've ridden nonstop," he said, then looked down at the bundle in my arms, slowly sinking onto the bed beside me. "And who is this?" he asked.

"Meet your daughter, Sorcha."

"Sorcha," Prasutagus said, blowing warm air into his hands before he lifted the child. "Hello, Sorcha. What are you doing so far away from home?" he asked, kissing her forehead. Prasutagus smiled at his tiny daughter, soaking in her looks as he touched the tiny fingers on her hand.

"Perhaps I should..." Aulus began.

Prasutagus looked up. "Please, be at rest. I am glad to find Boudica in the company of friends."

"I am here at the bequest of the priestesses," I told Prasutagus. "There was no time to wait. There had been a…misunderstanding. Governor Plautius did not know this was a sacred site and had sent a team for the trees. I arrived in time before more damage could be done. The governor was kind enough to ride out to talk to me, only he found me in the company of this one," I said, looking to the child.

Aulus laughed. "Had I suspected, I would have brought a gift. As it was, I was trying to convince your wife to return with me to the comfort of Camulodunum. Perhaps you will be more successful than I was in convincing her."

"I will have to decline as well. I would like to get Boudica and my daughter back to Venta. There is no sign of snow for the next few days."

"I'll have a wagon sent for you," Aulus said. "We have one that easily cuts through the snow. I would not have Boudica and the little one at the whims of the weather."

"I…very well. I would appreciate that, my friend," Prasutagus told Aulus.

Aulus nodded. "Then, if you will excuse me, I will rejoin my men and see that it's done. King Prasutagus, Queen Boudica," he said, then paused to look at the baby. "Princess Sorcha." He smiled lightly, then turned to go.

"Governor Plautius," I said, feeling oddly uncertain what to say.

He paused, then looked back at me, a restrained but broken expression on his face.

"You have my unending gratitude for your words here," I told him.

Aulus muttered something in a language I didn't recognize, running his hand over his mouth nervously, then exited the room, Pix following along behind him.

Confused, Prasutagus shook his head but said nothing.

On the other side of the curtain, I heard Aulus speak briefly to Brigantia before the door opened and closed.

Prasutagus leaned forward and kissed Sorcha on the forehead. Then, he looked up at me. "You protected Maiden Stones."

"I know there was a risk, but I had to take it. After everything we have been hearing... I gave the priestess Dynis my word that she could call on me if there was a need. And then, I dreamed. The greenwood called me here."

"I see," Prasutagus said with a nod. "How odd to find the governor in the place."

"Well, I threatened his men and demanded he come, so…"

At that, Prasutagus laughed. "My child's mother is a fierce protector of the land, the people, even the very stones."

I gave Prasutagus a soft smile.

"I think the governor is fond of you, Boudica."

"We shall use that to our advantage when and where we can."

"Be careful, my wife. Not everyone plays the game fairly."

"Who said *I* planned to play fairly?"

At that, Prasutagus grinned. "You hear that, my princess? Your mother would outsmart the Romans. You must watch her."

At that, the baby whined and then launched into a full cry.

Prasutagus tried to comfort her, but Sorcha would have none of it.

"Here," I said, reaching for her. "Perhaps she is hungry." Taking the child from him, I set her to my breast once more.

Sorcha instantly settled.

Prasutagus gazed long and lovingly at me. "My queen and my daughter," he said, his gaze lingering on me until his eyes grew soft. I watched as his expression changed, his vision shifting to some distant place. And then his words came, low and hollow, "May the Maiden protect you both. And may Rome weep for the violence that will be done to them if they ever put hands on either of you."

CHAPTER 61

I t was late in the day when Pix escorted a very
nervous Roman soldier to the priestess's house.

"Boudica, yer Roman was true to his word. The
wagon be here."

"It's a *carpentum*, actually," the soldier stammered
awkwardly.

Pix rolled her eyes at him. "No matter what it be called.
They be ready for ye."

"The governor didn't come?" I asked.

"No, Queen Boudica, but he sent us," the soldier
replied.

"I see. We'll be ready shortly," I told him.

"Come on," Pix told the Roman, then led him back
outside.

Still feeling the discomfort of the birthing, I redressed
then made ready to go. Prasutagus pulled my boots on for
me and helped me fasten my cloak.

"Druda..." I said.

"I will lead him," Prasutagus replied.

"Shall we say goodbye, Sorcha?" I asked the baby.

Prasutagus and I then joined the young priestesses in the main chamber.

"Maidens, will you give Sorcha your blessings?" I asked them.

The young priestesses, including Arian, gathered around, talking sweetly to the child, who stared at them in wonderment.

When they were done, I said, "I wish you all well. May the Maiden watch over you. If you ever need me, simply call," I said, then Prasutagus and I made our way outside, Dynis and Brigantia joining us.

Pix was waiting out front.

"Where did the Roman go?" I asked.

Pix pointed to the forest's edge.

"Let's hope he made it back to the others," I said with a laugh.

"Or not," Brigantia said, grinning lightly.

Outside, I found Raven and Druda prepared to depart. Nightshade, however, remained in the small corral.

"Pix," I said, looking back, confused.

"I will stay back a bit, make sure there be no more trouble here," she said.

I frowned.

"I'll be along shortly, one way or another."

"Queen Boudica," Brigantia said, gesturing to the spiral. "The spiral of Maiden Stones is a sacred place. Under certain conditions, it can lead one to memories of the past, to visions of the future, or simply to the heart of it all. At the center is the Triple Goddess stone. If you look, you will find the arms of the spiral form a triskelion. One arm is the path of the Maiden. One is for the Mother. One is for the Crone.

"As we walk the path, many times the gods speak. Given that she was born here, I would ask that we take Sorcha to the center of the stones and ask for the Triple Goddess's blessing upon her," she said, then turned to Prasutagus. "I know you studied in Mona, but like the sacred isle of Avallach, this is a place for women only."

"I understand," Prasutagus replied.

Brigantia nodded. "Come, Queen Boudica, let's walk the path of the Maiden in Sorcha's honor.

I nodded to her.

Brigantia led me to the entrance of the spiral.

The priestess lifted her hands in prayer. "Sacred Maiden. Now is the winter of your life. You lay nestled in the earth and will be reborn come spring. We honor you at this sleeping time. As flower bulbs sleep, as trees rest, so do you. It is the time of the Crone, but the Maiden shall awaken once more. We honor you, and we come to this spiral to ask your blessing on Princess Sorcha, daughter of Queen Boudica and King Prasutagus, protectors of these sacred stones."

With that, Brigantia and I began our path. The spiral was sided by rocks on the ground, the peaks of which stuck out of the snow. Tall monoliths also stood on either side of the path, following a swirling design.

Brigantia sang a song as we went in a language I didn't know.

I looked down at Sorcha. "This is for you. The Maiden calls you, Daughter," I whispered, then made my way behind the priestess. As I went, I felt the same odd presence I always felt when I was close to those of the Otherworld.

I looked back at Dynis, Prasutagus, and Pix, but saw no one. Everything looked blurry.

"Where have they—" I asked Brigantia, but the priestess gave me a knowing look and kept singing.

I looked down at Sorcha. "The Maiden... As once I was, now you are."

I heard giggling amongst the stones. When I looked, I saw a young girl peeking out at me from behind a stone. From behind another stone, I saw a young boy. My memory of the girl was vague, but the boy... I would know him anywhere.

"Gaheris..." I whispered.

The child giggled, then ran off.

When he did so, I noticed the land around me had somehow shifted.

Below my feet was green grass dotted with dandelions. On the branches of the nearby trees, I saw pink and white blossoms. Birds called, and a warm wind blew sweetly.

"Gaheris," I called, but he was gone.

Ahead of me, Brigantia—and not Brigantia, but a young woman no more than sixteen years of age but with the priestess's face—led me down the path toward the shrine's center.

As we neared the middle, a figure stepped out from behind a stone.

"Gaher—" I began in anticipation but stopped when I saw who had come. "Mother," I whispered.

Damara stood leaning against a stone, barely older than I was now. She wore a long, green dress trimmed with gold embroidery. She wore a simple ring of red roses and fragrant herbs on her head.

"Mother," I said, stopping. How like Brenna she looked.

"Boudica," the young Brigantia called, turning back to look at me. She smiled as she walked backward, her steps a half-skip. "You cannot stop in the spiral. They cannot cross over to you, and you will be lost if you cross to them. Come."

Damara smiled at me, her eyes going to her grandchild. She pressed her hands together and touched them to her lips, her eyes wet with unshed tears.

"She is Sorcha," I whispered, tears pricking at the corners of my eyes. "She is Sorcha." I continued on slowly.

My mother nodded but said nothing more.

I turned back for one last glance, but Damara was gone.

I swallowed hard, feeling the ache within me. But I also knew that seeing my mother, seeing Gaheris and his sister, Gwyn, was a blessing. They were watching over me—and over my daughter.

When I reached the center of the spiral, I found Brigantia as I knew her once more. At the center of the sacred space was an unusual altar with a pale pink stone at its center. The oval-shaped stone had streaks of white and gold. The unique stone was laid into the altar like a gemstone on a necklace.

"This is the stone of the Triple Goddess," Brigantia said, "sacred to the Trinovantes tribe, given to us by the Seelie court." Brigantia gestured to the glimmering stone. "Place Sorcha here."

I did as she told me.

Overhead, the birds chirped sweetly, and the sun shone down upon us. I caught the scent of apple blossoms in the air.

Brigantia raised her hands. "Maiden, Mother, and Crone, I call upon you to bless the child Sorcha, daughter of Queen Boudica and the druid King Prasutagus. Long ago, our tribe promised the Seelie they would watch over this place. Boudica stood before us like a shield where our kings have failed us. Give her child your blessings. Those beings of the greenwood who watch, give your blessings to Princess Sorcha. May she carry the light of the maiden in her."

Around me, the air seemed to shiver. A soft breeze wafted over the place. And then, I felt them draw close. Unseen things, standing just behind me, began to whisper.

"Sorcha, princess of the Greater Iceni, we gift you…

"The fiery heart of the spring sun…

"The passion of thunder and lightning…

"The power of the raging rivers…

"The ferocity of a mother bear…

"And the beauty of cherry blossoms…

"Sorcha.

"The light.

"The firebrand."

Then, the presence faded.

"The greenwood has spoken. The goddesses have cast this child's fate. May they be honored," Brigantia called, then gestured for me to pick up Sorcha once more.

The priestess then motioned me to follow her back out of the circle, leaving on a different path.

"We shall return on the Mother's path," Brigantia told me.

Before we departed, I looked back toward the path we had followed there.

I gasped when I saw Gaheris standing there, looking the way he had the last time I'd seen him, dressed in the fine tunic he'd worn when he'd asked my father for my hand.

"Gaheris," I whispered, unable to control the tears that rolled down my cheeks.

He raised his hand, giving me a soft smile, then looked toward Sorcha and nodded, giving me an approving grin.

I set my hand on my heart, Gaheris doing the same, and then he faded.

"Boudica," Brigantia called.

Holding Sorcha in one hand, I wiped my tears with the other and stepped onto the path, surprised to hear the crunch of dried leaves.

Overhead, the yellow and orange leaves shifted in the wind.

Brigantia smiled back at me. She looked much as she did now.

I followed her forward, pausing only when I saw one figure standing among the stones.

I did not recognize him at first. All my life, I had

known him as old. The man with long, auburn hair standing before me was a stranger—except for his eyes.

"Belenus," I whispered.

The druid raised his hands to his forehead in a gesture of respect.

"Grandfather," I whispered.

Belenus smiled, then gave me a soft nod.

His eyes went to Sorcha.

He drew a figure in the air, an ancient symbol I did not know, marking and blessing the child.

I passed him slowly so he could see her, then carried on behind the priestess.

When we neared the end of the path, Brigantia turned and looked back at me, gesturing for me to come along. Then, she took one more step, disappearing.

I looked down at Sorcha.

"My sweet girl. My sweet firebrand. Come, there is much to be done," I said, then stepped from the spiral into the snow.

CHAPTER 62

The ride home in the wagon, or *carpentum* as it was technically called, proved to be comfortable but slow. The enclosed wagon was filled with more finery than many people's houses. The cushions on the seat were made of silk and filled with feathers. Velvet drapes covered the windows. The roof on the carriage's interior was painted with half-dressed women holding massive wine jugs, Roman amphoras with handles on each side.

I pushed aside the curtain and called to one of the Roman soldiers Aulus had sent as an escort. While Aulus had not come, he had sent a chest with gifts for Sorcha. It sat unopened on the bench across from me.

"Soldier," I called.

The man reined his horse close to the cart. "Queen Boudica, is anything the matter?"

"No. Nothing at all. If anything, I am too comfortable. Whose *carpentum* is this?"

"It was used by the emperor when he was here in Britannia."

"It's finer than most homes I have seen."

The soldier smothered a laugh. "Yes, Queen Boudica."

Sitting back, I adjusted my grip on Sorcha, hoping to regain feeling in my left hand, then leaned back in the posh seat.

Riding at the head of the party, I could hear Prasutagus talking to one of the Roman soldiers.

I closed my eyes, my mind going back to the stones.

Prasutagus said he'd seen nothing. "You disappeared when you entered the spiral," he'd said. "I saw nothing within until you appeared once more."

As I thought back on the experience, Gaheris's expression came back to me.

"In the next life, my love," I whispered to the absent man. "In the next life."

The *carpentum* rocking me to sleep, I was surprised when I opened my eyes once more to find it was nearly dark. I pushed the curtain aside once more. "Prasutagus?"

I heard him click to Raven, and a moment later, the pair appeared by my side.

"Where are we?"

"We've just crossed into Greater Iceni territory. We will ride throughout the night, as long as you are comfortable."

"But the soldiers…"

"They are soldiers. They can carry on, as can I. I will see you safely home. Do you need anything? Are you warm enough?"

"We are as cozy as the emperor himself in here."

At that, Prasutagus chuckled. "Good."

Sorcha fussed.

"Sorcha, however, is complaining."

"Not even the finest Roman trappings are enough for you, Daughter?" Prasutagus asked.

"Perhaps she prefers our own things."

"Good," Prasutagus said. "Rest, my queen, I will have you home soon."

With a nod, I closed the curtain once more and settled back.

Nothing sounded better.

IT WAS DAWN WHEN I OPENED MY EYES ONCE MORE AND heard the familiar sounds of the market in Venta. The merchants and other villagers called to Prasutagus.

"King, who has come?"

"King Prasutagus, who is with you?"

"A princess," Prasutagus called to the crowd. "The Princess of the Greater Iceni!"

At that, I pulled aside the curtain. "Here she is," I called, lifting the child so the others could see.

"Queen Boudica's child is born," someone called to the crowd. "It is a princess."

At that, many people came close to the wagon for a look.

"What have you named her, Queen Boudica?" the

woman who had sold me the raspberries called.

"She is Sorcha."

"Hail, Princess Sorcha! All hail our new princess!" the old woman called.

The wagon rolled on, but the people raced to the window to look.

"Queen Boudica! Health to you, my queen. Health to you and the princess."

"Blessings upon you and your child, my queen!"

"The Maiden's blessings on you, Princess Sorcha!"

We rode through the village toward the king's house, a gaggle of children running alongside to look at Sorcha and call to me.

I waved to them as we went.

Soon, the wagon passed through the gates of the king's house and slowed to a stop.

I waited a moment for Prasutagus to appear. He opened the door with a smile. "May I take that blissful burden from you, my queen?"

I nodded and then handed Sorcha to him.

"Queen Boudica," I heard Brita call as she rushed outside. "By the goddess, it's the baby! Boudica," she said, then pushed her head inside the wagon. "Are you well? You had the baby already? Can I help you out?"

"Yes, yes, and yes," I said, reaching for her hand.

Ducking, I exited the *carpentum*, glad to be on my own two feet again.

Vian, Nella, Galvyn, Artur, and Ansgar also appeared, everyone crowding around Prasutagus and the child. Brita and I joined them.

"How sweet she is," Vian said, smiling. "What have you named her?"

"Sorcha," Prasutagus replied.

"Welcome home, Princess Sorcha," Galvyn told her.

"Let me get your things," Brita said, darting back to the wagon.

Artur came to me, wrapping his hands around my waist. He said nothing, but I could feel the worry leaving him.

"I'm here," I said simply, kissing him on the head.

"Let's get the queen inside," Ansgar said.

"Galvyn, send for Ariadne," Prasutagus said. "I will have her see them both, just to be sure."

"Yes, King Prasutagus."

"And our Roman escort..." Prasutagus said, pausing to look back at the men. "These men rode throughout the night to see the queen safely home. Food, drink, and rest for them."

Galvyn nodded to Prasutagus, then turned to the soldiers. "This way," he said, waving for them to follow him to the guesthouse.

We all made our way inside, settling in the common dining room, where everyone gathered around to meet Sorcha.

"Would you like to hold her?" Prasutagus asked Artur.

"Me?" the boy asked in surprise.

"She's your little sister. It is your job now to help keep her safe," Prasutagus said.

At that, Artur nodded. Moving gently, Prasutagus

helped Artur gently cradle the little one into his arms. "Hello, Sorcha. I'm Artur," he said.

I looked up at Prasutagus, who smiled gently at me.

And for a brief moment, a future unfolded before me that was happy. Even in these strange times, it was possible.

"Queen Boudica," Brita said, entering behind me. "Is this… I found this in that fancy wagon," she said, holding the chest.

"Ah," Prasutagus said. "The governor's gift. So, what has he sent for our little girl? I forgot to look."

Brita brought the box to Prasutagus, who opened it. Inside was a necklace made of gold and brilliant amber and rubies. The stones had been formed in the shape of a sun.

Brita gasped. "What a fine piece."

"Sorcha," Ansgar said. "Bright and shining. Seems the governor knows the meaning of the princess's name."

Prasutagus closed the box. He handed it off to Ansgar and then reached for Sorcha. "What are Roman baubles to a Celtic princess? I will make you a necklace from acorns, hagstones, and shells, sweet girl. And you will wear that with pride."

"May the old ones hear your prayers," Ansgar added.

When Prasutagus moved to kiss the baby on her head once more, I saw the look on his face, one he hid from the others. It was a strange mix of jealousy, anger, fear, and embarrassment. Prideful people. That is what we were. And Aulus's gift—a second of its kind—had wounded his pride.

"Brita, how about a bath," I said, redirecting the conversation. "I'm ready to wash away the last few days and go to bed. Prasutagus? A hand?"

He turned to me and then smiled. "My queen."

"My king."

"Welcome returns, Queen Boudica," Ansgar said. "Get your rest."

The others echoed him.

With Sorcha in his arms, Prasutagus and I returned to our bedchamber, where the maid worked busily. I was ready to get back into my own bed and enjoy the next chapter of my life.

CHAPTER 63

For a time, that dream seemed easily won. As winter dragged on, turning to spring once more, I spent my time tending to Sorcha. Worries about Rome faded into the background.

A rider finally arrived from Oak Throne.

A boy.

"Bran and Bec have named the child Bellicus," Cai told us. "In honor of ancient Belenus."

"It is good to see him remembered," I said. "Once the weather clears, I hope to see them both and meet Bellicus."

Cai, who had been holding Sorcha, smiled, then handed her back to me. "Bran will be glad to hear you are delivered safely. This winter was full of strange omens and happenings."

"Such as?"

"A pack of wolves found their way into the fort after dark and *after* the gates were closed. We were going to make ourselves nice cloaks out of them when Ula scolded us all until we felt like beaten children. Instead, we opened the gates and let them go. That and other odd things. Strange screams in the night. Stars falling from the sky toward the Wash." Cai shook his head. "I'm glad spring is upon us once more."

"As am I."

Cai smiled nicely at me, then scanned the room. "You seem to be one warrior maiden short..." he said, looking for Pix.

"She's ridden to King's Wood. I expect her to return any time now. She will be glad to see you."

Cai grinned. "She has an odd way of getting under one's skin."

I smiled at him. "You don't need to tell me."

"I promised Bran I would search the market for some Roman-style buckles he wanted. I will return by nightfall to see if that mad woman has made her way back."

"You are welcome to stay with us as long as you wish."

"Thank you, Boudica," he said, then paused. "It is good to see you again. I was recently in Frog's Hollow. I remembered all of our good times there, with you and Gaheris. Lynet sends her love."

I smiled at Cai. "He is in my thoughts these last few months as well," I told him. "Please return my love to Lynet when you see her next."

Cai nodded, then took his leave of me.

"You see," I told Sorcha. "With the winter departing, there will be much excitement. You will see."

As winter faded into spring, then spring into summer, Prasutagus began his work once more.

Building began in earnest in Venta, along with expanded farming on the western bank of the Tay. My husband also spent much of his time riding from Venta to Yarmouth, where they rebuilt the warehouse that had burned in winter and commissioned new boats. Luckily, they had managed to save many of the goods we'd stored for trade. It was not a total loss, but the village needed work. Along with the work in Yarmouth, the mining of silver and iron had increased tenfold in Greater Iceni territory, with new mines being explored.

Vian wisely encouraged Prasutagus to put the displaced Trinovantes settlers to work. To the northeast, not far from Northern Iceni borders, there was a mine that the elders swore was rich in silver. Prasutagus sanctioned the development of a new village just south of the mine. The people named it Camulan, after Camulos. Ansgar, Henwyn, and the other druids visited the site and performed a rite, calling upon Camulos to bless the new settlement.

Despite my hopes that I would soon see my family in Oak Throne, the year passed quickly. All of our time was spent building and raising our fierce little girl.

When autumn came again, Prasutagus returned from the harbor to find Pix and me walking alongside Druda, Sorcha sitting on the horse's back. The excited baby was clapping as she rode, me holding her waist so she didn't squirm her way into trouble. The autumn sunlight shimmered on her deep auburn hair, shining like the dark red of decaying oak leaves.

"Ah, here is my warrior maiden. Training her in spears and shields already?" Prasutagus asked Pix.

"Nay, Strawberry King, but she is eager to ride. However, that son of yours," Pix said, gesturing across the field where Artur was stabbing a straw dummy to death with a sword, "is quite another matter. He is ready to lead the Greater Iceni to battle."

Prasutagus laughed. "Artur," he called to the boy, waving to him.

The boy paused his onslaught a moment to wave to his father, then continued the battle.

"Da, da, da," Sorcha babbled at Prasutagus.

"What is it, my girl?"

"Dat, dat," she said, pointing to Druda.

"Yes, you are riding Druda. I see. I will have to find a Caledonian pony for my princess."

"They say those beasts can be ornery," I warned my husband.

"Then it will fit in with this barnyard full of personalities," Prasutagus said. "Speaking of which, any sign of Nightshade's foaling?"

"She whinnies at me e'ery time I leave her. E'en now, she's watching me," Pix said, pointing over her shoulder to where Nightshade was hanging her head over the fence. The horse's round belly protruded from both sides.

As if on cue, Nightshade whinnied at Pix and then kicked the fence.

"I suppose I best check on her. Want me to take this one?" Pix asked, gesturing to Druda.

I nodded, then lifted Sorcha off the horse.

"Come along, Druda," Pix said. "Yer girl be waspish."

I turned to Prasutagus, who took Sorcha from me.

"You are back early today," I said. Prasutagus had ridden out before first light to visit the harbor. Usually, he was not back until after the evening meal.

Prasutagus nodded. "There is a shipment leaving tomorrow morning for Londinium. I would like to sail with them."

I nodded. "Very well."

"Do you want to come?" he asked me.

"Me? But... Sorcha."

"We will only be gone a few days. She is eating well, and the others can watch over her. There are many rumors, Boudica. I would like to go and see for myself. I would be glad to have you alongside me."

"What rumors?" I asked.

"That Legate Vespasian is moving along the coast, crushing anyone resisting him. Some say he turns a blind eye to who is a friend and who is a foe to accomplish his goals. But the real worry is to our west. Governor Plautius has spent all summer penetrating into Dobunni and Cornovii lands hunting Caratacus. That would be no matter to us, but they say the Coritani are providing help to their Cornovii neighbors."

I frowned. Melusine's father would soon find his head on a pike if the rumors were true. "And Caratacus?"

"Still alive, from what I have heard."

"Again, this business with the Coritani," I said with a frown. "Anything about Caturix?"

Prasutagus shook his head. "Come to Londinium with

me, wife. Let's go see what these Romans are doing there. They say that city has grown times ten in the last year. Let's see for ourselves."

"All right. I will speak to Brita," I said, then took Sorcha's hand. "What about you, little lady. Will you be able to make do without your mother and father for a few days?"

"Nay," she said firmly, scolding me.

Prasutagus laughed.

When we went back inside, Prasutagus took Sorcha with him to his meeting chamber while I went to seek out Brita and explain the plan. I found her helping in the kitchens. There, I shared Prasutagus's idea.

"It is no trouble at all. I will see to my little princess," Brita reassured me. "Never worry, Queen Boudica. All will be well."

Vian, who was lingering nearby, moved to speak, then paused.

"Vian?"

"I... Do you think there would be room for me? I don't wish to intrude on your privacy, but I think that if I can see the port city, it may be helpful for planning."

"I will ask Prasutagus."

"What are you asking, my wife?" Prasutagus asked, entering the kitchens behind me, a fussy Sorcha in his arms.

"King Prasutagus," Betha said, looking flustered as she hastily tried to tidy up her work bench.

"This one is chewing on her hand," he said, looking to Sorcha. "Perhaps a biscuit, Betha?"

"Oh," the woman said, the red draining from her cheeks. "Of course," she added, then went to a basket of small biscuits she kept for when Sorcha's aching gums got the best of her. She handed one to the baby.

"What is it?" Prasutagus asked.

"Vian was wondering if she could join us."

Prasutagus grinned. "Have you ever been on a ship before, Vian?"

"No, King Prasutagus."

"It is not always easy on the stomach, but you are welcome to try. I would be glad to have your eyes looking about. But keep in mind, Londinium is not a place suitable for ladies."

"I understand. I'll refrain from being shocked."

At that, Prasutagus laughed. "Very well."

Sorcha, sated by her biscuit, grew quiet once more. Prasutagus and I returned to the private meeting room. Prasutagus stood before his map. I went to his side. The entire south was now covered in red pegs.

"Legate Vespasian is moving through Durotriges territory," Prasutagus said, moving the red pegs farther west along the coast.

"Resistance?" I asked.

Prasutagus nodded. "From the Durotriges and their neighbors, the Dumnonii, to the west." Prasutagus shook his head. "The Romans took the Isle of Wight over the summer. I just heard the news today. Vespasian is building a Roman encampment there."

"We have heard nothing from Aulus all summer," I

said, frowning at the Roman pegs pushing through Catuvellauni lands into Cornovii territory.

Prasutagus shrugged. "He needs nothing more from us."

Prasutagus's words caused a weird ping in my heart. Perhaps it was good the governor had turned his attentions away from Venta. The strange, unspoken feelings between us were good for neither of us. I loved Prasutagus. Nothing in this world would cause me to be untrue to him, but there was something about the Roman that was...*intriguing*. It was best if that kind of lure stayed well away from me. And, perhaps Prasutagus was right. Aulus had gotten what he wanted from the Iceni. Maybe his game with me had already been played through. I hated the thought that he had toyed with my emotions for political ends.

"Let Rome be Rome and Caratacus be Caratacus. We are Greater Iceni. So, we shall sail to Londinium and see how we can become even richer," I said. "But you must promise me one thing."

"What's that?"

"That if we see any elephants for sale, you will buy me one."

Prasutagus laughed. "You will have to ride it home, my queen. I have no ships to accommodate such a beast."

"Yet," I told him, planting a kiss on his cheek.

"Yet," Prasutagus replied with a grin.

CHAPTER 64

After a painful goodbye to Sorcha and many hugs with Artur, we rode to the harbor the following day. Pix, nervous about her horse and set on keeping an eye on the children, stayed behind. In Yarmouth, Prasutagus, Vian, and I boarded a ship, along with a handful of warriors. I was impressed at the wealth of goods on board. From furs to swords and everything in between, I could see the result of the massive work Prasutagus—and Vian—had been putting into the growth of the Greater Iceni's wealth.

Vian and I settled in at the front of the ship where we could get the best view and be out of the way.

"The weather is good today," Prasutagus told us. "The wind is on our side. It will take time, but we will soon be underway."

Within the hour, we set off, a group of three ships all laden with Greater Iceni goods. As we left the port, I noticed that Roman ships and those of the Parisii were docked in Yarmouth. Trade and sales were already under-way. As we sailed from the harbor, the symbol on another of the ships caught my attention.

"Prasutagus," I said, pointing. "Is that... Where is that ship from?"

"Menapii," he told me. "Some traders have come from Gaul with salt, gems, and other rare goods."

Reaching into my vest pocket, I pulled out the small leather pouch I had stored there. I removed the coin and looked from it to the pennant on the ship, noting the similarity in design. I handed the coin to Prasutagus.

"Aye, Boudica. I'm sorry. I had forgotten. We can talk to the ship's captain when we return if they are still in port. I'm sorry," he said, then handed the coin back.

"It's all right," I said, trying not to let my frustrations show.

Prasutagus gently set his hand on my shoulder, then rejoined the men.

I gritted my teeth. Prasutagus may have forgotten, but I had not. I struggled to quiet the flicker of annoyance I felt toward Prasutagus. Had those ships been coming for months, and he had said nothing? I didn't speak of Gaheris to Prasutagus. Despite my best efforts to live alongside Esu's memory, sometimes, I was overrun by it. I had chosen not to subject Prasutagus to the same thing. While Esu's memory was my constant companion, Prasutagus had forgotten that I still mourned a man whose murder went unpunished.

I sighed, then looked back out to sea.

"Is that... What is that you showed Prasutagus?" Vian asked.

I handed the coin to her. "There was an attack on the people of Frog's Hollow at the Wash several seasons ago. Did you hear of it at Holk Fort?"

"I... Yes, I remember Saenunos speaking of it."

"There was no sign of the attackers," I said, "except this. A single clue was left behind in the sand. A Menapii coin."

"No one survived the attack?"

"A child who cannot speak," I said, thinking warmly of Tristan. It had been too long since I had been home to see them all. "I was betrothed to a man from Frog's Hollow, Gaheris. He was the chieftain's son. He died in that attack."

"I never knew, Boudica. I'm so sorry," Vian said, handing the coin back.

I studied the coin in my hand. "One day, I will have an answer. May the gods have mercy on whoever took Gaheris from me because I will not."

Seeing the sea from land was nothing compared to experiencing it on waves. Prasutagus warned us that the boat would pitch and roll, and it did. Thankfully, it bothered neither Vian nor me. We rolled along with the rocking sea.

It was late in the night, the moon reflecting on the wave caps, when Prasutagus rejoined me.

"Can I prepare you somewhere to sleep? I am afraid it will be little more than a corner, but I can try."

"No. Not yet. I am just admiring the moon on the waves."

Prasutagus slipped in behind me, wrapping his arms around me. Vian slept curled up on the ship's deck not far from us.

"I miss Sorcha," Prasutagus said. "All I can think about is her laugh."

I chuckled lightly. "Yes. I know they will care for her, but still."

Prasutagus tucked his face into my neck.

I rested against him.

"You don't speak much of Gaheris. I'm sorry I didn't think of it."

"It's not a pain for you to carry."

"You are my wife. Your pain is my own. You have become a mother to Artur in everything but blood. I'm ashamed that I didn't think to tell you about the ships. Maybe… I guess I hoped you'd left your sorrow behind. And if I am honest, I hoped his memory had faded. I'm a jealous person. It's a flaw I'm not proud of."

I swallowed hard, then said, "Thank you for your honesty."

"I will do better."

But Prasutagus's confession reminded me that I wasn't so perfect either. Already, it had occurred to me that I may see Aulus in Londinium.

"Don't chide yourself," I told Prasutagus. "We are all only mortal. The gods did not create us as perfect beings. Why do we hold ourselves to such standards? But we can love one another, flaws and all."

"Flaws and all," Prasutagus said with a laugh, then kissed me on the side of the head. "Lean back, wife, and keep me warm. I will doze under the moonlight and dream of the gods of the sea."

I settled into Prasutagus's arms. "Good night, my love," I whispered to him.

"Good night, my May Queen."

WE REACHED THE MOUTH OF THE THAMES THE FOLLOWING day and began our journey upriver to Londinium. The green-brown waters of the Thames were sided by willow trees, their long branches with yellowed leaves drifting like a woman's hair onto the water's surface. A bevy of swans floated by our ships, making their way to a patch of tall cattails and water lilies on the river's edge. The scent of autumn was in the air, a light aroma of decaying leaves and smoke from fires on the breeze. We passed several farmsteads settled amongst the rolling hills as we went.

"The south bank is Cantiaci," Prasutagus told us. "At least, it was. Now, it is Rome's. The north of the river and the village itself is now the Trinovantes."

"Also, essentially, Rome," Vian said.

"Yes," Prasutagus replied.

Soon, the number of boats in the river increased, and we began to see signs of activity. A road sided the river, and on it, we passed wagons and units of Roman soldiers making their way to Londinium.

When we turned around a bend in the river, the great bridge spanning the Thames came into view.

On each side, we saw construction, but it was the north side of the river that looked like a swarm of ants. Roman workers were everywhere: digging ditches, erecting stone walls, and constructing new buildings. In addition to the soldiers, I saw many Roman commoners, distinguishable by their dress. Overseers watched the construction while merchants and workers hurried from place to place.

"So much for the shanty town of Londinium," Vian said.

"It's like a fungus growing on the side of the Thames," I said with a frown. "Behind us, the greenwood whispers. Here, it reeks of fish and bodies."

"You and Vian must be accompanied by guards at all times," Prasutagus told us. "Now, I must help the men bring us to port. It is a hideous place, that is certain, but we will leave it very wealthy. You will see," Prasutagus said, then turned back to the men. "Ah-hey-ho," he called, the men answering the same.

Vian and I sat side by side, looking at the throng of people.

"The Greater Iceni will survive Rome's friendship, but I don't know how the rest of our people will fare," Vian said, her eyes wincing as she watched a man lashing a slave. "But for what it's worth, I am glad that you, Prasutagus, and Caturix are wise enough to save us from *that* fate. But may the gods be with all the rest."

WHEN WE FINALLY MADE PORT, PRASUTAGUS SENT RUNNERS into the city to meet with merchants and then began unloading goods. I watched how deftly Prasutagus organized his men and took charge of the cargo. He knew who to talk to, who to send where, who to ignore. Several of the merchants on the docks came to meet with him.

Mostly, Vian and I just stayed out of the way. Finally, Beow, one of Prasutagus's men, joined us.

"Prasutagus asked that we take you to the market when we were done unloading. If you are ready, we can go now."

"We're ready."

Beow whistled to Prasutagus, who turned to look. Seeing we were preparing to go, Prasutagus excused himself from the men he was talking to and joined us.

"Keep that at hand," Prasutagus said, gesturing to my spear. "No one will bother you, especially when they realize who you are, but the city is a rough place. Expect to see a fair few fights and worse. And you will also see many things for sale at the market. You must temper your heart."

I nodded, understanding his meaning.

"We will spend the night on the ships and depart in the morning. Be back before dusk," Prasutagus told Beow.

"I'll keep them safe, my king."

Prasutagus clapped the man on the back, gave me a warm grin, and headed back to work.

"Queen Boudica," Beow said, gesturing for us to follow.

Vian and I then made our way into the market, four men with us.

Everywhere I looked, I saw construction. The new buildings looked like those being built in Camulodunum, in the Roman style. At one end of town, land was being prepared for a massive building project. In addition, several trading stations were being built. I watched as a group of men worked.

"They are not Roman," I said, observing the workers.

"They are Gauls. It looks like they are building a permanent home here. Several people are building similar trading stations," Vian said, pointing to a row of build-ings. "But the administrative buildings, those are Roman."

"Which means that Rome will oversee the town."

Vian nodded. "So much for Trinovantes lands."

We made our way past the ship-builders, admiring their fine work, as well as the impressive size of the ships they were crafting. New piers were being constructed in the harbor, slaves working in chest-high water to accom-plish the task. We heard people calling to one another in languages we didn't recognize. Roman soldiers passed us by, eyeing our party closely.

I heard the words, "Greater Iceni," whispered by one of the men. At that, they left us be.

Vian and I visited the animal market, where cattle, horses, mules, donkeys, and other beasts of burden were for sale. Vian and I stopped at a vendor where a man was selling puppies, including the marsh terries I'd seen in Stonea.

"You should know these dogs, lady," the vendor told me.

"Should I? How?"

"They be Northern Iceni, sent down with King Caturix's traders. You be Northern Iceni, ain't you?"

"This is Queen Boudica of the Greater Iceni," Vian told the man.

"I say. Queen," he said, bowing to me as he pulled off his cap. "They be fine dogs. The Romans pay a handsome price for them. All these pups are already purchased."

I lifted one of the little furry monsters and gave it a squeeze. "Be safe on your journey, little one."

"Yeah, I got great hounds, terriers, mastiffs, all manner of dogs here," the man said, gesturing to the pens behind him. "Anything you want, Queen Boudica, you will find in this market. Watch your coin purse, though. Thieves are just as likely to try to steal from you as from anyone else."

"Thank you for the advice, sir."

I gave the pup one last scratch, set him back with his littermates, then we carried on. The next vendor we approached was selling birds. He had every bird you could imagine from chickens, ducks, geese, falcons, songbirds, and more.

"Boudica, look," Vian said, tugging on my arm.

In the back was an oversized pen. Within were two birds with brilliant blue and green feathers, their long tail plumes resting on the ground. On the top of their heads was a crown of delicate quills.

"Sir, what are those?" I asked.

The vendor, who'd been tossing some feed to the geese, looked from me to the birds, suddenly perking up at the prospect of a sale.

"Those are peacocks, fine lady," he said, then lifted a long feather lying nearby. "This is one of their tail plumes. The feathers have the eyes of the gods within. Look," he said, handing it to me. "When they are in the mood, their plumage fans out like so," he said, waving his hands, his fingers spread wide. "Most beautiful birds you ever saw."

"Where have they come from?" Vian asked.

"Not sure, exactly. I got them from some traders in Gaul. They've come from some far-off place. I was hoping to sell them to some Roman senator, but no luck. Too expensive to buy to cook. It's a male and female pair here. The male has all the color."

"And their care… Are they difficult to tend to?" I asked.

"No, lady. They eat the same as any duck or chicken."

I grinned at Vian, who nodded to me.

"The price?" I asked.

The man named a ridiculous sum.

I laughed. "No fancy feather is worth that," I replied, handing the feather back, then motioned for us to go on.

"Wait. No, lady. No. You're right. Let me reconsider," he said, and then our bargaining began.

When we finally settled on a fair price, I handed over the coin.

"Three ships belonging to the Greater Iceni are in the harbor. Have them—and their feed as negotiated—delivered there."

"Yes, lady."

With that, we made our way onward, finally stopping at a makeshift tavern. Construction of a new building—a proper inn and tavern—was underway not far from us.

"Prasutagus can send us on guard duty again any time he wishes," Beow said as the tavern maid set down a massive tankard of ale and a plate of meat before him.

"It was a long trip," I said with a laugh.

As we ate, I was surprised when I spotted a familiar face in the crowd—Madogh.

The man gave me the briefest of glances, then disappeared into the mob.

Of course, Prasutagus would have his men everywhere —including the docks.

After we finished our food, we made our way to the textile and goods markets. There, the vendors were hawking their wares to Romans and Celts alike. I saw many fine wares. Selecting a few items such as spices, oils, and unusual pots and bowls of good quality for the kitchens, I pressed on. I stopped again, examining a tall vase that had been elaborately painted. I studied the image thereon. The image showed women on horseback, fighting with swords, slings, bows and arrows, against a field of soldiers. In the distance behind them was a walled city.

"The Amazons," the vendor, a man with thick black hair and an unusual accent, told me. "An ancient tribe of warrior women. They fought at the fall of Troy, where the Trojans and Greeks battled. Sadly, they fought for Troy against my people. Here is Artemis, their patron goddess, watching them from the heavens. See how she rains down arrows on the Amazon's enemies."

"All women?" Vian asked. "They had no men in their tribes?"

"Not for any longer than one night," the man answered Vian with a wink, making the girl's cheeks blush.

"Artemis..." I said, touching the image.

"The Romans call her Diana," the man explained.

"Isn't it odd how you can travel the wide world and discover the gods with different names but the same faces," I said, realizing that this goddess bore a striking resemblance to the Morrigu.

"You should see what I have seen, lady," the man said with a laugh but did not elaborate.

"I will have it," I said, then negotiated the price. The man neatly boxed up the vase, passing it off to one of the men.

"Queen Boudica," Beow told me. "It is near dusk. We should return to the boats."

Agreeing with him, we set off through the market once more.

"There is so much here," Vian said, her eyes wide as she took in the place. "We have barely seen half the things.

And so much construction. Look where they are digging," she added, pointing. "They are building a stone wall around the whole town."

"King Diras will be very pleased with his new city."

At that, Vian huffed a laugh.

She was right to laugh. "*Claudius* would be very pleased with his new city," I said.

"How long before there is any sign left of the Trinovantes people?" Vian said, looking around. All around us, buildings of Roman design sprung up like weeds.

"It is all Rome."

Vian nodded. "All Rome. So, too, are the Trinovantes."

CHAPTER 65

When we returned to the ships, we found Prasutagus and the others there. Along with Prasutagus was a Roman man wearing a fine toga, as well as two Roman soldiers. The Roman was a plump man with short, curly brown hair, a long nose, and a loud laugh. He clapped Prasutagus on the shoulder as he spoke.

Vian and I exchanged a questioning look.

"Ah, here is my wife," Prasutagus said, gesturing for me to join him.

I went to Prasutagus.

"Boudica, this is Praefectus Gaius Marcellus. We met when I last came to Londinium. He's here to oversee the construction."

"Sir," I said, inclining my head to him.

"I say, what a beauty. Well met, Queen Boudica. Yes, yes, you must agree, Prasutagus. She will be much more comfortable in my home."

"Very well. We thank you for the generous offer," Prasutagus said. "I must attend to some matters here, and then we will join you."

The praefectus nodded, then he and his men made their way down the dock.

I cocked an eyebrow at Prasutagus.

"He heard we were in port and thought it unseemly for a queen to sleep on a ship. I don't care what he thinks, but I care what he knows. Gaius's ability to gossip makes Titus look like a novice. He invited us to stay with him tonight. We must accept."

"Very well. He's overseeing the construction here. For who?"

"For King Diras, for Rome; they are one and the same."

"Ugh," I said with a groan.

"I'm sorry, Boudica. I know I should have consulted you, but—"

"No. It's not that. It's just…we ate at the tavern, and I'm still full. You know how the Romans are. All they want to do is eat. I'll never survive the night."

At that, Prasutagus laughed. "If that is the worst of our troubles, I'll take it."

"Queen Boudica," one of the men called from the ships. "What are these birds?" he asked, gesturing to the pens.

It was Prasutagus's turn to look confused. "Indeed, what are those?"

I grinned at him. "I couldn't find elephants, but I did find something."

We went to the ship where my peacocks sat waiting.

"They are called peacocks," I told them.

"Do you eat them?" the soldier asked.

"No. They are...well, they are too beautiful to be eaten."

"Bloody loud is what they are. Have you heard them?"

"How can you say such a thing about my lovely birds? Their call is as soft as doves." In truth, I had not heard anything from the birds and had no idea how they sounded.

At that, the men laughed. "You will see, Boudica. You will see."

AFTER HE MADE THE ARRANGEMENTS WITH THE MEN, Prasutagus, Vian, two guards, and I journeyed to the home of Praefectus Gaius Marcellus. The house itself was hidden from the street, surrounded by high walls. The enormous house was built very near the massive construction site. Once permitted inside the walls, we found the gates opened to a large courtyard. The ground was laid with stones, and a statue of a woman pouring water from a jug sat at the center of the garden. Flowering trees and other plants decorated the space. Torches sat in sconces on the walls, lighting the courtyard. On the other side of the courtyard was the house. A servant led us to the door.

When we got there, the guard extended his hand. "Your weapons."

Reluctantly, we disarmed.

The guard led our warriors away.

Prasutagus, Vian, and I were escorted inside the well-appointed house to a dining room where a young boy wearing a knee-length tunic sat playing a harp. The floor had been decorated with small tiles in intricate floral designs. Grapes, fish, and bread loaves were worked into the ornamentation. The walls, too, were painted with images of pastoral scenes. Already, food had been spread out on the table, and wine was flowing freely.

Gaius Marcellus rose when we entered. "King Prasutagus, Queen Boudica," he said, "Welcome. You are all welcome to my house. Come. Let's have some wine. Sit. Sit."

The table had been set for Gaius, Prasutagus, and me.

Perceiving that the Roman must have thought Vian was my slave, I turned to say something, but Vian held my arm. "Say nothing, Boudica," she whispered. "It is for the best. I will remain in the shadows so I may see and hear more," she said, then took a spot behind my chair.

Prasutagus quickly assessed the situation and said nothing.

The two of us sat.

"It is good to see you again, Prasutagus. It is so rare we receive such noble persons as yourself here in Londinium. I suspect everyone else thinks they will be robbed," he said, then let out a loud laugh, slapping the table. The silver serving pieces, floral arrangements, and painted dishes on the table shook.

Prasutagus chuckled lightly. "Well, I am eager to see

where the fruits of my labor are headed and discern what is missing in the market."

"So to better fill the gap?" Gaius asked.

"Yes."

Gaius lifted his cup to Prasutagus. "They say the King of the Greater Iceni is a smart man. Now, I know it to be true," he said, then turned to me. "And you, Queen Boudica, what have you found in Londinium to please you?"

"Sadly, there were no elephants to be had, but I did manage a pair of peacocks."

Gaius laughed and slapped his hand on the table again, making the wine goblets shake. "I, too, am in search of such birds, but I want white ones. They say that Queen Cleopatra had such a pair with her in Rome. Such birds are hard to come by, but I am determined to have a white pair —in honor of Diana."

"Are the birds sacred to her?"

"You will find white peacocks in all of Diana's temples in Rome. Perhaps, one day, we will even have a temple for her here. But for now, the governor has us building to Mithras, our god of war and obligations."

"The expansion of the town is impressive," Prasutagus said. "I don't recognize the place anymore."

"Londinium will become the market hub for all of Britannia," Gaius said proudly. "I have sworn it to the emperor himself. We have many great expansions planned. We shall bring Rome to this barbarian world."

"As it has to the Dobunni and Durotriges?" Prasutagus asked.

"Oh, yes. So you have heard?" Gaius said eagerly. "Legate Vespasian has done very well. Even the Isle of Wight has fallen to him. The island will be a great station for our military advances into Britannia. Your western coast is still wild and eludes us, but we will reach there."

"That will be easier when Caratacus is found," Prasutagus said.

Gaius lifted his cup to toast Prasutagus. "Indeed, it will. A thorn in the governor's side," the man said, then leaned forward. "It is whispered your Coritani kings are hiding him. But I have no worries. If anyone will find him, it is Aulus Plautius. The governor is a well-respected soldier. He succeeds in all his campaigns."

"I'm sure King Verica would agree," Prasutagus said.

"You have not heard," Gaius said, his face lighting up at the prospect of sharing some gossip. The man waved for his servants to pour us more wine. Once our glasses were full, he leaned forward. "Of course, you are friends with Rome, so there is no harm in telling. The news just reached me yesterday. King Verica took ill and died three days ago. His son, Cogidubnus, has been crowned king of the Atrebates."

"That is surprising news," Prasutagus said. I could hear the hint of alarm in his voice, but he tried to hide it.

"It is a good thing, a good thing. Cogidubnus may have been born of your people, but he has spent most of his life in Rome. He is a good soldier and will be a wise leader. I hear he is planning to wed a Regnenses princess. I forget her name. We will have a strong alliance across the south, King Prasutagus. And great prosperity for us all. Let us toast Fortuna," the Roman said, "for she brings wealth to us all. To Fortuna," he said, hoisting his glass.

"To Fortuna..." I began, "and in memory of King Verica," I added. "May he long be remembered as a great king of the Atrebates who retook his father's lands."

"To Fortuna and Verica," Gaius agreed.

And with that, we drank.

I looked at my husband over my cup.

All of the changes we faced came about in Verica's name.

And now, the king was gone.

But Rome was here to stay.

WE SPENT THE NIGHT TALKING WITH GAIUS, WHO SHARED HIS plans for the city. I tried to pace my intake of Roman wine, but by the end of the night, I found I had imbibed far more than I intended.

The Roman, it seemed, had intended it that way. We had finished several flagons of wine when the Roman finally set down to the business of asking questions.

"I understand the Northern Iceni are very close with the Coritani. King Caturix's wife is from that tribe, is she not?" he asked.

"King Caturix—my brother—has continued the peaceful relations with his neighbors that my father spent a lifetime to achieve," I said waspishly.

"Ah, King Caturix is your brother? Is that right? Yes, perhaps I had heard that before. Are you Caturix's only sibling, Queen Boudica?"

I sensed the probing nature of the question but decided it was safe to say, "No. I have another brother, Prince Bran, who resides in Oak Throne."

"And is he wed?"

"He is."

"Another princess?"

I grinned when I thought of Bec. "No. He is married to a commoner."

"Is that right?" Gaius asked in surprise. "Any other brothers?"

"Thankfully, no," I said, making the Roman laugh.

"Are you married, Gaius?" Prasutagus asked.

"I am. I am. My Lavinia remains in Rome. Your lands are too wild for her. She's a good friend to the governor's wife, in fact."

"The governor's wife?" I asked, trying to hide the surprise in my voice.

"Yes, Pomponia, wife of Governor Plautius, and Lavinia are very close. Pomponia is a wonderful lady. The two of them are thick as thieves. I have often joked that they have left us alone on purpose so they can spend our money and do as they please with us so far away."

He's married. He lied to me. Why did he lie to me?

Refocusing, I chuckled lightly. "I'm sure that's not the case. You must miss one another terribly."

"Well, there are ways to stem such longings," Gaius said knowingly, raising and lowering his eyebrows at

Prasutagus. He flicked his gaze to an attractive, blonde slave with ample breasts standing nearby.

I swallowed hard, trying not to show my disgust at the man's insinuation.

"Regardless," Gaius continued. "Wives have a way of turning a man's head. I'm sure Prasutagus can attest to that. We only hope that King Caturix's wife does not turn his head toward the Coritani way of viewing things."

"Queen Melusine is not that kind of queen," I told the man with irritation. "And my brother is a man of his word."

Unless you were Kennocha and Mara...

"I do hope so. As I understand it, the governor is planning to visit your brother. But I'm sure he will find everything in order. By the gods, it has grown very late. Both of you look dreary-eyed, and here I sit, talking of idle rumors."

Gaius clapped his hands, making Vian jump and his servants scurry.

"Let my people see you to your rooms. You will find a small closet therein for your slave, Queen Boudica. We shall see you in the morning. I understand we have a fine feast of oysters and quail eggs ready for tomorrow's morning meal. And if you have some time, I will show you the construction at the forum. You will find it most impressive."

"We look forward to it," Prasutagus said.

At that, the Roman servants motioned for us to follow them.

We were led away from the main hall and up a flight

of stairs to a second story. They led us into a room that was bigger than Ula's entire cottage. The servants opened the shutters on the windows so we could look out on the city.

"Your slave can stay in the antechamber through there," a servant told me, gesturing to a door connected to our room. "There is water, wine, and fresh linens. How else may we serve you?"

"We need nothing more. Thank you," I replied.

The man bowed, then exited, leaving Vian, Prasutagus, and me on our own.

Vian went to the window and looked out. You could easily see much of the town from this vantage point. She stood there for a long moment before she turned to me.

"Do you need any assistance, Boudica?"

"No, Vian. Thank you," I said, then went to the small door, opening it to reveal a windowless but comfortable enough room on the other side. "Well, there's a bed," I said with a sympathetic smile.

"I can take the room if you are frightened, Vian," Prasutagus offered.

She shook her head. "I will be all right, my king. I am only sorry I have nothing to write with. I'm trying to commit everything I see to memory."

"We'll find you something tomorrow," Prasutagus reassured her.

"Thank you," she told him, then went to look at the linens sitting on mine and Prasutagus's wide bed. "They have left you a bedgown, Boudica. Are you sure I can't help you?"

I glanced into the small room once more. "No, Vian. And are *you* sure about the bedchamber?"

Vian shrugged. "I'll be fine. The bed is larger than what I had in Holk Fort," she said with a slight laugh. "May the gods—our gods—watch over you both. Good night," she said, then went to the small room, closing the door behind her.

Prasutagus took Vian's spot by the window.

I joined him, both of us looking out at the budding city.

"This news about Verica is alarming," I said.

Prasutagus nodded.

"And I am worried for Caturix."

"As am I."

My husband wrapped his arms around me. The noise and smells of the city rose upward.

With a sigh, Prasutagus shut the casement and led me to bed. He lifted the fancy bedgown that had been left for me.

With a sigh, I took it from him, then began to undress. "If I didn't smell like the sea, I wouldn't bother with it."

"Well, you don't *have* to wear it," Prasutagus whispered.

I smiled at my husband, then removed all of my clothes and set them aside, slipping naked into the bed. The sensations of the silk linens and rich velvets felt good on my skin. Prasutagus, too, undressed, then slipped into bed with me. Prasutagus wrapped his arms around me, kissing my bare shoulder.

"It has been months since we were without Sorcha between us in the bed," he whispered.

Stubborn as she turned out to be, Sorcha would not sleep anywhere but in bed with Prasutagus and me. She would cry herself red-faced if we tried to have her sleep in the cradle. Prasutagus was right. This was the first we'd been without her.

We lay in the darkness of the Roman house, quietly kissing and touching one another until the streets began to grow silent. Through the wall, we heard the sound of Vian's soft breathing. Then, we joined one another in earnest. My hands roved across Prasutagus's strong back, feeling his muscles. Under the scent of the sea air clinging to his hair, I caught the light smells of fern, soap, and sage that always perfumed his skin. His lips tasted of wine and oils. Still dizzy from the wine, my head buzzed with antici-pation when Prasutagus gently squeezed and kissed my breasts, his hand playing between my legs. I swallowed the moans that wanted to escape my lips. Soon, he climbed atop me, and we began moving as one—man and woman, husband and wife, king and queen, lord and lady. It took everything within me not to call out loudly when Prasu-tagus brought me to the pinnacle of pleasure. Soon, he, too, reached the apex. Afterward, he lay with his head on my sweaty chest, gently touching my breast.

"In this life and all the others to come, I will always love you," Prasutagus whispered, then slipped off to sleep.

CHAPTER 66

The next morning, I woke with my head aching. We redressed and made our way back downstairs, where Gaius treated us to a hearty meal, then led us outside, Vian and our soldiers joining us once more.

As we went, I heard Vian whispering to the men. They had all been fed and comfortably lodged for the night—which I was relieved to discover.

"Now, come and see this," Gaius said, leading us to the massive square we had seen under construction. "This will be Londinium's forum, a major hub," he said, leading us into the gigantic, square construction site. "Here, we will have a marketplace with spaces for hundreds of vendors. A space for auctions. And on the far end, we shall build a great basilica. I can see it in my mind. A structure like nothing your people have ever seen."

"What is the function of a basilica?" I asked.

"It's used for the city's administration, for courts and

the like…state business," Gaius answered me absently. "But here, here is where Britannia's money will be made. You will see, Prasutagus. Keep those ships coming to Londinium. We shall make a space here just for your people. A permanent stall for the goods of the Greater Iceni. Already, you are a step ahead of your rival kings— the Greater Iceni will grow richer, faster than all the rest. Only Queen Cartimandua seems to have your shrewdness. She, too, sends regular shipments. Have you met the Brigantes queen?"

"Once, in Camulodunum."

"Ah yes, at the submission of the eleven kings. I hear she is very beautiful. Is it true?"

"Some would call her such."

"You have a loyal husband, Queen Boudica. He will not even betray you in his words. Come, let me show you the rest of the market. We have fine horses for sale, many sent from the Northern Iceni, Queen Boudica."

As we went, Gaius shared with us his plans to build temples, theaters, and public baths, which puzzled Prasutagus and me.

"And all the men come together to bathe?" Prasutagus asked, confused.

"Indeed, they do. It is excellent for the health. They are quite relaxing. And, of course, we are *tended* to by slaves of all shapes and sizes."

Neither Prasutagus nor I responded to his innuendo.

"You see," Gaius said. "We have slaves of every hair color, skin color, shape, and size," he said, gesturing to a slave market underway not far from us. There, I spotted several Romans purchasing slaves. Some people were foreign-looking, with darker skin or unfamiliar appearance, others looked Gaulish, but from the dress of the people there, I understood that most were Catuvellauni.

The sight of it stunned me.

But what had I expected? Caratacus had led his people into war. This was the result.

A group of Romans looked over a dozen or so strong-looking men, all bound at the wrists with irons on their necks.

Disgusted by the sight, I had just turned away when someone called my name.

"Boudica! Queen Boudica!"

Confused, I looked back.

A Roman soldier banged his sword against a wagon full of captives. "Shut up, you hag."

But someone in the wagon persisted. "Boudica! Boudica!"

I stared at the mud-stained faces looking back at me, hair matted with dirt and wild with knots.

And then, I saw.

"Priestess Dindraine," I whispered, then rushed across the square to the wagon, bypassing the Roman soldiers who shouted at me.

"Boudica," Prasutagus called, hurrying behind me.

I ran to the wagon, gripping the wooden railings.

"Dindraine," I said, barely recognizing the Catuvellauni priestess. She was a shadow of the woman Dôn had introduced me to at Arminghall on Beltane. "Priestess. Is that you?" Her black-and-silver hair was a disheveled mess. She had streaks of mud and blood on her face, the dried blood coming from a cut on her forehead. The kohl on her eyes had streaked down her face in a wretched mess.

"Boudica," the priestess said, reaching desperately for my hands. "Help us. They've taken all of us from the sacred temple. Help us…"

"Shut up, you," the Roman soldier said, swatting at her. Then, he grabbed my arm, "Mind your turn, woman."

I pulled the dagger from my belt with my free hand.

The Roman soldier's eyes widened when he felt my knife point pressed against his throat.

"Touch me again, Roman, and you'll find the point of my dagger sticking out of the top of your head."

"Get your hand off her, legionnaire," Gaius shouted. "Don't you know who that is?"

I shook the Roman's hand off my arm.

"I will have you whipped," Gaius told him. "That is Queen Boudica of the Greater Iceni, a dear friend of the governor. You there," Gaius shouted to another soldier. "Discipline this soldier."

"Praefectus," the man said, then pulled the soldier away.

Trying to regain my composure, I turned to Gaius. "There appears to have been some mistake here," I said, gesturing to the wagon holding the priestesses. "The women herein are part of a holy order."

Gaius tittered nervously. "I can't say where they come from, Queen Boudica. Governor Plautius's men send captives south. We don't know anything about where they've come from."

"Naturally, you would have no way of knowing. As I said, there has been some mistake. We've had the governor's word that none of our holy people would be touched."

"They're Catuvellauni," Gaius said.

"So they are. There appears to have been a mistake—nothing for which you are responsible—but I had the governor's promise."

"We don't want to cause you any trouble, Gaius," Prasutagus said. "Business is business. We will pay their purchase price. All of the women here."

"There are some very fine women there. Already, I've sold a few. Their price in silver…"

"We will pay it. With a friend's discount, of course. Boudica, will you please see to it? Gaius was going to take me to see the construction of the Temple of Mithras before we departed. I was looking forward to it."

Gaius smiled, looking relieved that what could have blown up into a massive conflict passed like a foul wind. "Thank you, King Prasutagus. Yes. A misunderstanding. Yes. I trust you understand *I* had nothing to do with it," he said, then he and Prasutagus moved off.

A moment later, the slavemaster joined us.

"These women. All of them. What is their price?" I asked.

When the man told me the sum in silver, I was shocked, not that the cost was so much, but because I had purchased horses for less.

Without another word, I handed over the silver.

"The praefectus said there were others. Where have they gone?" I asked.

"Two girls," the slavemaster said. "Went south, already. Back to Rome."

I felt like I might vomit. "Very well. Thank you."

Gesturing for a guard to step aside, the slavemaster unlocked the wagon.

"Come on, you lot," he told them.

Two of the younger priestesses stepped out first. They were a sorry sight, their beautiful blue robes ripped to tatters, their hair a mess, their faces and hands dirty and bloody. They stopped to help Dindraine out, reaching for her hands. It was then that I realized Dindraine had lashes on her back.

She stumbled as she tried to climb from the wagon.

A Roman moved to yank her up when Beow stepped forward to help.

"We will attend to it from here," I said sharply.

The Roman stepped back.

All in all, six girls plus Dindraine remained of their holy people. The girls were all bound at the wrists. I noticed that two of the girl's dresses had been ripped at the bodice. One of the women tried to hold the gaping front of her dress closed with her bound hands.

Beow unhooked his cloak and wrapped it around her.

Not looking back, we turned and made our way back toward the boats.

Dindraine was limping heavily. Her bare feet were scraped and bloody.

"Beow," I said, gesturing to the warrior

He needed no coaxing. "Forgive me, holy one," Beow told her, lifting the priestess.

"My boy, there is nothing to forgive, and even if there were, there is no forgiveness left in me," the priestess said, her voice sounding empty. She set her head against the man's chest and closed her eyes, tears streaming down her face.

CHAPTER 67

W hen we got to the ships, we removed the priestesses' bindings, and Vian and I quickly began tending to their wounds.

I turned to Beow. "From the market, I need yarrow, goldenseal, feverfew, and honey," I said. "And blankets," I added, pushing a pouch of silver toward him. "Do you know the herbs?"

He nodded. Without another word, the man hurried off.

Vian worked quickly, tending to the priestesses while I cleaned Dindraine's feet.

"What happened?" I asked the priestess in a low tone.

"The Romans were looking for Caratacus," she said. "We told them we had not seen the king, but they did not believe us. Our temple was raided. My priestesses... defiled," she said in a low whisper. "And I was questioned."

"By who? The governor?"

Dindraine shook her head. "No. I have not seen Governor Plautius. One of their soldiers. I didn't know him."

"May the Morrigu punish them for what they have done."

"There are none left to punish the Romans," Dindraine said in an empty voice. "They are a disease spreading across the land that cannot be stopped. Not even the gods can stop them now."

"Do not lose faith in the gods," I whispered, wiping the blood from her feet. "They are still with us. Rome cannot change that."

Dindraine laughed. Her tone was hard and painful. "Rome will pull down our gods as it pulls down our kings. Beware, Boudica, for one day, they will come for you too."

While I knew she was injured and angry, her words sent a shiver up my spine.

When Beow returned, I prepared an astringent for the wounds and a tonic to heal injuries.

"Clean the wounds with warm water as thoroughly as you can first, then apply the astringent. It will sting," I told Vian. "And make sure they drink the tonic. The herbs therein will heal and relax them."

"Boudica, after what happened at Maiden Stones... I thought the governor promised nothing like this would happen again," Vian said.

"He did. So, either there has truly been a mistake, or he is a liar."

It was becoming increasingly clear, Aulus *was* a liar. If

he would lie about having a wife or fail to keep his promises, what else was he lying about?

Vian said nothing more. The two of us merely got to work helping the women as the men finished their business so we could depart. Our people, unnerved by the sight of the holy women in such a state, hurried their work to be done with it as quickly as possible.

Dindraine, spent with exhaustion, said nothing as I treated the wounds on her back. She did not even wince when I applied the astringent, though I knew it must have hurt.

"I will cover them with clean cloths for now. When we get to Venta, I can treat them further."

Dindraine nodded mutely.

Most of the other priestesses were similarly quiet.

I stopped to give a tonic to the woman wrapped in Beow's cape.

She met my gaze and said, "Thank you, Queen Boudica. Surely, the Great Mother brought you to us. We are all grateful to you."

"We will see you safely back to Venta. I promise. What is your name?"

"Rue."

"I'm sorry for what happened to you."

"Do not be. It is King Caratacus's doing. He brought this upon us. And now, the gods have punished him."

"What do you mean?"

"The king's sister was amongst us. Caratacus left Princess Imogen in our care, thinking Rome would not touch her if she was hidden amongst our holy people. He was wrong."

"What happened to her?"

"Princess Imogen is very beautiful, Queen Boudica. She was raped many times by the soldiers. Not that the rest of us were not, Dindraine included, but Imogen faced the worst of it. But two days ago, a Roman bought her. He stripped her in the slave market for all to see. Many laughed and jeered. But Imogen paid no mind. Always, she lived in another world. The Roman took her on his ship... I do not have to say the life she has been sold into."

"May the Morrigu curse them all."

"Yes," Rue said absently. "But as for Imogen, I can only hope she dies."

IT WAS NEARLY DARK WHEN THE LAST OF THE MEN RETURNED to the ships. Prasutagus arrived shortly afterward. He went to Dindraine, kneeling on the deck before her.

"Wise one," he said, but Dindraine merely stared off into the distance.

I joined Prasutagus. "She has been like that since we got her settled. Give her some time. The best we can do for her now is get her away from here."

Prasutagus nodded. "I will see the ships readied. The other priestesses?"

"I treated their wounds as best I could and gave them

all a tonic. Those who could, ate. Beow fetched blankets and wraps for them."

"I am sorry it took so long. I tried to hurry, but it was difficult to shake Gaius. Once I did, I met with Madogh. I returned as quickly as possible.

"I'm sure you did your best. Prasutagus..." I said, then moved my husband away from the men, relaying what Rue had told me about Princess Imogen.

My husband's face contorted as he listened. "Caratacus thought she would be safe with them."

"He was wrong."

"And Governor Plautius is a liar," Prasutagus said stiffly.

"Yes."

Prasutagus nodded. "Let's set sail."

I nodded.

With that, Prasutagus and the men prepared to depart. Before we set sail, I went to the cage containing the peacocks. Scooping some feed from the bag, I reached into the cage to feed the birds. They huddled in the corner, away from me.

"Poor creatures," I said. "How far you have traveled from everything you know. Your journey will be over soon. You will be safe from harm. I promise."

In response, one of the birds sounded—loudly.

Its odd trumpet made everyone on the boat jump.

"Like a banshee wail..." Rue said. "May its keening be for Rome."

CHAPTER 68

The return trip to Yarmouth was a somber one. We were all horrified by what had happened to our holy women. In some of the men's eyes, I could see that glint of rage that was often followed by action. This was what had riled the other tribes to push back against Rome, but they had done so clumsily, without coordination. Caratacus had made too many enemies to get people to rally around him. Most of us had sympathized with King Verica's plight. Now...

I felt rage swirling in the pit of my stomach. I had to put myself between Rome and the priestesses of Maiden Stones. They were safe, but only because I intervened. Had I not been there, they would have shared the same fate as Dindraine and the others.

Aulus had promised not to touch our holy people.

He had lied.

One of the men had brought a lyre with him. On the

way home, he played, singing some old songs to comfort the priestesses.

He sang of the maiden Olwen, who had been taken captive by a giant who lived deep in the mountains on the borders of the Otherworld. An ordinary shepherd, Greater Iceni by our man's retelling, traveled there to free the golden-haired maiden. The giant forced the man to complete a series of impossible tasks, which no one could ever accomplish, but the shepherd did—with Olwen's help. After defeating the giant, the man returned to Venta with his new bride, a maiden so sweet and pure, white flowers bloomed everywhere she stepped.

Rue sat at the front of the ship and looked out at the moon-capped waves.

I went to Dindraine, taking her hand. "Dindraine?" I asked, searching her face.

"Boudica," she whispered. "The goddess sent you to us. I don't have the words to thank you. Granddaughter of Rian... Of course, it was you."

"I am so sorry. I don't know what to say. The governor promised me our holy people would not be touched. He has gone back on his word."

"They wanted Caratacus. They knew Imogen was there. They thought she would tell them where he was if she was threatened or if they threatened us. We told them she was mad. They didn't believe us—not until the temple was burned, the priestesses abused, and Imogen raped. Still, she spoke to them of chickens. Of chickens," Dindraine said with a sad laugh.

"You are not alone in your plight. They came for

Maiden Stones, but I convinced the governor to stay his hand."

"I was told that they are building a temple in Camulo-dunum over the ancient shrine of Camulos. No, Boudica, they do not respect our holy things—and they are marching west."

"West. Avallach. Mona."

Dindraine nodded. "You must send someone to Avallach and to Mona, tell them what is happening here. Venetia will be able to keep Avallach hidden. But Mona... the Romans have not forgotten what our druids did to them in the time of Julius Caesar. You must use your influence with the Romans. Do *whatever it takes* to protect Mona. It is the heart of our land. If Mona falls, so fall we all."

I entwined her hand in mine and pressed it against my forehead. "May the gods use me as they see fit and give me the strength to make Rome listen."

"Dear girl," Dindraine said. "You stand alone before a tidal wave."

MOST OF US SLEPT FITFULLY THAT NIGHT, OUR HEARTS unnerved by what we had seen. On the one hand, the Greater Iceni had been accepted as partners of Rome. Prasutagus had arranged with the praefectus to build a permanent trading station for the Greater Iceni in

Londinium. Like the Greater Iceni, other tribes successfully made their way in this new world. The Atrebates watched the Catuvellauni fall with smug satisfaction. The Parisii used their coastline as a trade advantage. The Brigantes, too, took every opportunity to grow their wealth. While I didn't know the extent of Caturix's plans, I saw his mind at work in the market. We had all grown more prosperous as a result of our alliance. But at what cost to the rest of our people?

I did not want to help Caratacus, but I didn't want to see his priestesses in chains either.

On the second day of our journey, ease washed over the priestesses as they slowly awoke from the trauma. When dawn broke, my peacocks found a way to puncture their sorrow.

The birds' incessant and grotesquely loud calls had all of us laughing.

"Boudica, you will keep all of Venta awake with those bloody birds," Beow told me. "Why did you buy such noisy things?"

"To begin with, I didn't know they were so loud. I felt sorry for the lovely things, seeing them like that."

"I hope their feathers are worth the trouble," Beow said.

"If not, Betha can cook them. That will silence their honking," Prasutagus told us.

"Poor creatures, leave them be," I chided them both.

With the wind in our sails, we arrived in Yarmouth late that afternoon.

The ships docked in the harbor once more.

"How much Yarmouth has grown," Dindraine said. "It was barely a fishing port. Now..."

I simply nodded. I would not wax poetic to the priestess about the increase in trade flowing through our port. She had just escaped becoming a commodity herself, a fact that made me feel ill.

"I will prepare a wagon to take us back to Venta, if that is all right with you, wise one," Prasutagus told Dindraine.

"Whatever you deem best, King Prasutagus. We are in your hands now."

Prasutagus bowed to her and then got underway.

"When we reach Venta, I can send word to Henwyn," I told Dindraine. But the priestess surprised me when she shook her head.

"No. I have considered it much of the trip," Dindraine said. "If you will help us, we will ride north to Dôn."

"I... Of course."

"Dôn has been my good friend these many years. Andraste's Grove is quiet, hidden. So near Venta, King's Wood and Arminghall are exposed. We will combine our sisters at the grove, for now, assuming Dôn and the Dark Lady Andraste are willing. The grove is very near the Wash. If there is ever need, escape comes easier."

Understanding, I set my hand on her arm. "As you wish."

Dindraine's gaze went to the priestesses. The women waited silently, seated on a bench, watching the men unload the goods. Rue, however, had walked to the end of the dock. The woman's dark hair blew in the breeze.

"I don't think all of us will continue on in service of the

goddess," Dindraine said. "I trust I can rely on you to help those whose paths end here."

"Yes."

We watched as Beow went to the priestess, speaking to her gently. Rue moved to give the cloak back to him, but he wouldn't take it. Instead, the pair stood together.

"The Maiden is mysterious in her ways," I said, sensing a future for the couple I saw before me.

Dindraine nodded. "She always seems innocent, but her pull is one of the most powerful things on earth. Her charms can bring down empires."

Once Prasutagus had the wagons ready, the priestesses loaded into one of the wagons. The goods, including my peacocks and the other supplies I had purchased in Londinium, were loaded into a second wagon.

I mounted Druda and then joined Prasutagus at the head of our party.

He whistled to the others, then we headed out.

"Madogh shared news of Verulam with me," Prasutagus said, referring to the seat of the Catuvellauni.

"Burned?"

Prasutagus shook his head. "Captured. As with Camulodunum, the Romans are using the fort as a staging point for further campaigns deeper into Catuvellauni territory."

"Prasutagus..." I said, feeling a heavy sensation in my chest.

"We are playing with fire. I know, Boudica. Right now, we are winning. But what if things change in Rome? They are always murdering their leaders. What if their next leader does not look kindly upon us here?"

"I would tell you not to think such things, but you are not wrong to wonder."

"Only time will tell if we have made the right decision."

"Dindraine... I will take her and the others north to the Grove of Andraste, as she has requested."

"Not to King's Wood?"

"No. And she has suggested we send envoys to Avallach and Mona, to tell them what is happening here... to warn them."

"The Romans would never dare touch our holy island," Prasutagus said.

"Nor would they defile the priestess of the Catuvellauni, nor Maiden Stones, nor build a temple over that of Camulos..."

Prasutagus's gaze grew dark. "I will speak to Ansgar."

I nodded.

"We return to Venta with one hand full of gold, the other filled with blood. These are the scales we play with, Boudica."

"We play with them because we would not see both hands bloody."

"Your brother..."

"May the gods watch over Caturix and keep him away from those who would lead him into harm."

WE MADE OUR WAY BACK TO VENTA. IT WAS A QUIET, SOMBER ride. The sun had set. The air had grown cold as winter approached. Overhead, the midnight-blue sky was filled with silver stars. I could smell the scent of woodsmoke in the air as we passed the farmsteads. It was deep in the night when we finally arrived at Venta.

The exterior gates to the city were closed and manned. I was relieved at the sight. As we had journeyed home, I had begun growing increasingly anxious about my family. I could not imagine myself leaving Sorcha alone again, even if I knew Pix could keep her safe.

"Hold," the watchman at the wall called. "Who approaches?"

Prasutagus rode forward. "It is Prasutagus."

"My apologies, King Prasutagus," the watchman answered, followed by a call of, "Open the gates," to the men below.

When the gates opened to the city, I felt a wave of relief pass over me.

Everything was fine.

Everyone was fine.

We were safe.

For now.

CHAPTER 69

W hen we arrived at the king's house, I immediately felt pulled in two directions. Thankfully, Pix appeared to greet us.

"Your wee one is sleeping," she told me. "She would not sleep for Brita the first night, but she ne'er had an issue with me. I kept her with me, talked her exhausted. I just woke Artur. He's in there snuggled beside her now."

"Thank you, Pix," I said, setting my hand on her shoulder.

"Ye have returned with others."

"Yes," I said darkly. "The Romans sacked the Catuvellauni shrine and took the priestesses as slaves."

"I warned ye, Strawberry Queen."

"So you did. But this is the result of Caratacus's foolishness—just like everything else. And on top of it, King Verica is dead," I said with a sigh. "Come, we must make the guesthouse ready," I told Pix.

"Ye and Vian take them. I will wake Ronat to get them something to eat. A kiss ought to get her up."

"Her mother will beat you with a broom."

"She has not done so yet, and Ronat likes my kisses. Don't be jealous. Ye can invite me to bed any time ye wish," Pix said, then headed back into the roundhouse to get help.

I went to the wagon where the men were helping the priestesses down.

I held out my hand for Dindraine. "We will see you housed in the guesthouse tonight."

Dindraine merely nodded.

"Queen Boudica... your noisy birds?" one of the warriors asked.

"Leave them by the chicken pens. I will see to them in the morning."

"If they fly away, Boudica, all of the Greater Iceni will curse you for letting loose a noisy scourge on them," the man told me with a laugh.

I chuckled.

Making my way across the green, I led the women to the guesthouse we used for important company. The place was small, but the priestesses would be comfortable together there. The roundhouse had been sectioned off with drapes. There was a large common area with benches, a table and chairs, and a firepit. Three additional areas with beds were hidden by the drapes.

"Pix and Ronat will be here in a moment with food and drink. Let me see to the fire," I said, then began working.

Outside, I heard Prasutagus and Galvyn talking, but neither man entered.

Rue knelt beside me. "Let me help you, Queen Boudica."

"You should rest," I told her.

"No," the woman said. "I will work. Just because Rome took my world from me, it doesn't make me an invalid. The spirit of the goddess resides in all of us. Each stage of life brings difficulty and change—girl to woman, maid to mother, mother to crone. We are facing those trials now. My sisters will go from this place to Andraste, where the fourth face, the dark face of the goddess, will lend them power. There, they will embrace the strength they need to go on."

"Your sisters will go. Not you?"

"Not me. If you permit it, I will stay in Venta."

"Should I speak to Henwyn?"

"No."

"Then perhaps a role for you here in the—"

"No, Queen Boudica. Thank you."

"If there is anything I *can* do for you, you need only ask. The village midwife, who delivered my daughter, is always short-handed. Can I make an introduction?"

Rue paused, then said, "Yes, thank you, Queen Boudica. You have given me my life back. What more can I ask for?"

I said no more. I felt sick about what had happened and so very angry. In the morning, I would try to discover where Aulus was stationed.

The governor and I would have words.

Pix and Ronat arrived shortly after that, carrying trays of food and drink.

Behind them came a sleepy-eyed Brita carrying extra blankets and clean dresses. In the pile, I recognized gowns that belonged to her, me, Ronat, Nella, and some of Ginerva's old gowns.

I swallowed hard, touched by the maid's unflinching kindness.

Pix also had the wherewithal to bring with her my satchel with my medicines and herbs and handfuls of clean linens.

"Some of the priestesses' wrists need ointment," I told Pix, handing her a container of salve. "Will you help?"

Pix nodded, then went on her way.

I took another jar of ointment and went to Dindraine, handing it to her. "Ula showed me how to make it. May I treat your back once more?"

Dindraine opened the jar, giving it a sniff, then nodded to me.

"Boudica," Brita said, handing me a shift and a gown— my pale purple dress I'd worn on the day Gaheris had asked for my hand. "I tried to choose from your older, more worn gowns. I hope you don't mind. Dindraine is most like you in size."

I nodded, taking the gown from Brita, then motioned for Dindraine to step into one of the curtained areas with me.

The priestess disrobed while I fetched warm water.

When I returned, I sat on the bed beside her and cleaned the wounds. She winced but said nothing. After the lashes were clean once more, I applied the salve and then wrapped her with bandages. Along with the bruises on her back, her arms and neck also had black-and-blue marks. When we were done, I redressed her in a shift, then pulled my gown over her head.

"It is a fine gown," Dindraine said, touching the sleeves.

"It fits you well," I said, willing the memories bubbling up from my heart to be quiet.

At that, we returned to the common room where the women sat eating and drinking.

"Sleep this night and get your rest tomorrow. I will arrange for us to travel north to the Grove of Andraste the day after. The king's house is walled and protected by guards, but I will ask two men to keep watch here."

"We thank you, Boudica," Dindraine told me. "I'd like to speak to Ansgar in the morning."

"I'll be sure to let him know. And I apologize in advance for the birds."

At that, some of the girls smiled, an expression that warmed my heart.

I looked to Pix.

"I'll stay a bit," she told me, her mouth full.

I nodded. "Good night, wise ones. And may the Great Mother watch over your sleep this night," I said, then departed.

Outside, I found Prasutagus waiting.

"Settled?" he asked.

"As well as can be. Let's set an extra guard on them tonight...for their comfort."

"I will see to it," Prasutagus said, then paused, pushing a stray hair behind my ear. Wordlessly, he pulled me close to him and kissed the top of my head. I could feel his unspoken fears in his embrace. What if... What if Rome turned on us? What if something changed and everything collapsed around us? What if we ended up like them?

After a long moment, Prasutagus let me go.

"I'll go check on our little ones," I told Prasutagus.

"I will join you soon."

And with that, we parted.

I slipped back into the king's house. Within, I smelled the scent of baking bread and cooking meat. Betha must have been working in the kitchen. I rounded the corner to go to Pix's chamber when I came across a tired-looking Nella. Her hair, which she usually pulled back into a tight bun, hung loosely around her shoulders, a mix of black, white, and the last hint of brown. She was wearing her night dress, a loose shawl pulled around her shoulders.

"Queen Boudica," she said, pausing. "I was just checking on the children."

"I am about to do the same."

"Sleeping...both of them. How Sorcha has taken to that wild woman of yours," she said with a frown, then refocused, adding, "Brita told me what happened. The priestesses..."

"Thank you for your help with the clothes."

"Is it true what the maid said? The holy site was destroyed?"

I nodded.

"May Andraste spill their guts," she said sourly. "If you wish it, I can see to them in the morning."

Nella had seemed lost since Ginerva's passing. Sorcha was not inclined toward her and struggled to be free whenever the woman tried to tend her. Artur had outgrown her. The truth was, Nella had no place in my household anymore. After the disaster with Ardra, her attitude toward me improved, but there was still animosity between us. Had I been a more spiteful woman, I would have sent her on her way. But as it was, she no longer had a role here and simply seemed to float.

"That would be greatly appreciated. We must discern what they need. They have left everything behind. I will take them north to the Grove of Andraste the day after tomo—"

"To the Northern Iceni? Not here?"

"As was their wish."

"I see. Well. Regardless. I will attend them."

"Thank you, Nella."

"Very good, Queen Boudica. Good night."

"Good night."

I went to Pix's door, opening it slowly. Within, I found Artur and Sorcha curled up together on Pix's bed. Artur had his arm wrapped around his little sister, pulling her close. The pair had become thick as thieves, Sorcha always protesting loudly when Artur left the room.

The child's curls wrapped around her ears. Her red hair had faded into a deep color that reminded me of roasted chestnuts, a red-and-brown mix. When the light caught her hair right, you could see the ruby flames in her locks. The pair looked so sweet, I hated to disturb them.

Instead, I slipped onto the bed behind Artur and pulled up the cover.

He stirred lightly in his sleep. "Mother?"

"It's Boudica," I whispered.

"Yes. I knew it was you. Welcome home."

CHAPTER 70

I woke the next morning, feeling groggy, my back aching. For a moment, I was confused about where I was—on a ship, in a Roman house, home? But then Sorcha sighed in her sleep, and I remembered. I was in Pix's bed with the children.

I rose quietly, slipping out of bed carefully so as not to wake them.

Leaving the room, I made my way back to my chamber so I could change.

When I entered, however, I was surprised to find Pix in bed beside Prasutagus.

My husband snored loudly in his sleep.

"Ye took my bed, so I took yers," Pix whispered, her eyes still shut.

"I hope that's all *ye* have taken tonight that's mine."

Pix grinned. "I'll let the Strawberry King tell ye when he wakes," she said in a whisper. "Now, leave me be. I was up half the night keeping watch over the priestesses."

"Or fooling around with Ronat. Or Prasutagus."

"Or both."

From the courtyard, I heard a loud honk. For a moment, I was confused.

"Yer new children be calling," Pix whispered with a giggle.

With a sigh, I went to my wardrobe and pulled out a clean tunic and trousers. I set a small pot of water on to heat, brushed out my hair, then undressed. As I washed up, I felt eyes on me.

I turned to find Pix grinning at me.

"Why don't ye come to bed?" she said, pushing aside the coverlets to reveal she was naked.

My response to the sight confused me. I wasn't angry she was in my bed—naked—with my husband. Instead, part of me felt pulled toward the idea. My eyes slipped over her body, her firm, pert breasts, the patch of golden hair between her legs. A longing tugged at me, but I turned away.

"My heart belongs to one person at a time."

"Ye and he are the same," Pix said with a sigh, then pulled up the covers once more.

I dressed quickly, then pulled my hair back into a braid. Grabbing my spear, I made my way out of the room, pausing to peek in on the children before going outside. Both were still asleep. I slipped down the hallway, finding the house quiet. I made my way outside.

Fog covered the king's compound. It was early morning, the sun just threatening to rise. I passed the guesthouse.

"Queen Boudica," the guards called, bowing to me.

I waved to them, then went on my way to the stables.

The mist must have lifted off the river. It drenched everything in fog so thick that I could barely see five feet in front of me. As I walked, the fog grew increasingly denser. And then, a realization washed over me. I should have made it to the stables by now.

I should have...

Stopping, I looked all around me.

Everywhere was mist, and there was a scent of bog in the air.

I had drifted between the worlds.

"Banshees be cursed." Ula had taught me better than this.

"Boudica?"

My skin rose in gooseflesh.

Who had found me here?

What had found me here?

I turned, seeing the silhouette of a man standing there. I recognized him at once by the muscular cut of his body.

"Aulus?"

He stepped toward me, the mist clearing just a little.

"Boudica... Where am I?"

"In Britannia, there are places where the veil thins. That is where you are. On the borders of the Otherworld. You must watch yourself here, Rome. This is the fey realm, and I am very certain they would be glad to keep you here for a hundred years."

"I am traveling. I thought of you as I walked into the mists, and now..."

"That is the way of things. You see me now, Rome."

"You seem angry."

"I *am* angry."

"Why?"

"Because I just plucked the holy priestesses of the Catuvellauni from a slave market in Londinium. They tell me their temple is sacked."

"I—"

"Don't *I* anything, Aulus. You lied to me."

"It is war, Boudica."

"And not just about that. Why didn't you tell me about your wife? Pomponia? Or have you forgotten you are married?"

Aulus winced. "It's not a happy marriage, Boudica. I'm glad to be away from her," he said, then stepped toward me. "I'm glad to be somewhere where women are smart, funny, fierce," he said, then reached out and gently touched my face, "and truly beautiful. In their hearts, not just in their faces."

I wanted to step back.

I truly did.

But I didn't.

"You lied to me," I repeated again, feeling tears well in the corners of my eyes. My reaction confused and angered me.

He held my gaze. "I *am* sorry."

"Aulus, I need you… I need you to protect our holy people. If you do not, they are lost. I need you to do this for me. I need you."

"And what will you do for me, Boudica?"

I swallowed hard. "What do you want?"

"You know what I want."

"I cannot give you what you're asking."

"Because you don't desire it?"

I hesitated.

"Your pause tells me everything," Aulus said, his finger drifting across my lips. "Rose of Britannia."

"I cannot..."

Aulus nodded. "Then, you cannot," he said, pulling his hand away.

The peacock sounded somewhere in the mist, its shrill, loud call piercing through the fog.

Confused, Aulus looked around.

The mist swirled around us. Within it, I saw shapes of others—the Seelie and more. Globes of blue light flickered around us.

"Boudica," Aulus said, a tremor of fear in his voice.

"Focus on something real, something tangible," I called to him. "Your horse. The stones under your feet. Your dog. Hear the birds. Focus on this world, *our* world, and you will find your way out of the mist."

"Boudica," Aulus called once more.

"Aulus, focus on the stones. On Britannia. Don't get lost in the mist," I called to him, but he was gone. My heart pounded in my chest.

He would be all right.

He would find his way out.

"Why do you care, Princess Boudica of the Northern Iceni," a voice asked from behind me.

"It's *Queen* Boudica of *Greater* Iceni," I said, turning to find myself face to face with the Seelie prince I had met near the Grove of Andraste. "Banshees be cursed," I whispered, realizing that I had told him my true name once more.

"*Queen* Boudica of the *Greater* Iceni," he said with a slick smile.

By the gods, how handsome he was.

"I ask you again, why do you care if we take the Roman? We would have such fun with him..."

"I... I don't know why."

The Seelie lowered his chin and raised his eyebrows. "You *do* know."

I swallowed hard. "The old chains...those that bind us from life to life. I *know* him."

"So you do. But what you see in *this* life is not all there is to him."

"What else is there?"

The Seelie prince stepped toward me. "Pain," he whispered in my ear.

Trembling, I closed my eyes.

"Beware, Queen Boudica of the Greater Iceni. It is not only *love* that follows you from life to life..."

The peacock squawked once more.

I opened my eyes.

I was standing on the green not far from the stables.

The sun had risen, the golden rays penetrating the mist that had swallowed the compound.

I squeezed my hand around my spear as I inhaled and exhaled slowly and deeply.

Great Lady. Andraste. Watch over me.

CHAPTER 71

Trying to calm my nerves and focus my attention on anything other than the encounter in the mists, I went to tend to my new birds.

Morfran, who apparently was as curious as I was, alighted on the fencepost nearby, watching as I knelt to fiddle with the cage.

He squawked at me.

"Convince them not to fly off," I told Morfran. "I will care for them here. In the woods, they will become some hunter's dinner and a wife's new cap."

Setting out bowls of food and water, I lifted the cage gate and stepped back to watch as the shy creatures slowly crept out. They eyed me carefully as they made their way to the feed. The male's long tail feathers dusted the ground as he walked. As the sun burned off the mist, it shimmered on the bird's brilliant plumage.

The female followed behind the male, both of them making their way to the feed.

They ate cautiously, observing me carefully.

When they were done, they moved out into the green space. The male shook his body then started preening.

Morfran cawed loudly at them, startling the birds.

To my shock, the male lifted his tail feathers, the massive plume of feathers fanning out in an impressive display.

"Like some fey thing," Ansgar called to me as he approached.

Realizing there was nothing to be alarmed about, the male calmed and lowered his plumes. The pair continued grooming themselves.

"What are they?" Ansgar asked, joining me. He folded his arms together, his hands within his robes, the hems of his long sleeves touching.

"They are called peacocks. They were so beautiful, I could not bear to leave them there in such conditions," I said, then sighed. "They are not the only ones."

Ansgar nodded slowly. "So it is true, what Galvyn has told me."

"Dindraine asked to speak to you this morning."

Ansgar nodded. "Shall we see if she is awake?"

I nodded, then the two of us made our way to the guesthouse.

"I am disturbed at this news. The governor expressly told you that our holy people would not to be disturbed."

"Yes. He promised me. It was a promise he could not or did not keep." *It is war, Boudica.*

"I am concerned about my brethren on Mona."

"As am I. Their safety is important to me, but also, my

sister is there. Someone should travel to Mona. And there is Avallach to consider as well.

"The priestesses of Avallach are very capable of keeping themselves hidden. Mona, however... Yes, you are right. Someone should go. Not an easy prospect now that the west is on fire."

"If one were to travel north through Coritani lands then sail from a Brigantes' harbor..."

Ansgar nodded. "Yes, that would work. I will go, Boudica, but I will not be able to return until spring."

"I wouldn't risk you if I didn't think it necessary. Thank you, Ansgar."

"Let me speak to Dindraine. Perhaps some of the priestesses would like to travel with me."

"Make whatever arrangements you need. We will see to it," I told the druid as we reached the door.

"Thank you, Boudica," he said, then knocked on the door. "It is Ansgar," he called.

A moment later, Dindraine opened the door. "Ansgar."

"Alas, dear sister..."

Dindraine stepped aside to let him in.

She paused, waiting for me.

"I need to see to my child, but I will return soon," I told her. "Do you need anything?"

Dindraine shook her head. "Your people have seen to our every comfort. Thank you, Boudica."

I bowed to her, then turned and made my way back to the roundhouse, forcing the thousand swelling emotions within me to be silent as they warred against one another: worry about Ansgar traveling so far, fear for the priestesses, the odd ache over seeing Dindraine in *that* gown, and then, Aulus's words.

You know what I want.

I did.

And I was angry at myself and ashamed to admit that it took everything within me to deny wanting it too.

BACK INSIDE, I HEARD VOICES AND HAPPY LAUGHTER COMING from the dining hall. Within, I found Prasutagus, Nella, Artur, Vian, and Galvyn at the table. Vian was working hard on something, drawing with a coal pen, several pieces of Roman parchment on the table in front of her. Brita entered, holding Sorcha.

"Look who just woke up," Brita told me. "Look, Sorcha. Here is your mother!"

When Sorcha saw me, she squealed with happiness and then reached out for me, moving so quickly that Brita had to grab her to keep her from tumbling.

Setting my spear aside, I went to her.

"Ah, here is my sweet girl," I said, taking her from the maid. I kissed the baby on her cheeks and then went to Artur, bending to kiss him on the head. "And my sweet boy. Good morning."

"Good morning, Boudica," Artur replied.

I turned back to Sorcha, tweaking her chin. "Look at you. I think you got bigger since I left."

Sorcha giggled, then pressed her face into my neck.

I gently stroked her head, kissing her, then went to Prasutagus, settling in on the bench beside him.

"I heard your birds. That's what woke me," he told me.

"Oh, *that's* what woke you?" I asked, raising an eyebrow at him.

Prasutagus chuckled, then gave me a knowing glance but said nothing more in front of the others.

Betha appeared from the back. "Brita? Can you give Ronat and me a hand?" she asked the maid, then turned to Prasutagus and me. "I will take food over to the priestesses now."

"Very good. They should take their rest this morning, but let us have evening meal here together and honor them as they deserve," Prasutagus said.

"Yes, King Prasutagus," Betha said.

"I will help," Nella said, rising. "And, as Queen Boudica requested, I will prepare a list of what they need, then go to the market to fetch it."

"Thank you, Nella," Prasutagus told her. "Let Galvyn know what coin is needed."

Nella nodded, then departed.

"Vian?" I called.

"Hmmm?" she replied without looking up.

"Did you remember to eat?"

"Mm-hmm," she said, reaching out for a hunk of bread with one hand while she continued drawing with the other.

I grinned, then turned to Sorcha. "See how Vian works?

Will you be busy like her, wild like Pix, or one with the gods, like Ansgar?"

Prasutagus grinned. "Perhaps, she should be a little of all," he said, tickling her chin. "After all, she will one day be the queen of the Greater Iceni."

"She will not need to be all of them," Artur chimed in. "I will be there to help her. Whatever she doesn't have time to be, I will be for her."

Prasutagus grinned at her. "You are a good brother, Artur."

Artur smiled.

"Speaking of brothers," Prasutagus said, turning to me. *Caturix.* "I will speak to Bran when I get to Oak Throne, see what he knows, but maybe I should ride to Stonea afterward."

"I should come north with you," Prasutagus said.

"My king, I would not dissuade you, but there is much here that needs your attention," Galvyn said.

Prasutagus frowned. "I was afraid that was the case."

"There is still time before the first snow flies," Galvyn said.

"It's not the snow I'm worried about," Prasutagus said darkly.

I nodded.

Vian paused. "Are you talking about the Coritani?"

Both Prasutagus and I looked at her.

"What do you mean, Vian?" I asked.

"In Londinium… I heard some soldiers gossiping about King Volisios. They said that if things don't improve with the Coritani, the legions may have to march north. Is that what you mean?"

"Caratacus is trying to bend them to his side. And with them, King Caturix."

"Sometimes I think you are the only rulers in this land with any sense," Vian told Prasutagus and me, then snapped up her papers. She turned to Galvyn. "I need a shovel."

Galvyn raised an eyebrow at her. "A shovel, Lady Vian?"

She nodded.

Chuckling good-naturedly, Galvyn rose. "Sense *and ingenuity*—something this house has in plenty."

CHAPTER 72

I stayed busy throughout the day, tending to Sorcha and showing her and Artur my new birds. I didn't know if they felt safe in their new home or just liked having feed nearby, but the birds did not try to flee. As it was, when they did fly, they could not lift off the ground very far. Noisy as they were, Sorcha paid them no mind. Instead, she spent most of her time trying to catch the feral kittens who lived in the stables.

To her luck, the kittens thought her dawdling steps as fun as she found them, so they played together.

Pix appeared mid-morning, yawning, a loaf of bread tucked under her arm.

"Ah, here ye are," she told Artur. "Ready?"

Artur nodded.

"Go get yer practice bow," she told him.

Artur turned to me. "Boudica…"

"Go ahead."

At that, he ran off to fetch the weapons.

"Finally up?" I asked Pix, who joined me.

She tore off a hunk of bread and handed it to me. "That bed be far softer than mine."

I rolled my eyes.

"And the Strawberry King be warm to snuggle up against."

"You would have been warmer if you'd been dressed."

"Ye didn't mind a gander. Though yer king was surprised when he gave me round arse a squeeze and realized it wasn't yers."

At that, we both chuckled.

"And then?" I asked.

"Jealous?"

"Of course."

"I'll leave that for you to find out," she said, then looked to Sorcha, who threw straw for the kittens to chase. "Firebrand, what ye be doing?"

Sorcha turned to her, pointing to the kittens. "Dat, dat, dat."

"I see them," Pix called back. "Wee fluffy things."

Sorcha giggled, then continued her play.

Artur returned a moment later, and he and Pix went off for target practice.

It was late in the afternoon when Vian appeared, shovel in hand, mud on the hem of her dress and smeared across her cheek, a determined expression on her face. "Do you know where Prasutagus is?" she asked.

I had been sitting outside with some of the priestesses —those not still sleeping—keeping the women amused with Sorcha's antics.

"He's within," I said, pointing back to the roundhouse.

She nodded then headed inside, shovel still in her hand.

Not long after that, Prasutagus reappeared, and he and Vian—still with her shovel—disappeared into the city. We did not see either of them again until that night when we had gathered for the evening meal. They both returned muddy, needing to redress and wash before dinner.

The priestesses gathered in our dining hall. Betha and Ronat had fixed an excellent meal, bringing platters of meat, cheese, two roasted geese, and apple tarts, and poured ale for the women. While their eyes were still haunted, the color had come back into some of the priestesses' cheeks.

Once Vian and Prasutagus joined us, Ansgar gestured for everyone to come to the table.

"Let us take hands," he said, motioning to everyone in the room, servants, guards, and all. "Tonight, we dine with our holy sisters. May the Great Mother watch over them in this trying time and in the coming days. May the food upon this table nourish them. And may the Dark Lady Andraste protect them. So mote it be."

"So mote it be," we answered.

We gathered around the table then—all of us—to share the meal with the priestesses.

"You have to tell us what you have been doing all day, Vian," I said.

Vian grinned. "I made an observation in Londinium about the water drainage from the city. I've been testing my ideas."

Prasutagus nodded. "Vian's ideas are proving very useful."

"I have other notes. Other ideas. I am still formulating," Vian said.

"Your birds did not fly away, Queen Boudica," Cait, one of the priestesses, said.

"Either Artur's raven convinced them to stay, or they like the feed."

"Or both," Cait replied.

"King Prasutagus," Dindraine said, her resolute voice silencing the table. "What news of King Caratacus? Where is the king of the Catuvellauni?"

Prasutagus set down his cup. He paused, then said, "It is whispered he is with the Dobunni, wise one."

"And what is he doing there?"

"We believe he is trying to raise support—from the Dobunni, the Cornovii, the Silures, even the Coritani—whoever he can get to listen."

"And has he been effective?"

"To some extent."

"And the southeastern tribes?"

"Caratacus made many enemies in his goal to expand his father's empire. With King Verica's line returned and the Romans coming on behalf of Aedd Mawr, no one wanted to get involved. You should know, Priestess, that King Verica is dead. His son has taken the Atrebates throne and married to the Regnenses."

Dindraine lifted her cup. "Caratacus and Togodumnus had all of their father's ambition and none of his wit," she said, then sipped. "But they did not expect Rome."

"None of us did," Ansgar said.

"We all made a terrible mistake, turning a blind eye to the south where Rome grew like an unweeded garden," she said, then turned to my husband and me. Her gaze shifted to Sorcha, who sat on my lap chewing on a hunk of bread. "You have chosen a path that has made you safe for now. It is the best path you could have chosen, King Prasutagus," she said.

"Thank you, wise one."

She nodded slowly, as if lost to her thoughts. "But if you value what you love," she said, reaching out to stroke Sorcha's cheek, "do not turn your back on them. After all, Rome was founded by a boy who was raised by a wolf."

"May the Morrigu protect us," I said.

"And fight alongside us when she cannot," Dindraine replied.

The priestess's words put a temporary damper on the evening, but Pix did her best by lightening the mood, sharing ridiculous but amusing tales, such as the tale of a maiden who was wooed by the charms of a goat. In the end, she had everyone laughing. By the time the priestesses were ready to retire for the evening, even Dindraine had smiled once more. I was glad about it.

"We will ride early in the morning," I told Dindraine as Pix made ready to escort the priestesses back to the guesthouse. "I will have everything prepared."

"Thank you, Queen Boudica," she told me, then departed with the others.

I turned to Prasutagus, who was holding a sleeping Sorcha against his chest. "She weighs as much as a sack of grain," he said, "and my arms are tired from all the digging. Let me go set her down."

"I'll come with you," I told him, and we went back to our bedchamber.

There, Prasutagus lay Sorcha down in the middle of our bed.

The child never stirred.

"Not the first time today you've had a spare woman in your bed."

"This is the first time I've invited one, though," Prasutagus said, then shook his head. "If anything, Pix is persistent."

"And did she win you over this time?"

Prasutagus huffed a laugh, then pulled me close to him. "No."

"Got a squeeze though, or so I hear."

Prasutagus chuckled. "In my defense, I thought it was you. But, yes."

At that, we both laughed.

When Sorcha stirred in her sleep, we silenced our giggles.

"My arms are aching, but I have some work to do. You, however, should rest. You will ride early tomorrow."

I nodded.

Prasutagus touched my chin gently. "I love you, Boudica. I will do whatever it takes to keep my family safe," he said, then kissed me gently.

"I love you too."

CHAPTER 73

The ride to the Grove of Andraste came as a welcome relief. It had been too long since I had been home, and with each mile north I put between Venta and me, I began to feel more at ease. Even Druda's steps had a perkiness that they didn't always contain.

Pix and I rode at the front of our party, taking turns holding Sorcha before us.

Pix sang old songs, making Sorcha clap her hands.

We bypassed Oak Throne, going directly to the grove.

We arrived at dusk.

The pack of hounds who watched over the place raised the alarm as the horses drew near. I was not surprised to find Tatha, fully armed, right behind them.

"Boudica," Tatha said in confusion. "What are you..." she said, then her gaze drifted behind me where she spotted Dindraine. She turned to Grainne, who was hurrying across the square to meet me, a smile on her face. "Fetch Dôn," she told the girl.

Grainne's smile faded as she took in the sight of the priestesses. She turned and hurried toward Dôn's cottage.

I dismounted and then greeted the dogs.

"I am glad to see you all too," I told them, giving them pats, then went to Tatha.

"Well met, Priestess," I said, giving her arm a squeeze.

"Boudica," she said. "I am glad to see you." Her gaze went behind me. "I think you come with bad news."

"For the Catuvellauni, yes."

Understanding, Tatha nodded.

"Come here, you," I called, turning to Pix and Sorcha. I reached out for the child, taking her from Pix. "Let's help Dindraine and the others from the wagon," I told Sorcha, then turned to Tatha. "Tatha, this is Sorcha. Sorcha, this is the priestess Tatha.

"Tah-ha," Sorcha said.

Tatha smiled and took her hand. "Hello, little princess."

Sorcha grinned at her.

Tatha, Pix, and I went to the back of the wagon and helped the women out.

"Sisters," Tatha said. "You are welcome at the Grove of Andraste."

"I sent along supplies as well," I told Tatha. "There is grain and other goods here. I will go to Oak Throne from here. I will be sure Bran sends supplies along, but do not hesitate to ask if you need anything."

Tatha nodded, then stepped forward to help Dindraine.

"Honorable Mother," she said, reaching out for Dindraine's hands. "Welcome."

"Thank you, Priestess."

Pix and I joined the other priestesses as we passed through the stone monoliths guarding the grove and into the little grouping of huts there. Dôn appeared from within her small house. Walking with a staff, she made her way to us.

Dindraine went to her, the priestess's eyes growing wet with tears.

When she reached Dôn, she fell to her knees and took Dôn's free hand.

"Our shrine has fallen to Rome," she said, pressing Dôn's hand against her forehead. "Help us, Sister." And then, Dindraine wept loudly. It was as if she had been keeping everything bottled up within her. In the safety of Dôn's presence, it came out all at once.

"Oh, Sister," Dôn said, wrapping her arms around the woman. Dôn pressed her cheek against the woman's head and whispered to her in a low tone.

Dindraine nodded.

Sorcha, noticing Dindraine's upset, grew teary-eyed. Giant tears began to fall down her cheeks.

"It's all right," I whispered to her. "You are good to see their pain. It will be all right. They are safe now," I told the little girl.

Dindraine rose and wiped the tears from her cheeks.

Dôn turned to the others. "Come. All of you. You are welcome here in the Grove of Andraste. The Dark Lady has led you home to us."

Behind Dôn, the other priestesses of the grove appeared.

"I will get the supplies unloaded," Pix said.

"Let me assist you," Tatha said, the pair of them going back to the wagon.

I stood for a moment, unsure what to do.

"Come, Boudica. You and the princess," Dôn called to me.

The women gathered around the fire, taking seats on the benches. Grainne and the other women of the Grove worked quickly to bring more benches for everyone to sit on. Sorcha on my lap, I settled in on a tree stump.

The women of the grove sat and listened as Dindraine recanted what had befallen them. The tale of what had happened to Imogen and the others, including Dindraine, brought tears to Dôn's eyes. The old woman listened as Dindraine spoke, and I swore I saw her spirit grow dimmer with each moment. The tale of fire, abuse, and pain they had endured made me feel ill.

All for Caratacus's ambition...

All for a king who put himself before his people...

When Dindraine stopped speaking, everyone was silent.

After a long time, Dôn spoke, "It is the will of the gods that Boudica came when she did. Andraste weaves. In the fires, I have seen your face many times these last weeks, but did not know why. We will expand our numbers here. We will become a safe haven for our holy people. Boudica, you will tell Bran to send men. We must have three more houses built before winter."

"Yes. Of course."

Dôn looked at me expectantly. "Well, go and get it done."

I chuckled lightly, then rose. "Of course, *Ancient* Dôn."

At that, Dôn smirked at me, then rose. "I will return in a moment," she told the priestesses, then came to accompany me back to the horses.

"Boudica," Dindraine said, rising. She cleared her throat, but I heard a waver in her voice when she spoke again. "May the goddess watch over you. We owe our lives to you. Thank you."

"May she keep you all safe," I told them, then turned to walk with Dôn.

"Well, little princess," Dôn said, tickling Sorcha's chin. "You have finally come to the Grove. I wish you had brought her under better circumstances so I could sit and pat her soft hair all day."

"I am sorry to meet you again under such conditions."

"It was good of you to bring them here. Dindraine and I were close friends long ago on Mona. We will do as the goddess bids and make things work here—with the help of the house of Aesunos."

"I will see it to it."

"Boudica," Dôn said, then paused. "What of Rome? Are we in danger here? Tell me the truth."

"As long as the Northern Iceni stay true to their word to Rome and do not interfere, you are safe. But there is a rumor that the Coritani are sympathetic to Caratacus. They are trying to convince Caturix to join their side. I will ride to Stonea hereafter. You must use any influence you have to keep Caturix out of it. He is too easily swayed by others. That is good and bad. He must be swayed *by us* if we are to keep the people safe."

"Ah, how the Dark Lady weaves. You will find Caturix at Oak Throne."

"He's there?"

Dôn nodded. "Tell him to come to me before he returns to Stonea. We will let Andraste put the fear of fire into him," she said, her gaze going back toward the circle of trees at the top of the hill. Dôn reached out and tickled Sorcha's chin. "I would have thought you would have named her Damara."

"There is already one child named for my mother," I said in a low tone.

Dôn considered for a moment. "Mara? The child of Kennocha?"

"Caturix's daughter."

"That explains much. Such is as the goddess wills," Dôn said, her gaze going to Pix. "That ancient thing still fluttering around you?"

"She is."

"Wild, lost thing," Dôn said, then shook her head. "I trust I will see you again in better days, Boudica."

"That is my hope as well."

"Then let it be so. Farewell for now," she said, then took Sorcha's hand and kissed it. "Farewell, little princess."

Sorcha grinned at her.

With that, I went to Druda. One of the men came to

hold Sorcha so I could mount, then handed the girl up to me.

With everyone settled, we turned the wagon and prepared to ride out once more.

"Be well, daughter of Damara," Dôn called to me.

"Be well, Wise Mother," I called in reply.

Pix turned, lifting her hands to her forehead in respect.

And with that, we rode off. I was not a priestess, but with every fiber in me, I wanted to stay and be of help. Even though I wasn't a priestess, I *was* a queen. My brother, king of this land, was waiting at Oak Throne. It was up to me to ensure that he did what was right.

May the Dark Lady be with me.

CHAPTER 74

I t was after dark when we arrived at the gates of Oak
Throne. Like Venta, the city was closed. Torches illuminated the guard posts. There were far more
guards on the walls than I ever remembered.

"Hold there," a voice called from the wall. "Who
comes?"

"Yer princess, now Prasutagus's queen," Pix answered
for me.

"Boudica? Is that you?"

"It is, my friends," I called.

"Open the gates!"

When we rode through the gates, I saw a runner rush
off in the distance toward the roundhouse. Druda, excited
to be home, snorted and pranced.

"Welcome home, Queen Boudica," a voice called from
the wall.

We rode on, passing the oak tree, to the roundhouse. As
we went, I looked down the lane for any sign of Ula, but

the old woman did not appear. I did notice the smoke coming from the roof of her home. That little sign of life was enough to reassure me.

When we reached the roundhouse, Bran and Bec appeared.

"Boudica," Bran called, rushing to take Druda's reins. "Welcome, Sister. And hello, Druda," he said, giving the horse's neck a pat.

"Here, let me help," Bec said, reaching for Sorcha. "Come to me, little princess."

Sorcha, whom I'd secured around me, half woke as Bec lowered her. She whimpered lightly.

"It's all right, sweet girl. I've got you," Bec told her.

Balfor appeared behind Bran and Bec. "Boudica. Welcome home."

"Thank you, Balfor."

Balfor scanned my party. "I will see to your men. Your wagon is empty, Boudica."

"Freshly so. But I carry a tale no wagon can bear."

Balfor sighed heavily. "I am hearing too many such tales these days. Gentlemen, welcome to Oak Throne. Come with me," he said, then led my men away.

Young Tadhg appeared from the stables. "Queen Boudica... I can see to Druda and the others."

"Tadhg, you are a foot taller."

The boy laughed, then gestured to Sorcha. "You too, Queen Boudica."

I chuckled.

With that, the boy led the horses to the barn.

"Pix," Bran said. "I am glad to see you again."

"And ye, Prince," Pix said, then turned her gaze to Bec. "Priestess."

Bec smiled at her.

A moment later, Caturix appeared in the doorway. His body was framed by the light within, making a silhouette. How familiar the scene was...the same, but so very different all at once.

"Boudica," he said, unable to hide the surprise in his voice.

"Hello, Brother."

"It was a long ride, and the night air is cool. Let's get Sorcha inside," Bec said, then turned and went back into the house, Caturix stepping out of her way. Pix and Bran followed along behind her.

I met my brother at the door.

"Boudica... is all well?"

"Decidedly not. With you?"

"Decidedly not." My brother sighed heavily. "Come, Sister. Let's see what troubles the world has thrown our way."

And with that, we made our way inside.

Within, I found Bec waiting with a sleeping Sorcha on her shoulder. The child's lips had formed into a perfect circle, jutting out sweetly.

"Children first, tribes after," Bec told Bran and Caturix, then waved for me to follow her. "Bellicus is asleep. Riona just got him down. Is it all right if we put her down in your old bed? You and Pix can sleep there, of course."

"Yes. That will work."

I went ahead of Bec, opening the door to my chamber.

The smell of the place immediately sucked me back in time and made me ache for my sister.

"Here," I told Bec, gesturing to my bed.

Bec gently set Sorcha down. She squirmed a little, then fell back to sleep. I covered her, ensuring she was safe in the low bed, then turned to Bec.

Bec stared down at her. "Her hair is darker than yours, more like Bran's and Brenna's.

"She looks like our mother."

"She is a beauty."

"Can I see Bellicus?"

Bec nodded then we made our way to my father's old room. There, on a small cot at the foot of the bed, slept a sweet boy with shaggy brown hair. He was asleep sprawled out, his mouth open wide. He still had a smear of dirt on his face.

"He wouldn't let Riona clean him up, so she gave up and put him to bed like this, clothes, shoes, dirt and all. Ula swears he is a changeling."

I grinned. "I'm glad to see him and you, Priestess."

"And I, you, Princess."

At that, Bec pulled me into an embrace. "Boudica, I'm so glad you are here. Bran needs you. You must step between him and Caturix. Thank the Mother you have come."

I squeezed her tight, then pulled back. "What's happening?"

"King Volisios has Caturix's head twisted. You must make him hear reason."

"As I feared."

"Caturix is insisting Bran does what Caturix says in the matter. Bran will not agree. There was a terrible argument right before you arrived."

I took Bec's hand. "Let's not delay."

Bec nodded, then studied me. "You have news. I can see it in your eyes."

"Yes, but not the good kind."

"I will get you some ale..." she said, then led me back to the dining hall.

There, Pix was seated at the bench, pouring herself a mug of ale and chewing on a twist of dough.

"Boudica. Sit. Rest," Bran said, gesturing.

I took my seat at the table with the others. It was strange to be there with my brothers, all of us taking up the spots at the table we had occupied as children. I could feel the tension in the air between them.

Pix handed me a mug of ale. "Ye'll be needing this, I think," she told me with a wink.

I smiled at my brothers. "I feel Brenna's absence," I said, scanning the table where my sister should have been.

"Let's toast her," Bec suggested, "so she feels remembered in our thoughts. To Brenna," she said, hoisting her cup.

"To Brenna," we all answered.

Bran gave Caturix a sidelong glance. In it, I felt the tension that remained between them. I was glad Bec had warned me of the source of it.

There was a long silence.

After a moment, Pix laughed, then said, "All of ye are in a bind, no one wanting to share yer bad news first. I cannot think of a more somber place to be than with all of ye," she said then rose. Grabbing another two knots of bread and refilling her cup, Pix moved to leave.

"Where are you going?" I asked.

"To find that good-looking boy. Ye can hash out the troubles of the lands. But I warn ye, no matter which way ye turn, left or right, yer head is already in the noose. Now ye just need to figure out how to break the rope before it's too late."

CHAPTER 75

"Boudica," Bran began. "I'm glad to see you, but why have you come?"

I recanted the tale of our trip to Londinium and what we had seen and learned there—from the construction to the death of King Verica to the rumors from the west and on to the discovery of the priestesses and what had befallen them.

As I told them about the priestesses, tears drifted down Bec's cheeks.

"They didn't want to stay at Arminghall," I said. "Dôn and Dindraine have known one another for many years, and Dindraine felt safer here at the grove. Dôn asks you send men to construct three new houses before winter. We brought food supplies from Venta, but they will need more," I told Bran.

Bran looked stunned. "Of course. I will see to it first thing tomorrow. How horrible. Caratacus just left his sister there? And now…" I could see from the look on Bran's face that he felt guilty. If he had wed Princess Imogen, she wouldn't be a Roman slave now. Of course, that fate was not meant to be. But in a way, Bran's near-miss made him feel a kinship for the girl and evoked his deep sympathy.

"Caratacus thought she would be safe with the priestesses," Caturix said darkly. "Rome promised not to harm our holy people.

It is war, Boudica.

"Yes. A fact about which I will discuss with the governor when I see him next," I said waspishly.

"How well did that discussion go after the mess at Maiden Stones?" Caturix asked sourly.

"Governor Plautius called Maiden Stones a mistake. His men did not inform him it was a holy site. The priestesses have not been bothered again. I am sorry for Dindraine, I truly am, but it is Caratacus who brought that terror upon them."

"And continues to bring it wherever he goes," Bran said, giving Caturix a sharp look.

Caturix glared at him.

"What is it?" I asked my brothers, looking from one to the other.

"Tell her," Bran told Caturix with annoyance.

I turned my attention to Caturix, raising an eyebrow at him.

"Caratacus came to Stonea," Caturix said.

I felt my heart thumping in my chest. I willed my hands not to shake with rage.

"He has been speaking to the Coritani. Volisios and the others will join him, but they are rallying secretly. Come spring, they will advance upon the Romans."

I swallowed hard, then said, "And they ask you to join them?"

"Yes."

"And are squeezing you hard because of Melusine?"

My brother nodded slowly. "Caratacus warns that it is the last chance we have to stand against Rome. If we do not act now, we will all perish in time."

"Let me remind you, Brother, that Caratacus all but put a knife to Father's throat," Bran said angrily. "If I were king—"

"You are *not* king," Caturix told him, slapping his hand on the table, making all of our drinks shake.

"Who else? Who else will stand against Rome? The Brigantes?" I asked.

Caturix shook his head. "Cartimandua will not hear from Caratacus. She won't even receive his messengers. She has them executed."

"Parisii?"

"No."

"Ordovices?"

"No, but he has support. The Dobunni, Cornovii, Silures…"

"Rome is already penetrating into the lands of the Dobunni and Cornovii. And they are failing in their resistance."

"Caratacus hopes with the help of the Coritani... They

are a large tribe, Boudica. Together, if they resist, they *can* beat back the Romans."

I stared into my cup. I had barely touched the ale. It tasted off tonight. *Everything* felt off tonight. My body ached, my head hurt, and I was tired...

I looked at my brother. "Caturix, there is no one alive on this island who wants the Romans here—save, perhaps, the line of Verica. *I* do not want the Romans here. They have used their war with Caratacus as an excuse to grab land. I am not blind to it. But here is one thing I do know... Caratacus is no military leader. He will lead his people and those who follow him to their deaths. He will doom those who stand with him to the same fate he doomed his sister. We have two choices. Both of them are bad ones. But one leads the Iceni to status and wealth in the larger world, and the other puts the Iceni in chains. If you follow Caratacus, you doom every person in Stonea, Holk Fort, Oak Throne, Frog's Hollow, and all the rest to the same fate as Imogen. Will you see your wife raped, flogged, sold off as a slave?"

"Why are you so certain we will lose?" Caturix asked, banging his fist on the table. "You and Prasutagus are the same, preaching peace when war is already here."

"War is here for Caratacus and those who stand beside him. It is not here for us. The Atrebates grow. The Brigantes grow. The Iceni grow. In choosing to support Verica, we chose Rome. And we chose Rome because Caratacus and Togodumnus came for us—*they came for our father*. Or have you forgotten that, Brother? Our father is dead because Saenunos was whipped into action by the Catuvellauni. And you dare to pound your fist at us," I said, feeling my anger boiling over. I rose. "Our father died like a dog on the side of the road because the Catuvellauni bent our uncle to their will. And with him, Belenus, our grandfather. And now, you would throw in your lot with Caratacus. The fact that you even received him disgusts me."

"Boudica," Caturix said, lifting his hands. "Boudica, please."

My gaze went to Bran, who pleaded with me with his eyes not to go.

I sat once more with an exhausted huff. "I am heartsick at what has happened to Dindraine and the others. It makes me ill to my core—and I *will* discuss it with the governor, face-to-face, as we sit here now. I *will* extract a promise from him that no more of our holy people will be harmed, no matter their tribe."

"Can you, Boudica? Do you have that influence over him?" Bec asked.

"I do," I said, and I meant it. I knew what Aulus wanted from me. I would find a way.

Bran turned to Caturix. "I cannot support a move to help Caratacus. I have Bellicus to think of. I cannot do anything that puts him in harm's way. Rome has left us be, as they promised. Oak Throne grows as a result. Our trade here has increased tenfold," Bran said, then turned to me. "You will see tomorrow. New granaries. New ships. Why would we risk all of that because Caratacus asks us to? This is his war, not ours."

"What if Caratacus and the others succeed? Then what? They will turn on us," Caturix said.

"What chances do they really have, Brother?" Bran asked.

Caturix frowned.

I swallowed hard, then said, "I do not want Rome here. No one does. But our duty is to our people. Our duty is to keep our people safe. Caratacus has failed. His sister is sold. His priestesses were abused. The Cantiaci threw their warriors before Rome, and they died. You must go back to Volisios and help him see. If he moves with Caratacus, he condemns his people to death and slavery. Keep all those you love from Stonea to Oak Throne safe and *stay out of this*."

Caturix sat for a long time, staring silently into the space before him, then got up. "I need air," he said. "If you will excuse me. I... I need air," he said, then made his way out of the dining room.

"Caturix," I called. "Dôn asked to see you."

My brother nodded in acknowledgment and then left.

We sat in silence, waiting until the door opened and closed, then Bran exhaled deeply.

"Thank the gods. Thank all the gods you came, Boudica. No matter what we said, we could not convince him. Volisios is like a poison in his ear, Caratacus doubly so."

I clenched my jaw hard. "Perhaps it is time the Iceni does more to help Rome put an end to this."

"What do you mean?" Bran asked.

"We deliver Caratacus to Rome."

Bran nodded.

Bec shifted in her seat, then said, "Boudica, if Rome's

greed ever gets the better of them and they turn on the Iceni, what will we do then?"

"Pray to Andraste and the Morrigu for strength. Because if that happens, it will be as Pix says, and we will all hang."

CHAPTER 76

Caturix did not return that night. Exhausted from the long ride and the abundance of bad news, I went to bed and curled up beside my little one, pulling her close to me and trying to forget everything.

As I slowly drifted to sleep, my thoughts turned to Aulus. I needed to find a way to extract a promise that would stick. But at what price? I would never betray Prasutagus. How could I convince a man to give to me when I could never give him what he wanted in return?

I kissed the back of Sorcha's head.

For her sake and for everyone else's, I would find a way.

I MUST HAVE SLEPT DEEPLY BECAUSE NOT EVEN PIX'S EXCESSIVE snoring woke me that night. Instead, I woke to find a toddler breathing loudly into my face. I kept my eyes closed, praying that Sorcha would go back to sleep. But then, I felt sticky fingers creeping across my cheek. Beside me, Sorcha turned in her sleep.

Confused, I opened my eyes to find a little boy with jam-covered fingers playing with a curl on my forehead.

"Good morning, Bellicus," I whispered.

The child grinned at me, revealing four tiny white teeth.

Across from us, Pix snored loudly, making Bellicus and me both jump.

I giggled. "She is a dragon. Be careful."

"Bellicus," Riona scolded the child in a whisper. "What are you doing in here, child? I'm sorry, Boudica. I swear, once he found those little legs of his, he gets everywhere."

"It's no matter," I said with a grin, kissing the boy's grubby hand.

I sat up slowly, Sorcha waking along with me.

She whined, fussing at being woken.

"Look, Sorcha," I said, shifting so she could see. "Look who has come."

"Oh! Oh!" Bellicus called, spying Sorcha for the first time.

Sorcha grinned, then laughed.

"By the Maiden, she's a twin of your mother," Riona said. "This is Sorcha?"

"It is."

"Hello, Princess," Riona said, lifting her. "Oh dear, we

have a wet one. Well, don't you worry, Princess. I am here now. Old Riona will take care of you as I took care of your mother. Where are her things, Boudica?" Riona asked, looking around. When she spotted my bag on the floor, she huffed loudly. "Like a soldier, slinging your garments about. You never change. Take Bellicus back to his mother. She's in the dining hall. I'll get this princess dressed for the day."

"What about me?"

"Suppose I can shake out a tunic for you too," Riona said, then looked at Pix. "She sleeps like she's in a mound and roars like an ox. How did you sleep with her in here?"

I laughed, then slipped out of bed and took Bellicus's hand. "Let's find your mother."

Grinning, the boy dawdled, leading me out of the room.

I grinned at his uneven steps, his belly and head leading him more than his feet. We made our way back to the main chamber, where I found Bec and Cidna.

"Boudica," Cidna called. "They told me you had come. Oh, and you found my Belli. Come here, boy," Cidna said, opening her arms wide for him.

Leaving me, Bellicus went to her.

"Cidna is his favorite," Bec told me. "She plies him with sweets."

"Do not. I am his favorite come naturally."

"As you say."

"Don't give me sass, Priestess."

Bec chuckled. "Bran and Caturix have gone to get

supplies ready for the grove. Can I get you anything, Boudica?"

I shook my head. "I will clean up and visit my own cantankerous Northern Iceni woman," I said, lifting my voice so Cidna could hear me.

"I heard that, Boudica. You'd best put on your best boots."

"Why?"

"Because Ula needs her arse kicked from one side of Oak Throne to the other for her sheer stubbornness. Couldn't get her to take a sack of grain all year. She'd rather eat roots and acorns."

"Banshees be cursed," I grumbled. "Cidna, prepare me a basket. Give me enough to keep her for a few months."

"I'll do you better. But get your ears ready. She will box them."

"What else is new?"

Both Cidna and Bec chuckled, and Cidna disappeared to the back, taking Bellicus with her.

"How are you otherwise, my friend? How is your life in Venta?" Bec asked me. "Are you happy with Prasutagus?"

I nodded. "It is a good life. It took some adjusting for his household. Esu left a son behind. My arrival was hard for him. The tensions in our lands aside, I *am* happy."

"To be honest, I worried you wed too quickly after Gaheris. I'm glad to hear my worries were for nothing."

"Gaheris lives in my blood, but Prasutagus has his place alongside Gaheris's memory."

Bec nodded.

"And you, Priestess? Abused by your cooks and tending a child as wild as his father…"

Bec smiled a genuine and honest smile. "I cannot imagine a happier life."

"I'm glad."

"I only hope Caturix does nothing to upset it."

"I will speak to him again."

Bec nodded.

"Let me make myself presentable," I said, motioning to the back.

"I'll be here. Bellicus likes to feed—and chase—the chickens in the morning. And I should make sure Cidna isn't letting him eat jam by the handful."

I chuckled, then went back to my chamber. Riona was gone, but my clothes were laid out. I quickly redressed and then headed out. When I appeared in the hallway once more, I found Riona and Sorcha. Sorcha was dressed, her hair wet from being combed, her face cleaned.

"What a sweet child," Riona said, kissing her cheek. "Bellicus is as wild as a fey thing, but Sorcha…what a fine girl you have."

"You hear that, my firebrand?" I asked the baby, reaching out for her.

Sorcha grinned at me.

The three of us returned to the main hall. Cidna waved to me from the front door. "Come here, Boudica."

I stepped out of the house to find that Cidna had loaded a wagon with enough grain and supplies to see Ula through the winter.

"Albie will help you pull," Cidna said.

I ruffled the kitchen boy's hair. "You and Tadgh are racing. I can't wait to see which of you will be taller," I told Albie.

"Bran said I can join his warriors next year."

"Very good!" I told him. "Now, this will be your first test. Steel yourself. We shall face the most fearsome creature in all of Northern Iceni territory."

At that, Albie laughed.

I settled Sorcha into the wagon between two sacks of grain. "Hold on," I told her, then we headed off, tugging the wagon behind us.

Sorcha giggled as we walked down the lane to Ula's house. Many greeted me with smiles, waving to my daughter as we went.

When we finally arrived at Ula's door, I noted her fire was burning—she was inside.

I knocked on the door. "Ula," I called. "There is a firebrand on your doorstep."

Some pots rattled about inside, and the door opened. Ula peered outside.

"What are you doing in Oak Throne?" she asked.

"That…is a topic better discussed inside."

Her eyes went to the wagon. "Take that back."

I lifted Sorcha. "You can't take a child back. That's not possible, and you know it," I said, then shoved Sorcha at her, forcing Ula to hold her or Sorcha would fall.

"Okay, Albie. Bring it all inside," I said, then lifted a sack of grain and carried it in, forcing Ula and Sorcha to step aside so I could pass.

"Boudica," Ula grumbled at me. "What is all this? I

don't need all this. I'll be chasing mice out of it all winter."

"Better than eating those mice. Seems like an excellent reason to get a cat. Any kittens to be had in the market, Albie?"

"Marin has a litter. White and gray. Very cute."

"When we're done, go fetch one for Ula."

"What am I supposed to do with a cat?" Ula demanded.

"Teach it to chase mice," I said, setting down my heavy bag and then going for another.

"I should get a switch and swat you both," Ula told Albie and me as we began carrying another load inside.

"Nay," Sorcha told Ula firmly, pointing in the old woman's face. "Nay, nay, nay."

Albie and I both chuckled.

At that, Ula paused. "What, Princess? Don't want me to scold your mother?"

"Nay," Sorcha told her firmly.

"I see. Loyal, are you? Good. Good. Boudica needs those who are loyal about her. As it is, she is swimming with eels."

"I hear the Romans eat them," Albie quipped.

"They do. I saw them on the table in Camulodunum. Served with millet and garlic. I didn't try it myself, but the Romans seemed to love them."

"Is it true that their emperor wears a gown like a woman?"

"A toga. That's what they call it. And yes, he does. It was made with the whitest white fabric I ever saw and trimmed in a deep purple, the color of their rulers."

"What does he look like?"

"He is an ugly man with close-set eyes that are small and beady. And he had a bald head and a bulbous nose."

At that, Albie laughed.

"It's true," I said, setting down another sack and then lifting one more.

"Listen to your mother, talking about the emperor of Rome while carrying sacks of beets," Ula told Sorcha, then tickled her chin, making the girl giggle.

I carried the bag into the house, then paused for a rest.

Albie carried in the last two sacks. "Done, Boudica. I'll be back with that kitten shortly," he said, then rushed away, the cart jangling behind him.

Ula grunted with annoyance, then closed the door. She went to look at all the bags. "What am I supposed to do with all this?"

"Eat it, I presume."

"Always a smart reply," Ula said, then sat down, Sorcha in her lap. "Now, let me look at you," Ula said, her eyes meeting Sorcha's. "Hair like the Morrigu. And I see her flicker sleeping inside you."

"What *do* you see, Ula? She is a princess, but she is the granddaughter of a priestess. What do you see for her?"

Ula rose and handed the child back to me. With that, she went to her table and rummaged around a bit, returning to the fire once more. "I will ask Andraste to speak. Let's see what she says."

With that, Ula banked up her fire and added some leaves that made a thick smoke that filled the room. Sorcha watched with curiosity but did not fuss. Once the flames were going, Ula began to whisper in a low tone. She drew a spiral symbol into the cold ashes spread across the flagstones near the fire before her. From her pocket, she removed a pouch and poured small talismans—stones, bits of bone, gems, acorns, and more—into her hands. She shook her hands as she whispered.

Sorcha looked from Ula to me.

"Shh," I whispered, putting my finger to my lips.

The child stared at the fire.

My head felt woozy, the scent of the smoke getting to me as well. I held Sorcha even more tightly, fearful I would drop her. I pressed the child against me.

"Dark Lady Andraste," Ula called, her voice gravelly. "Red-cloaked Morrigu. Crone. It was you who first showed me the child of Boudica. Now, guide us. Show us what path you would have her take," Ula said, then tossed the talismans on the ground before her.

My eyes grew heavy.

Closing them for just a moment, I saw someplace far from here. White houses with tile roofs crowded the streets. A great building with tall columns stood on a hill. Around me, I heard bells ringing in alarm. On the street, I saw a woman wearing a hooded cape, a dagger in her hand—it dripped with blood.

My eyes snapped open.

"Avenger," Ula whispered in a voice not her own. "Avenger... Boudica, Queen of the Greater Iceni, put a blade in Sorcha's hand. This is the word of the Dark Lady Andraste. Heed it."

CHAPTER 77

I spent the rest of the morning with Ula, sharing with her all I had seen, from the visits to Camulodunum and Londinium to the news of the Catuvellauni priestess.

At some point, there was a knock on the door.

Ula opened it to find a fluffy gray-and-white kitten sitting there.

Sorcha squealed with delight.

"Bah," Ula said, then let the kitten inside, shutting the door behind her. She went to her table and opened a crock from which she took out a hunk of chicken which she broke into small bits.

Sorcha sat on the ground, letting the little kitten rub all over her.

"What a sweet thing, Ula. Look at it."

"Useful for hunting mice," Ula said.

"How can you say that? Look at," —I lifted the kitten,

checking— "him. His face his gray, but his body is all white. What will you call him?"

"Cat."

"Ula!"

"*You* name him."

"Look at your sweet gray face. Graymalkin. He's Graymalkin."

"Come, then, Graymalkin," Ula said, setting down the dish of chicken. "And do not fuss about it. That's all there is."

The kitten waddled over to the dish and sat down to eat. Sorcha went to him, patting the kitten as he ate.

"Caratacus is trying to whip up the Coritani—and Caturix," I told her.

"It was a mistake for that boy to keep his seat in Stonea."

"He was trying to keep Melusine from Kennocha and Mara."

"And brings trouble on all of us in the process."

"Melusine lost a child. She was pregnant the same time Bec and I were."

Ula stared into the flames. "She will not bear. Not now. Not ever."

"Ula…"

Ula shook her head. "A pity."

I frowned.

"What, girl? You cannot control the fate of others. Not everything that comes to pass is good. Ask Dindraine."

"I will seek out Aulus. I must get him to listen."

"You won't have to look hard. He, too, seeks you."

"What do you mean?"

"You know what I mean, girl. You can win us a slice of safety with what's between your legs. Give the Roman what he wants."

"Ula! You know I cannot."

"Do you think yourself so precious?"

"I would not betray Prasutagus."

"You will betray all of us if you cannot get the Roman to give you his word—and mean it. He is a shadow on your spirit, Boudica. I see his shade upon you, from life to life."

"Why?"

"An old pact. An old wound," Ula said, looking deep into the flames. "So far back, I see myself as young," she said, then laughed. "And at your side, along with that mad girl. A different place. A different time. It will take seven lifetimes to undo it, Boudica. You will not be rid of him any time soon. Now, you must face the consequences since you didn't listen to the hollow hills. There is still time to act. You will meet the Roman. Already, he desires you to the point of love. You must stoke that flame for all our sakes."

"I cannot forsake the oath I have sworn to Prasutagus."

"Events are already in motion, Boudica. Do what you can. That is all I can say. For once, I will not chide you."

"You see, the kitten has softened you already."

Ula laughed lightly, then looked back into the fire. As she stared, her eyes grew watery. She wiped her unshed tears away without saying a word and then rose. She dug through her things once more, pulling out a biscuit, which she handed to Sorcha.

"Here, firebrand. Munch on this," she said. "It's good you came to Oak Throne, Boudica. You should come more often."

"Are you saying you missed me?"

"Bah."

"I missed you too, Ula."

"Winter will be upon us soon. It will be a long, cold one. As the mother sleeps, so shall we. Let us see what comes in spring. Now, go on with you. There is work that must be done."

I nodded, then scooped up Sorcha. "Come along, wee one."

Ula followed me to the door.

"Stop being so stubborn with Cidna," I told her. "If she has something for you—supplies, or anything else—take it. We all just want to look after you."

"Bah," Ula said, waving for me to go.

"Bah, yourself. You sound like a sheep," I replied, then stepped outside. "Be well, Ula," I said, pecking her quickly on the cheek.

"Troublesome girl. Be well, Boudica. And you, little firebrand," she said, then closed the door.

Feeling ill at ease by Ula's unexpected softening, I was lost in my thoughts as I made my way back toward the market. I had passed the oak tree and was close to the vendors when someone called my name.

"Boudica?"

"Di-di-ca!" another little voice echoed.

I looked to find Kennocha and Mara making their way toward me. Mara looked so much like Caturix that I stopped for a moment, taking it in.

Melusine would never bear a child...

Mara was my brother's only heir...

This meant that unless Caturix acknowledged Mara, Bellicus would inherit the throne of the Northern Iceni.

"Mara," I said, bending to receive the little girl running toward me. I gave her a hug, then set Sorcha down so she and Mara could get a good look at one another. When Kennocha grew closer, another realization washed over me. She was pregnant once more.

"Kennocha, it is good to see you."

"And you, Boudica. Is this Sorcha?"

"It is."

Kennocha bent to look at her. "Well met, Princess. I am Kennocha, and this is Mara."

The girls grinned at one another.

Kennocha kissed Sorcha's hand, then rose. "I am glad to see you here. Is everything well?" she asked.

"I... yes and no. I have brought some women—priestesses from the Catuvellauni—to stay with Dôn. It is a complicated mess."

"I saw Bran and Caturix loading wagons with building supplies this morning. I didn't know the reason."

I nodded, then looked her over. "You are looking... well?" I asked, then arched an eyebrow.

Kennocha smiled, her hand drifting over her stomach. "Mabon, perhaps."

"Is it..."

She looked around to ensure we were alone. "Another niece or nephew for you."

"I wish you well. No delaying calling Ula for help when it is time. But if she is too cantankerous, Bec can help."

"It has been very good having Bec here. She and Bran are doing very well ruling Oak Throne. I hope you will forgive me for saying it, but I think the people are happier now than under your father."

"My father could be a hard man."

"Bran wins everyone to his side with a joke and a smile."

I grinned, glad to hear that Bran was doing well in Oak Throne. "I know Caturix is here, but do you need anything? Is there anything I can do for you?"

Kennocha shook her head. "No. I am quite content today," she said, then looked behind me, a smile alighting on her face.

I turned to find Caturix approaching.

My brother froze a moment, then pulled himself together and joined us. To my surprise, he bent to scoop up both girls at once.

"Beautiful maids of the Iceni," he said, smiling at them.

Kennocha laughed lightly.

Who is this person? I never saw my brother look like that before.

"Shall I walk you home?" Caturix asked Kennocha, who nodded.

"That means you are coming with me," I said, taking Sorcha from him.

I met my brother's gaze, giving him a puzzled glance, but he said nothing.

"Come on, Mara," Caturix said, reaching out to take the basket Kennocha was carrying with his free hand. "Let's see you home. Boudica, we'll speak later."

"All right."

As my brother walked away, I puzzled at his choices. Already, people whispered about Kennocha. Had Mara's paternity become an open secret? And now, there was another child on the way. What was he thinking?

He loved her.

He loved Kennocha and Mara.

That was what he was thinking.

The marriage to Melusine hadn't changed that.

But was there more?

"You see. Mara is your cousin," I whispered to Sorcha. "See Mara?" I asked.

Sorcha pointed.

I nodded. "Yes. That is her. We will all be sure to take good care of her in the future. Including you," I said, poking Sorcha in the belly, making her giggle.

I walked with the little girl down to the river. There, I found that three new docks had been constructed. While many of the vendors and fishermen there were Northern Iceni, I noticed some strangers, including a man in a distinctly Roman barge. His men were unloading his goods onto the dock.

I went to him. "Hello, sir," I called.

The man turned, eyeing me over. "Lady," he said. "It's

is a good day to be in Oak Throne. I will have my goods unloaded for you to peruse tomorrow."

"Where have you come from?" I asked.

"Sailed from Londinium."

"What is the news? I heard Governor Plautius was in Londinium," I said, fishing for information.

"No, lady. That is wrong. His men have pulled back to Verulam for the oncoming of winter."

"Is that so?"

"Indeed, lady. Saw them myself not a week back. Camped all around the fort, they are. Tell your maid to come in the morning. I have many fine Roman silks, perfumes, looking glasses, beads, all you can desire."

I nodded to him. "Thank you, sir."

And with that, I turned and headed back.

Now, where was Pix?

Perhaps it was an excellent time to see what had become of Verulam.

CHAPTER 78

I t took some convincing, but finally, Caturix and Bran
agreed to give some additional men to accompany
Pix and me to Verulam. It was still early enough in
the day to get underway. I did not want to delay in case I
missed Aulus.

"Fly both standards," Caturix said. "Let him know you
are coming to discuss our holy people for both of us. And
take the roads controlled by the Romans. You don't know
what you will encounter amongst the Catuvellauni. Take
the Kenna Route south through Northern then Greater
Iceni territory. From there, it is not a long ride to Verulam."

"I still think I should go," Bran said.

"You are needed here," I reminded him, then turned to
Bec. "Are you sure it will not be too much trouble to watch
Sorcha?"

"Of course not, Boudica. Riona and Cidna are here to
help me," she said, then grinned. "And there is always
Ula."

"Thank you, Bec. We'll be back in a few days."

"Caturix," I said, pulling my brother aside while Pix and the warriors settled in. Now came the hard part. If I could get Caturix to speak what I guessed he already knew, I could make a move that may save us all. "Brother, you must be honest with me."

"About what?" Caturix asked, his brows narrowing.

"I will need to convince the governor it is in his best interest to help us, to keep his word about our holy people. And I need to show him the Northern Iceni are still with him, no matter what he has heard."

"What do you mean?"

"Aulus has spies everywhere. He knows that Volisios is talking to you. They are watching the Coritani. The Romans already know that the Coritani will betray them. The governor is no fool. Volisios will walk into a trap. You will lead the Northern Iceni to ruin if you walk with him. It's not too late to undo this mess and show Rome that the Northern Iceni are true to their word."

"What do you want, Boudica?" Caturix asked, his voice dark with expectation.

"Where is Caratacus?"

Caturix paused.

He knows.

"Caturix."

My brother sighed. "He has a wife and child amongst the Dobunni. They are living in a small fort called Stokeleigh near the Avon Gorge."

"Are you certain?"

Caturix nodded.

"If the Romans find him, that puts an end to every-thing. You know that. There is no further reason for them to advance. And if they do—"

"Then they are liars."

I nodded.

"You are playing with fire, Boudica."

"We both are, Brother. Let's hope neither of us gets caught by the flames."

With that, my brother—unexpectedly—pulled me into an embrace. "Be careful, Sister."

"And you, Brother."

With that, I turned from him and mounted Druda.

Bran came to me, petting Druda on the neck. "You have the clout of a queen, but these are uncertain times. Watch yourself on the road."

"It's not the road ye need to be worried about," Pix mumbled.

Bran glanced at her, then said, "Be careful *everywhere* you go."

Bec brought Sorcha to me. I leaned in the saddle, taking her hand and kissing it. "Be good for Bec. I will return in a few days."

"We will have fun with Bellicus. You will see, Sorcha," Bec said.

I adjusted the spear behind me, then looked back at the warriors assembled. In addition to the men from Venta, Cai and Bran's band of warriors had joined us.

"We will ride with you, Boudica," Cai told me.

I nodded to him, grateful to have someone I trusted with me. I gestured to the party, then we rode out.

I turned back in my saddle to wave to Sorcha. Bec waved her hand to me. When I saw the sad look on her face, I suddenly felt sorry. But Bran had seen it too. He took Sorcha from Bec's arms. Holding Sorcha, Bran began chasing Bellicus, Sorcha in front of him. The boy ran from my brother and daughter, laughing as he dawdled as quickly as his little legs could carry him.

My gaze went to Caturix, who watched the happy scene, a pinch of pain on his face.

At that moment, it became clear that my brother regretted his choices.

He had an adorable daughter and another child on the way. Would he acknowledge them? Could he? What would happen with Melusine if he did? Would he discard Melusine to marry Kennocha? Doing so would destabilize everything between the Northern Iceni and the Coritani. In the one moment, I realized that these were the thoughts running on an endless loop through Caturix's head. Add in the political tensions…

Caturix was unsettled.

That was a perilous place for him to be.

I turned back in my saddle and faced the road once more.

I had to do everything I could to make things right, not just for our holy people but for the Northern Iceni. Because if my guess was correct, Caturix was in danger.

WE RODE THROUGHOUT THE AFTERNOON AND INTO THE night, crossing into Greater Iceni territory well after sundown. Finding a quiet glade off the road, we made our camp. Gathered around the campfire, the men ate and drank and told funny stories, including one I had never heard before that had taken place at a Midsummer festival when I was a girl.

"We were sure one of us would win the wrestling match and catch your or Brenna's attention," Cai told me. "All of us were in love with either you or your sister," Cai said with a laugh. "But Gaheris was the most determined. He knew you were giving out the prizes. He swore he would pull you into a muddy embrace and steal a kiss from you."

"Gaheris told us he would wrestle a bull to win if he had to," Davin added with a grin.

"But did he win?" I asked. "I don't remember."

"He did! But when it came time to get his prize, old Belenus gave out the gifts. We teased him mercilessly for not claiming his kiss," Cai said, laughing.

I chuckled. "Don't worry. He got his prize. If not then, later. So you can laugh all you like, but he still won."

"Aye, Boudica. We all wish he was still here to claim it. To Gaheris," Cai said, lifting his cup. "May he be long remembered until we all meet again."

"To Gaheris," we called.

I sipped the liquid, the brew tasting sour, then set it aside. All day, everything I put in my mouth tasted wrong. Cidna's food was never spot-on, but I had grown up with the taste. Still, it all tasted off somehow. And yet, I kept dreaming of roasted hazelnuts. Wasn't it nearly time for them? I would watch for hazelnut trees as we rode tomorrow.

That night, I lay down to sleep under the shelter of the leaves, moon, and stars, thinking of Gaheris.

Had he lived, where would I be now? Would I be in Frog's Hollow? How many things would have gone differently if I had been Gaheris's wife? Would we still have befriended Rome, or would the Greater and Northern Iceni already have fallen as the Cantiaci and Catuvellauni had?

That night, I slept soundly. It had been too long since I had been in the forest, under the trees. I missed the feel of the wind on my face as I slept. I slept so deeply that I was surprised when Pix shook my shoulder the following day.

"Up, Strawberry Queen. Bel doesn't wait upon ye."

We struck camp and got on the road once more. If we traveled throughout the day, we could reach the Catuvellauni seat of Verulam by nightfall. None of us wanted to be on the road in Catuvellauni territory at night.

I quickly readied Druda, stuffed a bit of bread and cheese in my mouth, then made ready. Once more, we took to the road, this time at a trot.

We rode throughout the day, only stopping for a brief rest, but as we rode, we saw what war had wrought: burned farms and villages, families in threadbare clothing rushing from the road and into the woods to hide from riders, and more. As we came closer to Verulam, even the road showed a Roman stamp. The road had been widened and flattened. We saw units of men working in the forest cutting trees. Roman overseers watched their work.

"Catuvellauni," Pix said, lifting her chin in their direction. "In chains."

I nodded.

As we rode past another group of Romans and their captives, some people began to shout to us.

"Iceni. It is the Iceni. Queen Boudica, where is our king? Where is King Caratacus, Queen Boudica? Save us!"

"Silence," a Roman shouted, his voice followed by the crack of a whip.

It was nearly nightfall when Verulam came into view. Like Camulodunum, the city was a shadow of itself. Seated on a hilltop, Verulam looked out over a deep valley. In that valley were hundreds of tents.

"May Taranis protect us," Cai said from behind me.

I swallowed hard, steeling myself to the sight, then led the party ahead. We rode toward the hilltop stronghold. Romans manned the walls of the ancient fortress. As we approached, the gates swung open.

On the other side stood Aulus, king of this mountain. Beside him sat his massive black dog—Victory.

Aulus scanned over the party, then met my gaze.

Then, he smiled, and something ancient in my spirit lit up in a way it had no business doing.

Dark Lady Andraste, what are you weaving for me?

CHAPTER 79

We rode into the fort, the doors swinging closed behind us. Aulus met me, taking Druda's reins so I could dismount.

"Queen Boudica," he said politely. "This is a surprise."

"Governor Plautius," I replied, then dismounted. I bent to pat the dog. "Hello, Victory. What a great big boy you have become."

The dog wagged his tail and licked my hand.

Aulus chuckled, then eyed my party. "I see the banners of the Greater and Northern Iceni here."

"I come on behalf of both."

"I see," Aulus said. "And here, I just thought you missed me."

"Maybe I did."

"*I* did not, Rome," Pix quipped.

"Likewise," he replied to her.

"Friends," Aulus called to the party. "My men will see you have food and drink. Rest yourselves."

680

One of Aulus's men came to take Druda and the other horses. Soldiers met with Cai and the others. "Your weapons, gentlemen."

Cai looked toward me.

I nodded.

Reluctantly, they handed them over. A boy came to take my spear and Pix's weapons. As I disarmed, I looked over the fort. Everywhere I looked, I saw Roman soldiers, servants, and Catuvellauni in chains.

"Admiring the fort that could have been yours?"

"Mine?"

"They tell me your father was planning to wed you to Caratacus. Or was it Togodumnus? Or both?" he said, then laughed. "You *and* your sister."

I swallowed hard. He had found out about Brenna. "Yes, that was the rumor."

"Funny, I didn't know you had a sister, Queen Boudica."

"She is among our holy people," I replied.

"Ah," Aulus said, his tone suggesting he had just put the final piece of a puzzle together. "I see. Let's not bandy about in the courtyard. Caratacus left me a perfectly good dining hall. Come," he said, then offered me his arm.

Victory trotting alongside us, we made our way inside, Pix following behind us.

Aulus glanced at her over his shoulder. "This one follows you like a shadow."

"Easier to keep my eye on ye, Rome," Pix told him.

Aulus huffed a laugh.

We wound through the narrow hallways of the fort.

The ancient place had been built on a rocky hilltop. It was an unusual building. The natural boulders formed part of the walls, rocks and clay filling in the gaps. The halls jutted off at odd angles. The stonework was carved with elaborate Celtic knotwork and other symbols of our people.

Aulus led me to a dining room. Therein, I spotted his secretary.

"Narcissus, have a bedchamber readied for Queen Boudica and her maid," he told the man, then turned to Pix. "Maid, why don't you take your queen's things and ready her chamber," he said, gesturing for Pix to go with Narcissus.

Pix frowned hard at Aulus, then turned to me.

"I'll be along later," I told her.

Pix met my gaze and held it. In it, I saw her warning, but she said nothing more.

"This way, lady," Narcissus said, motioning for Pix to follow along.

Once they had gone, Aulus turned to the table and poured us two goblets of wine.

I scanned the room. Cave walls made up the ceiling and one side of the room. Stone had been laid in other places to separate the rooms. The stonework had been carved. At the center of the room was a deep firepit around which benches were set.

Aulus handed me a goblet, then motioned for us to sit by the fire.

He lifted his cup in a toast. "Who do you want to toast, Boudica?"

"Hmm," I mused. "To Mithras, your god of war *and obligation.*"

Aulus arched an eyebrow at me. "Then, to Mithras," he said, then we drank.

Victory took the opportunity to lie down by the fire.

"What do you think?" Aulus asked, gesturing around him.

"It is a fine fort...an ancient stronghold."

"Part cave," Aulus said. "Lots of twisting tunnels leading to chambers deep in the mountain. It would have been hard to take the fort if its king had been here to protect it. Sadly for the Catuvellauni, Caratacus left it open to attack. We were able to take the fort without much bloodshed. Once we got here, we cleared the place from hiding Catuvellauni. Although I must admit, some of my men were half afraid to go after them down into those tunnels in the dark."

"They should be. There are ancient things in our caves. I am surprised you didn't end up a man or two short."

"Who's to say I didn't?" Aulus replied, then drank once more.

"Well, I guess you always have more men," I replied. "Thousands, from what I can see."

Aulus nodded. "Yes," he said, then tapped his ring on the side of his cup, his head bobbing in unison as he thought. I could see in his eyes he had fallen down a well of deep thoughts. How often had I noticed the same expression on Vian's and Prasutagus's faces? But the Roman's blue eyes looked haunted. Something he was thinking of vexed and saddened him.

"You're not here anymore," I said.

Aulus blinked hard, then looked up. After a moment, he chuckled lightly. "Following the thread of a problem. Sometimes, a thread leads to an answer. Other times, to a knot."

I grinned. "And what was it this time?"

"Ah, I always find knots for this particular problem," he said, then winked at me.

A moment later, a fleet of servants appeared carrying platters of food. They quietly laid the table.

"Governor," the Roman servant said, "shall we attend upon you and the queen?"

"No," Aulus replied. "We will have privacy."

The man bowed, then disappeared.

Aulus rose. "You must be hungry. I'm sure it was a long ride from..."

"Iceni territory," I replied with a grin.

Aulus chuckled. "Iceni territory. Come, let me serve you," he said, then pulled out a chair at the table for me.

I settled in, Aulus adjusting my seat for me. Then, he lifted a silver spoon and began serving me. "I've traveled all across the Roman Empire, and I have to tell you something, Boudica, but I hope you will not be offended."

"And that is?" I asked.

"The cuisine on your island is the worst," he said with a laugh.

"And to think, I was fed from a table supplied by— notoriously—the worst cook in all of the Northern Iceni lands," I said with a chuckle.

At that, he laughed loudly. "Then I hope you don't find

this fare too rich for your tongue. My servants make it to my taste."

I eyed my platter, on which I spotted a roasted dove in a golden sauce alongside small fruits and berries. The bread he laid on the side of my platter was made with herbs and a purple-colored fruit I didn't recognize. The scent wafting off the bread was like nothing I had ever smelled before. Once my plate was prepared, Aulus fixed his own dish and then sat.

For a moment, I felt small.

When we had met with the emperor, I noticed the care their party had taken in eating, the ladies in particular. I had done my best then to eat in a refined manner. But in my daily life, I never much thought about it. I was just as happy to plunk down on the grass with a chicken leg in one hand and a mug of ale in the other. Now, I was faced with a dish I wasn't sure how to eat without embarrassing my ancestors.

And I didn't want to look foolish in front of Aulus.

Instead, I sipped the wine.

For the first time in days, something actually tasted good. In fact, it was the best wine I had ever tasted.

"Do you like it?" he asked, gesturing to the wine.

I nodded. "Love it, in fact. I've never had a wine quite like this before."

Aulus smiled widely. "I have a large vineyard. It's a beautiful place with rolling hills, cypress trees, and miles upon miles of grapevines. My villa is there. The vineyard has been in my family for many years. It has grown, thanks to my father's success and now mine. We brew excellent wines there. This is a bottle from my winery."

"Your wine? From your family?"

He nodded.

"It's perfect," I said, then set the cup down. "And your wife... Does she share your interest in wine?"

"How did you learn about my wife?"

"How did you learn about my sister?"

Aulus sipped his wine once more, then said, "Pomponia... I can't say my wife has ever seen my vineyard," he said as he considered. "No. She hasn't unless she's gone there in my absence. She's not particularly interested in nature. Although, she does enjoy the fruits of its labor. Pomponia is a creature of Rome, distantly related to the emperor himself. She spends most of her time gossiping with anyone who will listen, sleeping with whatever man will have her, and spending my gold on gowns and jewels."

Stunned by his admission, I said, "It's a pity she doesn't see her husband as the rest of the world does."

"And how is that, Queen Boudica? How does the world see me?"

"As a man who should be respected."

He gave me a soft, honest smile. I could see that my words had touched his heart. But I had not intended them as flattery. I meant what I said. Aulus was to be respected... feared but respected.

"That is my secret. Now you will tell me yours. But eat first," he said, gesturing to my plate.

I chuckled and then took a bite of bread. In it, I tasted

the sweet tang of basil, rosemary, and olive oil. The food melted in my mouth. "What is this?" I asked, gesturing to the purple fruit pressed into the bread.

"That is an olive."

"Purple?"

He nodded. "I have many olive trees at my vineyard, as well as fig, orange, and cherry trees. There is a little pond on the property. Fig trees grow all around it. I would climb the trees and sit in the branches, eating figs and watching the swans.

Lifting a serving spoon, he set a piece of fruit on my plate. "A fig. Taste it."

I popped it into my mouth. It was dense and chewy. The flavor reminded me of honey. "Very sweet," I said.

"They are better fresh, but too delicate to be shipped here."

"Your vineyard sounds like a beautiful place."

"It is. There are times that I miss it very much."

"Such as today, I think."

"Today, I am dreaming."

"Of?"

"Of what my life would be like if I lived on my land with a woman I loved."

I paused. "No one likes to live in lack. Be it lack of love or anything else."

Aulus nodded. "Yes. That's right," he said. Then, he smiled once more, shaking off whatever thoughts had clouded around him. "Especially, lack of good food. Eat, dear Boudica. Because if what you say is true about your childhood cook, I wouldn't keep you from another decent bite."

We finished the meal in idle talk, Aulus telling me of his time as a boy at the vineyard, where it seemed to me he was raised mainly by servants. But it also became abundantly clear that, like me, he was a wild annoyance to those who tried to parent him, his antics rivaling my own.

"Luckily for me, the vineyard was so large, they could never find me. So I would escape with a loaf of bread and round of cheese and sleep under the stars."

I laughed. "For me, it was the Wash," I said. "That was where I escaped. To swim. To ride..."

"Isn't the Wash far from Oak Throne?"

"Yes, it is," I said with a laugh.

Aulus chuckled. "Your father must have been worried."

"I cannot say if he was worried. I *can* say he was cross."

"Then he was worried. That is how fathers show it."

"Maybe."

"And did you escape alone to such places?"

"At first, yes. Later, I found a partner for my mischief."

"Your wild friend?" he asked, gesturing in the direction where Pix had gone.

"No," I said, then paused. "No. A man. Gaheris. He was a chieftain's son and my first love."

At that, Aulus paused. "Your first love, but not your husband."

"Gaheris was killed mere months before we were to wed. There was an attack on his fishing camp at the Wash. Everyone was butchered."

"I'm sorry for your loss. When did this happen?"

"Late summer in the year before your landing."

"At the Wash?"

I nodded.

Aulus nodded slowly, then reached out to take my hand. "I'm sorry for your loss."

"Did you... Did you ever have anyone like that? Before your wife."

Aulus paused. "No. I was waiting."

"For a suitable match?"

He laughed lightly. "When I was a young man, I went to the temple of Venus, our goddess of love, to speak to an *augur* who read the signs. She told me I would love only one woman in this life. So, I waited for the woman she described."

"Then your wife—"

"Pomponia is *not* that woman. She is a woman with connections my father appreciated. She is a loathsome creature, low in wit, easily manipulated by zealots, vain and gossiping. I hate everything about her. I was forced to wed."

"I..." I said, then paused, unsure what to say. "I'm sorry. I almost met the same fate, becoming the lady of this hall."

"Wed to Caratacus."

"Or Togodumnus. Or both..." I said in an effort to make him smile, forcing away the dark clouds that had covered his heart.

It worked. He smiled lightly and then asked. "How did you escape that fate?"

"Narrowly. I credit the gods for intervening and my father for listening."

"Which is how you came to be the wife of Prasutagus."

"Yes."

"And your sister?"

"Brenna. My sister was nearly wed to one or the other, but our druids intervened on her behalf. Now, she is with our holy people... which is, in part, why I am here."

"I dreamed... I dreamed we spoke of this. In the mist."

"It was no dream, Aulus," I said, then rose. Taking my wine goblet with me, I went to Aulus's work area at the back of the room. There, I fingered through the papers on his desk, including maps of our lands.

Aulus came to join me, looking over my shoulder as I looked through his papers. I pulled out a map, looking at his notes thereon. There, I saw Mona marked and with it, noted: *Stronghold of the druids.*

My eyes scanned the paper to the area where the Isle of Avallach was hidden in the mist. There were no markings around it.

Safe.

Secret.

May the Mother be thanked.

"My sister is here," I said, pointing to Mona. "It is our most sacred place. Every druid in our land is trained here —people from *all* the tribes. It is a place of prayer and learning, with sacred groves and stones. This is why I need you to be true to your promise. This is why I need you to honor your word to me. It is not only my people but my sister that I must keep safe."

Aulus placed his cup on the table, then set his hand on my arm.

"What do your druids learn there?"

"Music. Law. The language of our ancient ones. Spells, such as enchantments that will make a Roman emperor order his men to collect seashells then march home. And they learn to make prophecies, like the *augur* you spoke of."

Aulus slowly stroked my arm. "Prophecy."

"Yes."

"Do you want me to tell you what the priestess of Venus whispered to me?"

I felt an ache inside me, feeling him so close, his hand on my bare skin. Against all reason, I whispered, "Yes."

His hand slid up my arm, over my shoulder, to my neck, which he cradled softly. He leaned toward me, setting his other hand on my hip, pulling me back toward him. I could feel him, aroused, pressed against me.

"She told me I would know my love when I saw her. She told me the woman's hair would be as red as roses, that she would have a fierce fire within her. The priestess warned me that the woman's fire would burn me from the inside out, that she would be a wild thing, unlike any woman I'd ever known. She also warned that while I would long for her like nothing I had ever wanted before, she would be out of my reach," he said, gently pulling me closer to him, his fingers pressing on my hipbones. "And that no matter how much I wanted her, I would not be able to have her."

My heart pounded in my chest. It was so loud, I could hear it ringing in my ears.

"Is that true?" I whispered. "Did the priestess really tell you that?"

"Yes," he said, his lips gently touching my neck.

I swallowed. "Aulus..."

"I want you, Boudica. As my wife. In my bed. I want you in that picture I painted of my vineyard, laughing wildly, your red curls bouncing in the sunshine, running barefoot in the grass. That is where you belong. Not here. Not in this place."

"You have a wife."

"A word, that is all I need to speak, and Pomponia stumbles down the stairs or dies of poison. She is a canker on my life. Incestuous woman, closer to her brother than a woman should be in all the venial ways. I am cursed with her. Stay with me, Boudica. I can sail to Rome, take you back with me. Vespasian can have the governorship. Come back to Rome with me."

"I cannot," I whispered. "I have a child. My people. My family. And I love Prasutagus."

"Even though you want me as I want you."

"I..."

"You said you wanted there to be truth between us. Let's have it," he said, pulling me closer, his hand reaching around me to cup my breast. "You want me as I want you."

I closed my eyes and bit my bottom lip, suppressing a groan. What he said was true. I did want him. But I loved Prasutagus. I could not. I would not.

"Boudica…"

"I cannot."

"But you want me."

"I… Yes."

"Then don't deny me," he said, his fingertips touching my nipple, which hardened at his touch. "Don't deny what you feel between us," he said, kissing my neck.

"I cannot," I whispered, hearing the pain in my voice.

Moving gently, he turned me to face him, but he knocked the drink sitting on the table when he did. The red wine splattered over the map, seeping from the ocean into Cantiaci and Trinovantes land and across to the Catuvellauni, the Atrebates, and west. The whole map was soaked red with wine. And in the last, the Iceni lands faded red too.

The sight of it was so abhorrent that I stepped back.

"Blood on the land," I whispered. "Blood on the land."

Aulus turned to me. "Boudica?"

I met his gaze. "You *are* right. I *yearn* for you. I *want* you. But it cannot be in this life. It cannot be. Too much separates us, and I will not dishonor Prasutagus. Do you remember what I told you? About how we believe a soul lives many lives? When you reach your Elysium, find the mist… Find the mist and come back to me. In the next life, I will come to you."

"Swear it," Aulus said.

"I swear it. I swear it by the Great Mother. I swear it by the Forest Lord. I swear it by the Dark Lady Andraste. May they hear my words. I swear it. It cannot be in this life. But I swear, we will be together in the next."

Aulus swallowed hard, then reached out for my hand.

I embraced him, wrapping my arms around him, laying my head on his chest.

"I love you, Boudica, even if you cannot be mine. And I will do what I can to keep you, and all you love, safe."

"Aulus," I whispered, closing my eyes. "I *am* sorry. I truly am."

But then, my head felt woozy. For a moment, I saw another world, another life. Aulus and I stood on the roof of a tall fort. Around me, I heard the sounds of battle. And then... he fell. He fell from the wall down into the arms of trees. And as he met his death, his eyes stayed fast upon me.

I shuddered, then pulled back, meeting Aulus's gaze once more.

"I cannot give you myself," I said, then turned to the map. "But I *can* give you Caratacus."

CHAPTER 80

A ulus and I leaned over the map as I explained what I had learned of Caratacus's movements. As I did so, I willed my heart to be quiet. I truly lamented Aulus's pain—and my own. The pull I felt toward him was as strong as I had felt for Prasutagus and Gaheris.

But it had to be ignored.

It could not come to pass.

Everything Aulus was asking of me was impossible.

I could not leave my people to become a bride of Rome. I could not leave my daughter, my family, or my husband. The shame was too much to even consider...no matter how beautiful a picture Aulus had painted.

And it had been a beautiful one.

"Where is this Stokeleigh?" Aulus asked, his hand resting gently on my back as we looked at the map.

"Here," I said, pointing. "It is a small fort overlooking the Avon Gorge. I don't know much more. This would be a smaller, seemingly unimportant encampment. He is there with his wife and child. He will not think you will look there."

Aulus nodded. "I can reach him before the winter sets in. How did you come to know this, Boudica?"

"Caturix. Caratacus is bending my brother's ear, but Caturix hasn't forgotten the Catuvellauni's role in our father's murder. He wanted you to know," I said, sounding more confident than I felt.

"I understand," Aulus said, then stepped back. "I... There is much I need to do, but," he said, then studied my face. He didn't want to leave me.

I smiled gently at him. "I'm tired. I need to ride out in the morning. I should take my rest now."

"Yes," he said, then smiled gently at me. "I've kept you awake very late, and you've ridden so far to bring me this news."

I held his gaze. "Aulus, what we discussed about Mona, the holy people there and everywhere else in our lands. They *must* be protected."

"I promise you, Boudica. By all that lies untouched between us, I promise you they will not be harmed under my watch."

I set my hand on his cheek. "Thank you."

He took my hand and placed a kiss thereon as he breathed in slowly and deeply. Then, he let me go.

"Let me call a servant," he said, then lifted a bell, ringing it gently.

A moment later, Narcissus appeared once more.

"Have Queen Boudica taken to her chamber, then

return at once."

"Yes, Governor."

I met Aulus's gaze once more.

He gave me a soft smile. "Good night, Boudica."

"Good night, Aulus."

Turning, I joined Narcissus and followed the man from the room.

"The governor looks happy," Narcissus said as we wound down the narrow hallway. "Funny, he only smiles like that when you are around."

"He likes my sense of humor," I replied with a grin, making the man laugh.

"I'm sure there is something about you he likes, Queen Boudica," he said, then led me down the hall to a door. He opened it, revealing a fine bedchamber suitable for a lady. A ping of pain washed over my heart when I realized this might have been Imogen's room.

"Your maid is—" Narcissus began when Pix appeared.

"Here," Pix said, an irritated expression on her face.

"She has a chamber beside yours," Narcissus told me. "I've had refreshments already sent," he added, waving to a tray on a table. It was laden with food and drink. "Do not hesitate to call for a servant if you want anything else. Good night, Queen Boudica."

"Good night, Narcissus."

The man left, closing the door behind me.

"Well," Pix said, eyeing me over. "Clothes still on, not too many hairs out of place."

"What did you expect?" I asked her waspishly.

"What did I expect? That he would catch ye in his snare this time."

A wave of annoyance washed up in me. "He is no worse than you. In fact, of the two of you, you are the one who reaches too far too often."

The moment I said it, I regretted my words. "Pix, I'm sorry. I—"

"Nay, say nothing more. Did ye get what ye came for?"

"Yes."

"Then that is all that matters. Good night, Strawberry Queen," she said, then disappeared behind the flap separating the main bedchamber from the maid's quarters.

With a heavy sigh, I sat down at the table where a generous spread of food was laid out—at least, what was left of it. I lifted a piece of bread, smelling—was that lavender?—the array of herbs and spices baked into the bread. I spread it with thick butter and spooned honey on the bread. I sat eating, piece after piece, and thinking of Aulus's villa.

I could hear the hum of the bees.

I could smell the scent of grapes in the air.

I could feel the crunch of green grass under my feet.

No war.

No hardships.

No cold winters.

Just flesh on flesh, pleasure, delight.

I closed my eyes, envisioning myself in a fine bed with Aulus, with soft silk sheets and warm summer breezes fluttering through the windows. I felt his hand on my arm, his breath on my neck.

But it was not to be.

I popped the last bite in my mouth. How good it had tasted. Everything on the table tasted better than anything I'd ever eaten before.

Frustrated, I rose and went to bed, not even bothering to change my clothes.

I closed my eyes and wished all the beautiful visions away.

They were not to be.

They could never be.

There was no sense in dreaming of Aulus.

There was no sense imagining his lips on my skin.

No sense wondering how his mouth tasted.

No sense dreaming of a life with him.

This was my life. Cold winters. Smokey houses. Hard work. Stables that smelled of animals and mud...

"*And fire,*" a crackling voice whispered to me. I recognized it as the voice of the Dark Lady Andraste. "*And fire!*"

CHAPTER 81

I slept deeply that night. My stomach was overfull, my emotions overwrought. I did not wake until the following morning when I heard a knock on the door.

"Queen Boudica?" a woman's voice called. "I have hot water."

"Come," I called.

A female servant entered, Catuvellauni by her dress. She set the water and linens down and then tidied up the tray. Another servant came in behind her with a small tray of a steaming- hot drink and morning meal.

"Master Narcissus said to call when you are ready to return to the stables."

"Where is the governor?" I asked sleepily, sitting up.

"In the camp," the girl said. "Do you need anything else?"

"No. Thank you."

With that, the girl departed.

Pix flung the curtains back with a tired yawn. "I dare say, I am ready to be done with this haunted place. Felt like I slept with a hundred ghosts last night."

"I heard nothing at all."

"Ye had too much wine. Now, let me see," Pix said, clapping her hands together as she looked over the meal.

"Leave me something. Nothing has tasted good these many days except this Roman fare."

"Cidna's cooking ne'er tastes right. 'Tis not you."

I joined Pix at the table, joy pricking my heart when I spotted blackberry jam and creamy butter. "It started before that," I said. "Every mug of ale I drink tastes like horse piss."

At that, Pix laughed. "Then you be with child again."

"No."

"Ye and the Strawberry King be fornicating like rabbits in spring whenever ye can, even if ye don't invite me."

I paused, a swell of guilt waving through me. "Pix, about what I said last night…"

She raised her hand. "I will hear nary a thing about it. 'Tis right what you said. We will leave it at that. Now, hand me that plate of ham. I will fill myself on Roman spoils, then let's get out of here."

I slathered a piece of bread with jam and butter and then sat down to eat. From below, I heard the sounds of soldiers. I went to the window, opening the casement.

The view that met me was startling. The Roman army was spread long and wide, so far that they became a blur of white tents.

Pix joined me. "More than at Camulodunum."

I nodded. "Yes."

"Like mold on old bread. Soon, won't be anything left of Catuvellauni. Some movement there," she said, pointing below.

I spotted Aulus with a group of soldiers. They wore heavy cloaks like the Catuvellauni people but were armored underneath.

"Where do you suppose he is going?" Pix asked.

"For Caratacus."

"Told you, did he?"

"No."

"Then..."

"*I* told *him*."

"Told him what?"

"Where Caratacus is hiding."

Pix looked at me. "Why did ye do that?"

"Because if they catch Caratacus, there is no more excuse for this war."

Pix bobbed her head as she considered, then turned and went back inside and added more food to her place.

"What, no playful quip to add?"

"Nay."

"Why not?"

Pix shrugged. "If they catch Caratacus, it may end the war, or it may not."

"Meaning?"

"Do ye really think they'll stop fighting once they have him? Soon, we will see why they are really here."

I stared down at Aulus, watching him walk across the

square. He paused a moment, then turned, looking up at me. I smiled and waved to him.

He bowed to me, then turned back to his men.

"Fate brought them here," I told Pix, my voice low.

"And fate brought me this ham. If ye want any, Boudica, ye best sit down, else I will eat it all."

I joined her at the table, piling food onto my own plate. I kept loading and loading the dish, finally realizing I had more than Pix.

I paused. "I can't really be with child again, can I? Sorcha is barely weaned. She still nurses when she can."

Pix shrugged. "Ye had yer courses again?"

"Once."

"When was the last?"

"Well... It's been a while."

Pix laughed, then put some of her ham on my plate. "Good thing ye didn't lie with that Roman last night. Come next summer, ye wouldn't know whose child ye had in yer belly."

"Pix."

"Or did ye?"

"Did I what?"

"Lie with the Roman."

"No."

"But ye wanted to."

I looked back toward the window but didn't answer.

"Eat," Pix said, pointing. "A thought is not a thing. Eat, and be glad ye are stronger than me."

AFTER I FINISHED MY MORNING MEAL AND WASHED UP, PIX and I packed up our things and made ready to go. The horses had already been brought out and the saddlebags repacked. Narcissus led us back outside. There, I found Cai and the others waiting.

Two Roman soldiers appeared, returning our weapons to us.

Aulus joined me, taking my spear from a servant and handing it to me. "It's a weighty weapon. Weapons from Britannia are prized in Rome and sell for a heavy stack of gold. Even a simple dagger can cost a fortune."

I was well aware that eyes were on me, and I would not shame myself by flirting with the Roman before my men. There were many things I wanted to say, but none that could be spoken in such company. "Thank you for your hospitality, Aulus. I enjoyed the dinner and your wine. I think the taste will linger with me for a long time."

He inclined his head to me. "Safe travels back to…Iceni territory."

"Iceni territory."

He turned, looking briefly toward his men. "We, too, are about to set off."

I lowered my voice. "He will have many warriors with him. They will look the part of farmers. You need more men."

Aulus grinned. "Very well, General Boudica, I will keep that in mind."

I chuckled lightly, then exhaled deeply. "I wish you luck."

"And I wish you safe travels."

With that, I went to Druda and mounted.

"Open the gates," a soldier called.

I gave Aulus a wave, then motioned for the others to follow. With that, we rode out...away from the Catuvellauni stronghold and from the dream of a beautiful life that was never meant to be.

CHAPTER 82

Т he ride back to Oak Throne left me feeling on edge. Part of me felt guilty for throwing Caratacus's wife and child in the way of Rome to end the war. But on the other hand, how many other wives and children would be spared if we could do just that?

When we camped that night, I dipped into my saddlebag to find several surprises: a jar of deep purple olives, honey, herbed bread, a sack of figs, and a single bottle of wine.

I felt torn for a long moment, then took the olives, honey, and bread to the men gathered at the fire. I left the wine and figs where they were.

I passed around the goods, letting Cai and the others try the olives.

"They grow on trees?" Cai asked, chewing as he considered.

I nodded.

"They have a good taste," Divin said, taking another. "Here," he added, handing the jar to the others.

"Better than the porridge they gave us," Aterie said with a laugh.

"Don't complain. You have a fine cook at home to feed you," Cai told Aterie.

"A fine cook?" I asked.

"Finola came from Holk Fort," Aterie told me. "We wed a month back."

"My congratulations. I will share the news with Vian."

Aterie smiled. "Thank you, Queen Boudica."

I sat with my hunk of bread, using my knife to spread honey across it as I stared into the fire. I ate slowly, letting the taste of the honey linger in my mouth.

"Did your meeting... Everything go all right, Boudica?" Cai asked.

Forcing a smile, I said, "Everything I do, I do for the good of our people, to keep the Iceni—Northern and Greater—safe. I hope I succeeded in that task."

Cai nodded. "No doubt you did. No one is more insistent and stubborn than you."

I chuckled. "I will take that as a compliment."

"As intended. As intended."

We slept in the forest that night and made our way back to Oak Throne in the morning. It was just before dusk when we rode through the fort's gates.

Bran and Bec greeted us before the roundhouse, Bec holding Sorcha. I slipped off my horse, grabbed my bag, and went to my daughter.

"Aye, sweet girl, come here, you," I said, taking Sorcha from Bec.

Sorcha squealed with delight, hugging me tightly.

"Caturix?" I asked Bran.

"He spoke to Dôn then departed for Stonea."

I nodded.

"Come inside, Boudica," Bec said. "You look tired." Bec turned to the men. "All of you are welcome within. Come for ale and meat."

Carrying Sorcha, I headed inside with the others.

Pix took my things while I made my way to the dining hall.

Cidna chatted lightly to the men as she placed a platter of simple bread rounds and roasted lamb on the table. The scent of it turned my stomach.

I turned my attention instead to Sorcha. "Did you have fun while I was away? Did you play with Bellicus?"

"Bell-ee!"

I smiled at her. "Yes, Bell-ee."

She pointed to the back to the bedchambers.

"Has Bellicus gone to bed?"

"Bell-ee!"

I chuckled, smoothed her hair, and then kissed her cheek.

Bec settled in beside me. She pushed a curl behind Sorcha's ear. "She was a very good girl for us. She and Bellicus wore all of us exhausted."

"Did you, sweet Sorcha?"

"Do you want anything to eat?" Bec asked, turning toward the table.

I shook my head.

"Maybe something else? A soup or..." she said, then lowered her voice. "*I can fix you something.*"

I chuckled, then shook my head. "No, I'm just tired. It was an exhausting series of events."

"Of that, I have no doubt. Did all go well?"

"I think so."

"Good."

Riona appeared a moment later. "Boudica, I set out a sleeping gown for you and prepared a bath. All I could do to keep that wild woman of yours from crawling into it. Don't blame me if you find her there. Now, Princess, come to Riona so your mother can rest a moment."

"I..." I began in protest.

"Go ahead, Boudica. We'll see to Sorcha," Bec reassured me.

Rising, I turned to the men. "Thank you all. Thank you for coming with me," I told them. "Good night," I said, then headed to the back.

When I arrived in my chamber, I found my bag sitting on the foot of my bed, my clothes laid out. Riona had filled the washing basin. Despite her warning, Pix was not there. I undressed, slipping into the water. I cleaned my body, washed my hair, and then sat in the water, feeling it chill as time passed.

My hand moved to my belly.

Was Pix right? Was it possible I was with child again? It could be. More than a month had passed, and my moon-blood had not come.

But even that possibility was not what played at the forefront of my mind.

Closing my eyes, I inhaled deeply and then slid under the surface. Comforted by the silence, I held onto the moment and remembered.

The feel of his breath on my skin.

His hand on my breast.

The sensation of his manhood pressed against me.

How my hips nestled so perfectly against his.

When I exhaled, I would let it go.

I would let it all go.

I was the wife of Prasutagus, and I loved my husband.

I would leave it all behind me, let the water take it from me, and think on it no more.

Great Mother.

Lady Epona.

Dark Lady Andraste.

Help me forget.

I stayed underneath until my lungs burned, the image of that sunny villa so far away fading as my body screamed for air.

And then, with a gasp, I broke the water's surface. I rose, grabbed a drying cloth, then stepped out of the water and did not look back.

THE FOLLOWING DAY, PIX AND I MADE READY TO DEPART. THE men from Venta yoked the wagon once more, then we prepared to set off.

Bec pulled me into an embrace, then kissed Sorcha on the cheek.

"I will see you soon, sweet girl," Bec told her.

Sorcha merely giggled.

Bran, who was holding Bellicus, reached for my hand. "Be safe, Boudica. And do not keep us in the dark. Caturix still thinks of me as a child. He tells me what *he thinks* I need to know, and we don't see things the same. I would not have the Romans march on me for my brother's choices."

"I understand," I told him. Without saying as much, Bran judged Caturix's choices as king and found him lacking. Bran would never lift a hand against my brother, but for all Bran's wild ways, he somehow saw things better than Caturix. And for that, I was glad for my people.

Bran walked with me when I went to mount Druda.

"Boudica, did all go well with the governor? When you returned, you looked...distraught."

"Everything is fine. It went well."

"Are you certain?" Bran asked, studying my face.

I had forgotten how well Bran saw through me.

"I think I'm pregnant again," I told my brother in a whisper. "I was, truly, tired."

At that, Bran smiled. "Then it is good news."

"It is early days yet."

Bran nodded. "I will pray to the Mother."

"Thank you, Brother," I said, then handed Sorcha to

him so I could mount. Once I was settled, he handed the girl up to me.

"Winter will soon be upon us. Stay safe and warm," Bran told me.

"And you." I turned back to the others who had gathered. "Be well, friends."

Riona, Cidna, Balfor, and the others came to wave goodbye.

With that, we made our way from the fort. As we passed the lane leading to Ula's house, I looked but did not see her. As we passed through the market, Eiwyn, Birgit, Phelan, and the other children appeared.

"Boudica," Birgit called breathlessly.

Grinning at them, I slipped my hand into my bag and pulled out a small sack, which I tossed to her.

The other children gathered around her as she opened the satchel. From inside, she pulled out a dry fig.

"What is it?" she asked.

I chuckled. "A fig. You eat it."

"Where did it come from?"

"Rome."

"Is it poisoned?"

"I hope not. It was a gift to me."

At that, they laughed, then tried the fruit.

"It's faerie food!" Birgit called.

"A fey feast!" Phelan agreed.

"Let's go show the others," Eiwyn called, then the children ran off.

"Thank you, Boudica!" they called in unison, then disappeared.

As we crossed over the bridge, I looked downriver.

To my surprise, I saw the washer there.

She sat, the tips of her long, golden hair trailing into the water. The bottom of her dress was lost beneath the waves. She wailed, her sorrowful sound sending a shiver down my spine, then went back to washing once more.

I turned, looking behind me at Pix to see if she had seen her too, but Pix was busy chewing on an apple and talking to her horse.

I paused a moment, letting the others pass, then watched.

The washer sang in her foreign tongue, washing blood from the clothes in her hands. I trembled, feeling like all my blood had left me.

The washer lifted her gaze and looked directly at me.

"Masterwort," I whispered, then dipped into my pocket to see if I had anything on me, but Sorcha spoke up.

"Dat. Dat!" She pointed toward the river.

I followed her gaze. She was looking at the washer.

"You see her too?"

"Dat!"

"Miserable fey. No one wants to hear you."

In my satchel, I had a small packet of herbs. Within, I found a bundle of Masterwort. Breaking off the tiniest of pieces, I stuck one into Sorcha's mouth and another in my own.

"Gack," Sorcha said, spitting it out.

Cringing at the bitter taste, tears coming to my eyes, I forced myself to swallow.

When I looked back, the woman and her blood-stained clothes were gone.

I had tried not to look but had seen all the same.

It had been a man's clothing she had washed.

The last time I had seen her, Gaheris had died.

Steeling my heart, I reached into my bag once more and pulled out the bottle of wine. Pulling out the cork, I turned the bottle upside down and emptied its contents onto the ground. When it was done, I tossed the bottle into the river, where it disappeared below the dark waves, then clicked to Druda.

It was time to go home.

CHAPTER 83

When we arrived in Venta, we were greeted by waves and smiles. The sight of it warmed my heart. Beyond our borders, war ravaged the land. But here, we were safe. Here, we were thriving. We rode through the city to the king's compound.

Brita, Artur, and Galvyn exited the roundhouse to meet us.

Pix had carried Sorcha on the last leg of the ride. She sat sleeping, pressed against Pix.

Galvyn came to me, Brita and Artur going to help Pix.

"Queen Boudica, welcome home," Galvyn told me.

"Thank you, Galvyn," I said as I dismounted.

"The king is in the fields. I sent a boy to fetch him."

"Thank you."

"Lady Dindraine and the others safely delivered?"

"To Andraste's hands."

"May she rest safely there," Galvyn said with a nod.

"Ansgar set off while you were gone. He took a small party of warriors with him."

I exhaled deeply. "May the gods keep him safe."

When I dismounted, Galvyn and I joined Pix. Brita was holding Sorcha.

"You'd best go on to the stables, Pix. That mare of yours has been ready to foal since yesterday. She won't let anyone near her save Artur, whom she let take her some grain and water. She tries to kick or bite everyone else," Galvyn told her.

"Ye hear that, Druda? Yer offspring be coming," Pix said, taking the horse's reins and heading off.

Artur and Brita joined me. I held out my arm to the boy, pulling him close to me.

"All well?" I asked him.

He nodded.

"Brita?"

"We are well here, Queen Boudica, only anxious for your return. Vian has been keeping Prasutagus distracted digging ditches," she said with a chuckle, "leaving the rest of us to assuage our own worries."

"Well, we are here now. And I have no interest in going anywhere unless the gods call me."

"Which they seem to do far too often, my queen. Come inside. You are home now."

We made our way back into the roundhouse, and while Oak Throne still felt like home, Venta represented my new life, one I shared with my husband and daughter—and perhaps, another child soon.

The truth was, I was shaken by what had happened at

Verulam. I felt like a part of myself I didn't know or didn't understand lay sleeping inside me. Whoever that Boudica was, she was dangerous. She could ruin everything. I didn't trust her. But I had left her behind, thrown away with the wash water, never to be thought of again.

I took Sorcha from Brita's arms and went to mine and Prasutagus's chamber. I lay the sleeping child down in the bed. Moving as quietly as possible, I removed my riding clothes and washed up. When I was done, I went to redress. Opening my trunk, I remembered that my purple gown and a few others were gone, given to the priestesses.

Fingering through my things, I pulled out a dark blue frock, trimmed with yellow and red flowers on the hem. I ran a comb through my wild hair. I was home. I was back with my husband. Nothing could touch me here.

Slipping from the room, I went back to the main hall.

Everything was quiet.

Only Nella remained. She was tidying up.

"Queen Boudica," she said, curtseying to me. "Welcome home."

"Thank you, Nella."

"Everyone has gone to see about that mare. Artur has been living in the stables since yesterday."

I chuckled. "It is an exciting time, but I am weary of excitement. Let them have it."

At that, Nella chuckled lightly.

From outside, I heard the sound of horses, and one of the stable hands called, "King Prasutagus."

Feeling like the sun had warmed me from within, I turned and made my way outside. There, I spotted a very grubby Prasutagus. He wore a pair of buckskin trousers and a white tunic, the laces undone at the top. He'd pulled his long, red hair back from the temples into a small knot at the back of his head.

He smiled the moment he saw me, then dismounted quickly, crossing the square to take me in his arms.

"Boudica," he whispered, pressing me against him. "Thank the Mother you are back. I dreamed…I dreamed you were in Verulam," he whispered.

My stomach quaked a moment, then I said, "I was."

He paused and pulled back to look at me, his gaze meeting mine. He studied my face for a long moment, then pulled me close once more. "But you are here now. You are here with me. *My* wife. *My* love." What had Prasutagus seen? Had the gods warned him? Why? But then, the truth dawned on me. Just as Aulus and I were tied, so were Prasutagus and I. And if that was so, this would not have been the first life where these two men would find themselves at odds with one another when it came to me. Prasutagus was as tied to Aulus as me.

"I am here, and I will *always* be at your side."

"Boudica," he whispered, kissing the top of my head. "My queen. Welcome home."

CHAPTER 84

That night, as we lay in bed, I shared with Prasutagus what Caturix had told me and why I had gone to Verulam, including the news that I had given away Caratacus's hiding spot.

"You are right," Prasutagus told me, pulling me close to him. "If they have Caratacus, there is no excuse for war."

"And if they continue their expansion, it's all been a lie."

"I don't like this news that they know of Mona."

"I saw the governor's maps. They don't yet know of Avallach. But I extracted the governor's word. There will be no more affronts to our holy people."

"Do you think he will keep his promise this time?"

I paused. "Yes."

For a long time, Prasutagus said nothing, then pulled me close, kissing my shoulder.

Wanting to break the tension, I said, "I have other, far more interesting news."

"I can feel you smiling in the darkness."

"Can you guess why?"

"With you, my May Queen, there is no telling."

I slipped his hand to my stomach. "It is not certain, but..."

"A child? You're with child?"

I rolled over and smiled at him. In the dim light of our bedchamber, lit only by a small brazier, I found Prasutagus smiling down at me.

"My courses are uncertain since Sorcha is still weaning, but..."

"Any illness? Dizziness as before?"

I shook my head. "Not yet. Everything just tastes strange."

Prasutagus stroked my cheek. "Sweet wife, in the middle of all this chaos, what joy you have brought me." He planted a kiss on my lips, and then another, and another, and another. Soon, those kisses grew hungrier, more wanting. My hands roved over Prasutagus's body. I pulled his tunic off, touching and kissing him, the taste of his salty skin on my lips. I inhaled deeply of his scent, my head spinning.

I loved Prasutagus.

Gaheris may have been my first love, and some echo of love lingered for Aulus, but my heart beat for Prasutagus. I felt whole in his arms.

King and queen.

Earth and sky.

We were twin spirits, two dancing flames who would love one another forever.

And ever.

And ever.

In the weeks after my return to Venta, the first snow fell, and with it, everything grew silent. Nightshade gave birth to a healthy young colt who was a dapple like his father, but his coat was darker like his mother. Along with their young one, the child growing in my belly soon made itself more well known by causing me to vomit at least half a dozen times a day, no matter what I ate.

"Sweet Sorcha was easy on you, Queen Boudica," Betha told me, setting a pot of chicken broth before me. "I swear, I couldn't get a bite in me for six months when I carried Ronat. I always say she took out her mischief in the womb so she could come out a sweet daughter. Never had trouble with Ronat. Always been a good girl. Perhaps it will be the same for you."

I groaned. "I certainly hope so," I said, leaning over the pot to smell the broth. While my stomach was growling hungrily, the scent of the soup sent a wave of nausea through me.

"By the Mother, how pale even the smell makes you," Ronat said, her hands on her hips as she considered.

Frowning, Pix rose and started pulling on her cloak.

"Where are you going?"

"Into Venta. I will go see that midwife. Last time ye were with child, Ula gave you herbs that helped. Maybe they have the same."

"But it's snowing."

"Aye, and it will keep snowing for the next few months. Doesn't change the fact that ye need it," Pix said as she eyed the broth. "Give her something sweet," she told Betha.

"But all she eats is sweet. We must get something else into her."

"Better than nothing," Pix replied.

"Let me see if I have anything left, Boudica," Betha said, then headed into the kitchens.

Pix patted me on the shoulder, making my stomach wave, then headed out.

I sighed heavily, setting my hands on my stomach. "Sweet one, whatever you are plotting in there, go easy on your poor mother. And if you have this much mischief in you, try giving it out a little at a time," I said with a laugh, then leaned over the pot once more.

My stomach revolted the moment I inhaled, sending me running for a bucket.

It was going to be a very long winter.

BY THE TIME WE REACHED SORCHA'S FIRST BIRTHDAY, HER little sibling had stopped tormenting me. The teas Rue and Ariadne sent had helped. I was glad when my stomach settled enough for me to eat once more.

News was slow coming as winter carried on. But for once, it was a relief. Part of me didn't want to know what was happening beyond our borders. I didn't want to know Caratacus's fate. I didn't want to know what tribes had rallied or fallen. I didn't want to hear what the Coritani had decided. I didn't want any of it.

Prasutagus, too, seemed glad of the quiet.

He and Vian spent much time poring over designs and drawing in his workroom as he planned for the spring.

"We should talk to a Roman builder," Vian told Prasutagus. "Perhaps we can send someone to Camulodunum. There are tricks in their designs I cannot see," Vian said as she marked, erased, marked, and erased one sketch over and over again. "I have an idea to improve the water catchment system the Romans use, but I will need to test it...once the rain falls again."

Prasutagus, who'd been looking over his own work, nodded. "I will go to Londinium in the spring to work on the construction of our warehouse and market stall. I'm sure I can find someone there."

Sighing, Vian sat back, then rubbed her eyes. "I need air."

"Pix is with Artur and Sorcha outside."

Vian nodded, then rose. "I'll join them. Do you need anything, Queen Boudica?"

"Honey. Peaches. Cherries. Blackberries. Olives..."

Vian laughed. "Mutton for supper it is."

I groaned.

With a laugh, Vian departed.

Prasutagus set his work aside and came and sat beside me. He pushed a stray hair behind my ear. "You look tired."

"I *am* tired, and it is not yet midday."

"Rest, Boudica. This child takes much from you. Why don't you get some sleep?"

I chuckled. "I've done nothing all day," I said, setting aside my sewing.

"Well," Prasutagus said with a grin. "I never took you for the weaving type."

"Nor am I. Look," I said, showing him the deranged-looking kitten I had sewn on a frock for Sorcha.

"It's a good likeness of a donkey."

"It's a kitten!"

At that, we both laughed.

"All right," I said, rising, my back aching when I did. "I'll sleep. But wake me for the midday meal. I don't want to miss my mutton."

Prasutagus set a kiss on my cheek, then I headed off, my back and feet aching. I would be very glad when the weather broke and this child came.

Great Mother Goddess, get me to that day.

CHAPTER 85

With the end of winter came the beginning of news. The first came in the form of Madogh, who arrived one night in early spring looking cold, exhausted, and nursing a shoulder wound.

"Arrow, Queen Boudica, caught as I was making my way out of Catuvellauni territory," he said. "I stopped at King's Wood on my way here, and the priestesses saw to it."

"Roman or Catuvellauni?" I asked.

"Catuvellauni. They are all stirred up."

"What's happened?" Prasutagus asked as he poured the man a cup of strong spirits.

Madogh sipped the brew. "Tastes of anise."

Prasutagus nodded. "One of our people in Venta started brewing it last summer."

"It's good," Madogh said. "The Romans surprised Caratacus. They discovered his whereabouts somehow.

They swept into the village where he was hiding during the night."

"Do they have him?" I asked.

Madogh shook his head. "The king slipped away. Left his wife and young child behind so he could save his own throat."

"He escaped?" I asked, sitting down.

I failed.

The plan has failed.

Madogh nodded. "They went after him but met resistance in Silures territory. Many Romans were killed."

"The governor?" I asked, trying to hide the tremor of emotion in my voice.

Madogh shook his head. "No. He's fine. But Governor Plautius has Caratacus's family. Word is he will send them to Rome. If Caratacus cares anything about his wife and child, things will shift soon."

"*If* he cares anything for them," I said, "which I doubt. What news of the Romans? Are they preparing to go after him?"

Madogh sipped once more, then set his cup down. "The answer to that is why I dragged myself across half-frozen rivers and muddy fields to get here. Word reached the Romans that the Coritani were amassing. Governor Plautius was preparing to go north. Legate Vespasian is pressing across the southwest."

"North," I whispered.

"And Caratacus?" Prasutagus asked.

"A man I traded a lot of money with says he's on the

Catuvellauni's border with the Coritani, if not in Coritani lands themselves. The governor has his own people hunting Caratacus. Roman gold is flowing, buying bounty hunters everywhere."

"The Coritani," I said, looking to Prasutagus.

"News of King Caturix? Are the Romans advancing on the Northern Iceni?" Prasutagus asked.

Madogh paused. "There were whispers that the queen's brother is complicit, but there has been no movement in Stonea."

"I need to get word to Caturix. If Volisios warped his mind, he would drag the Northern Iceni into war. Banshees be cursed!"

"Anything else?" Prasutagus asked.

"Cogidubnus's Regnenses wife is with child. The Atrebates annexed most of the southern Catuvellauni lands. In late winter, they sent many, many Catuvellauni slaves to Gaul."

"And Broc? Has he had any luck finding Princess Imogen?" Prasutagus asked.

I turned to my husband, surprised by the question.

"He is due to return from Gaul later this month," Madogh said. "I will travel to Londinium to meet him. I hope to discover some news there."

Prasutagus nodded. "Thank you, Madogh. Let me call Galvyn so you can take your rest," he said, gesturing for the man to follow him.

They left the room, Prasutagus returning a few moments later.

"Princess Imogen?" I asked.

"I tasked Broc to try to locate her and free or purchase her if he can. I hoped I could have her taken to Mona."

"Then you have already done more for her than her brother."

"She is an innocent in this mess."

"The Coritani… What if Caturix fell prey to Coritani maneuvering?"

"It's not possible to pass through the fens yet. There will be too much flooding in the bogs."

"I could send Pix…the old way."

"If she will go, send her," he said, then sighed. "War does not wait upon summer. They are marching," Prasutagus said, then sighed heavily. "And here, I was dreaming of crops of sunflowers and new babies," he said, setting his hand on my round stomach.

"I like your vision of the world much more than theirs."

"May we stay at peace long enough for it to become a reality."

But Prasutagus's dream was not to be.

Spring passed into summer, and with it came dire news.

Pix left us in the spring before the thaw. Despite seeking word of her everywhere, no one had seen her. It was past Midsummer, on the day that I felt the first pangs of labor, that she finally returned. She stumbled into the king's compound, looking sick from hunger and thirst.

"Queen Boudica, come quickly," Galvyn had called.

"Pix," I said, rushing to her. "Pix, what happened to you?"

"Me? Look at ye. Ye be as big as a flea that has feasted on flesh."

"Of course I am. It's past Midsummer. Where have you been?"

"Past Midsummer?"

I nodded.

"Aye, it's the way of it. I tried to hurry, but the old way is confusing. By the time I got to Stonea..." she began, then looked toward Galvyn.

"I will go fetch the king," Galvyn said, then disappeared.

The two of us walked slowly, making our way inside.

"By the time you got to Stonea..." I said, gesturing for her to continue.

"By the time I got there, it was too late to warn King Caturix. He had gone, taking the Fen folk north with him."

"Banshees be cursed. What is he thinking? Melusine?"

"I warned her war would be upon her if the Romans discovered Caturix had turned on them. She swore he went in secret and had not raised the Northern Iceni banner."

"Why did it take you so long to get back?"

"The way through the stones is confusing, Boudica. I was...lost for a time."

"Let's get you inside. You look half-starved."

"Ne'er eat nor drink faerie foods. I did not—this time—but I am the worse for it."

Pix and I went inside. I ignored the ache in my lower back and the pressure on my groin. Of all the times to have a confluence of events, why now?

I sent Newt running to the kitchens to fetch food for Pix, sitting her down in a comfortable chair.

"Artur, Sorcha…" Pix asked.

"Both well. Artur has worried for you. We all have. They will be back soon, I am sure. Brita has taken them to see some baby lambs," I said, then winced.

"Ye look near upon it."

"Your arrival is certainly a portent," I replied, pressing my fists into my back.

Prasutagus opened the door. "Pix," he said, a worried expression on his face. "Are you hurt? What happened?"

"I'm intact, Strawberry King, merely lost in the mists for a time. I took the old way. Ye know how that be."

Prasutagus nodded.

"Caturix has gone, took the fighters of the Fen folk north with him," I told my husband.

"By Cernunnos's horns," Prasutagus swore.

"He didn't raise the banner calling all the Northern Iceni warriors," I added.

"That will not matter to Rome. We must get word to Bran. Bran must not rise, no matter what happens. That is the only thing that will protect them. He must show himself in defiance of his brother. Boudica, there was word this morning of fighting on the borders of the Coritani and Cornovii lands. The governor has engaged them there."

"We must send someone north to Bran at once. I can do nothing to save Caturix from his stubborn ignorance... but Oak Throne. Bran must reach out to the druids at Holk Fort. They, too, must make ready to reject Caturix's call to war—if it comes."

"It will come," Prasutagus said darkly. "Rome will creep across the land until the cattails burn like torches amongst the fens."

Pix and I both stared at Prasutagus.

After a moment, he shook himself from his vision. "I'll go to Bran myself, but Boudica..."

"This child will come whether you are here or not. Go, Prasutagus. Oak Throne is my home. The Grove of Andraste, Frog's Hollow, Holk Fort...they must be protected." Tears came to my eyes, and I couldn't tell if it was from the birthing pains, the frustration with Caturix, or my fear for my people.

"Dammit," Prasutagus said, then came to me, setting a kiss on my lips, then turned and rushed from the room.

Feeling ill, I sat.

"Yer Roman will not be able to spare Caturix if he discovers him in battle. Caturix will not give him a choice, no matter how much the Roman may want to spare ye from the pain."

I looked into the fire. "Caturix has chosen his fate. Now, I can only think of those who will be harmed in his wake...including Melusine," I said, then grunted with pain.

"Boudica," Pix said.

Newt returned a moment later with a large tray, Betha and Ronat following behind him.

"Pix," Ronat called, rushing to her and giving her a hug. When Ronat let her go, Betha embraced her as well.

"You're skin and bones," Ronat chided her.

"Then ye best get another platter ready because I be ready to eat."

Ronat laughed, then looked at me. "Boudica, you look white."

"I...Ronat, can you go to the village for me?"

"Boudica?"

"Send for Ariadne. Don't let Prasutagus know where you have gone."

"Where is the king going? I just made a bag for him," Betha said, confused.

"North," I said.

"But your child is coming," Betha said.

I waved my hand. "There are more important matters now. Pix, you eat. I'm going to go..." I said, then gestured to my bedchamber.

"Go on. Quickly," Betha told her daughter, then Ronat rushed off.

"Queen Boudica, I am right behind you," Betha told me.

With that, I made my way to my bedchamber, where my laying in would soon begin.

As I sat down on my bed, kicking off my slippers, I swore to the gods.

Dark Lady Andraste.

Hear my prayers.
Protect Caturix.
And deliver Caratacus to the Romans.
If you cannot, deliver him to me.
I will end what he has started.

CHAPTER 86

As I lay down in bed, I heard Raven's hooves kick up in the square outside, the others following behind Prasutagus as he rode north to Bran.

Why, Caturix? Why?

My father had been right. Caturix was always too eager to follow the word of men he perceived as wiser or stronger than himself.

I had hoped to make him see that Prasutagus was the one to follow.

More, I had hoped he would learn to follow his own heart.

Be he hadn't.

Volisios was Melusine's father. He had a rope around Caturix's neck. In agreeing to wed a woman he didn't care about and forsaking the one he did love, Caturix's weakness had led him into this mess in the first place.

Aulus would spare Bran as long as Bran did not rise.

Aulus would spare Bran for me.

But Caturix...

I winced hard, setting my hand on my stomach.

"Oh, dear one... Why now?"

Ariadne arrived shortly after Prasutagus departed.

"The child's time is upon you, Queen Boudica. All we can do now is wait. I will prepare some herbs to make the birthing easier. Priestess Rue is here with me. May she help?" Ariadne told me after she had examined me.

"Yes, of course."

Ariadne went to the door and let Rue in.

I was glad to see the priestess. She was dressed as a commoner now, but the ancient markings on her forehead gave away the fact she had once lived a life of a holy person.

"Queen Boudica. It is good to see you again," she told me.

"Rue. Are you well?"

She nodded. "I have settled into Venta. It is my home now. If it is acceptable to you, I will aid Ariadne. I am apprenticing to become a midwife."

"Apprentice is not exactly the right term. You know herbcraft far better than me," Ariadne told her.

"Good for visions. Not great for laboring women. That said, I *do* have herbs I can burn to help the child's passing," Rue told me.

I nodded. "Very well," I said, in too much pain to say more.

The passage of time began to slow. At one point, I heard Artur outside the door, but the women did not let him in. Others drifted in and out of the room, including Brita, Ronat, Betha, Vian, and Nella.

I also heard Sorcha, who sparked a tantrum in response to not being allowed inside.

"Try to rest," Rue said, setting a gentle hand on my forehead. "Sleep, if you can. The child is slow to come. It will be a long night."

I floated in and out of sleep, the pain wracking me. Ariadne checked my progress throughout the night, but still, my body did not ready itself for birth.

I heard Pix in the room at one point. Her voice sounded alarmed.

"But it should be done? What's wrong?"

I heard Ariadne answer her, but her tone was too low for me to hear.

When Rue and Pix exited the bedchamber, I caught the expression on Pix's face. Something wasn't right.

"Pix," I said weakly.

"I will be right outside the door, Boudica. I'm not far from ye."

The labor went on and on. But the pain felt different this time. It was an odd pinching pain, unlike what I had experienced with Sorcha. Something wasn't right. I was sorry I had let Prasutagus go.

The two women talked in hushed tones, and I could hear the worry in Ariadne's voice.

"What is it?" I asked as I writhed in pain on the bed. "Tell me the truth. What's wrong?"

Ariadne came to me. "Your child is too slow to come, Queen Boudica. Your body is not making way. I can give you a draught that will help, but it will be painful. Very painful."

"And if I don't take it?"

Ariadne inhaled deeply, then exhaled slowly. "If not, then many times, both mother and child die. The draught is the last recourse."

"I trust you," I whispered to her.

I lay, wincing in agony, as the women prepared the drink. Shortly thereafter, they brought it to me, Rue helping me sit up to help me drink.

"It will taste very bad," Ariadne told me. "But drink it all."

I nodded, then took the cup. Forcing myself to swallow, I finished it. The taste reminded me of brews Ula had given me before, with sharp flavors of herbs and mushrooms. I suppressed the urge to vomit. A few moments later, I began feeling dizzy.

"Ariadne?"

"Lie back, Boudica, and make ready to push," Ariadne told me, then turned to Rue. "Keep close to her. Watch her. Once the child is out, give her the second draft."

I felt a massive urge to push.

The pain was like nothing I'd ever felt before.

I screamed.

"Almost time, Boudica. Almost there," Ariadne told me.

My heart was racing, and I heard ringing in my ears.

Black dots swam before my eyes.

"Gaheris," I whispered, swearing I saw him standing at my bedside.

Time felt like it had slowed to a stop. My back cramped, arching hard.

"Now, Boudica. On the count of three, push. One, two, three..." Ariadne called.

I pushed hard, feeling like my spirit was coming loose from my body.

"Again!"

I pushed again.

We repeated the process over and over again.

"One last time. Now," Ariadne called.

I pushed hard.

"There! There you are. Come on, little one. Come on. Rue, give her the tonic. Now."

"Queen Boudica," Rue said. "Gulp this down. We must stem the flow of blood. Now," she said, setting a drink to my lips.

I drank the bitter brew, then collapsed backward.

Ariadne gasped.

Rue left me, joining her. "By the Mother," the priestess whispered.

"Quickly. My knife," Ariadne said.

The women worked fast. At what, I couldn't see.

I listened, waiting for a cry, but heard nothing.

"What is it?" I asked, tears slipping down my cheeks. "What's happening? Is my baby dead?"

No one answered.

"Is my baby dead?" I screamed at them.

"There we go. There we go. Come, little one," Ariadne said.

And a moment later, I heard a shrill cry.

"It is a little girl, Queen Boudica," Ariadne said. "She was born with a caul. We have her free now. May the Mother be praised, she is well."

"May the Mother be praised," Rue said, then took my hand. "She was born in a bubble. What a special child she will be."

"What is the new princess's name?" Ariadne asked me.

"Olwen," I whispered. "Olwen. Like the maiden who outsmarted the giant."

CHAPTER 87

T he next several days passed in a blur of sleep and caring for Olwen.

"Being born with a caul is a strong sign from the gods," Rue told me. "The Great Mother wraps the child in a veil so she may grow eyes to see the Otherworld. Olwen will be a child of the greenwood."

"Is that so, little one?" I asked the baby, gently stroking her cheek.

Sorcha sat on the side of my bed, singing songs for her sister and me.

The birth had taken much from me. I was unable to rise without assistance. Ariadne warned me that I might not easily conceive again after such a difficult birth.

"The tonic I gave you is a shock to the woman's system. It will force the labor, but can sometimes come at a cost. Many women do not conceive again," she warned me.

"I have two beautiful daughters," I said. "The Mother has already blessed me twice. I would not ask for more."

Ariadne smiled gently at my girls. "Indeed, they are a blessing. The future queen of the Greater Iceni and her noble sister. Born with a veil, she will be destined for Mona."

I smiled. "I will have to put a lyre in her hands and see if she shares my sister's skill in music."

Ariadne smiled.

There was a commotion in the hallway, and a moment later, the door opened, revealing Prasutagus.

"Late again," he said, smiling at me.

"Da-da. Look. Dat," Sorcha said, pointing to Olwen.

"Olwen or Antedios?" Prasutagus asked.

"Olwen," I said with a smile.

Prasutagus came to my bedside, lowering himself to his knees. "Another princess. Hello, sweet Olwen."

"Your daughter was born with a veil, King Prasutagus," Ariadne told him. "The gods have blessed her."

"Such blessings are welcome in times like these," Prasutagus replied, meeting my gaze. "May the Great Mother be praised. Both of you are well?"

"It was not an easy birth," Ariadne told him.

"This one did not want to leave her safe cocoon," I said, stroking Olwen's cheek.

Prasutagus's brows knitted with worry. "Are you... Are you all right now?"

I nodded. "I will need some rest."

"Let us leave the king with his wife," Ariadne said. "We will be nearby, Boudica."

With that, the midwife and priestess departed.

Prasutagus picked Sorcha up, playing with the small bows Brita had affixed in her hair.

"No, Da-da," Sorcha scolded him.

Prasutagus chuckled, then took his hand away. "I'm sorry, my princess," he said, then sat down beside me, setting Sorcha on his knee. "Boudica, *are* you well?" he asked, a nervous tremor in his voice.

"The child would not come. Ariadne had to resort to harder measures. There is a chance I will not be able to have more children," I said, my voice catching. While I had meant what I had said, that I was blessed as it was, the news was still hard to share.

"No matter," Prasutagus said, shaking his head. "No matter. As long as you are both well," he said, leaning over to kiss me on the forehead, then kissing Olwen and planting another on Sorcha's face. "My girls."

I smiled, but the beauty of the moment faded as my thoughts turned north. "Bran?"

"Caturix has told him nothing. But Bran is good at talking. He's learned from traders that Aulus has split his army, half going to chase Caratacus, the other half into Coritani lands where they are burning villages and taking hostages."

I swallowed hard.

"Bran is far wiser than Caturix gives him credit for. He hates to see echoes of the conflict between your father and uncle in himself and Caturix, but he will not rise, no matter what Caturix says. He will ride to Holk Fort and speak to the druids."

I nodded. "I cannot help Caturix now. I can only pray to Taranis that he is successful in his efforts. May the gods go with him."

PRASUTAGUS AND I SPENT THE ENTIRE SUMMER WAITING WITH bated breath for news that never came. Fall passed, and finally, we heard word. King Dumnocoveros, the western-most king of the Coritani, had been defeated. His fort had fallen to the Romans. But still, no news came of Caturix and the Northern Iceni.

As Aulus took over the tribal lands, he disarmed the Coritani people. There were stories of weapons being confiscated from homes and markets. King Dumnocoveros had been taken in chains and sent back to Rome.

As fall came once more, things grew quiet.

I heard nothing.

Not from Aulus.

Not from Caturix.

The only news came from Bran, sharing that all was well in Oak Throne, and that Bec was with child once more.

When winter came, we settled in and braced ourselves for the long, dark days. The Greater Iceni had managed to stay free of conflict, focusing instead on expanding our harbors, establishing ourselves in Londinium, and build-ing, making, and growing. Prasutagus's dreams of sunflower fields had come to fruition. And we spent the year in silence, raising our girls as war raged around us.

The dark days of winter passed in silence.

But in the spring that followed, news began to bubble up from everywhere.

Soldiers were arriving from Gaul. Massive ships filled with men landed to the south in Regnenses territory and in Camulodunum. Prasutagus had gone to Londinium, where word spread like wildfire that Aulus had Caratacus on the run, cornering him in Silures territory. Given the massive number of men at his disposal, it had become increasingly clear that the emperor wanted Caratacus captured.

But that was not to be.

The year passed in war.

And still, I heard nothing from Caturix.

IN THE SPRING OF 47 CE, HOWEVER, EVERYTHING CHANGED.

I walked with Sorcha, Olwen, and Artur from the roundhouse to the stables when I heard a call from the gate.

"Riders! Riders approaching. Rome," the watchman called.

I turned to Artur. "Send a rider. Fetch Prasutagus."

Prasutagus had gone for the day to King's Wood. Henwyn had grown ill with fever, and the druids feared her end was coming. Soon, they would have to select a new leader. Prasutagus had wanted to tell the old woman farewell and speak to the druids about the plans for their future.

Artur, now a muscular young teen molded by Pix's hard training, nodded. "I will go myself," he said, then made his way to the stables.

Olwen whimpered when the gates opened.

I picked her up. "It's all right," I said, comforting the girl.

"Don't worry," Sorcha told her in a childlike but bold voice. "I have my dagger," she said, wielding the wooden weapon Pix had carved for her. "I will stab those Romans if they get too close."

"Sorcha," I said. "The Romans are our friends."

I stood waiting, watching.

When Aulus rode through the gates, my heart fluttered, and I felt heat rise up in my cheeks. I willed myself to be calm. I was queen of the Greater Iceni. I was no blushing maiden. I was being ridiculous.

And yet, as he rode toward me, all I could think about was the fact that I had spent the morning weaving garlic and that I was wearing an old gown. I hadn't even fixed my hair that morning. I smelled of the kitchens and was dressed no better than a servant.

The stable hands rushed out to meet the party.

Aulus rode to us, his eyes on me.

I met and held his gaze.

Years had passed since that moment in Verulam. And while I'd left the longings I'd felt for him behind me, their echoes remained. The moment I set eyes on him, I could see it was the same for him.

"Queen Boudica," he said, gathering himself. Smiling, he looked at Sorcha and Olwen. "And Princess Sorcha," he said, inclining his head to my elder daughter. "That is a fine sword there, Princess."

"It is a dagger, Roman," Sorcha snipped at him.

"Sorcha," I scolded her.

Aulus laughed, his gaze going to Olwen.

"I heard you had another child. I am sorry, young princess, I don't know your name."

Olwen buried her face in my neck.

"She is Olwen," I said, stroking my younger daughter's straw-colored hair.

"Princess Olwen," Aulus said with a soft smile.

"You are welcome in Venta, Governor. Please, won't you come inside? My people will see to your horses and men."

"Queen Boudica," Brita said, appearing from the roundhouse. "Here, my queen. Let me. Come along, girls. Your mother has an important visitor."

At that, Brita took Olwen from my arms and reached out for Sorcha.

Sorcha paused a moment, sticking her tongue out at Aulus, then went with the maid.

Aulus laughed, then joined me.

When he drew close, however, his expression changed. The pleasant demeanor he always wore dropped.

"Boudica, it is urgent," he said.

Nodding, I motioned for him to come inside.

We went to the formal meeting room.

When the door was closed behind us, Aulus came to me, gently grabbing my shoulders. "I am being recalled to Rome."

I felt like my heart had sunk into my stomach. "W-what?"

"Word will spread that I am being called home to enjoy my honors, and I *will* be honored, but let there be truth between us. Claudius is displeased. He wants Caratacus captured and the other tribes bent into submission. Publius Ostorius Scapula has arrived to replace me. Boudica, if your people think me harsh, they have seen nothing. I knew your brother was supporting the Coritani. I have kept it to myself. But Scapula is not me. He has discovered the truth. Already, he is moving north into Northern Iceni territory."

"You're leaving?"

"Boudica, have you heard a word I've said?"

"I have, I just..."

"My orders were to return to Camulodunum and prepare to sail at once. I only came to Venta to warn you. I'm not supposed to be here. Scapula is a dangerous man, Boudica. Do not cross him. Do not cheat him. Do nothing to displease him. You and Prasutagus must remind him that you are friends to Rome. Prasutagus is the most respected of your kings. Do whatever you can to keep that trust."

"Aulus..."

"Boudica, do you hear me?" he asked, shaking me gently.

"I do. It's just…"

"It is too late to warn Caturix, but you can step between Scapula and Bran. You and Prasutagus. You must convince Scapula that it was not the Northern Iceni who have risen but Caturix acting alone. Already, I have tried to plant these seeds in Scapula's mind. Now, you must stoke the fire."

"Yes… Yes. I will. Bran… You're leaving?"

Aulus held my gaze, his blue eyes searching mine. "I'm leaving."

"Will you be all right? Claudius…"

"Claudius assures me that I will be honored upon my return. After all, I am the one who brought him a victory here."

"You're going home."

"I'm going home."

We stared at one another.

"Then I will think of you at home, amongst your grapevines and olive trees," I said, feeling unbidden tears well in my eyes. "With the sun shining upon you. Your bare feet in the grass."

Aulus stared at me for a long time, then took my face into his hands and kissed my lips passionately. I caught the light taste of wine on his mouth and the scents of freshly washed linens and leather—the scents of him. Two opposing instincts cried out: one telling me to push him away and the other telling me to run with him.

When he finally let me go, he stared at me for a long moment.

"Farewell, Britannia," he said, then turned and left the room.

I listened as his footsteps made their way around the bend and out the front door.

I stood, frozen in place, listening to his voice outside as he called for his horse.

Then, hoofbeats and the sound of the watch calling for the gates to open.

Afterward, silence.

I stood, staring at the blank space in front of me.

Gone.

He was just...gone.

And Caturix was in terrible danger.

CHAPTER 88

Prasutagus returned a few hours later. I could see by the lingering shadows of sorrow in his eyes that Henwyn had passed.

I waited for him in our private meeting chamber. Sorcha and Olwen sat together on the floor, rolling a ball between them and giggling.

"Dada!" Sorcha called, jumping up to greet him, hugging Prasutagus's knees. Olwen followed behind her. Although she was nearly two, Olwen never talked. Both Ariadne and Rue had looked her over and found nothing physically wrong. She simply did not speak. But she was a bright girl. She often laughed and giggled at things that no one else saw. Pix swore it was the greenwood playing games with her. I had no doubt she was right.

Prasutagus bent, kissing and hugging both girls, then turned to me.

"Boudica," Prasutagus said. "They said the governor was here. Where is Aul—"

"Gone."

"Gone?"

"Gone. Gone from Venta. Gone from our island. Gone." Prasutagus sat beside me. "What do you mean?"

"Emperor Claudius has summoned him back to Rome. A new governor has arrived and is already marching north. Aulus came to warn us. This new man, Publius Ostorius Scapula, is a hard man. Aulus knew about Caturix. He stayed his hand, but Scapula will not."

Prasutagus's brow furrowed. "Why would Governor Plautius turn a blind eye to Caturix?"

"Prasutagus, Scapula is *already* marching north," I said, refocusing his attention. "And he knows about Caturix. What can we do? My brother…"

Prasutagus was silent for a long moment. "We must now look to our own future. We must keep what we have here safe. Our daughters must be our chief concern."

I felt like an invisible hand was tightening around my throat. There was no way to get word to Caturix now, and I wouldn't risk Pix again. She nearly died in her last attempt to cross the barrier. Prasutagus was right. We needed to protect what was ours, but that included the Northern Iceni for me.

"I will send word to Bran at first light," I said.

"Boudica…" Prasutagus began, an odd tremor in his voice, but he did not finish. Whatever he wanted to ask, he let it die in his throat. "Henwyn has passed. The druids will hold the rites at Arminghall tonight. We must be there."

"Dada," Sorcha said, tugging on Prasutagus's leg. "Play with us."

Prasutagus paused, searching my face. I gestured for him to join the girls.

He sat on the floor with them. "What is your game, my princesses?"

"I roll the ball to Olwen," Sorcha told him. "She rolls to me."

"Can I play?"

"You have to be fast," Sorcha told him.

"I will do my best to keep up with you."

The three of them sat playing. I watched their game and tried to calm my wild heart.

Inside, I was screaming.

No matter how much I twisted and turned my mind around all of it, there was no escaping the fact that our world was changing, and there was nothing we could do to stop it.

LATE THAT NIGHT, ALL OF US AT THE KING'S HOUSE WENT TO Arminghall to honor Henwyn's passing.

A bonfire had been prepared for her within the semi-circle of the henge. The priestly order, including Ansgar, gathered around.

Flames flickered in the darkness as we prepared to send the priestess onward.

Prasutagus, dressed in his finest clothes, stepped forward. The golden torc on his neck shimmered in the firelight.

"My people," he called. "Tonight, we celebrate the passing of the priestess Henwyn who long served the gods at this sacred nemeton. This night, she begins her passage to the Otherworld where she will take her rest before rejoining us in her next life once more."

Sorcha stood beside Brita. She held the maid's hand, her eyes wide as she watched her father.

Olwen, however, clung to me. She shivered in the cool of the night. I pulled her close to me, kissing her on the cheek to comfort her.

"Life is a circle," Prasutagus called. "It is never-ending. We spin like a wheel. Our time in this mortal realm is limited, but our spirits are endless. Even when we lose those we love in this life, we can take comfort in the knowledge that the wheel will spin, and we will see them again."

I closed my eyes, letting Prasutagus's words resonate in my chest. Grief was stuck there and did not want to let go. It was a silent thing I could not give voice to.

Gone.

Gone.

And just like that...gone.

And now, my brother was in danger.

My people were in danger.

"Great Mother, Forest Lord, Sacred Bel, Wise Brigid, tonight we send Henwyn to the fires. May her ancestors and all those who have served alongside her, in this life or another, greet her as friend, mother, sister, on the other side."

Ansgar stepped forward. "Honorable Henwyn," he called. "I commit you to Bel's fires. May the Sun Lord light your way home," he said, then set her pyre aflame.

We all stood, watching as the wood caught fire. Henwyn's tiny body had been wrapped in a drape, her body adorned with flowers. Soon, the entire pyre caught flame, embers circling upward into the night.

"Ahh," Olwen gasped loudly, as if she saw something startling.

I followed her gaze, watching the embers as they twisted upward. Olwen pointed at the sky, but her eyes moved beyond the embers, watching something unseen. I saw a flash of iridescent light reflected in Olwen's eyes, but when I looked, I saw nothing.

"Ohh," Olwen said, her voice a soft whisper, and then she looked back toward me. She set her small hand on my cheek then watched above us.

"Farewell, Henwyn," I whispered into the sky.

Staring at the stars for a long moment, I said, "May Mithras keep you safe and guide you home."

But my words had not been for the priestess.

The priestesses and druids came together then, singing, their hands upraised. Prasutagus joined them. In a language I did not know, they began their funeral chant.

A soft breeze blew across the glade.

A voice called my name in a soft whisper from somewhere behind me.

"Boudica...

"Boudica..."

Olwen exhaled softly in surprise, then looked behind us.

"Do you hear it too?" I asked her.

She nodded.

"Boudica...

"Boudica..."

I turned to Brita. "I'll be back in a moment," I whispered. "Can you watch Olwen?"

Brita nodded. "Everything all right?"

"Yes," I said, in something of a lie, then stepped away from the others.

A few heads turned, watching me, but I signaled that all was well.

Pix, however, moved to come along.

I shook my head, then retreated into the darkness.

I walked down the hill away from the nemeton. Once more, the wind blew. On it, I smelled the heavy scent of fire. But it was not coming from the nemeton. It came from somewhere in the hills beyond.

My heart began to thump in my chest. I made my way through the valley and across the water to the other side, climbing toward the top of the hill.

"Boudica...

"Boudica..."

The wind whipped around me.

The voices at the nemeton faded to a low hum as I made my way up the hill on the other side of the valley. I looked back, seeing the pyre burn, the druids gathered there. Amongst the group, I could make out Prasutagus.

"Boudica...

"Queen of oak...

"Queen of stone...

"Come.

"Quickly.

"Come."

I raced up the hill to the mountain's peak, then looked over to find...nothing. There was nothing. No army. No danger. No fire. Only trees, grass, wind, moonlight, and the King Stone. The dark trees swayed in the moonlight.

The breeze blew once more.

On it came the sounds of battle. I heard screams, clashing arms, and the sound of muffled crying.

My skin rose in gooseflesh.

I turned and looked at the King Stone. The stone was illuminated by a golden halo, light radiating all around it.

My hands shaking, I walked slowly toward the stone.

The stone's surface began to waver like water, the engraved images thereon disappearing. An image formed on the stone. It was murky at first, like looking into a dark pool filled with muddy water, but as I stepped closer, shapes became sharper.

On the other side of the stone—*through* the stone—I saw fire and embers floating through the air.

The pyre?

I looked across the valley below me, but it was not that. It was something else.

I moved closer.

Screams grew louder. I heard sword upon sword. I heard voices calling out in agony. But most of all, I heard weeping.

I peered into the stone. Beyond it, I saw a small ring of menhir. Their shapes were familiar. At the very center of the stones was a pool. The space was shadowed in darkness, but behind them, I saw a village on fire.

No...

Not a village.

A woman wept, then looked out from behind the stones. Her face marred with mud and blood. A bloody tool in her hand, she was nearly unrecognizable.

But then, I saw her eyes.

Melusine.

Stonea was on fire.

Melusine stared in horror around her.

"Melusine," I called.

She turned as if confused to hear a voice.

A rider appeared behind her. Dressed in full Roman armor, the rider lowered his spear and rode hard toward Melusine.

"Melusine. Melusine!" I called. I rushed to the King Stone and reached for Melusine.

My hand felt like it had been dipped in liquid light.

Dark Lady Andraste, help me!

I reached for Melusine, catching the fabric of her sleeve, then pulled hard.

Her weight falling toward me, I yanked her from beyond, the pair of us tumbling to the ground.

It took me a moment to reorient myself.

I looked back at the King Stone, but it had gone dark. The light, the voices, the fire, everything was gone.

It was simply stone once more.

I rose and went to Melusine, helping her stand.

Her eyes wild, she stared at me. "Boudica," she gasped. "Boudica... The Romans... The Romans... Caturix is dead! The Northern Iceni have fallen!"

"Boudica...

"Queen of oak...

"Queen of stone...

"Queen of ash and iron...

"Rise."

Continue Boudica's saga in *Queen of Ash and Iron: A Novel of Boudica*, the Celtic Rebels book 3. Available on Amazon.

Made in the USA
Monee, IL
24 February 2023